梁英君

郭灵云 编

【高校英美文学专业学习丛书】

经典英美小说选读

THE SELECTED READINGS
IN BRITISH AND AMERICAN
CLASSIC NOVELS

知识产权出版社

全国百佳图书出版单位

内容摘要

　　本书积累了作者十年的英美文学教学经验，以细腻的笔触分析了英美文学史上最经典的小说。编者选取了英美文学史上数十部众所周知的经典小说，附以思考题、详细的赏析、中文注释和译文，方便学生阅读同时有助于学生提高文学作品的鉴赏能力。该书适合作为英美文学的爱好者或英美文学教师的参考资料，也适合作为英语专业的选修课教材。

责任编辑：殷亚敏　　　**责任校对：**董志英
封面设计：刘　伟　　　**责任出版：**卢运霞

图书在版编目（CIP）数据

　　经典英美小说选读/梁英君，郭灵云编.—北京：
知识产权出版社，2012.12
　　ISBN 978-7-5130-1767-1

　　Ⅰ.①经…　Ⅱ.①梁…②郭…　Ⅲ.①小说–文学欣
赏–英国②小说–文学欣赏–美国　Ⅳ.①
1561.074②I712.074

　　中国版本图书馆 CIP 数据核字（2012）第 305160 号

经典英美小说选读

The Selected Readings in British and American Classic Novels

梁英君　郭灵云　编

出版发行：知识产权出版社

社　　址：北京市海淀区西外太平庄 55 号		邮　　编：100081	
网　　址：http：//www.ipph.cn		邮　　箱：bjb@cnipr.com	
发行电话：010-82000860 转 8101/8102		传　　真：010-82000860 转 8240	
责编电话：010-82000860 转 8126		责编邮箱：yinyamin@cnipr.com	
印　　刷：北京科信印刷有限公司		经　　销：新华书店及相关销售网点	
开　　本：787mm×1092mm　1/16		印　　张：18.5	
版　　次：2013 年 1 月第 1 版		印　　次：2013 年 1 月第 1 次印刷	
字　　数：318 千字		定　　价：39.00 元	

ISBN 978-7-5130-1767-1/I · 256 （4619）

Prelude

Is it necessary to read English novels for college students? For some students, the study of English means only learning some English texts and reading a few books on grammar and vocabulary. You may think that reading a novel is something a waste of time.

We can not escape the task of reading the classical English and American authors when we want to study English well. While you are reading the English classic works, you will find all that best language finds its expression in literature. Some say that dictionary is a best tool to master a language. Dictionaries tell us about the spelling, pronunciation and definitions of words. But dictionaries can't show all subtle shades of meaning of a word. The best way to study the meaning of a word is that of learning it between the lines in the British and American novels of classic authors. These novels have gone through times and proved to be the best of all literary works.

How to carry out an effective reading of classics? Firstly, build up your vocabulary and language foundation by every possible means; secondly, make yourself love novels. If you do not love any books, the study of novels would be a painful business for you; thirdly, the most important thing is to read the representative works of major writers, or " classics ", that is, universally acknowledged good works of literary arts. Reading classics can perfect your language skills and in return you will have greater interest in classic novel reading.

In conclusion, you must go through the whole process, step by step, all by yourself with the help of teachers and some reference books such as a dictionary or the books like this book.

This book, with vivid illustration of pictures and detailed explanation and Chinese version presents you the best works of the best and will help you have a profound understanding the classics. I hope that this book, though not exhaustive, may lay a basis for your further exploration and debate.

Liang Yingjun

March 2012

Contents

中文参考译文

Unit 1
Daniel Defoe (1660~1731)

Life

Daniel Defoe was born at the end of summer of 1660 in London. His father, James Foe, was a London butcher. The future novelist kept his father's family name until 1703, when he added the aristocratic prefix "De" with which we have been familiar.

Daniel was sent to one of the "dissenting" academies, an institute where different and unconventional views and subjects such as English composition and science, are taught. There he received a good education.

Daniel was a jack-of-all-trader before he became a novelist. His father wants him to become a member of the Puritan clergy, but after leaving school, he became a clothes business agent, namely a merchant, dealing between manufacturer and retailer.

In addition to his business dealings, Defoe involved himself in Politics. In 1685 he joined in an unsuccessful attempt to place the Protestant Duke of Monmouth on the throne instead of the natural heir, the Catholic James II, and in 1688, he joined

William III's successful army in the Glorious Revolution, which put a Dutch protestant on the throne of England. By 1690, Defoe had a number of shipments moving back and forth across the English channel from one European market to another. But as a result of his adventurous speculations, or of the general depression caused by the war with France, he was thrown into bankruptcy in 1692 and put into prison. Defoe, was, however, a resourceful businessman. He managed to settle his debts and kept himself out of prison. In 1697 he published *An Essay Upon Projects*, proposing a national highway system, a national banking system, simple laws for shipwreck and fire insurance—measures that all modern industrialized states have put into practice. In short, Defoe is a social economist.

Defoe's experience as a journalist paves a way for his novel-writing career. Defoe is the first important English novelist. When he was nearly 60 years old, he wrote his first novel, *Robinson Crusoe*, which was published in 1719. Then he produced a number of other novels. Of all his works, *Robinson Crusoe* is his masterpiece.

Defoe produced more than 500 written works in his lifetime, including social criticisms, poems, pamphlets, and novels. Besides *Robinson Crusoe*, there are some other novels including *Captain Singleton*, *Moll Flanders*, *Colonel Jack* and *Roxana*. The last four novels show the writer's sympathy for the poverty-stricken people. He has portrayed a series of realistic and ordinary characters in simple and ordinary language.

Plot of *Robinson Crusoe*

As Defoe's masterpiece, *Robinson Crusoe* is one of the few books in English literature that have been enjoying an undiminished popularity for centuries. The novel consists of three parts, but only the first part has been widely read. The plot of the novel is based upon the real experience of Alexander Seilkirk, a Scottish sailor, who was ever deserted on an uninhabited island after he had quarreled with the captain. He had lived there in solitude for five years before he was rescued by a passing ship. On his return to England in 1709, his experience became widely known after it was reported in many periodicals.

Inspired by the adventurous experience of this Scottish sailor, Defoe successfully characterizes Robinson Crusoe as the protagonist of the novel. The whole story of Robinson Crusoe covers three parts. In the first part, Crusoe, a slave trader meets with his most unfortunate shipwreck. He is cast by the cold waves upon the shore of an uninhabited island, where he manages to live for 28 years because there is no possible opportunity for him to escape. In order to live in the wilderness, he swim back to the ship to search and bring back the remaining food, clothing, household tools and guns, and then builds a simple cottage to shelter himself against the possible attacks of wild animals. He grows barley and rice in spring and harvests when the autumn comes. He rescues a savage, whom he names Friday and makes his servant. Crusoe tries his best to teach Friday to speak and read English, while Friday serves his teacher and master in every possible way. After having lived on the island for 28 years, they are rescued by a passing ship, which carries them back to England. The first part of story ends with Crusoe sending women and supplies to the island to establish a regular colony there.

The second part is a series of adventures of Crusoe on his 11 year business trip to different parts of the world, especially his return to the island where he lived for 28 years to set up a colony and simultaneously spread English views of religion and morality. Because of its less unified and more monotonous plot, the second part has been considered as inferior to the first part, and together with the third part, another dull narration of Crusoe's adventures have few readers.

Some Comments on *Robinson Crusoe*

The novel can be read in different ways. Most simple, it is a story of sea adventures. Its thrilling incidents: the shipwreck, the earthquake, the meeting with Friday, the clash with the savage natives—have attracted millions of readers, including young children. To read it politically, we may interpret the story as a process of colonial expansion. Crusoe, supported by advanced technology represented by gun, conquers a less civilized people represented by Man Friday. Though they become good friends, Friday has remained a servant to his master—Crusoe since the first day they met.

To read it socially, we find that Crusoe's adventures imply different Western Cultural values. The novel sings a song of "the dignity of labor", a slogan as a disguise to justify the bourgeoisie's bloody accumulation of wealth. Robinson is a self-made man. He succeeds in creating a new life all through his own efforts.

The novel also explores the theme of "back to nature". Industrialization brought England material wealth, but it also ended with the peaceful life in the countryside and created poverty and disturbance in the city. The novel expresses a desire to go back to a more economic and humble life style. After four years on the island, Robinson starts to like its idyllic life: "I looked now upon the (civilized) world as a thing remote, which I had nothing to do with, no expectation from, and indeed no desire about..."

There is also the theme of "religious devotion." Completely separated from civilization, Crusoe reflects upon man's frailty and God's mercy. He has a fuller undersanding of the power of religion. Crusoe find the need, after being thrown into the deserted island, for prayer and repentance, and finds that inner peace does not come from material possessions in civilized world but from communication with God.

Robinson Crusoe is written in almost colloquial language. Though it is a novel of the 18th century, we have no difficulties in understanding its story. It is narrated in the first person singular. The narration of this novel is true and realistic to life, like a person telling his own experience to his friends. Simple language, realistic narration and real background of the story, for it is based on a sailor's real experience, all these elements make Robinson Crusoe's adventures more believable, convincing and exciting.

Symbolism pervades in this novel. In general, the whole story symbolizes the whole process of human development: from the primitive stage, to feudal period to the capital society. The tools fetched by Crusoe and offering him great help symbolize the civilization, which is necessary to the survival of a person on a desolate island. The island itself has symbolic significance because it is the physical conditions, which changed Crusoe to stop wandering (Crusoe is a merchant, loving sailing adventures). The confinement on the island is mostly responsible for the physical and mental growth, which took place within Crusoe. In the case of Robinson Crusoe, it was this solitude that essentially changed him and made him less of a wanderer, both spiritually and physically, for he found faith in God and no longer was able to aimlessly wander due to the confinement on the island.

In *Robinson Crusoe*, the narrator develops to form an optimistic outlook towards an unfortunate situation, however, that a man isolated himself from society and lived on an uninhabited island for 28 years is still a myth, as Aristotle said such as man, if he exists, is either a beast or a God.

Robinson Crusoe is so influential that it is not only appreciated in European countries but in China. In 1905, Chinese translator Lin Shu translated *Robinson Crusoe* with simple language, concise description and well-knit plot construction. In the Chinese version, it is narrated in the first singular person with realistic psychological description. Therefore, the Chinese readers have a chance to read it and think about it.

Major Characters

Robinson Crusoe is one of the protagonists most successfully portrayed in English novels. Through his characterization of Crusoe, Defoe depicts him as a hero struggling against nature and human fate with his strong will and hand, and Defoe eulogizes the creative physical and mental labor. From an individual laborer to a master and colonizer, Crusoe seems to have gone through various phases of human civilization—primitive stage, feudal society and the capitalistic in the 18th centrury, creating a picture of how man's history has developed. That is the vital significance of the novel.

However Crusoe is not portrayed as a great hero in epic adventure to win readers of generations. He does not boast of his courage in getting rid of the difficulties and fear on the uninhabited island, and he is always in an un-heroic feeling of fear or panic, as when he first finds the footprint on the beach. Crusoe prefers to depict himself as an ordinary sensible man, never as an epic hero. It is his perseverance in spending months making a canoe that makes his adventures praiseworthy. Additionally, his resourcefulness in building a home, dairy, grape arbor, country house, and goat stable from practically nothing is clearly remarkable. The Swiss philosopher Jean-Jacques Rousseau applauded Crusoe's do-it-yourself independence, and he recommends that children be taught to imitate Crusoe's life.

Crusoe is very interested in possessions and power. He has an ambition of possessions and power. When he first calls himself king of the island, he really does consider himself king, so he describes the Spaniard as his subject. His teaching Friday to call him "Master," even before teaching him words for "yes" or "no" is annoying for any grown-up, who is taught in that way. In conclusion, Crusoe's virtues tend to be private: his industry, resourcefulness, courage and do-it-yourself independence make him an excellent individual. His vices are social, and his urge to control others is highly objectionable. By bringing both sides together into one complex character, Defoe gives us a fascinating glimpse into the contradictions of a modern man.

Friday is probably the first nonwhite character to be given a realistic and humane portrayal in the English novel. Crusoe represents the first colonial mind in fiction, and Friday represents all the natives of America, Asia, and Africa who would later be oppressed in the age of European imperialism. At the moment when Crusoe teaches Friday to call him "Master", Friday becomes an enduring political symbol of racial injustice in a modern world.

Friday is a key figure within the context of the novel. In *Robinson Crusoe*, he is much more charming and colorful than his master. Indeed, Defoe stresses the contrast between Crusoe's and Friday's personalities. In his joyful reunion with his father, Friday exhibits far more emotion toward his family than Crusoe who never mentions missing his family or dreams about the happiness of seeing them again. Friday's expression of loyalty in asking Crusoe to kill him rather than leave him is more touching than anything Crusoe ever says or does. In short, Friday's emotional directness has a sharp contrast with Crusoe's emotional numbness.

Introduction to Chapter IV

The most successful and significant portion of the novel is the story of the hero's first adventures on the uninhabited island, especially when he is alone and before he has Friday as his servant (Chapter IV). Here the hero is not a colonizer or a foreign trader but is depicted as a man struggling against nature and living through a seemingly primitive environment. Here we see the glorification of the new bourgeois man who has the will and courage to face hardships and the determination to preserve himself and improve on his living conditions. Here we even see the glorification of physical and mental labor, which enables the hero to gradually create a favorable environment for himself. This part provides the possible conditions for the probability of a single man managing to live on in a deserted place and soon to improve his living conditions. Without many useful things (stand for products of human civilization of many centuries), which he got from the wrecked ship, he could not even have survived at all. It is told in a simple, straightforward style, and this adds to the realistic effect of the story.

Chapter IV

My thoughts were now wholly employed about securing myself against either savages, if any should appear, or wild beasts, if any were in the island; and I had many thoughts of the method how to do this, and what kind of dwelling to make, whether I should make me a cave in the earth, or a tent upon the earth; and, in short, I resolved upon both, the manner and description of which it may not be improper to give an account of.

I soon found the place I was in was not for my settlement, particularly because it was upon a *low moorish ground*[1] near the sea, and I believed would not be *wholesome*[2]; and more particularly because there was no fresh water near it. So I resolved to find a more healthy and more convenient spot of ground.

I consulted several things in my situation, which I found would be proper for me. First, health and fresh water, I just now mentioned. Secondly, shelter from the heat of the sun. Thirdly security from *ravenous*[3] creatures, whether men or beasts. Fourthly, a view to the sea, that if God sent any ship in sight I might not lose any advantage for my deliverance, of which I was not willing to banish all my expectation yet.

In search of a place proper for this, I found a little plain on the side of a rising hill, whose front towards this little plain was steep as a house-side, so that nothing could come down upon me from the top; on the side of this rock there was a hollow place, worn a little way in, like the entrance or door of a cave; but there was not really any cave, or way into the rock at all.

On the flat of the green, just before this hollow place, I resolved to pitch my tent. This plain was not above a hundred yards broad, and about twice as long, and lay like a green before my door, and at the end of it descended irregularly every way down into the low grounds by the seaside. It was on the NNW[4]. side of the hill, so that I was sheltered from the heat every day, till it came to a $W.$[5] and by S[6]. sun, or thereabouts, which in those countries is near setting.

Before I set up my tent, I drew a half circle before the hollow place, which took in about ten yards in its semi-diameter from the rock, and twenty yards in its diameter from its beginning and ending. In this half circle I pitched two rows of strong *stakes*[7], driving them into the ground till they stood very firm like *piles*[8], the biggest end being out of the ground about five feet and a half, and sharpened on the top. The two rows did not stand above six inches from one another.

Then I took the pieces of cable which I had cut in the ship, and laid them in rows one upon another, within the circle, between these two rows of stakes, up to the top, placing other stakes in the inside leaning against them, about two feet and a half high, like a spur to a post; and this fence was so strong that neither man or beast could get into it, or over it. This cost me a great deal of time and labor, especially to cut the piles in the woods, bring them to the place, and drive them into the earth.

The entrance into this place I made to be not by a door, but by a short ladder to go over the top; which ladder, when I was in, I lifted over after me, and so I was completely fenced in, and fortified, as I thought, from all the world, and consequently slept secure in the night, which otherwise I could not have done; though as it appeared afterward, there was no need of all this caution from the enemies that I apprehended danger from.

Into this fence or fortress, with infinite labor, I carried all my riches, all my provisions, ammunition, and stores, of which you have the account above; and I made me a large tent, which, to preserve me from the rains that in one part of the year are very violent there, I made double, *viz.*[9], one smaller tent within, and one larger tent above it, and covered the uppermost with a large *tarpaulin*[10], which I had saved among the sails. And now I lay no more for a while in the bed which I had brought on shore, but in a *hammock*[11], which was indeed a very good one, and belonged to *the mate of the ship*[12].

Into this tent I brought all my provisions, and everything that would spoil by the wet; and having thus enclosed all my goods I made up the entrance, which, till now, I had left open, and so passed and repassed, as I said, by a short ladder.

When I had done this, I began to work my way into the rock; and bringing all the earth and stones that I dug down out through my tent, I laid them up within my fence in the nature of a terrace, so that it raised the ground within about a foot and a half; and thus I made me a cave just behind my tent, which served me like a cellar to my house.

It cost me much labor, and many days, before all these things were brought to perfection, and therefore I must go back to some other things which took up some of my thoughts. At the same time it happened, after I had laid my scheme for the setting up my tent, and making the cave, that a storm of rain falling from a thick dark cloud, a sudden flash of lightning happened, and after that a great clap of thunder, as is naturally the effect of it. I was not so much surprised with the lightning, as I was with a thought which darted into my mind as swift as the lightning itself. O my powder! My very heart sunk within me when I thought that at one blast all my powder might be destroyed, on which, not my defence only, but the providing me food, as I thought, entirely depended. I was nothing near so anxious about my own danger; though had the powder took fire, I had never known who had hurt me.

Such impression did this make upon me, that after the storm was over I laid aside all my works, my building, and fortifying, and applied myself to make bags and boxes to separate the powder, and keep it a little and a little in a parcel, in hope that whatever might come it might not all take fire at once, and to keep it so apart that it should not be possible to make *one part fire another*[13]. I finished this work in about a fortnight; and I think my powder, which in all was about 240 pounds weight, was divided in not less than a hundred parcels. As to the barrel that had been wet, I did not apprehend any danger from that, so I placed it in my new cave, which in my fancy I called my kitchen, and the rest I hid up and down and in holes among the rocks, so that no wet might come to it, marking very carefully where I laid it.

In the interval of time while this was doing, I went out once, at least, every day with my gun, as well to divert myself, as to see if I could kill anything fit for food, and as near as I could to acquaint myself with what the island produced. The first time I went out, I presently discovered that there were goats in the island, which was a great satisfaction to me; but then it was attended with this misfortune to me, viz., that they were so shy, so subtle, and so swift of foot, that it was the difficultest thing in the world to *come at*[14] them. But I was not discouraged at this, not doubting but I might now and then shoot one, as it soon happened; for after I had found their haunts a little, I laid wait in this manner for them. I observed if they saw me in the valleys, though they were upon the rocks, they would run away as in a terrible fright; but if they were feeding in the valleys, and I was upon the rocks, they took no notice of me, from whence I concluded that, by the position of their optics, their sight was so directed downward, that they did not readily see objects that were above them. So afterward I took this method: I always climbed the rocks first to get above them, and then had frequently a fair mark. The first shot I made among these creatures I killed a she-goat, which had a little kid by her, which she *gave suck to*[15], which grieved me heartily; but when the old one fell, the kid stood stock still by her till I came and took her up; and not only so, but when I carried the old one with me upon my shoulders, the kid followed me quite to my enclosure; upon which I laid down the *dam*[16], and took the kid in my arms, and carried it over my *pale*[17], in hopes to have *bred it up tame*[18]; but it would not eat, so I was forced to kill it, and eat it myself. These two supplied me with flesh a great while, for I eat sparingly, and saved my provisions, my bread especially, as much as possibly I could.

Having now fixed my habitation, I found it absolutely necessary to provide a place to make a fire in, and fuel to burn; and what I did for that, as also how I enlarged my cave, and what conveniences I made, I shall give a full account of in its place. But I must first give some little account of myself, and of my thoughts about living, which it may well be supposed were not a few. I had a dismal prospect of my condition; for as I was not cast away upon that island without being driven, as is said, by a violent storm, quite out of the course of our intended voyage, and a great way, viz., some hundreds of leagues *out of the ordinary course of the trade of mankind*[19], I had great reason to consider it as a determination of Heaven, that in this desolate place, and in this desolate manner, I should end my life. The tears would run plentifully down face when I made these reflections, and sometimes I would expostulate with myself, why *Providence*[20] should thus completely ruin its creatures, and render them so absolutely miserable, so without help abandoned, so entirely depressed, that it could hardly be rational to be thankful for such a life.

But something always returned swift upon me to check these thoughts, and to *reprove*[21] me; and particularly one day, walking with my gun in my hand by the seaside, I was very *pensive*[22] upon the subject of my present condition, when reason, as it were, *expostulated*[23] with me t'other way, thus: "Well, you are in a desolate condition it is true, but pray remember, where are the rest of you? Did not you come eleven of you in the boat? Where are the ten? Why were not they saved, and you lost? Why were you singled out? Is it better to be here, or there?" And then I pointed to the sea. All evils are to be considered with the good that is in them, and with what worse attends them.

Then it occurred to me again, how well I was *furnished*[24] for my subsistence, and what would have been my case if it had not happened, which was a hundred thousand to one, that the ship had floated from the place where she first struck and was driven so near to the shore that I had time to get all these things out of her; what would have been my case, if I had been to have lived in the condition in which I first came on shore, without necessaries of life, or necessaries to supply and procure them? "Particularly," said I aloud (though to myself), "what should I have done without a gun, without ammunition, without any tools to make anything or to work with, without clothes, bedding, a tent, or any manner of covering?" and that now I had all these to a sufficient quantity, and was in a fair way to provide myself in such a manner, as to live without my gun when my ammunition was spent; so that I had a tolerable view of subsisting without any want as long as I lived. For I considered from the beginning how I would provide for the accidents that might happen, and for the time that was to come, even not only after my ammunition should be spent, but even after my health or strength should decay.

I confess I had not entertained any notion of my ammunition being destroyed at one blast—I mean, my powder being blown up by lightning; and this made the thoughts of it so surprising to me when it lightened and thundered, as I observed just now.

And now being to *enter into a melancholy relation of a scene of silent life*[25], such, perhaps, as was never heard of in the world before, I shall take it from its beginning and continue it in its order. It was by my account, the 30th of September when, in the manner as above said, I first set foot upon this horrid island, when the sun being to us in its *autumnal equinox*[26], was almost just over my head, for I reckoned myself, by observation, to be in the latitude of 9 degrees 22 minutes north of the line.

After I had been there about ten or twelve days it came into my thoughts that I should lose my reckoning of time for want of books and pen and ink, and should even forget the *Sabbath days*[27] from the working days; but to prevent this, I cut it with my knife upon a large post, in capital letters; and making it into a great cross, I set it up on the shore where I first landed, viz., "I came on shore here the 30th of

September 1659." Upon the sides of this square post I cut every day a *notch*[28] with my knife, and every seventh notch was as long again as the rest, and every first day of the month as long again as that long one; and thus I kept my calendar, or weekly, monthly, and yearly reckoning of time.

Notes

[1] 低洼的沼泽地

[2] healthy

[3] 饥饿的

[4] north-north west

[5] west

[6] south

[7] 木桩

[8] 桥桩

[9] that is to say.也就是,即

[10] 防水油布

[11] 吊床

[12] 大副

[13] 一部分火药引爆另一部分火药

[14] approach

[15] 喂奶,哺乳

[16] 母羊

[17] 栅栏,及鲁滨逊的家

[18] 把它(羔羊)驯养大

[19] 人迹罕至之处

[20] 上帝

[21] blame severely

[22] 沉思的

[23] 规劝;告诫

[24] provide

[25] 预想到将来的生活忧郁而寂寞

[26] 秋分;秋分点

[27] 安息日

[28] 凹痕

Questions

1　How does Robinson Crusoe keep himself secure and find a proper place for living?

2　How difficult is it to hunt a goat?

3　If you were thrown on a deserted island in 17th century, what would your feelings and thoughts be and what would you do?

4　What is the psychological development of Robinson Crusoe?

5　What do you learn from reading this passage?

Analysis of Chapter IV

This chapter gives some details to the readers about how Robinson, by sheer will power, hard manual labor, perseverance and resourcefulness, begins to build up a new life for himself on the desolate island.

Chapter IV is not only a vivid description of Crusoe's manual labor but also his psychological description. How he built a shelter for himself and how he relieved himself from depression and desperation and formed a realistic idea and plan for his future life are realistically presented in this selection. Being abandoned on an uninhabited island, Crusoe was in great depression and upset. "*I had a dismal prospect of my condition.*" For this accident had cut his normal connection with the outside human world. Robinson rebuked the determination of Heaven. It was the determination of Heaven that made him so miserable, helpless and depressed. So "*It could hardly be rational to be thankful for such a life.*"

But "*something always returned swift upon me to check these thoughts and reprove me.*" Robinson suddenly realized what he thought before was mistaken. He began to blame himself for what's in his mind. In his reconsideration, he found God/Providence had offered him a lot of mercy. He compared the destiny of his fellow men on the ship and his destiny. Though thrown on the island, he survived rather than be drowned.

"*Then it occurred to me again, how well I was furnished for my subsistence and what would have been my case if it had not happened, which was a hundred thousand to one, that the ship floated from the place where she first struck, and was driven so near the shore that I had time to get all these things out of her?*" "a thousand to one" refers so small a chance for the ship to float from the place, so near the shore. The use of the feminine pronoun "she", not "it" proves Robinson's affectionate feelings for the ship and what the ship offers him. Therefore Robinson feels lucky to be able to fetch many things from the wrecked ship, such as an iron bar, a cask of gunpowder, any guns, boards, etc, all of which are well employed and furnished. Thus he blames no more. "So that *I had a tolerable view of subsisting, without any want, as long as I lived*". Robinson became realistic and considered how to deal with future accidents such as the exhaustion of ammunition and the decay of health and strength.

A lightning destroys his gunpowder. Such an accident made Crusoe decide to put everything into order. "*I shall take it from its beginning, and continue it in its order.*" According to the sun position, he settled the date, the time.

The latter part of this chapter focuses a psychological development of Robinson Crusoe, from depression to confidence by finding comfort from God. Then he holds a tolerable view towards the unfavorable conditions. Finally because of accidents, he made a pragmatic and realistic decision to settle everything in order.

Unit 2
Jonathan Swift (1667 ~ 1745)

Life

Jonathan Swift was born of English parents in Dublin, on Nov. 30 1667. His father died before he was born; his mother was poor and Swift was compelled to accept aid from others. With the help of an uncle he was educated at Trinity College, Dublin.

At college, he detested the curriculums and studied only what appealed to him. After graduation, he became a secretary of a distant relative, Sir William Temple, a retired statesman in London, but he treated Swift as a servant. He spent about ten years (1689 ~ 1699) with Temple. During these years he read widely and started to write.

After Temple's death, Swift returned to Ireland, and served the church faithfully. Swift made great efforts to better the condition of unhappy people around him. Afterwards he entered the strife of party politics. At first, he served the Whig party, but in 1710 he changed over to the Tories. For several years, especially from 1710 to 1713, Swift was one of the most important figures in London. The Whigs feared the lash of his satire; the Tories feared to lose his support. In truth, Swift despised both parties; his chief object was to win for himself the masterful position in church for which, he believed, his talents had fitted him. In 1713 Swift was made Dean of St. Patrick's Cathedral. He has written a number of pamphlets against the Whig government in London, showing his sympathy for Irish people. He gradually became an Irish Patriot.

Swift was a master of satire. He wrote a great deal of prose, chiefly in the form of pamphlet. Now Swift remains the most powerful English satirist, his counterparts consider him a rare combination of cold intellect, acid satire and sincerity. His most famous works are *The Battle of Books* (1697), a satire on the intellectuals and *A Tale of a Tub* (1704), a satire on the various churches of the day.

Swift's fame rests largely upon his *Gulliver's Travels*. The book was published in 1726, and soon it was in everyone's hands. And it is still read with interest and pleasure all over the world.

In 1745 he died in Dublin. When his will was opened it was found that he left all his property to found asylum for lunatics and incurable.

Plot of *Gulliver's Travels*

Gulliver's Travels can be ranked among the greatest satirical works of world literature. It was published anonymously in 1726 after his 6-year labor at it since 1720. It consists of four voyages of Gulliver, the protagonist, respectively to Lilliput, to Brobdingnag, to Laputa and other strange lands, and to the country of the

Houyhnhnms, four major remote and fantastic countries after he has met with shipwrecks or pirates or other unfortunate happenings on the sea.

In the first part, Lemuel Gulliver, a surgeon on Lilliput, where the inhabitants are six inches high. But they are greedy and vicious. The Emperor thinks himself the terror of the world, though he is only as big as Gulliver's thumb. The English political parties and religious dissension are satirized in the description of the wearers of high heels and low heels and of the controversy on the fantastic question whether eggs should be broken at the big or small end.

In the second part, Gulliver comes to Brobdingnag, where he finds himself among wise giants sixty feet high. The king of Brobingnag makes the observation that European history is "only a heap of conspiracies, rebellions, murders, massacres, revolutions, banishments; the very worst effects that avarice, faction, hypocrisy, cruelty, madness, hatred, envy, lust, malice, and ambition could produce." His conclusion: "I can not but conclude the bulk of your natives to be the most pernicious race of little odious vermin that nature ever suffered to crawl upon the surface of the earth." That is to say the people lived in England is so harmful a race. Because of their devastating effects, the nature is greatly suffered. "Crawl upon" is employed to compare human being to disgusting beasts or insects or worms. So it is a sharp satire on the society in times.

The third part provides readers a series of adventures at several places. Again on a ship, captured by pirates and set adrift in a small canoe, he lands on the floating island of Laputa. This visit to the flying island of Laputa and other strange lands offer him chances of meeting the king and the nobles who are described as a group of absent-minded philosophers and astronomers engrossed in extremely abstract and absurd discussions. It is a skillful satire upon philosophers, men of science, historians, and projectors. Their behavior is abstract and laughable because the projectors are engaged in projects such as extracting sun-shines out of cucumbers, turning ice into gunpowder and making cloth from cobweb (the net work made by spiders).

The satire in the fourth part is the sharpest and bitterest. Again, Gulliver as captain of a ship was cast upon an unknown island, the land of Houyhnhnms (so

named because the word sounds like the long-pitched cry or neighing of a horse).
Here are horses born with reason and possessed of all good and admirable qualities,
and they are the ruling class. The rest of the inhabitants are Yahoos, a species of
hairy, naked and wild animals, disgusting creatures shaped like human beings, who
are the embodiment of every conceivable evil. Then after learning the language of the
Houyhnhnms, Gulliver is asked to tell about the conditions of England and Europe.
First he remarks on the causes of furious and bloody wars, and then he tells about the
unjust legal system and self-seeking lawyers in England. The greed for money
prevalent in the English society of his time, and the exploitation of human labor as
well as the idle life led by the noble men in his country are mentioned in his talk. He
admires the Houyhnhnms. Finally Gulliver expresses his wish to stay forever with the
Houyhnhnms, but it is not granted him. So he builds a canoe and sails to an
uninhabited island, and there he is seized and carried by force into a Portuguese
ship. Eventually he returns to England. Because he is so disgusted with the Yahoos
that when he returns to England he looses consciousness when his wife kisses him. For
he recognizes his wife as a vicious Yahoo in the shape of the human, so disgusting to
him. Gulliver's illusion is getting worse and worse: he has difficulty in figuring out
human beings and he thinks that horses speak to him.

Some Comments on *Gulliver's Travels*

In *Gulliver Travels*, from different angles, Swift's social satire touches upon the
political, religious, legal, military, scientific, philosophical as well as literary
institutions in his England and the men who made their careers there.

It exposes the ugly appearances of the English ruling classes, showing their
hypocrisy and greed, their intrigue and corruption, their ruthless oppression and
exploitation of the common people. It criticizes the declining feudalism and the new
capitalist relations, ridiculing the predominance of money in human relations in that
society. It also attacks the aggressive wars and colonialism in the 18th century.

Satire, as a most distinct feature of Swift's *Gulliver Travels*, is a kind of writing
that holds up to ridicule or contempt the weakness and wrong doings of individuals,

groups, institutions, or humanity in general. The aim of satirists is to set a moral standard for society, and they attempt to persuade the readers to see their point of view through the force of laughter.

The most famous and representative satirical work in English literature is Jonathan Swift's *Gulliver Travels*. In the distant land of Brobdingnag, where the people are twelve times as tall as a normal human being, Gulliver is brought before the King to describe the English people. Swift satirizes the English people through the King's response: *He (the king) was perfectly astonished with the historical account I gave him of our affairs during the last century, protesting it was only a heap of conspiracies, rebellions, murders, massacres, revolutions, banishments; the very worst effects that avarice, faction, and so many evils could produce.* A similar expression will be read in part IV from our selections.

Major Characters

Lemuel Gulliver is the narrator and protagonist of the story. Gulliver is a bold, intelligent and well educated adventurer who visits a multitude of strange lands. He has courage for he undergoes some experiences of nearly being devoured by a giant rat, taken captive by pirates, shipwrecked on faraway shores, and shot in the face with poison arrows. His sixteen-year isolation from humanity is really hard to bear, however, he rarely shows such feeling and emotional attachment to family. In addition, Gulliver is quite different from other great travelers, such as Odysseus, who get themselves out of dangerous situations by exercising their wit and ability to trick others. He seems too dull for any battles of wit and too unimaginative to think up tricks, and thus he ends up with passive situations.

Houyhnhnms are rational horses and masters of land. They are the ruling class. They process all the virtues—reason, wisdom, knowledge, manners and self-control. Their thoughts and behavior are wholly governed by reason and truthfulness—they do not even have a word for "lie" in their language. They maintain a simple, and peaceful society. Houyhnhnms are like ordinary horses, except that they are highly intelligent and deeply wise. They live in a sort of socialist republic, with the needs of the community put before individual desires. They are the masters of the Yahoos, the savage humanlike creatures in Houyhnhnmland. In all, the Houyhnhnms have the greatest impact on Gulliver throughout all his four voyages. The meeting with Houyhnhnms becomes Gulliver a "human-hater" and he is grieved and unwilling to leave them. Even when he goes back in England he relates better with his horses than with his human family. He is certainly, in the end, a horse lover.

Yahoos, a species of hairy, naked, filthy and wild animals, disgusting creatures shaped like human beings. The men are characterized by their hairy bodies, and the women by their low-hanging breasts. They are extremely primitive in their eating habits. They are servants to Houyhnhnms, pulling their carriages and performing manual tasks. Though they are in the shape of human but behave exactly like animals. They have all the conceivable beastly qualities that Gulliver's own countrymen have—violent, evil and base. Despite Gulliver's disgust for these creatures, he ends his writings referring to himself as a Yahoo, just as what the Houyhnhnms do in the end—expel him from their realm. Thus, "Yahoo" becomes another term for human, at least in the mind of Gulliver at the end of his fourth journey.

Introduction to Chapter VI

This selection is from the fourth part of the novel, in which Gulliver tells, in the first person singular, his experiences when traveling in the land of Houyhnhnms, the noble horses. The Houyhnhnms, who are moral, intelligent, and noble-minded, stand in striking contrast to the Yahoos who are hairy, uncultivated, and infamous for their savagery, although they inhabit the same land with the Houyhnhnms. It is obvious that Swift throws his acid satire upon the corruption, hypocrisy, avarice, treachery, and other kinds of social evils of early 18th century England in Chapter VI. Moreover, he not only pours his antipathy to the realities, but exhibits a strong desire for an ideal society, as is clearly illustrated by his description of the sharp contrast between the Houyhnhnms and Yahoos in Chapter VIII.

Chapter VI

[A continuation of the state of England under Queen Anne. The character of a first minister of state in European courts.]

My master was yet wholly at a loss to understand what motives could incite this race of lawyers to perplex, disquiet, and weary themselves, and engage in a confederacy of injustice[1], merely for the sake of injuring their fellow-animals; neither could he comprehend what I meant in saying, they did it for 'hire'. Whereupon I was at much pains to describe to him the use of 'money', the materials it was made of, and the value of the metals; that when a *Yahoo* had got a great store of this precious substance, he was able to purchase whatever he had a mind to; the finest clothing, the noblest houses, great tracts of land, the most costly meats and drinks, and have his choice of the most beautiful females. Therefore since 'money' alone was able to perform all these feats, our *Yahoos* thought they could never have enough of it to spend, or to save, as they found themselves inclined, from their *natural bent*[2] either to profusion or avarice; that the rich man enjoyed the fruit of the poor man's labour, and the latter were a thousand to one in proportion to the former; that the bulk of our people were forced to live miserably, by labouring every day for small wages, to make a few live plentifully. I enlarged myself much on these, and many other particulars to the same purpose; *but his Honour was still to seek*[3]; for he went upon a supposition, that all animals had a *title*[4] to their share in the productions of the earth, and especially those who presided over the rest. Therefore he desired I would let him know, what these costly meats were, and how any of us happened to *want*[5] them? Whereupon I enumerated as many sorts as came into my head, with the various methods of *dressing them*[6], which could not be done without sending vessels by sea to every part of the world, as well for liquors to drink as for sauces and innumerable other *conveniences*[7]. I assured him that this whole globe of earth must be at least three times gone round before one of our better female *Yahoos* could get her breakfast, or a cup to put it in. He said that must needs be a miserable country which cannot furnish food for its own inhabitants. But what he chiefly wondered at was, how such vast tracts of ground as I described should be wholly without fresh water, and the people put to the necessity of sending over the sea for drink. I replied, that England (the dear place of my nativity) was computed to produce three times the quantity of food more than its inhabitants are able to consume, as well as liquors extracted from grain, or pressed out of the fruit of certain trees, which made excellent drink, and the same proportion in every other convenience of life. But, in order to feed the luxury and intemperance of the males, and the vanity of the females, we sent away the greatest part of our necessary things to other countries, whence, in return, we brought the materials of diseases, folly, and vice, to spend among ourselves. Hence it follows of necessity, that vast numbers of our people are compelled to seek their livelihood by begging, robbing, stealing, cheating, pimping, flattering, suborning, forswearing, *forging*[8], *gaming*[9], lying, fawning[10], hectoring[11], *voting*[12], *scribbling*[13], *star-gazing*[14] poisoning, whoring, canting, libelling, *freethinking*[15], and the like occupations; every one of which terms I was at much pains to make him understand.

That 'wine' was not imported among us from foreign countries to supply the want of water or other drinks, but because it was a sort of liquid which made us merry by putting us out of our senses, diverted all melancholy thoughts, begat wild extravagant imaginations in the brain, raised our hopes and banished our fears, suspended every *office*[16] of reason for a time, and deprived us of the use of our limbs, till we fell into a profound sleep; although it must be confessed, that we always awaked sick and dispirited; and that the use of this liquor filled us with diseases which made our lives uncomfortable and short.

But *beside*[17] all this, the bulk of our people supported themselves by furnishing the necessities or conveniences of life to the rich and to each other. For instance, when I am at home, and dressed as I ought to be, I carry on my body the workmanship of a hundred tradesmen; the building and furniture of my house employ as many more, and five times the number to adorn my wife.

I was going on to tell him of another sort of people, who get their livelihood by attending the sick, having, upon some occasions, informed his honour that many of my crew had died of diseases. But here it was with the utmost difficulty that I brought him to apprehend what I meant. He could easily conceive, that a *Houyhnhnm*, grew weak and heavy a few days before his death, or by some accident might hurt a limb; but that nature, who works all things to perfection, should suffer any pains to breed in our bodies, he thought impossible, and desired to know the reason of so unaccountable an evil. I told him, we fed on a thousand things which operated contrary to each other; that we ate when we were not hungry, and drank without the provocation of thirst; that we sate[18] whole nights drinking strong liquors, without eating a bit, which disposed us to sloth, inflamed our bodies, and *precipitated or prevented digestion*[19]; that prostitute female *Yahoos* acquired a certain malady, which bred rottenness in the bones of those who fell into their embraces; that this, and many other diseases, were propagated from father to son; so that great numbers came into the world with complicated maladies upon them; that it would be endless to give him a catalogue of all diseases incident to human bodies, for they would not be fewer than five or six hundred, spread over every limb and joint-in short, every part, external and intestine, having diseases appropriated to itself. To remedy which, there was a sort of people bred up among us in the profession, or pretence, of curing the sick. And because I had some skill in the faculty, I would, in gratitude to his honour, let him know the whole mystery and method by which they proceed.

But, besides real diseases, we are subject to many that are only imaginary, for which the physicians have invented imaginary cures; these have their several names, and so have the drugs that are proper for them; and with these our female *Yahoos* are always infested.

One great excellency in this tribe, is their skill at 'prognostics', wherein they seldom fail; their predictions in real diseases, when they rise to any degree of malignity, generally portending death, which is always in their power, when recovery is not: and therefore, upon any unexpected signs of amendment, after they have pronounced their sentence, rather than be accused as false prophets, they know how to approve their sagacity to the world, by a seasonable dose.

They are likewise of special use to husbands and wives who are grown weary of their mates; to eldest sons, to great ministers of state, and often to princes.

I had formerly, *upon occasion*[20], discoursed with my master upon the nature of government in general, and particularly of our own excellent constitution, deservedly the wonder and envy of the whole world. But having here accidentally mentioned a minister of state, he commanded me, some time after, to inform him, what species of *Yahoo* I particularly meant by that appellation.

I told him that a 'first' or 'chief minister of state', who was the person I intended to describe, was the creature wholly exempt from joy and grief, love and hatred, pity and anger; at least, makes use of no other passions, but a violent desire of wealth, power, and titles; that he applies his words to all uses, except to the indication of his mind; that he never tells a truth but with an intent that you should take it for a lie; nor a lie, but with a design that you should take it for a truth; that those he speaks worst of behind their backs are in the surest way of preferment; and whenever he begins to praise you to others, or to yourself, you are from that day forlorn. The worst mark you can receive is a promise, especially when it is confirmed with an oath; after which, every wise man retires, and gives over all hopes.

There are three methods, by which a man may rise to be chief minister. The first is, by knowing how, with prudence, to dispose of a wife, a daughter, or a sister; the second, by betraying or undermining his predecessor; and the third is, by a furious zeal, in public assemblies, against the corruption's of the court. But a wise prince would rather choose to employ those who practise the last of these methods; because such zealots prove always the most obsequious and subservient to the will and passions of their master. That these ministers, having all *employments*[21] at their disposal, preserve themselves in power, by bribing the majority of a senate or great council; and at last, by an expedient, called an '*act of indemnity*' [22] (whereof I described the nature to him), they secure themselves from *after-reckonings*[23], and retire from the public laden with the spoils of the nation.

The palace of a chief minister is a seminary to breed up others in his own trade: *the pages, lackeys*[24], and porters, by imitating their master, become ministers of state in their several districts, and learn to excel in the three principal ingredients, of insolence, lying, and bribery. Accordingly, *they have a subaltern court paid to them by persons of the best rank*[25]; and sometimes by the force of dexterity and impudence, arrive, through several gradations, to be successors to their lord.

He is usually governed by *a decayed wench*[26], or favourite footman, who are *the tunnels through which all graces are conveyed*[27], and may properly be called, in the last resort, the governors of the kingdom.

One day, in discourse, my master, having heard me mention the 'nobility' of my country, was pleased to make me a compliment which I could not pretend to deserve: that he was sure I must have been born of some noble family, because I far exceeded in shape, colour, and cleanliness, all the *Yahoos* of his nation, although I seemed to fail in strength and agility, which must be imputed to my different way of living from those other brutes; and besides I was not only endowed with the faculty of speech, but likewise with some rudiments of reason, to a degree that, with all his acquaintance, I passed for a prodigy.

He made me observe, that among the *Houyhnhnms*, the white, the sorrel, and the iron-gray, were not so exactly shaped as the bay, the dapple-gray, and the black; nor born with equal talents of mind, or a capacity to improve them; and therefore continued always in the condition of servants, without ever aspiring *to match out of their own race*[28], which in that country would be reckoned monstrous and unnatural.

I made his honour my most humble acknowledgments for the good opinion he was pleased to conceive of me, but assured him at the same time, that my birth was of the lower sort, having been born of plain honest parents, who were just able to give me a tolerable education; that nobility, among us, was altogether a different thing from the idea he had of it; that our young noblemen are bred from their childhood in idleness and luxury; that, as soon as years will permit, they consume their vigour, and contract odious diseases among *lewd females*[29]; and when their fortunes are almost ruined, they marry some woman of mean birth, disagreeable person, and unsound constitution (merely for the sake of money), whom they hate and despise. That the productions of such marriages are generally scrofulous, rickety, or deformed children; by which means the family seldom continues above three generations, unless the wife takes care to provide a healthy father, among her neighbours or domestics, in order to improve and continue the breed. That a weak diseased body, a meagre countenance, and sallow complexion, are the true marks of noble blood; and a healthy robust appearance is so disgraceful in a man of quality, that the world concludes his real father to have been a groom or a coachman. The imperfections of his mind run parallel with those of his body, being a composition of spleen, dullness, ignorance, caprice, sensuality, and pride.

Without the consent of *this illustrious body*[30], no law can be enacted, repealed, or altered: and these nobles have likewise the decision of all our possessions, without appeal.

Notes

[1] series of unlawful injustice

[2] natural inclination or tendency 天性

[3] but still my master was to seek an answer, i.e., he still did not understand; his Honour, his majesty, the title of emperor, here refers to master in the land of Houyhnhnm.

[4] right; claim

[5] lack

[6] preparing them for cooking, i. e., adding spices such as ginger, pepper, cinnamon, etc.

[7] material comforts; goods; here, articles of food.

[8] making counterfeit money 造假币

[9] gambling

[10] 奉承

[11] threatening

[12] to vote for money or manipulate elections

[13] writing carelessly as a hack writer

[14] the occupation of an astrologer

[15] rejecting traditional religious belief, hence, in this context, behaving oneself loosely, immorally

[16] function

[17] besides

[18] sate-sat

[19] caused us to suffer from loose bowels or constipation 便秘.

[20] on suitable opportunity or sometimes.

[21] official posts, here implying profitable jobs.

[22] An act of this sort was usually passed at each session of Parliament, to protect holders of public office from the possible consequences of any official acts done illegally but in good faith.赦免条例

[23] later reckonings, i.e., reckonings of illegal gains after retirement from public office.

[24] low servants; men servants

[25] they, of inferior rank themselves and their court are subjected to those of the highest ranks for they and their court are paid by them.

[26] an immoral, corrupt young woman, perhaps a servant girl who is getting old.

[27] the secret channels through which all favours are handed out.

[28] to marry outside of their own race

[29] unchaste women

[30] the noblility

Questions

1 What social evils and what professions are attacked by the author in Chapter VI?

2 How does a chief minister achieve his position?

3 How is the "nobility" described by the author?

4 According to your understanding, what are the similarities between Gulliver's native countrymen and Yahoos?

Analysis of Chapter VI

Chapter VI, from Part IV of *Gulliver's Travels* is to give Gulliver's master "master in the land of Houyhnhnms" a continual accounts of the state of England and England's first prime minister. All these descriptions have deeply confused the master.

Gulliver's natives are yahoo-like human beings. They are crazy about "hire". Here it means promotion of position and they are also crazy for money with which they can buy whatever they want. Their nature is profusion and avarice. The rich men are the minority of society depending on the fruit of the poor. After Gulliver's description, the master did not understand why the man of England are so greedy and horrible like that. Therefore, Gulliver goes on explaining to the Master what these "costly meats (In Chapter VI, 1st paragraph, Line 8, it means human being or natives of England)" were—such as: How the female cook breakfast; how they get water and make excellent drink (wine); the inequality between the poor and rich can be read. The poor provide the greatest part of our necessary things to other countries so as to feed the "luxury and intemperance of the males, and the vanity of the females", however in return, we brought the materials of disease, folly, and vice. In order to live we have to beg, rob, steal, cheat, pimp, forswear, flatter... and so on. Gulliver lists more than 20 words of evils. These parallelled words make readers at tense reading it, feeling horrible to live in the world where evils are prevalent in every corner and Gulliver himself "was at much pains to make him understand. (In Chapter VI last line of 1st paragraph)"

Gulliver's "Introduction of wine" in next paragraph is impressive and profound. It is a sort of liquid which made us merry, get rid of melancholy thoughts by putting us out of our senses; get wild extravagant imaginations in brain, raised our hopes and banish our fears, make us unreasonable for a time, result in unconscious limb and sound sleep. Eventually, wine made our lives uncomfortable and short.

Above all, English natives live an extravagant life. Though at home, one will dress as he ought to be, "I carry on my body the workmanship of a hundred tradesmen. (In Chapter VI 3rd paragraph)" In social intercourse, one must be able to use different arts to communicate with different persons, which makes one person a hundred tradesman. In result, one becomes hypocritical person of diverse personalities. In the following words "the building and furniture of my house employ as many more, and five times the number to adorn my wife." The structure "as many more" and the number "5 times to adorn" are a little exaggerated and absurd. However, to some extent, it is a satire reflecting the sick psychology of his contemporary Englishmen, a kind of wine and extravagant life.

"I was going on to tell himself of another sort of people". Here, "another sort of people" refers the diseased people. It is difficult for Master of Houyhnhnm to understand; because on the land of Houynhnhns, a Houyhnhnm grew weak and heavy a few days before his death or by accident might hurt a limb. According to the master, if making good use of our natural organs, it is impossible for us to suffer pains. Gulliver illustrates instances to satisfy master's curiosity about causes of diseases in human body. E.g. we feed on a thousand things, which operated contrary to each other; such as bad habits, amoral behavior (the propagation of malady from female prostitute) thus, numerous and endless diseases permeate in human world. statistics have been employed to specify the seriousness of malady: *could not be fewer than 5 or 6 hundred spread over every limb and joint; those diseases are incurable* though a sort of people—doctors pretend to cure the sick.

Besides real diseases, they have imaginary disease and imaginary cures. Doctors are good at predictions. When they predict that somebody is of malignity (of fatal disease) and going to die, they are in the power, while the patients are at doctor's mercy.

In the latter part of Chapter VI, Gulliver explained the *nature of government and Minister of state* was *a creature wholly exempt from joy and grief, love and hatred, pity and anger*. The Minister is emotionless and passionless. What he pursues is wealth, power and titles. He is a liar, *whenever he begins to praise you to others or to yourself, you are from that day forlorn.* That is to say when you are praised in front of others by the prime minister, from that moment on, you are deserted or wrecked, and you are devastated. The prime minister is unreliable. If a wise man receives his promise, he will give up hopes and withdraw.

Gulliver presents three methods of seizing the position of Minister. One way is to dispose of a wife, a daughter or a sister (abandon wife, daughter or sister to devote to the scheme of rising to chief minister's position); another way is betraying or undermining the predecessors and the third way is to be enthusiastic or crazy about the public assemblies against the corruption of the court. "A wise prince", king or governor will choose those who practice the last of three methods, because such zealots prove always obedient and loyal to the will and passions of their master. Moreover, these "ministers" have their official authoritative posts. These posts are profitable. In order to preserve their power, they bribe the majority of a senate or great council. If the ministers preserved their office, they still have preserved ways of making money—"(at the bottom the 10th paragraph) *by an expedient called an' act of indemnity' "...they secured themselves from after reckoning.* "after reckoning" means later reckoning. The ministers make sure that they could be free from reckoning of illegal gains after their retirement from the governmental offices. Therefore, the ministers retired with wealth and the nation was burdened with the spoils.

For the ministers had set bad examples, their subordinates would follow them, imitate them and become the "ministers of street." The persons who are inferior to the ministers follow their master's footprints and even excel them in three principal ingredients of insolence, lying and bribery. *They have a subaltern court paid to them by persons of the best rank* (In Chapter VI 11th paragraph). They, still, refer to the inferior officers. These officers and their court are subjected to those of higher ranks, who pay them and their court. Someday in the future, the inferior officers may be successors to their masters through several grades of promotion. However, Gulliver himself is considered as man from noble, so from many aspects, he is different from what Yahoos look like. Yahoos, in the land of Houyhnhnms, are servants of Houyhnhnms. They are lower than Houyhnhnms, because Yahoos are different from Houyhnhnms in the aspects of appearance, talents and capacity. The Houyhnhnms are forbidden to marry out of their race. For other races are considered monstrous and unnatural. This rule keeps the Houyhnhnms pure and unpolluted.

At the end of the conversation between Gulliver and Master of Houyhnhnms, Gulliver makes a distinct explanation of the different connotation of "nobility" in English and in the language of the Houyhnhnms. The concept of nobility in English is so superficial and shallow. In the last paragraph of this chapter, the author points out this noble race, the Houyhnhnms is the truly ruling class on the land.

Gulliver's Travels, Swift's achievement in literature, is thus a satire on the whole English society of 18th century. Especially in this part, English life is shown to resemble the despicable social life of the Yahoos and to contrast with the nobility of the Houyhnhnm.

Unit 3
Jane Austen（1775~1817）

Life

　　As a great novelist of realism, Jane Austen, the sixth child of the family of seven was born in a small village in 1775. Her father was a churchman, a learned man who encouraged his daughter both in her reading and writing. She received a good education at home. She is a vigorous reader and her family spent much time in group reading and performing theatricals. In such environment, Jane Austen's literary talent was being cultivated and developed. She never married in her life and she never lived apart from her family. She lived a quiet and uneventful life. Her closed friend was her sister, who also remained unmarried. Aside from doing domestic chores at home, Austen spent nearly all her time composing and revising. So because of many times of her revision, the year of the publication usually is not correspondent with the year when she wrote the work. However, almost every novel produced by her is very impressive, especially on the mind of women readers.

Sense and sensibility was published in 1811. It relates the story of two sisters and their love affairs. Elinor is a woman of good sense, while Marianne is the creature of sensibility. When they find the men they love have other lovers, one controls her emotion and the other lets the emotion control her action. It seems that Austen was offering her advice to young girls that they should never lose their reasoning power in dealing with men. She also criticized the selfish and irresponsible behaviors of both men and women in choosing marriage partners.

Mansfield Park (1814), *Emma* (1816), and *Persuasion* (1818) deal with the romantic entanglements of their strongly characterized heroines. *Mansfield Park* is more solemn and moralistic than Austen's early novels. Poor Fanny Price is adopted by her rich uncle, the stern but kind-hearted Sir Thomas Bertram. In the Mansfield Park, Fanny finds her cousin Edmund an only friend. When the sophisticated Henry Crawford and his sister Mary visit the Mansfield neighborhood, the moral sense of each marriageable member in the Bertram family is tested in various ways. Fanny proves herself an honest and virtuous woman and finally wins the heart of Edmund.

Emma, presents the story of the beautiful, charming and clever Emma Woodhouse in a more relaxed atmosphere. She is eager to plan a future for Harriet Smith, an orphan girl. The Woodhouse treat her as a member of the family. Emma first prevents her from marrying Robert Martin, an eligible young farmer, and then helps her in several failed attempts to pursue an ideal husband. She herself becomes the victim of her "clever" plan when she is surprised to learn that Harriet intends to marry Mr. Knightly, with whom Emma is in love. Eventually, Emma realizes how she again and again ruined Harriet chances to happiness, and she has learnt her lesson through the events. In the end Mr. Knightly proposes to Emma and Harriet happily accepts Robert Martin as her husband.

Persuasion has more psychological depth than her previous novels. *Northanger Abbey* (1818) tells the story of the unsophisticated and sincere Catherine Morland, who learns to distinguish between the excessively emotional life in Gothic novels and the realities of ordinary human existence. The novel voiced Austen's subtle criticism of the highly popular Gothic romances of the late 18th century.

Another two, published posthumously are fragments and early drafts of Jane

Austen including *Lady Susan* (1871) *The Watsons* (1871) and *Sanditon* (1925), which are less known to readers.

  Pride and Prejudice (1813) is the most popular of her novels. The characters are remarkably portrayed and they come alive under her pen: the long-winded (talkative) mother; the flattering churchman; the clever and quick-minded Elizabeth, whose "prejudice" is matched with Darcy's "Pride"; the empty-headed and flirtatious Kitty and Lydia; the modest and unselfish Jane; and the good natured Mr. Bennet. The conflict between Elizabeth and Darcy is the conflict between two equally wrong views on people's worth. Elizabeth is not the ideal woman to be Darcy's wife at first sight because she does not have a pretty face. But a woman's value should not be judged from the surface. Darcy will soon find her a woman with special charm and beauty. He loves her for her intelligence and integrity. But his proposal is rejected. His pride hurt, yet he had learnt his lesson. Elizabeth finally discards her prejudice and accepts the man as her husband.

Plot of *Pride and Prejudice*

  The first sentence of the novel sets the tone of it: *It is truth universally acknowledged, that a single man in possession of a good fortune must be in want of a wife.* Mr. and Mrs. Bennet are the parents of five unmarried daughters. The only aim of Mrs. Bennet is to find a husband for each. Mr. Bennet, is a gentleman of bookish nature, is disdainful of his wife and indifferent to his daughters, except Elizabeth, because she is intelligent and witty. An estate near the Bennets is leased by Mr Bingley, a wealthy bachelor, who brings with him his friend Mr. Darcy, likewise wealthy and unmarried. Bingley makes a good impression, but the arrogant Darcy is much disliked, especially by Elizabeth. Bingley and Sweet-tempered Jane Bennet fall in love, but Darcy temporarily frustrates their courtship. The fact is, however, that Darcy and Elizabeth also love each other, though neither realizes it. Darcy is blinded by his pride and Elizabeth is blinded by her prejudice against Darcy. Finally after Darcy has saved the reputation of silly Lydia, who has eloped with a never-do-well officer (Wickham), Darcy and Elizabeth realize their errors of judgment and become engaged, and Jane and Bingley are reunited.

The plot, like Austen's others works such as *Emma* and *Persuasion*, is simple and naturally has grown out of the characters and their ordinary relations. It deals with the everyday life of small and big landlords and their families in the English countryside, particularly with the love and marriage of the younger members of those families. The story centers round the heroine Elizabeth Bennet (who stands for "Prejudice") and the hero Fitzwilliam Darcy (who stands for "pride") and a minor couple, her sister Jane and his friend Charles Bingley. The incidents of the lives of these characters, including teas and visits and walks and dances and conversations and other expected or unexpected happenings, finally lead to the happy unions of the two couples.

Some Comments on *Pride and Prejudice*

The novel begins with a conversation at Longbourn, the Bennet household, regarding the arrival of Mr. Bingley, "a single man of large fortune" to Netherfield Park, a nearby estate. Mrs. Bennet sees Mr. Bingley as a potential suitor for her daughters, and attempts to persuade Mr. Bennet to visit him. There are five daughters in the Bennet family. Mr. Bennet seems to prefer Elizabeth, the second oldest, because of her intelligence, while Mrs. Bennet seems fonder of the oldest, Jane, because of her beauty, and the middle child, Lydia, because of her good humor.

The first line of the novel—"*It is a truth universally acknowledged, that a single man in possession of a good fortune, must be in want of a wife"*—is among the most famous first lines in literature. It not only calls the reader's attention to the central place that marriage will have in the plot of the story, but also introduces the reader immediately Jane Austen's use of **irony**. While the focus of the line is on "a single man ... in want of a wife," the real emphasis in the novel and in the society of the late-eighteenth and early-nineteenth centuries is the need for young women to find a husband in possession of a good fortune. The purely economic, utilitarian motive for marriage will come under attack in the novel. This strange social trend in marriage leaves many women with little choice but to marry for the sake of economic survival.

Our first glimpse of the Bennett family is enough to provide us with a fairly accurate sketch of their characters. Mrs. Bennett is chatty, frivolous and obsessed with marrying off her daughters, while Mr. Bennett is rather detached and ironic, not overly involved with the cares of the family. Jane is beautiful, amiable and good-natured, and always assumes that others are as good-natured as she. Elizabeth, good-looking but not as beautiful as her sister, however she has a sharp wit and prides herself on her keen perception of others' characters.

From the very first pages of the novel Austen's tendency to favor dialogue over narration is clearly manifested. Critics have acclaimed Austen has ability to bring characters to life by having them reveal themselves to the reader through their actions and dialogue, not through detailed narrative descriptions. Critic George Henry Lewes, a contemporary of Jane Austen, praises her because *"instead of description, the common and easy resource of novelists, she has the rare and difficult art of dramatic presentation instead of telling us what her characters are, and what they feel, she presents the people, and they reveal themselves."*

Her skillful art of the treatment of conversation is shown in this opening chapter. The characters are made to reveal themselves through their own words, and Jane Austen is always able to find the precise expression that accurately fits the character and the occasion. She is possessed of a neat humor and a satirical touch.

Her style is an almost perfect instrument for her purpose—simple, clear, quiet, precise, keen, suggestive and mildly ironical.

Major Characters

Elizabeth Bennet　The protagonist of the novel and the second oldest of five sisters, Elizabeth is lively, quick-witted, sharp-tongued, bold and intelligent. Elizabeth is good-looking, and is especially distinguished by her fine eyes. The importance of her eyes may be symbolic of her abilities of perception. She has pride in her abilities to perceive the truth of situations and of people's characters. However, her perceptive abilities fail her frequently because she judges people so rashly. By the end of the novel she overcomes her prejudice through her dealings with Darcy. Elizabeth is concerned with propriety, good manners, and virtue, but is not impressed by mere wealth or titles.

Mr. Darcy　An extremely wealthy aristocrat, Darcy is proud, haughty and extremely conscious of class differences at the beginning of the novel. He does, however, have a strong sense of honor and virtue. His first proposal to Elizabeth is refused. Elizabeth's rebukes help him to recognize his faults. It is, in fact, precisely because Elizabeth is not so fearful of his high social status and she is not afraid to criticize his character that he is attracted to her. The self-knowledge acquired from Elizabeth's rebukes and the desire to win Elizabeth's love spur him to change and judge people more by their character than by their social class.

Jane Bennet　Jane is the oldest in the family. Beautiful, good-tempered, sweet, amiable, humble and selfless, Jane is universally well liked. She refuses to judge anyone badly, always making excuses for people. Jane is a static character as she is basically a model of virtue from the beginning, there is no room for her to develop in the novel.

Charles Bingley　Mr. Bingley, much like Jane, is an amiable and good-tempered person. He is not overly concerned with class differences, and Jane's poor family connections are not a serious obstruction to his attachment to her. Bingley is very modest and easily swayed by the advice of his friends, as seen in his decision not to propose to Jane as a result of Darcy's belief that Jane does really love him. Also like Jane, Bingley lacks serious character faults and is thus static throughout the novel.

Mr. Wickham An officer in the regiment stationed at Meryton, Wickham is quickly judged to be a perfectly good and amiable man because of his friendliness and the ease of his manners. He initially shows a preference for Elizabeth, and she is pleased by his attentions and inclined to believe his story about Darcy. Yet while Wickham has the appearance of goodness and virtue, this appearance is deceptive. His true nature begins to show itself through his attachment to Miss King for purely mercenary purposes and then through Darcy's exposition of his past and through his elopement with Lydia, deceiving her to believe that he intends to marry her. But for Elizabeth's maturity and intelligence, she may also have been the prey of Wickham.

Mrs. Bennet Mrs. Bennet is a foolish and frivolous woman. She lacks all sense of propriety and virtue. She has no concern for the moral or intellectual education of her daughters. She is a totally illiterate housewife. From the beginning of the novel her sole obsession is to marry off her daughters. She is perfectly happy with Lydia's marriage, and never once blames her daughter for her shameful conduct or for the worry she has caused her family. Her impropriety is a constant source of mortification (侮辱，悔恨，遗恨) for the Elizabeth, and the inane nature of her conversation makes her society so difficult to bear that even Jane and Bingley decide to move out of the neighborhood a year after they are married.

Mr. Bennet An intelligent man with good sense, Mr. Bennet made the mistake of marrying a foolish woman. He takes shelter in his books and seems to want nothing more than to be bothered as little as possible by his family. That is to say for Mr. Bennet, anything is better than being bothered by the trivial family matters. His indolence leads to the neglect of the education of daughters. Even when Elizabeth warns him not to allow Lydia to go to Brighton because of the moral danger of the situation, he does not listen to her because he does not want to be bothered with Lydia's complaints.

Lydia Bennet The youngest of the Bennet sisters, Lydia is foolish and flirtatious. She is given up to indolence and the gratification of every strange idea. She is the favorite of Mrs. Bennet, because the two have something in common. Lydia is constantly obsessed with the officers in the regiment, and sees no purpose to life beyond entertainment and diversion. She lacks no sense of virtue, propriety or good-judgment, which can be observed in her elopement with Wickham and her complete lack of remorse afterward.

Catherine (Kitty) Bennet   Kitty seems to have little personality of her own, but simply to act as a shadow to Lydia, following Lydia's lead in whatever she does. The end of the novel provides hope that Kitty's character will improve by leaving from the society of Lydia and her mother and being taken care of primarily by Jane and Elizabeth.

Mary Bennet   The third oldest of the Bennet sisters, Mary is strangely solemn and pedantic. She dislikes going out into society, and prefers to spend her time studying. In conversation, Mary is constantly moralizing or trying to make profound observations about human nature and life in general.

Introduction to Chapter I

Chapter I is the opening chapter of *Pride and Prejudice* and it is also the most well-known beginning of British classics. In this chapter, all major characters leave a rough impression on readers' mind and the theme of the novel does appear in the first chapter. This is rare in novel. Reading chapter I, readers learn the author is good at conversation and she presents a vivid picture of 19th century life of middle class.

Chapter I

It is a truth universally acknowledged, that a single man in possession of a good fortune must be in want of a wife.

However little known the feelings or views of such a man may be on his first entering a neighbourhood, this truth is so well fixed in the minds of the surrounding families, that he is considered as the rightful property of some one or other of their daughters.

"My dear Mr. Bennet," said his lady to him one day, "have you heard that *Netherfield Park*[1] let at last?"

Mr. Bennet replied that he had not.

"But it is," returned she; "for Mrs. Long has just been here, and she told me all about it."

Mr. Bennet made no answer.

"Do not you want to know who has taken it?" cried his wife impatiently.

"*You* want to tell me, and I have no objection to hearing it."

This was invitation enough.

"Why, my dear, you must know, Mrs. Long says that Netherfield is taken by a young man of large fortune from the north of England; that he came down on Monday in *a chaise and four*[2] see the place, and was so much delighted with it that he agreed with *Mr. Morris*[3] immediately; that he is to take possession before *Michaelmas*[4] and some of his servants are to be in the house by the end of next week."

"What is his name?"

"Bingley."

"Is he married or single?"

"Oh! single, my dear, to be sure! A single man of large fortune; four or five thousand a year. What a fine thing for our girls!"

"How so? How can it affect them?"

"My dear Mr. Bennet," replied his wife, "how can you be so tiresome! You must know that I am thinking of his marrying one of them."

"Is that his design in settling here?"

"Design! nonsense, how can you talk so! But it is very likely that he *may* fall in love with one of them, and therefore you must visit him as soon as he comes."

"*I see no occasion for that*[5]. You and the girls may go, or you may send them by themselves, which perhaps will be still better; for, as you are as handsome as any of them, Mr. Bingley might like you the best of the party."

"My dear, you flatter me. I certainly *have* had my share of beauty, but I do not pretend to be any thing extraordinary now. When a woman has five grown up daughters, she ought to give over thinking of her own beauty."

"In such cases, a woman has not often much beauty to think of."

"But, my dear, you must indeed go and see Mr. Bingley when he comes into the neighbourhood."

"*It is more than I engage for, I assure you.*[6]"

"But consider your daughters. Only think *what an establishment*[7] it would be for one of them. Sir William and Lady Lucas are determined to go, merely on that account, for in general, you know they visit no new comers. *Indeed you must go, for it will be impossible for us to visit him, if you do not.*[8]"

"You are over-scrupulous, surely. I dare say Mr. Bingley will be very glad to see you; and I will send a few lines by you to assure him of my hearty consent to his marrying which ever he chases of the girls; though I must throw in a good word for my little *Lizzy*[9]."

"I desire you will do no such thing. Lizzy is not a bit better than the others; and I am sure she is not half so handsome as *Jane*[10], nor half so good humoured as *Lydia*[11]. But you are always giving *her* the preference."

"They have none of them much to recommend them," replied he; "they are all silly and ignorant like other girls; but Lizzy has something more of quickness than her sisters."

"Mr. Bennet, how can you abuse your own children in such way? You take delight in vexing me. You have no compassion on my poor nerves."

"You mistake me, my dear. I have a high respect for your nerves. They are my old friends. I have heard you mention them with consideration these twenty years at least."

"Ah! you do not know what I suffer."

"But I hope you will get over it, and live to see many young men of four thousand a year come into the neighbourhood."

"It will be no use to us if twenty such should come, since you will not visit them."

"Depend upon it, my dear, that when there are twenty I will visit them all."

Mr. Bennet was so odd a mixture of *quick parts*[12], sarcastic humour, reserve, and caprice, that the experience of three and twenty years had been insufficient to make his wife understand his character. *Her* mind was less difficult to *develop*[13]. She was a woman of mean understanding, little information, and uncertain temper. When she was discontented, she fancied herself nervous. The business of her life was to get her daughters married; its solace was visiting and news.

Notes:

[1] an estate in the neighbourhood of the home of the Bennets

[2] a carriage drawn by four horses

[3] the estate-agent

[4] a festival celebrated on Sep. 29, the feast day in honor of the archangel St. Michael. Usually on this day, a contract will be signed

[5] I see no need for that

[6] It is more than I can promise

[7] what a marriage(多好的一门亲事)

[8] This is because it was the etiquette of the time for the male head of a family to pay the first visit to a newly-moved-in neighbour. It would have been a shocking breach of etiquette for a mother and her daughters to call first.

[9] Elizabeth, Mr. Bennet's second daughter

[10] Mr. Bennet's eldest daughter

[11] Mr. Bennet's youngest daughter

[12] abilities or intelligence

[13] unwrap; unfold; hence in the present context, understand.

Questions

1　How do you understand the first sentence of this chapter?

2　What had happened to Mrs. Bennet?

3　According to this chapter, give sketches the Bennets' daughters.

4　Describe the personality of Mr. Bennet and Mrs. Bennet in your own words.

Analysis of Chapter I

The selection given here is the first chapter of the novel in which the parents of the Bennet girls are busy considering the prospects of their daughter's marriages, shortly after hearing of the arrival of a rich, unmarried young man as their neighbor. Mild satire may be found here in the author's seemingly matter-of-fact description of a very ordinary, practical family conversation, though unmistakable sympathy is given here to both Mrs. Bennet and Mr. Bennet.

Unit 4
Charlotte Brontë (1816 ~ 1855)

Life

Charlotte Brontë was born in 1816, the third daughter of the Rev. Patrick Brontë and his wife Maria. Her brother Patrick Branwell was born in 1817, and her sisters Emily and Anne in 1818 and 1820. In 1820, too, the Brontë family moved to Haworth, Mrs. Brontë dying the following year.

In 1824 the four eldest Brontë daughters were enrolled as pupils at the Clergy Daughter's School at Cowan Bridge. The following year Maria and Elizabeth, the two eldest daughters, became ill, left the school and died; Charlotte and Emily, understandably, were brought home.

In 1831 Charlotte became a pupil at the school at Roe Head, but she left school the following year to teach her sisters at home. She returned to Roe Head School in 1835 as a governess; for a time her sister Emily attended the same school as a pupil, but became homesick and returned to Haworth. Ann took her place from 1836 to 1837.

In 1838, Charlotte left Roe Head School. In 1839 she accepted a position as governess in the Sidgewick family, but left after three months and returned to Haworth.

Upon her return to Haworth the three sisters, led by Charlotte, decided to open their own school after the necessary preparations had been completed. In 1842 Charlotte and Emily went to Brussels to complete their studies. After a trip home to Haworth, Charlotte returned alone to Brussels, where she remained until 1844.

Upon her return home the sisters embarked upon their project for founding a school, which proved to be a failure: their advertisements did not receive a single response from the public. The following year Charlotte discovered Emily's poems, and decided to publish a selection of the poems of all three sisters: 1846 brought the publication of their Poems, written under the pseudonyms of Currer, Ellis and Acton Bell whose first letters stand for their genuine names. Charlotte also completed *The Professor*, which was rejected for publication. The following year, however, Charlotte's *Jane Eyre*, Emily's *Wuthering Heights*, and Ann's *Agnes Grey* were all published, still under the Bell pseudonyms.

In 1848 Charlotte and Ann visited their publishers in London, and revealed the true identities of the "Bells". In the same year Branwell Brontë, by now an alcoholic and a drug addict, died, and Emily died shortly thereafter. Ann died the following year.

In 1849 Charlotte, visiting London, began to move in literary circles, making the acquaintance, for example, of Thackeray. In 1850 Charlotte edited her sister's various works, and met Mrs. Gaskell.

In 1854 Charlotte caught pneumonia. It was an illness which could have been cured, but she seems to have seized upon it (consciously or unconsciously) as an opportunity of ending her life, and after a lengthy and painful illness, she died, probably of dehydration.

1857 saw the posthumous publication of *The Professor*, which had been written in 1845~46.

Plot of *Jane Eyre*

Jane Eyre is a young orphan being raised by Mrs. Reed, her cruel, wealthy aunt. One day, as punishment for fighting with her bullying cousin John Reed, Jane's aunt imprisons Jane in the red-room, the room in which Jane's Uncle Reed died. While locked in, Jane, believing that she sees her uncle's ghost, screams and faints. She wakes to find herself in the care of Bessie, a considerate servant and the kindly apothecary Mr. Lloyd, who suggests to Mrs. Reed that Jane be sent away to school. To Jane's delight, Mrs. Reed agrees.

Once at the Lowood School, Jane finds that her life is far from being idyllic. The school's headmaster is a cruel, hypocritical, and abusive man. At Lowood, Jane befriends a young girl named Helen Burns, whose strong, martyr-like attitude toward the school's miseries is both helpful and displeasing to Jane. A massive typhus epidemic sweeps Lowood, and Helen dies of consumption. After a group of more sympathetic gentlemen takes Brocklehurst's place, Jane's life improves dramatically. She spends eight more years at Lowood, six as a student and two as a teacher.

After teaching for two years, Jane yearns for new experiences. She accepts a governess position at a manor called Thornfield, where she teaches a lively French girl named Adèle. The distinguished housekeeper Mrs. Fairfax presides over the estate. Jane's employer at Thornfield is a dark, impassioned man named Rochester, with whom Jane finds herself falling secretly in love. She saves Rochester from a fire one night, which he claims was started by a drunken servant. Jane sinks into despondency when Rochester brings home a beautiful but vicious woman named Blanche Ingram. Jane expects Rochester to propose to Blanche. But Rochester instead proposes to Jane, who accepts almost disbelievingly.

The wedding day arrives. As Jane and Mr. Rochester prepare to exchange their vows, the voice of Mr. Mason cries out that Rochester already has a wife. Mason introduces himself as the brother of that wife—a woman named Bertha. Mr. Mason testifies that Bertha, whom Rochester married when he was a young man in Jamaica, is still alive. Rochester does not deny Mason's claims, but he explains that Bertha has gone mad. He takes the wedding party back to Thornfield, where they witness the insane Bertha Mason scurrying around on all fours and growling like an animal. Rochester keeps Bertha hidden on the third story of Thornfield. Knowing that it is impossible for her to be with Rochester, Jane flees Thornfield.

Penniless and hungry, Jane is forced to sleep outdoors and beg for food. At last, three siblings who live in a manor alternatively called Marsh End and Moor House take her in. Their names are Mary, Diana, and St. John Rivers, and Jane quickly becomes friends with them. St. John is a clergyman, and he finds Jane a job teaching at a charity school in Morton. He surprises her one day by declaring that her uncle, John Eyre, has died and left her a large fortune: 20,000 pounds. When Jane asks how she received this news, he shocks her further by declaring that her uncle was also his uncle: Jane and the Riverses are cousins. Jane immediately decides to share her inheritance equally with her three newfound relatives.

St. John decides to travel to India as a missionary, and he urges Jane to accompany him—as his wife. Jane agrees to go to India but refuses to marry her cousin because she does not love him. St. John pressures her to reconsider, and she nearly gives in. However, she realizes that she cannot abandon forever the man she truly loves when one night she hears Rochester's voice calling her name over the moors. Jane immediately hurries back to Thornfield and finds that it has been burned to the ground by Bertha Mason, who lost her life in the fire. Rochester saved the servants but lost his eyesight and one of his hands. Jane travels on to Rochester's new residence, Ferndean, where he lives with two servants named John and Mary.

At Ferndean, Rochester and Jane rebuild their relationship and soon marry. At the end of her story, Jane writes that she has been married for ten blissful years and that she and Rochester enjoy perfect equality in their life together. She says that after two years of blindness, Rochester regained sight in one eye and was able to behold their first son at his birth.

Some Comments on *Jane Eyre*

Themes

Love versus Autonomy

Jane Eyre is very much the story of a quest to be loved. Jane searches, not just for romantic love, but also for a sense of being valued, of belonging. Thus Jane says to Helen Burns: "to gain some real affection from you, or Miss Temple, or any other whom I truly love, I would willingly submit to have the bone of my arm broken, or to let a bull toss me, or to stand behind a kicking horse, and let it dash its hoof at my chest" (Chapter 8). Yet, over the course of the book, Jane must learn how to gain love without sacrificing and harming herself in the process.

Her fear of losing her autonomy motivates her refusal of Rochester's marriage proposal. Jane believes that "marrying" Rochester while he remains legally tied to Bertha would mean rendering herself a mistress and sacrificing her own integrity for the sake of emotional gratification. On the other hand, her life at Moor House tests her in the opposite manner. There, she enjoys economic independence and engages in worthwhile and useful work, teaching the poor; yet she lacks emotional sustenance. Although St. John proposes marriage, offering her a partnership built around a common purpose, Jane knows their marriage would remain loveless.

Nonetheless, the events of Jane's stay at Moor House are necessary tests of Jane's autonomy. Only after proving her self-sufficiency to herself can she marry Rochester and not be asymmetrically dependent upon him as her "master." The marriage can be one between equals. As Jane says: "I am my husband's life as fully as he is mine... To be together is for us to be at once as free as in solitude, as gay as in company... We are precisely suited in character—perfect concord is the result" (Chapter 38).

Jane Eyre is critical of Victorian England's strict social hierarchy. Brontë's exploration of the complicated social position of governesses is perhaps the novel's most important treatment of this theme. Like Heathcliff in *Wuthering Heights*, Jane is a figure of ambiguous class standing and, consequently, a source of extreme tension for the characters around her. Jane's manners, sophistication, and education are those of an aristocrat, because Victorian governesses, who tutored children in etiquette as well as academics, were expected to possess the "culture" of the aristocracy. Yet, as paid employees, they were more or less treated as servants; thus, Jane remains penniless and powerless while at Thornfield. Jane's understanding of the double standard crystallizes when she becomes aware of her feelings for Rochester; she is his intellectual, but not his social, equal. Even before the crisis surrounding Bertha Mason, Jane is hesitant to marry Rochester because she senses that she would feel indebted to him for "condescending" to marry her. Jane's distress, which appears most strongly in Chapter 17, seems to be Brontë's critique of Victorian class attitudes.

Jane herself speaks out against class prejudice at certain moments in the book. For example, in Chapter 23 she chastises Rochester: "Do you think, because I am poor, obscure, plain, and little, I am soulless and heartless? You think wrong! —I have as much soul as you—and full as much heart! And if God had gifted me with some beauty and much wealth, I should have made it as hard for you to leave me, as it is now for me to leave you." However, it is also important to note that nowhere in *Jane Eyre* are society's boundaries bent. Ultimately, Jane is only able to marry Rochester as his equal because she has almost magically come into her own inheritance from her uncle.

Jane struggles continually to achieve equality and to overcome oppression. In addition to class hierarchy, she must fight against patriarchal domination—against those who believe women to be inferior to men and try to treat them as such. Three central male figures threaten her desire for equality and dignity: Mr. Brocklehurst, Edward Rochester, and St. John Rivers. All three are misogynistic on some level.

Each tries to keep Jane in a submissive position, where she is unable to express her own thoughts and feelings. In her quest for independence and self-knowledge, Jane must escape Brocklehurst, reject St. John, and come to Rochester only after ensuring that they may marry as equals. This last condition is met once Jane proves herself able to function, through the time she spends at Moor House, in a community and in a family. She will not depend solely on Rochester for love and she can be financially independent. Furthermore, Rochester is blind at the novel's end and thus dependent upon Jane to be his "prop and guide." In Chapter 12, Jane articulates what was for her time a radically feminist philosophy:

Women are supposed to be very calm generally: but women feel just as men feel; they need exercise for their faculties, and a field for their efforts as much as their brothers do; they suffer from too rigid a restraint, too absolute a stagnation, precisely as men would suffer; and it is narrow-minded in their more privileged fellow-creatures to say that they ought to confine themselves to making puddings and knitting stockings, to playing on the piano and embroidering bags. It is thoughtless to condemn them, or laugh at them, if they seek to do more or learn more than custom has pronounced necessary for their sex.

Images of fire and ice appear throughout *Jane Eyre*. The former represents Jane's passions, anger, and spirit, while the latter symbolizes the oppressive forces trying to extinguish Jane's vitality. Fire is also a metaphor for Jane, as the narrative repeatedly associates her with images of fire, brightness, and warmth. In Chapter 4, she likens her mind to "a ridge of lighted heath, alive, glancing, devouring." We can recognize Jane's kindred spirits by their similar links to fire; thus we read of Rochester's "flaming and flashing" eyes (Chapter 25). After he has been blinded, his face is compared to "a lamp quenched, waiting to be relit" (Chapter 37).

Images of ice and cold, often appearing in association with barren landscapes or seascapes, symbolize emotional desolation, loneliness, or even death. The "death-white realms" of the arctic that Bewick describes in his *History of British Birds* parallel Jane's physical and spiritual isolation at Gateshead (Chapter 1). Lowood's freezing temperatures—for example, the frozen pitchers of water that greet the girls each morning—mirror Jane's sense of psychological exile. After the interrupted wedding to Rochester, Jane describes her state of mind: "A Christmas frost had come at mid-summer; a white December storm had whirled over June; ice glazed the ripe apples, drifts crushed the blowing roses; on hay-field and corn-field lay a frozen shroud ... and the woods, which twelve hours since waved leafy and fragrant as groves between the tropics, now spread, waste, wild, and white as pine-forests in wintry Norway. My hopes were all dead...." (Chapter 26). Finally, at Moor House, St. John's frigidity and stiffness are established through comparisons with ice and cold rock. Jane writes: "By degrees, he acquired a certain influence over me that took away my liberty of mind.... I fell under a freezing spell" (Chapter 34). When St. John proposes marriage to Jane, she concludes that "as his curate, his comrade, all would be right.... But as his wife—at his side always, and always restrained, and always checked—forced to keep the fire of my nature continually low, to compel it to burn inwardly and never utter a cry, though the imprisoned flame consumed vital after vital—this would be unendurable" (Chapter 34).

An important symbol in "*Jane Byre*" is the red-room. It can be viewed as a symbol of what Jane must overcome in her struggles to find freedom, happiness, and a sense of belonging. In the red-room, Jane's position of exile and imprisonment first becomes clear. Although Jane is eventually freed from the room, she continues to be socially ostracized, financially trapped, and excluded from love; her sense of independence and her freedom of self-expression are constantly threatened.

The red-room's importance as a symbol continues throughout the novel. It reappears as a memory whenever Jane makes a connection between her current situation and that first feeling of being ridiculed. Thus she recalls the room when she is humiliated at Lowood. She also thinks of the room on the night that she decides to leave Thornfield after Rochester has tried to convince her to become an undignified mistress. Her poverty-stricken condition upon her departure from Thornfield also threatens emotional and intellectual imprisonment, as does St. John's marriage proposal. Only after Jane has asserted herself, gained financial independence, and found a spiritual family—which turns out to be her real family—can she marry Rochester and find freedom in and through marriage.

Major Characters

Jane Eyre is an orphan and a girl with strong mind. In the novel, readers read a biographical description of Jane, from her childhood to her adulthood. She is a new woman image in 19th century. She is brave enough to express her feelings and thoughts. She is independent by supporting herself as a governess. She voices her desire for love based on equality and mutual attraction and understanding. Jane has overcome barriers in her way to happiness. During her life, she has to fight against the control and oppression of three men, i. e. Brocklehurst in Lowood School, Rochester and St. John Rivers. She is not a pretty girl. However, her character is charming and attractive. Such image has overturned the previous women images. Women images in the past are described as angels and they try their efforts to satisfy men. All of them are submissive. It seems that submission is a virtue for women of 19th century. So the image of Jane is significant for later writers who depict women characters. After all, appearance is not the only standard to comment on women.

Rochester is the master of Thornfield, a passionate man with Stern manner. He is not particularly handsome. Rochester wins Jane's heart, because he is the first person to offer Jane lasting love and a real home. Although Rochester has economical and social superiority, at the end of the novel, he has been blinded by the fire. He has become weaker while Jane has grown in Strength. Jane Claims: they are equals.

Introduction to Chapter XXXVII

Chapter 37 is getting near to the end of the story. Jane returns to Thornfield and she finds that Bertha died in fire and Rochester became handicapped. She decided to stay with Rochester and marry him when he is in the greatest difficulty. In this chapter, Jane and Rochester express mutual affection for each other. Jane tells Rochester her experience when she ran away from Thornfield on the wedding day. Rochester proposes to Jane and she agrees to be Rochester's wife.

Chapter XXXVII

Very early the next morning I heard him up and *astir*[1] , wandering from one room to another. As soon as Mary came down I heard the question: "Is Miss Eyre here?" Then: "Which room did you put her into? Was it dry? Is she up? Go and ask if she wants anything; and when she will come down."

I came down as soon as I thought there was a prospect of breakfast. Entering the room very softly, I had a view of him before he discovered my presence. It was mournful, indeed, *to witness the subjugation of that vigorous spirit to a corporeal infirmity*[2] .He sat in his chair—still, but not at rest: expectant evidently; the lines of now habitual sadness marking his strong features. His countenance reminded one of a lamp quenched, waiting to be re-lit—and alas! It was not himself that could now kindle the *luster*[3] of animated expression: he was dependent on another for that *office*[4] ! I had meant to be gay and careless, but the powerlessness of the strong man *touched my heart to the quick*[5] : still I *accosted*[6] him with what vivacity I could. "It is a bright, sunny morning, sir," I said." The rain is over and gone, and there is a *tender shining*[7] after it: you shall have a walk soon."

I had wakened the glow: his features beamed.

"Oh, you are indeed there, my skylark! Come to me. You are not gone: not vanished? I heard *one of your kind*[8] an hour ago, singing high over the wood: but its song had no music for me, any more than the rising sun had rays. All the melody on earth is concentrated in my Jane's tongue to my ear (I am glad it is not naturally a silent one): all the sunshine I can feel is in her presence."

The water stood in my eyes to hear this *avowal*[9] of his dependence; just as if a royal eagle, chained to a perch, should be forced to entreat a sparrow to become its *purveyor*[10] . But I would not be *lachrymose*[11] : I dashed off the salt drops, and busied myself with preparing breakfast.

Most of the morning was spent in the open air. I led him out of the wet and wild wood into some cheerful fields: I described to him how brilliantly green they were; how the flowers and hedges looked refreshed; how sparklingly blue was the sky. I sought a seat for him in a hidden and lovely spot, a dry stump of a tree; nor did I refuse to let him, when seated, place me on his knee. Why should I, when both he and I were happier near than apart? *Pilot*[12] lay beside us: all was quiet. He broke out suddenly while clasping me in his arms—

"Cruel, cruel deserter! Oh, Jane, what did I feel when I discovered you had fled from Thornfield, and when I could nowhere find you; and, after examining your apartment, ascertained that you had taken no money, nor anything which could serve as an equivalent! A pearl necklace I had given you lay untouched in its little casket; your trunks were left *corded*[13] and locked as they had been prepared for the bridal tour. What could my darling do, I asked, left *destitute*[14] and penniless? And what did she do? Let me hear now."

Thus urged, I began the narrative of my experience for the last year. I softened considerably what related to the three days of wandering and starvation, because to have told him all would have been to inflict unnecessary pain: the little I did say *lacerated*[15] his faithful heart deeper than I wished.

I should not have left him thus, he said, without any means of making my way: should have told him my intention. I should have confided in him: he would never have forced me to be his mistress. Violent as he had seemed in his despair, he, in truth, loved me far too well and too tenderly to *constitute*[16] himself my tyrant: he would have given me half his fortune, without demanding so much as a kiss in return, rather than I should have flung myself friendless on the wide world. I had endured, he was certain, more than I had confessed to him.

"Well, whatever my sufferings had been, they were very short," I answered: and then I proceeded to tell him how I had been received at Moor House; how I had obtained the office of schoolmistress and the accession of fortune, the discovery of my relations, followed in due order. Of course, St. John Rivers' name came in frequently in the progress of my tale. When I had done, that name was immediately taken up.

"This St. John, then, is your cousin?"

"Yes."

"You have spoken of him often: do you like him?"

"He was a very good man, sir; I could not help liking him."

"A good man. Does that mean a respectable *well-conducted*[17] man of fifty? Or what does it mean?"

"St John was only twenty-nine, sir."

" ' *Jeune encore*[18] ,' as the French say. Is he a person of low stature, *phlegmatic*[19] , and plain. *A person whose goodness consists rather in his guiltlessness of vice, than in his prowess in virtue*[20] ."

"He is untiringly active. Great and exalted deeds are what he lives to perform."

"But his brain? That is probably rather soft? He means well: but you shrug your shoulders to hear him talk?"

"He talks little, sir: what he does say is ever to the point. His brain is first-rate, I should think not impressible, but vigorous."

"Is he an able man, then?"

"Truly able."

"A thoroughly educated man?"

"St. John is an accomplished and profound scholar."

"His manners, I think, you said are not to your taste? —*priggish and parsonic*[21] ?"

"I never mentioned his manners; but, unless I had a very bad taste, they must suit it; they are polished, calm, and gentlemanlike."

"His appearance,—I forget what description you gave of his appearance;—*a sort of raw curate, half strangled with his white neckcloth, and stilted up on his thick-soled high-lows*[22] , eh?"

"St. John dresses well. He is a handsome man: tall, fair, with blue eyes, and a Grecian profile."

(Aside.) "Damn him!"—(To me.) "Did you like him, Jane?"

"Yes, Mr. Rochester, I liked him: but you asked me that before."

I perceived, of course, the drift of my *interlocutor*[23] . Jealousy had got hold of him: she stung him; but the sting was salutary: it gave him *respite*[24] from the gnawing *fang*[25] of melancholy. I would not, therefore, immediately charm the snake.

"Perhaps you would rather not sit any longer on my knee, Miss Eyre?" was the next somewhat unexpected observation.

"Why not, Mr. Rochester?"

"The picture you have just drawn is suggestive of a rather too overwhelming contrast. Your words have delineated very prettily a graceful Apollo: he is present to your imagination,—tall, fair, blue-eyed, and with a Grecian profile. Your eyes dwell on a *Vulcan*[26] ,—a real blacksmith, brown, broad-shouldered: and blind and lame into the bargain."

"I never thought of it, before; but you certainly are rather like Vulcan, sir."

"Well, you can leave me, ma'am: but before you go" (and he retained me by a firmer grasp than ever), "you will be pleased just to answer me a question or two." He paused.

"What questions, Mr. Rochester?"

Then followed this cross-examination.

"St. John made you schoolmistress of Morton before he knew you were his cousin?"

"Yes."

"You would often see him? He would visit the school sometimes?"

"Daily."

"He would approve of your plans, Jane? I know they would be clever, for you are a talented creature!"

"He approved of them—yes."

"He would discover many things in you he could not have expected to find? Some of your accomplishments are not ordinary."

"I don't know about that."

"You had a little cottage near the school, you say: did he ever come there to see you?"

"Now and then?"

"Of an evening?"

"Once or twice."

A pause.

"How long did you reside with him and his sisters after the cousinship was discovered?"

"Five months."

"Did Rivers spend much time with the ladies of his family?"

"Yes; the back parlour was both his study and ours: he sat near the window, and we by the table."

"Did he study much?"

"A good deal."

"What?"

"*Hindostanee*[27]."

"And what did you do meantime?"

"I learnt German, at first."

"Did he teach you?"

"He did not understand German."

"Did he teach you nothing?"

"A little Hindostanee."

"Rivers taught you Hindostanee?"

"Yes, sir."

"And his sisters also?"

"No."

"Only you?"

"Only me."

"Did you ask to learn?"

"No."

"He wished to teach you?"

"Yes."

A second pause.

"Why did he wish it? Of what use could Hindostanee be to you?"

"He intended me to go with him to India."

"Ah! Here I reach the root of the matter. He wanted you to marry him?"

"He asked me to marry him."

"That is a fiction—an impudent invention to vex me."

"I beg your pardon, it is the literal truth: he asked me more than once, and was as stiff about urging his point as ever you could be."

"Miss Eyre, I repeat it, you can leave me. How often am I to say the same thing? Why do you remain *pertinaciously*[28] perched on my knee, when I have given you notice to quit?"

"Because I am comfortable there."

"No, Jane, you are not comfortable there, because your heart is not with me: it is with this cousin—this St. John. Oh, till this moment, I thought my little Jane was all mine! I had a belief she loved me even when she left me: that was an atom of sweet in much bitter. Long as we have been parted, hot tears as I have wept over our separation, I never thought that while I was mourning her, she was loving another! But it is useless grieving. Jane, leave me: go and marry Rivers."

"Shake me off, then, sir,—push me away, for I'll not leave you *of my own accord*[29]."

"Jane, I ever like your tone of voice: it still renews hope, it sounds so truthful. When I hear it, it carries me back a year. I forget that you have formed a new tie. But I am not a fool—go—"

"Where must I go, sir?"

"Your own way—with the husband you have chosen."

"Who is that?"

"You know—this St. John Rivers."

"He is not my husband, nor ever will be. He does not love me: I do not love him. He loves (as he CAN love, and that is not as you love) a beautiful young lady called Rosamond. He wanted to marry me only because he thought I should make a suitable missionary's wife, which she would not have done. He is good and great, but severe; and, for me, cold as an iceberg. He is not like you, sir: I am not happy at his side, nor near him, nor with him. He has no indulgence for me—no fondness. He sees nothing attractive in me; not even youth—only a few useful mental points. —Then I must leave you, sir, to go to him?"

I shuddered involuntarily, and clung instinctively closer to my blind but beloved master. He smiled.

"What, Jane! Is this true? Is such really the state of matters between you and

Rivers?"

"Absolutely, sir! Oh, you need not be jealous! I wanted to tease you a little to make you less sad: I thought anger would be better than grief. But if you wish me to love you, could you but see how much I DO love you, you would be proud and content. All my heart is yours, sir: it belongs to you; and with you it would remain, were fate to exile the rest of me from your presence for ever." Again, as he kissed me, painful thoughts darkened his aspect.

"My scared vision! My crippled strength!" he murmured regretfully.

I caressed, in order to soothe him. I knew of what he was thinking, and wanted to speak for him, but dared not. As he turned aside his face a minute, I saw a tear slide from under the sealed eyelid, and trickle down the manly cheek. My heart swelled.

"I am no better than the old lightning-struck chestnut-tree in Thornfield orchard," he remarked *ere long*[30]. "And what right would that ruin have to bid a budding *woodbine*[31] cover its decay with freshness?"

"You are no ruin, sir—no lightning-struck tree: you are green and vigorous. Plants will grow about your roots, whether you ask them or not, because they take delight in your bountiful shadow; and as they grow they will lean towards you, and wind round you, because your strength offers them so safe a prop."

Again he smiled: I gave him comfort.

"You speak of friends, Jane?" he asked.

"Yes, of friends," I answered rather hesitatingly: for I knew I meant more than friends, but could not tell what other word to employ. He helped me.

"Ah! Jane. But I want a wife."

"Do you, sir?"

"Yes: is it news to you?"

"Of course: you said nothing about it before."

"Is it unwelcome news?"

"That depends on circumstances, sir—on your choice."

"Which you shall make for me, Jane. I will abide by your decision."

"Choose then, sir—HER WHO LOVES YOU BEST."

"I will at least choose—HER I LOVE BEST. Jane, will you marry me?"

"Yes, sir."

"A poor blind man, whom you will have to lead about by the hand?"

"Yes, sir."

"A crippled man, twenty years older than you, whom you will have to wait on?"

"Yes, sir."

"Truly, Jane?"

"Most truly, sir."

"Oh! my darling! God bless you and reward you!"

"Mr. Rochester, if ever I did a good deed in my life—if ever I thought a good thought—if ever I prayed a sincere and blameless prayer—if ever I wished a righteous wish,—I am rewarded now. To be your wife is, for me, to be as happy as I can be on earth."

"Because you delight in sacrifice."

"Sacrifice! What do I sacrifice? *Famine for food, expectation for content*[32]. To be privileged to put my arms round what I value—to press my lips to what I love—to repose on what I trust: is that to make a sacrifice? If so, then certainly I delight in sacrifice."

"And to bear with my infirmities, Jane: to overlook my deficiencies."

"Which are none, sir, to me. I love you better now, when I can really be useful to you, than I did in your state of proud independence, when you *disdained*[33] every part but that of the giver and protector."

"*Hitherto*[34] I have hated to be helped—to be led: *henceforth*[35], I feel I shall hate it no more. I did not like to put my hand into a hireling's, but it is pleasant to feel it circled by Jane's little fingers. I preferred utter loneliness to the constant attendance of servants; but Jane's soft ministry will be a perpetual joy. Jane suits me: do I suit her?"

"To the finest fibre of my nature, sir."

"The case being so, we have nothing in the world to wait for: we must be married instantly."

He looked and spoke with eagerness: his old *impetuosity*[36] was rising.

"We must become one flesh without any delay, Jane: there is but the *licence*[37] to get—then we marry."

"Mr. Rochester, I have just discovered the sun is far declined from its meridian, and Pilot is actually gone home to his dinner. Let me look at your watch."

"Fasten it into your *girdle*[38], Janet, and keep it henceforward: I have no use for it."

"It is nearly four o'clock in the afternoon, sir. Don't you feel hungry?"

"The third day from this must be our wedding-day, Jane. Never mind fine clothes and jewels, now: all that is not worth a *fillip*[39]."

"The sun has dried up all the rain-drops, sir. The breeze is still: it is quite hot."

"Do you know, Jane, I have your little pearl necklace at this moment fastened round my bronze *scrag*[40] under my *cravat*[41]? I have worn it since the day I lost my only treasure, as a memento of her."

"We will go home through the wood: that will be the shadiest way."

He pursued his own thoughts without heeding me.

"Jane! you think me, I daresay, an irreligious dog: but my heart swells with gratitude to the beneficent God of this earth just now. He sees not as man sees, but far clearer: judges not as man judges, but far more wisely. I did wrong: I would have sullied my innocent flower—breathed guilt on its purity: the Omnipotent snatched it from me. I, in my stiff-necked rebellion, almost cursed the *dispensation*[42]: instead of bending to the decree, I defied it. Divine justice pursued its course; *disasters came thick on me*[43]: I was forced to pass through the valley of the shadow of death. HIS chastisements are mighty; and one *smote*[44] me which has humbled me for ever. You know I was proud of my strength: but what is it now, when I must give it over to foreign guidance, as a child does its weakness? Of late, Jane—only—only of late—I began to see and acknowledge the hand of God in my doom. I began to experience remorse, repentance; the wish for reconcilement to my Maker. I began sometimes to pray: very brief prayers they were, but very sincere.

"Some days since: nay, I can number them—four; it was last Monday night, a singular mood came over me: one in which grief replaced frenzy—sorrow, sullenness.

I had long had the impression that since I could nowhere find you, you must be dead. Late that night— perhaps it might be between eleven and twelve o'clock—ere I retired to my dreary rest, I *supplicated*[45] God, that, if it seemed good to Him, I might soon be taken from this life, and admitted to that world to come, where there was still hope of rejoining Jane.

"I was in my own room, and sitting by the window, which was open: it soothed me to feel the *balmy*[46] night-air; though I could see no stars and only by a vague, luminous haze, knew the presence of a moon. I longed for thee, Janet! Oh, I longed for thee both with soul and flesh! I asked of God, at once in anguish and humility, if I had not been long enough desolate, afflicted, tormented; and might not soon taste bliss and peace once more. That I merited all I endured, I acknowledged—that I could scarcely endure more, I pleaded; and *the alpha and omega of my heart's wishes*[47] broke involuntarily from my lips in the words—'Jane! Jane! Jane!'"

"Did you speak these words aloud?"

"I did, Jane. If any listener had heard me, he would have thought me mad: I pronounced them with such frantic energy."

"And it was last Monday night, somewhere near midnight?"

"Yes; but the time is of no consequence: what followed is the strange point. You will think me superstitious,—some superstition I have in my blood, and always had: nevertheless, this is true— true at least it is that I heard what I now relate.

"As I exclaimed 'Jane! Jane! Jane!' a voice—I cannot tell whence the voice came, but I know whose voice it was—replied, 'I am coming: wait for me;' and a moment after, went whispering on the wind the words—'Where are you?'

"I'll tell you, if I can, the idea, the picture these words opened to my mind: yet it is difficult to express what I want to express. *Ferndean*[48] is buried, as you see, in a heavy wood, where sound falls dull, and dies unreverberating. Where are you?' seemed spoken amongst mountains; for I heard a hill-sent echo repeat the words. Cooler and fresher at the moment the gale seemed to visit my brow: I could have deemed that in some wild, lone scene, I and Jane were meeting. In spirit, I believe we must have met. You no doubt were, at that hour, in unconscious sleep, Jane: perhaps your soul wandered from its cell to comfort mine; for those were your accents—as certain as I live—they were yours!"

Reader, it was on Monday night—near midnight—that I too had received the mysterious summons: those were the very words by which I replied to it. I listened to Mr. Rochester's narrative, but made no disclosure in return. The coincidence struck me as too awful and inexplicable to be communicated or discussed. If I told anything, my tale would be such as must necessarily make a profound impression on the mind of my hearer: and that mind, yet from its sufferings too prone to gloom, needed not the deeper shade of the supernatural. I kept these things then, and pondered them in my heart.

"You cannot now wonder," continued my master, "that when you rose upon me so unexpectedly last night, I had difficulty in believing you any other than a mere voice and vision, something that would melt to silence and annihilation, as the midnight whisper and mountain echo had melted before. Now, I thank God! I know it to be otherwise. Yes, I thank God!"

He put me off his knee, rose, and *reverently*[49] lifting his hat from his brow, and bending his sightless eyes to the earth, he stood in mute devotion. Only the last words of the worship were audible.

"I thank my Maker, that, in the midst of judgment, he has remembered mercy. I humbly entreat my *Redeemer*[50] to give me strength to lead henceforth a purer life than I have done hitherto!"

Then he stretched his hand out to be led. I took that dear hand, held it a moment to my lips, then let it pass round my shoulder: being so much lower of stature than he, I served both for his prop and guide. We entered the wood, and *wended*[51] homeward.

Notes

[1] get up

[2] 看到他那么旺盛的精神竟受制于肉体上的残弱。Subjugation (to): surrender; corporeal: 肉体的, 身体的。Infirmity: 虚弱; 病症

[3] 光辉

[4] function

[5] 深深地触痛了我的心。Quick:痛处

[6] 走近跟……讲话

[7] 柔和明媚的阳光

[8] 你的同类。指云雀。因上文罗切斯特将简比成云雀,"同类"便由此而来。

[9] 公开表示;坦率承认

[10] provider

[11] 爱哭的

[12] 罗切斯特养的狗

[13] 用绳捆扎好的

[14] 匮乏的,一无所有

[15] 撕裂;折磨

[16] 构成;形成

[17] well-behaved

[18] (法语)still young

[19] 迟钝的;冷漠的

[20] 一个人,其好处仅仅在于没有罪过,而并非品行出众。Prowess:杰出的才能,高超的本领。

[21] 古板自负的,一副牧师腔。

[22] 一个没有经验的助理牧师,差点让自己的白领巾给勒死,踩着一双厚底高帮靴。curate:助理牧师。

[23] 对话者

[24] pause

[25] (毒蛇的)毒牙

[26] 伏尔甘,古罗马宗教信奉的火神,最初象征破坏性的火,如火山和火灾,后来成为铁匠的守护神。

[27] 印度斯坦语

[28] 固执地;执著地

[29] of one's willingness

[30] 不久。ere:在……之前

[31] 五叶铁线莲;忍冬

[32] sacrifice famine for food, sacrifice expectation for content.牺牲饥饿以得到食物,牺牲渴望以得到满足。

[33] contempt

[34] 到目前为止;迄今

[35] 从此以后

[36] 急躁;冲动

[37] marriage licence

[38] (女子的)紧身褡

[39] 微不足道的东西

[40] 脖子

[41] (旧式的)领结或领带

[42] 天命;神的安排

[43] 灾难接连落到我的头上

[44] (past tense of "smite") hit, punish

[45] 恳求;乞求

[46] 芬芳的;柔和的

[47] all the wishes in my heart. alpha:the first; omega：the last one.

[48] 桑菲尔德庄园被烧毁后,罗切斯特的住所

[49] 恭敬地,虔敬地

[50] maker; Jesus Christ

[51] 行,走

Questions

1 In the eyes of Jane, what great changes have taken place on Rochester?

2 What had happened to Jane when she left Thornfield?

3 There is a sharp contrast between Jane's description of St. John Rivers and Rochester's imagination of St. John. What about the difference?

4 Why does Jane frequently mention St. John?

5 From the end of this chapter, what do you think of the end of the story?

Analysis of Chapter XXXVII

Jane returns to Thornfield and discovers it was ruined in fire. She and Rochester live in Ferndean, during which Jane and Rochester are able to marry at last.

It is possible to question *Jane Eyre*'s feminism on the grounds that Jane only becomes Rochester's full equal (as she claims to be in the novel's epilogue-like last chapter) when he is physically infirm and dependent on her to guide him and read to him—in other words, when he is physically incapable of mastering her. However, it is also possible that Jane now finds herself Rochester's equal not because of the decline Rochester has suffered but because of the autonomy that she has achieved by coming to know herself more fully.

No woman was ever nearer to her mate than I am: ever more absolutely bone of his bone, and flesh of his flesh. I know no weariness of my Edward's society: he knows none of mine, any more than we each do of the pulsation of the heart that beats in our separate bosoms; consequently, we are ever together.

Another problem that troubles some critics is the fact that Jane finds happiness in the novel only through marriage, suggesting that marriage constitutes the only route to contentment for women. It could be argued that, in returning to Rochester, Jane sacrifices her long-sought autonomy and independence. Another way of looking at Jane's marriage is that she doesn't sacrifice everything, but enters into a relationship in which giving and taking occur in equal measure. Indeed, in order to marry Rochester Jane has had to reject another marriage, a marriage that would have meant a much more stifling and suppressed life for her. Moreover, in declining to marry St. John, Jane comes to the realization that part of being true to "who she is" means being true to her emotions and passions; part of what makes her *herself* is manifested in her relationships with *others*—in the giving of herself to other human beings. By entering into marriage, Jane does indeed enter into a "bond," but in many ways this "bond" is also the "escape" that Jane has sought all along.

Brontë seems to suggest a way in which a woman's quest for love and a feeling of belonging need not encroach upon her sense of self—need not restrict her intellectual, spiritual, and emotional independence. Indeed, Brontë suggests that it is only after coming to know oneself and one's own strength that one can enter wholly into a well-rounded and loving relationship with another.

Unit 5
Emily Brontë (1818~1848)

Life

The life of Emily was extremely uneventful, living at a boarding-school, teaching as governess, losing her health because of illness, remaining a single to the end of her life. She was unhappy a great deal of the time, but she pursued for all her life independence, which never came. Emily seems to have been more liberty-loving than her sisters, as Charlotte (novel writer—*Jane Eyre*) wrote, "liberty was the breath of Emily's nostrils: without it she perished".

As for the life and personality of Emily, some critics in China compare her with the talented authoress of China, Xiao Hong(萧红), who also died young. Her masterpiece is *The Scene of Life and Death*《生死场》. Xiao Hong has compared herself to Xiangling, a female character in *The Dream of the Red Mansion*, whose fate is described as "the destruction of poetry".

Emily's life was narrow: she lived most of her life, in Haworth, a bleak country town in Northern England. She owed her success to her father's somewhat enlightened view about his children's education. The two obstacles lying on her way to success were poverty, which followed her heels all her life, and the difficulty in finding a publisher, which was finally overcome. Xiao Hong was not so happy as Emily, she was born in a feudal family, in a secluded county in Northeast China, in 1911. Her father was a landlord and petty official, narrow-minded and hard-hearted. He treated her ill. The enlightened education is impossible. At 20, she was forced by her father to marry a "young master" of a rich family. She refused and ran away. But the "young master" cheated her and seduced her, and then abandoned her all alone with a heavy debt unpaid. Under the threat of being sold to a whore-house by the hotel she lived in, in emergency she wrote to a local newspaper. Xiao Jun, then a wanderer in Harbin came to her rescue and saved her out of the misfortune. Under the encouragement of Xiaojun and other writers, Xiao Hong began to write short stories and prose works. In 1935, her masterpiece, The *Scene of Life and Death* was published in Shanghai, and she became a famous authoress in China. Her road to success appears like a chivalric Romance.

Emily's character was reserved, stubborn and unbending. While Xiao Hong was open-hearted, honest, sympathetic and eager to help others, sometimes she could be self-willed. She and Xiao Jun was a suitable pair, but they parted because she could not endure his overbearing attitude towards her. She died in a lonesome state at 31 in Hong Kong.

Emily's talent had been fully manifested in her *Wuthering Heights*, as what Xiao Hong in her *The Scene of life and Death*. We feel regret for their early death, but no regret for their work.

Emily's literary career is short. It began at an early age, but she did not publish anything until the appearance of *Poems by Currer, Ellis, and Acton Bell*, in which some of her poems were included. In her verses there was not only good technique but a sturdy, vigorous note that was characterized of the lover of freedom who had written the verses. But Emily's literary fame now chiefly rests upon *Wuthering Heights* the only novel she wrote. It was published in 1846 in one volume together with *Agnes Gray* by Anne, her younger sister.

Plot of *Wuthering Heights*

Wuthering Heights is a somber story of love and sorrow and revenge. In the novel, the central figure is the stormy Heathcliff, a gypsy waif of unknown parentage. The story starts with Mr. Earnshaw's discovery of homeless Heathcliff in the street. Mr. Earnshaw brings Heathcliff to his own estate whose name is the title of the novel, Wuthering Heights. The old gentleman brings him up together with his own children. Heathcliff grows up under the care and guardianship of Mr. Earnshaw.

The death of Mr. Earnshaw is followed by his son's mistreatment of Heathcliff, when Hindley, the son of Mr. Earnshaw, gets to know that his younger sister Catherine falls in love with Heathcliff, he thinks it beneath his family dignity for her sister to marry a gypsy waif and therefore, Hindley cruelly separates two lovers. Heathcliff is forced to leave Wuthering Heights. He returned three years later when he has had the possession of considerable wealth. The fact that Catherine has married Linton determines Heathcliff to revenge, at first by resuming love with Catherine and she soon dies of grief and remorse, secondly by marrying Linton's sister whom he never loves but treats inhumanly because of her brother's marriage to Catherine, finally by forcing Catherine's daughter Cathy to marry his sickly son in order to get the Linton estate into his own possession. After he has possessed all the property through powerful means, he turns himself to the oppressor and treats Hindley and Hindley's son as cruelly as Hindley treated him long time ago. At the close of the story Heathcliff grows old, and he at last came to see the pointlessness of his violent revenge on the Earnshaws and the Lintons, when the death of his sickly son is followed immediately by a happy union of Cathy and Hareton. His disappointment and passionate love for Catherine leads to his own death.

Some Comments on *Wuthering Heights*

There is a realistic story of the relations between the oppressor and the oppressed and the revenge that results from these relations. Heathcliff in the novel is at first the oppressed person and then he himself becomes the oppressor, but at the end of the book, the oppressor weakens and breaks down. The final failure of Heathcliff suggests, according to Arnold Kettle a modern British critic, Heathcliff has at last "come to see the pointlessness of his fight to revenge himself on the world of power and property through its own values," for Kettle comprehends in profundity that the novel is not merely a story of personal love and revenge but "an expression in the imaginative terms of art of the stresses and tensions and conflicts, personal and spiritual, of nineteenth-century capitalist society."

Wuthering Heights belongs to the tradition of Gothic novels. The choice of the Gothic style suits well the theme of the novel. Gothic literature has always been associated with the abnormal and absurd. The setting is often in a remote or an alien soil. Actions take place in ruined, deserted castles. Old and empty house that once with creepers and grasses. Gothic novels pursue the creation of a grotesque atmosphere through the depiction of a rather bizarre and terrifying natural environment. The Gothic literature represented by Horace Walpole's *The Castle of Otranto*, Mary Shelley's *Frankenstein* and Mathew Lewis *The Monk*.

Wuthering Heights has a contemporary setting but it bears a similar strange Gothic quality. There were steep hills and precipitous slopes stretching far and deep ridges stood high like some giants on the landscape. Leafless trees stood on bare rocks and strong winds howled across the moor.

The gothic novel strives to create feelings of horror caused by the terrifying transformation of human character. It deals with the unconventional, the uncommon aspects of human nature. *Wuthering Heights* provides an effective environment in which the dark side of human nature is put under careful examination. Human passion can be constructive and destructive as well. In the novel, various human weaknesses are exposed: Catherine is selfish, Edgar weak, Heathcliff Savage, Isabella ill tempered and Cathy willful. Their weakness generates fearful results that nearly destroy every character involved. But Emily did not condemn the characters. Emily seemed to emphasize that it was fate that drove them together, and under a special environment, human love is a source of tragic disaster.

It is noticeable that the narration of the story is unconventional. Different from the first person singular or the third person omniscient, the story is told chiefly by two characters in the story: Mr. Lockwood, one of the tenants of Heathcliff, and Nelly Dean, a Housekeeper in the service of Catherine, in addition some supplementary aids, like Catherine's diary. The unusual way of narration adds much to the truthfulness of the story and the complexity of its plot.

Major Characters

Heathcliff is a foundling taken in by Mr. Earnshaw and raised with his children. Of unknown descent, he seems to represent wild and natural forces, which often seem amoral and dangerous for society. His almost inhuman devotion to Catherine is the moving force in his life. His vindictive hatred for all those who stand between him and his beloved makes him cruel but magnificent readers can never forget that at the heart of the grown man lies the abandoned, hungry child of the streets of Liverpool.

Mr. Earnshaw is the father of Catherine and Hindley, a plain, fairly well-off farmer with few pretensions but a kind heart. He is a stern father. He takes in Heathcliff despite his family's protests.

Catherine (or Cathy) Earnshaw is Mr. Earnshaw's daughter and Hindley's sister. She is also Heathcliff's foster sister and beloved. She marries Edgar Linton and has a daughter, also named Catherine. Catherine is beautiful and charming, but she is never as civilized as she pretends to be. In her heart she is always a wild girl playing on the moors with Heathcliff. She regards it as her right to be loved by all, and has an unruly temper. Heathcliff usually calls her Cathy; Edgar usually calls her Catherine.

Hindley Earnshaw is the only son of Mr. and Mrs. Earnshaw, and Catherine's older brother. He is a bullying, discontented boy who grows up to be a violent alcoholic when his beloved wife, Frances, dies. He hates Heathcliff because he felt his father's affection for him has been taken away by another boy, and Heathcliff in return hates him even more.

Edgar Linton is Isabella's older brother, who marries Catherine Earnshaw and fathers Catherine Linton. In contrast to Heathcliff, he is a gently bred, refined man, a patient husband and a loving father. His faults are certain effeminacy (女人气), and a tendency to be cold and unforgiving when his dignity is hurt.

Isabella Linton is Edgar's younger sister, and marries Heathcliff to become Isabella Heathcliff; her son is named Linton Heathcliff. Before she marries Heathcliff, she is a rather shallow-minded young lady, pretty and quick-witted but a little foolish (as can be seen by her choice of husband). Her unhappy marriage brings out an element of cruelty in her character: when her husband treats her brutally, she rapidly grows to hate him with all her heart.

Ellen (or Nelly) Dean is one of the main narrators. She has been a servant with the Earnshaws and the Lintons for all her life, and knows them better than anyone else. She is independently minded and high spirited, and retains an objective viewpoint on those she serves. She is called Nelly by those who are on the most equalitarian terms with her: such as Mr. Earnshaw, the older Catherine, Heathcliff.

Lockwood is the narrator of the novel. Heathcliff's tenant at Thrushcross Grange. He is a gentleman from London, in distinct contrast to the other rural characters. He is not particularly sympathetic and tends to patronize his subjects. That is to say, he treats the servants lower than him as if he were a master.

Hareton Earnshaw is the son of Hindley; he marries the younger Catherine. For most of the novel, he is rough and rustic and uncultured, having been carefully kept from all civilizing influences by Heathcliff. He grows up to be superficially like Heathcliff, but is really much more sweet-tempered and forgiving. He never blames Heathcliff for having disinherited him.

Catherine（or Cathy）Linton who marries Linton Heathcliff to become Catherine Heathcliff, and then marries Hareton to be Catherine Earnshawis the daughter of the older Catherine and Edgar Linton. She has all her mother's charm without her wildness, although she is by no means submissive and spiritless. Edgar calls her Cathy.

Linton Heathcliff is the son of Heathcliff and Isabella. He combines the worst characteristics of both parents, and is effeminate, weakly, and cruel. He uses his status as an invalid to manipulate the tender-hearted younger Catherine. His father despises him. Linton marries Catherine and dies soon after.

　　※ **Connection of two generations：**

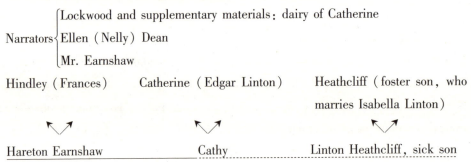

Narrators
- Lockwood and supplementary materials: dairy of Catherine
- Ellen（Nelly）Dean
- Mr. Earnshaw

Hindley（Frances）　　　Catherine（Edgar Linton）　　　Heathcliff（foster son, who marries Isabella Linton）

Hareton Earnshaw　　　　　Cathy　　　　　Linton Heathcliff, sick son

Hareton and little Cathy fall in love with each other and united after the death of Heathcliff's sick son, Linton Heatheliff.

Introduction to Chapter 15

　　Chapter 15 is the climax of the whole novel. There is the final meeting of Cathy and Heathcliff. Their love is passionate and wild, however, to be tortured by the betrayal of the love for Heathcliff, Cathy only wants to die. Cathy died and Heathcliff starts his mad revenge on those who are the barriers of Cathy and him. First he marries Isabella, sister of Linton but he doesn't love her. He tortures her for it is her brother married Cathy. He snatched Linton's heritage by asking Linton's daughter to marry his sick son. So this chapter is turning point of the story. After this chapter, Heathcliff turns himself from a person being oppressed to an oppressor.

Chapter 15

Another week over and $I^{[1]}$ am so many days nearer health, and spring! I have now heard all *my neighbour's*$^{[2]}$ history, *at different sittings*$^{[3]}$, as the *housekeeper*$^{[4]}$ could spare time from more important occupations. I'll continue it in her own words, only a little condensed. She is, on the whole, a very fair narrator, and I don't think I could improve her style.

In the evening, she said, the evening of *my visit to the Heights*$^{[5]}$, *I knew, as well as if I saw him, that Mr. Heathcliff was about the place*$^{[6]}$; and I shunned going out, because I still carried *his letter*$^{[7]}$ in my pocket, and didn't want to be threatened or teased any more. I had made up my mind not to give it till my master went somewhere, as I could not guess how its receipt would affect Catherine. The consequence was, that it did not reach her before the lapse of three days. The fourth was Sunday, and I brought it into her room after the family were gone to church. There was a manservant left to keep the house with me, and we generally made a practice of locking the doors during the hours of *service*$^{[8]}$; but on that occasion the weather was so warm and pleasant that I set them wide open, and, *to fulfil my engagement*$^{[9]}$, as I knew who would be coming, I told my companion that the mistress wished very much for some oranges, and he must run over to the village and get a few, to be paid for on the morrow. He departed, and I went up-stairs.

Mrs. Linton sat in a loose white dress, with a light shawl over her shoulders, in the recess of the open window, as usual. Her thick, long hair had been *partly removed*$^{[10]}$ at the beginning of her illness, and now she wore it simply combed in its natural tresses over her temples and neck. Her appearance was altered, as I had told Heathcliff; but when she was calm, there seemed unearthly beauty in the change. The flash of her eyes had been succeeded by a dreamy and melancholy softness; they no longer gave the impression of looking at the objects around her: they appeared always to gaze beyond, and far beyond-you would have said out of this world. Then, the paleness of her face-its haggard aspect having vanished as she recovered flesh-and the peculiar expression arising from her mental state, though painfully suggestive of their causes, *added to the touching interest which she awakened*[11]; and-invariably to me, I know, and to any person who saw her, I should think-refuted more tangible proofs of convalescence, and stamped her as one doomed to decay.

A book lay spread on the sill before her, and the scarcely perceptible wind fluttered its leaves at intervals. I believe Linton had laid it there; for she never endeavoured to divert herself with reading, or occupation of any kind, and he would spend many an hour in trying to entice her attention to some subject which had formerly been her amusement. She was conscious of his aim, and in her better moods endured his efforts placidly, only showing their uselessness by now and then suppressing a wearied sigh, and checking him at last with the saddest of smiles and kisses. At other times, she would turn petulantly away, and hide her face in her hands, or even push him off angrily; and then he took care to let her alone, for he was certain of doing no good.

Gimmerton chapel[12] bells were still ringing; and the full, mellow flow of the beck in the valley came soothingly on the ear. It was a sweet substitute for the yet absent murmur of the summer foliage, which drowned that music about the Grange when the trees were in leaf. At Wuthering Heights it always sounded on quiet days following a great thaw or a season of steady rain. And of Wuthering Heights Catherine was thinking as she listened: that is, if she thought or listened at all; but she had the vague, distant look I mentioned before, which expressed no recognition of material things either by ear or eye.

'There's a letter for you, Mrs. Linton,' I said, gently inserting it in one hand that rested on her knee. 'You must read it immediately, because it wants an answer. Shall I break the seal?' 'Yes,' she answered, without altering the direction of her eyes. I opened it—it was very short. 'Now,' I continued, 'read it.' She drew away her hand, and let it fall. I replaced it in her lap, and stood waiting till it should please her to glance down; but that movement was so long delayed that at last I resumed—'Must I read it, ma'am? It is from Mr. Heathcliff.'

There was a start and a troubled gleam of recollection, and a struggle to arrange her ideas. She lifted the letter, and seemed to peruse it; and when she came to the signature she sighed: yet still I found she had not gathered its import, for, upon my desiring to hear her reply, she merely pointed to the name, and gazed at me with mournful and questioning eagerness.

'Well, he wishes to see you,' said I, guessing her need of an interpreter.'He's in the garden by this time, and impatient to know what answer I shall bring.'

As I spoke, I observed a large dog lying on the sunny grass beneath raise its ears as if about to bark, and then smoothing them back, announce, by a wag of the tail, that some one approached whom it did not consider a stranger. Mrs. Linton bent forward, and listened breathlessly. The minute after a step traversed the hall; the open house was too tempting for Heathcliff to resist walking in: most likely he supposed that I was inclined to shirk my promise, and so resolved to trust to his own audacity. With straining eagerness Catherine gazed towards the entrance of her chamber. He did not hit the right room directly: she motioned me to admit him, but he found it out ere I could reach the door, and in a stride or two was at her side, and had her grasped in his arms.

He neither spoke nor loosed his hold for some five minutes, during which period he bestowed more kisses than ever he gave in his life before, I daresay: but then my mistress had kissed him first, and I plainly saw that he could hardly bear, for downright agony, to look into her face! The same conviction had stricken him as me, from the instant he beheld her, that there was no prospect of ultimate recovery there—she was fated, sure to die.

'Oh, Cathy! Oh, my life! how can I bear it?' was the first sentence he uttered, in a tone that did not seek to disguise his despair. And now he stared at her so earnestly that I thought the very intensity of his gaze would bring tears into his eyes; but they burned with anguish: they did not melt.

'What now?' said Catherine, leaning back, and returning his look with a suddenly clouded brow: her humour was a mere vane for constantly varying caprices. 'You and Edgar have broken my heart, Heathcliff! And you both come to bewail the deed to me, as if you were the people to be pitied! I shall not pity you, not I. You have killed me—and thriven on it, I think. How strong you are! How many years do you mean to live after I am gone?'

Heathcliff had knelt on one knee to embrace her; he attempted to rise, but she seized his hair, and kept him down.

'I wish I could hold you,' she continued, bitterly, 'till we were both dead! I shouldn't care what you suffered. I care nothing for your sufferings. Why shouldn't you suffer? I do! Will you forget me? Will you be happy when I am in the earth? Will you say twenty years hence, "That's the grave of Catherine Earnshaw? I loved her long ago, and was wretched to lose her; but it is past. I've loved many others since: my children are dearer to me than she was; and, at death, I shall not rejoice that I are going to her: I shall be sorry that I must leave them!" Will you say so, Heathcliff?'

'Don't torture me till I'm as mad as yourself,' cried he, wrenching his head free, and grinding his teeth.

The two, to a cool spectator, made a strange and fearful picture. Well might Catherine deem that heaven would be a land of exile to her, unless with her mortal body she cast away her moral character also. Her present countenance had a wild vindictiveness in its white cheek, and a bloodless lip and scintillating eye; and she retained in her closed fingers a portion of the locks she had been grasping. As to her companion, while raising himself with one hand, he had taken her arm with the other; and so inadequate was his stock of gentleness to the requirements of her condition, that on his letting go I saw four distinct impressions left blue in the colourless skin.

'Are you possessed with a devil,' he pursued, savagely, 'to talk in that manner to me when you are dying? Do you reflect that all those words will be branded in my memory, and eating deeper eternally after you have left me? You know you lie to say I have killed you: and, Catherine, you know that *I could as soon forget you as my existence*[13]! Is it not sufficient for your infernal selfishness, that while you are at peace I shall writhe in the torments of hell?'

'I shall not be at peace,' moaned Catherine, recalled to a sense of physical weakness by the violent, unequal throbbing of her heart, which beat visibly and audibly under this excess of agitation. She said nothing further till the paroxysm was over; then she continued, more kindly—

'I'm not wishing you greater torment than I have, Heathcliff. I only wish us never to be parted: and should a word of mine distress you hereafter, think I feel the same distress underground, and for my own sake, forgive me! Come here and kneel down again! You never harmed me in your life. Nay, if you nurse anger, that will be worse to remember than my harsh words! Won't you come here again? Do!'

Heathcliff went to the back of her chair, and leant over, but not so far as to let her see his face, which was livid with emotion. She bent round to look at him; he would not permit it: turning abruptly, he walked to the fireplace, where he stood, silent, with his back towards us. Mrs. Linton's glance followed him suspiciously: every movement woke a new sentiment in her. After a pause and a prolonged gaze, she resumed; addressing me in accents of indignant disappointment:—

'Oh, you see, Nelly, he would not relent a moment to keep me out of the grave. THAT is how I'm loved! Well, never mind. That is not MY Heathcliff. I shall love mine yet; and take him with me: he's in my soul. And,' added she musingly, 'the thing that irks me most is *this shattered prison*[14], after all. I'm tired of being enclosed here. I'm wearying to escape into *that glorious world*[15], and to be always there: not seeing it dimly through tears, and yearning for it through the walls of an aching heart: but really with it, and in it. Nelly, you think you are better and more fortunate than I; in full health and strength: you are sorry for me—very soon that will be altered. I shall be sorry for YOU. I shall be incomparably beyond and above you all. *I WONDER he won' be near me!*' She went on to herself. '*I thought he wished it*[16]. Heathcliff, dear! you should not be sullen now. Do come to me, Heathcliff.'

In her eagerness she rose and supported herself on the arm of the chair. At that earnest appeal he turned to her, looking absolutely desperate. His eyes, wide and wet, at last flashed fiercely on her; his breast heaved convulsively. An instant *they held asunder*[17], and then how they met I hardly saw, but Catherine made a spring, and he caught her, and they were locked in an embrace from which I thought my mistress would never be released alive: in fact, to my eyes, she seemed directly insensible. He flung himself into the nearest seat, and on my approaching hurriedly to ascertain if she had fainted, he gnashed at me, and foamed like a mad dog, and gathered her to him with greedy jealousy. I did not feel as if I were in the company of a creature of my own species: it appeared that he would not understand, though I spoke to him; so I stood off, and held my tongue, in great perplexity.

A movement of Catherine's relieved me a little presently: she put up her hand to clasp his neck, and bring her cheek to his as he held her; while he, in return, covering her with frantic caresses, said wildly—

'You teach me now how cruel you've been—cruel and false. WHY did you despise me? WHY did you betray your own heart, Cathy? I have not one word of comfort. You deserve this. *You have killed yourself*[18]. Yes, you may kiss me, and cry; and wring out my kisses and tears: they'll blight you-they'll damn you. You loved me—then what RIGHT had you to leave me? What right—answer me—for the poor fancy you felt for Linton? Because misery and degradation, and death, and nothing that God or Satan could inflict would have parted us, YOU, of your own will, did it. I have not broken your heart—YOU have broken it; and in breaking it, you have broken mine. So much the worse for me that I am strong. Do I want to live? What kind of living will it be when you—oh, God! would YOU like to live with your soul in the grave?'

'Let me alone. Let me alone,' sobbed Catherine. 'If I've done wrong, I'm dying for it. It is enough! You left me too: but I won't upbraid you! I forgive you. Forgive me!'

'It is hard to forgive, and to look at those eyes, and feel those wasted hands,' he answered. 'Kiss me again; and don't let me see your eyes! I forgive what you have done to me. I love MY murderer—but YOURS! How can I?'

They were silent—their faces hid against each other, and washed by each other's tears. At least, I suppose the weeping was on both sides; as it seemed Heathcliff could weep on a great occasion like this.

I grew very uncomfortable, meanwhile; for the afternoon wore fast away, the man whom I had sent off returned from his errand, and I could distinguish, by the shine of the western sun up the valley, a concourse thickening outside Gimmerton chapel porch.

'Service is over,' I announced. 'My master will be here in half an hour.'

Heathcliff groaned a curse, and strained Catherine closer: she never moved.

Ere long I perceived a group of the servants passing up the road towards the kitchen wing. Mr. Linton was not far behind; he opened the gate himself and sauntered slowly up, probably enjoying the lovely afternoon that breathed as soft as summer.

'Now he is here,' I exclaimed. 'For heaven's sake, hurry down! You'll not meet any one on the front stairs. Do be quick; and stay among the trees till he is fairly in.'

'I must go, Cathy,' said Heathcliff, seeking to extricate himself from his companion's arms.'But if I live, I'll see you again before you are asleep. I won't stray five yards from your window.'

'You must not go!' she answered, holding him as firmly as her strength allowed.'You SHALL not, I tell you.'

'For one hour,' he pleaded earnestly.

'Not for one minute,' she replied.

'I MUST—Linton will be up immediately,' persisted the alarmed intruder.

He would have risen, and unfixed her fingers by the act—she clung fast, gasping: there was mad resolution in her face.

'No!' she shrieked. 'Oh, don't, don't go. It is the last time! Edgar will not hurt us. Heathcliff, I shall die! I shall die!'

'Damn the fool! There he is,' cried Heathcliff, sinking back into his seat. 'Hush, my darling! Hush, hush, Catherine! I'll stay. If he shot me so, I'd expire with a blessing on my lips.'

And there they were fast again[19]. I heard my master mounting the stairs—the cold sweat ran from my forehead: I was horrified.

'Are you going to listen to her ravings?' I said, passionately. 'She does not know what she says. Will you ruin her, because she has not wit to help herself? Get up! You could be free instantly. That is the most diabolical deed that ever you did. We are all *done for*[20]—master, mistress, and servant.'

I wrung my hands, and cried out; and Mr. Linton hastened his step at the noise. In the midst of my agitation, I was sincerely glad to observe that Catherine's arms had fallen relaxed, and her head hung down.

'She's fainted, or dead,' I thought: 'so much the better. Far better that she should be dead, than lingering a burden and a misery-maker to all about her.'

Edgar sprang to his unbidden guest, blanched with astonishment and rage. What he meant to do I cannot tell; however, the other stopped all demonstrations, at once, by placing the lifeless- looking form in his arms.

'Look there!' he said.'Unless you be a fiend, help her first—then you shall speak to me!'

He walked into the parlour, and sat down. Mr. Linton summoned me, and with great difficulty, and after resorting to many means, we managed to restore her to sensation; but she was all bewildered; she sighed, and moaned, and knew nobody. Edgar, in his anxiety for her, forgot her hated friend. I did not. I went, at the earliest opportunity, and besought him to depart; affirming that Catherine was better, and he should hear from me in the morning how she passed the night.

'I shall not refuse to go out of doors,' he answered; 'but I shall stay in the garden: and, Nelly, mind you keep your word to-morrow. I shall be under those larch-trees. Mind! or I pay another visit, whether Linton be in or not.'

He sent a rapid glance through the half-open door of the chamber, and, ascertaining that what I stated was apparently true, delivered the house of his luckless *presence*[21].

Notes

[1] Mr.Lockwood, Mr. Heathcliff's tenant at Thrushcross Grange
[2] Mr. Heathcliff
[3] during our different conversation
[4] Nelly Dean, Catherine's servant
[5] Nelly Dean's visit to Wuthering Heights a week before
[6] I knew, as surely as if I saw him, that Mr. Heathcliff was prowling about Thrushcross Grange in the hope of getting a chance to break in and talk to Catherine.
[7] Heathcliff's letter to Catherine. He had made Nelly agree to carry to her mistress.
[8] religious service
[9] Nelly had engaged to carry Heathcliff's letter to Catherine and arrange for their meeting.

[10] partly cut off

[11] 使她格外令人怜恤

[12] 吉默吞教堂,在画眉山庄附近

[13] I can not forget you just as I can not forget my existence.我无法忘记你,就如同我无法忘记自己的存在。

[14] this world, which is a shattered prison for me.

[15] the next world

[16] I am surprised he won't be near me! I thought he wished to be near me.

[17] they kept away from each other.

[18] This refers to Catherine's luckless marriage with Edgar Linton.

[19] And there they held each other fast again.

[20] ruined; finished

[21] the presence of Heathcliff

Questions

1　How ill Cathy is?

2　What words show Cathy and Heathcliff's love is wild and mad?

3　In this chapter what personality does Ellen, as an on-looker, reveal to readers?

4　What does the last paragraph mean?

Analysis of Chapter 15

　　The selection here is taken from Chapter 15, which depicts the final meeting between Heathcliff and Catherine. This meeting is the climax of the whole story. What follows the meeting is Heathcliff's uncontrollable revenge on those who he thinks are related to his love failure.

　　This part is narrated by Nelly Ellen. She is the housekeeper in the service of Catherine and her observation and narration are usually objective and unbiased. One Sunday Ellen visits *Wuthering Heights*. She finds excuses for not being able to give Heathcliff's letter to Catherine, for she kept it in her pocket for 3 days. The fourth day, Sunday, most of the people went to church and Ellen found it is a perfect chance for her to complete the assignment. She gave Catherine Heathcliff's letter.

Catherine was changed by her sickness: there is a vivid description of Cathy in serious illness. She was beautiful in an unearthly way and her eyes *"appeared always to gaze beyond, and far beyond. You would have said out the world."* Judging from her mental and physical state, Ellen draws a conclusion, Catherine doomed to decay. Having been in her service for many years, Ellen was quite familiar with Catherine and Linton, so *"A book lay spread on the sill before her"*—*"I"* believe *Linton had laid it there*; And Catherine's attitude toward Linton changes according to her mood and feelings. She is bad tempered, however, Linton tries everything to make her happy. There is a concise depiction of natural scenery at Wuthering Heights. " The ringing bell in chapel; murmur of the summer foliage when the trees were in leaf was now substituted by the Chapel bells' sound." In a few words the author depicts the quiet winter days of Wuthering Heights; a great thaw or a season of steady rain (spring) and murmur of summer foliage (sounds of trees in leaf in summer). Ellen gives the letter to Catherine. After she has learnt it was a letter from Heathcliff, her reaction to the sudden visit of her former lover is realistically portrayed. Here Cathy was astonished and confused. It was Ellen who gave her an interpretation of the letter by saying *"He wishes to see you. He is in the garden by this time and impatient to know what answer I shall bring."* Ellen had left the door open, so Heathcliff walked in and Catherine eagerly waited for him to find the right room she lives. *"In stride"*, *"had her grasped in his arms"*, and *"hold for 5 minutes without speaking"* show Heathcliff's deep yearning and affection for Catherine. His manner of showing his love for Cathy is so passionate and almost crazy about her. Their reunion was bitter-sweet: though passionately glad to be reunited, embrace, kisses and sweek words such as *"O Cathy My life! How can I bear it"* can't prevent Heathcliff from expressing his sufferings to Cathy. It is a bitter scene. In the eyes of Ellen *"The two, to a cool spectator made a strange and fearful picture"*. Catherine accused Heathcliff of having killed her, and Heathcliff warned her not to say such things when he would be tortured by them after her death besides, she had been at fault by abandoning him. She asked him to forgive her, since she would not *"be at peace"* after death, and he answered: *"It is hard to forgive, and to look at those eyes, and feel those wasted hands... I love my murderer* but yours! (*but your murderer*) *How can I* (*How can I be your murderer?*)?" They held each other closely and wept until Ellen warned them that Linton was returning by saying that *service is over; my master will be here in half an hour*. Heathcliff wanted to leave, but Catherine insisted that he stay, since she was dying and would never see him again. He consented to stay, and "*in the midst of the agitation,* [*Ellen*] *was sincerely glad to observe that Catherine's arms had fallen relaxed... She's fainted or dead, so much the better...* (*she loses consciousness*)." Linton came in, Heathcliff handed him Catherine's body and told him to take care of her: "*Unless you be a fiend, help her first, then you shall speak to me*!" He told Nelly he would wait outside for news of Catherine's welfare (health information), and left. (Heathcliff promise to come again the next day without consideration of the existence of Linton.); here the subtle action shows delicate and considerate thoughts of Heathcliff for Catherine: "I" stated: *she's fainted or die*, While before Heathcliff left, it says *delivered the house of his luckless presence* which means the presence of Heathcliff has disburdened Mr. and Mrs. Linton and Ellen, for his stay was luckless to them all, because it was his presence that accelerates Catherine's death.

Unit 6
Thomas Hardy (1840~1928)

Life

    Thomas Hardy was born on June 2, 1840, in the village of Upper Bockhampton, located in Southwestern England. His father was a stone mason and a violinist. His mother enjoyed reading and relating all the folk songs and legends of the region. Between his parents, Hardy gained all the interests that would appear in his novels and his own life: his love for architecture and music, his interest in the lifestyles of the country folk, and his passion for all sorts of literature.

    At the age of eight, Hardy began to attend Julia Martin's school in Bockhampton. However, most of his education came from the books he found in Dorchester, the nearby town. He learned French, German, and Latin by teaching himself through these books. At sixteen, Hardy's father apprenticed his son to a local architect, John Hicks. Under Hicks' guidance, Hardy learned much about architectural drawing and restoring old houses and churches. Hardy loved the apprenticeship because it allowed him to learn the histories of the houses and the families that lived there. Despite his work, Hardy did not forget his academics: in the evenings, Hardy would study with the Greek scholar Horace Moule.

In 1862, Hardy was sent to London to work with the architect Arthur Blomfield. During his five years in London, Hardy immersed himself in the cultural scene by visiting the museums and theaters and studying classic literature. He started his literary career from poetic writing. Although he did not stay in London, choosing to return to Dorchester as a church restorer, he took his newfound talent for writing as well.

From 1867, Hardy wrote poetry and novels, though the first part of his career was devoted to the novel. At first he published anonymously, but when people became interested in his works, he began to use his own name. Like Dickens, Hardy's novels were published in serial forms in magazines that were popular in both England and America. His first popular novel was *Under the Greenwood Tree*, published in 1872. The next great novel, *Far from the Madding Crowd* (1874) was so popular that with the profits, Hardy was able to give up architecture and marry Emma Gifford. Other popular novels followed in quick succession: *The Return of the Native* (1878), *The Mayor of Casterbridge* (1886), *The Woodlanders* (1887), *Tess of the D'Urbervilles* (1891), and *Jude the Obscure* (1895). In addition to these larger works, Hardy published three collections of short stories and five smaller novels, all moderately successful. However, despite the praise Hardy's fiction received, many critics also found his works to be too shocking, especially *Tess of the D'Urbervilles* and *Jude the Obscure*. The outcry against Jude was so great that Hardy decided to stop writing novels and return to his first great love, poetry.

Over the years, Hardy had divided his time between his home, Max Gate, in Dorchester and his lodgings in London. In his later years, he remained in Dorchester to focus completely on his poetry. In 1898, he saw his dream of becoming a poet realized with the publication of Wessex Poems. He then turned his attentions to an epic drama in verse, *The Dynasts*; it was finally completed in 1908. Before his death, he had written over 800 poems, many of them published while he was in his eighties.

By the last two decades of Hardy's life, he had achieved fame as great as Dickens' fame. In 1910, he was awarded the Order of Merit. New readers had also discovered his novels by the publication of the Wessex Editions, the definitive versions of all Hardy's early works. As a result, Max Gate became a literary shrine.

Hardy also found happiness in his personal life. His first wife, Emma, died in 1912. Although their marriage had not been happy, Hardy grieved at her sudden death. In 1914, he married Florence Dugale, and she was extremely devoted to him. After his death, Florence published Hardy's autobiography in two parts under her own name.

After a long and highly successful life, Thomas Hardy died on January 11, 1928, at the age of 87. His ashes were buried in Poets' Corner at Westminster Abbey.

Plot of *Tess of the D'Urbervilles*

Tess Durbeyfield is the daughter of a poor country pedlar, who learns that he is a descendant of the ancient, noble D'Urberville family, sends his daughter to "claim kin" with a distant relative. There she is seduced by the young master, Alec, and returns home pregnant and disgraced. After the death of her baby, she leaves home and goes to work as a dairymaid at a distant farm, where she meets Angel Clare, son of a clergyman. The two young people fall in love and are married. But on the wedding night, upon hearing Tess's confession of her past, Clare deserts her and goes to Brazil. Left alone, Tess somehow ekes out a miserable existence. Then Tess's father dies and the family are thrown out on the street. To support her mother and her younger sisters and brothers, Tess is therefore forced to go back to Alec to be his mistress. Meanwhile, Clare, now regrets and was longing to reunite with Tess, returns to England to seek for her. Believing that Alec has ruined her for a second time, Tess kills him in despair, and runs away with Clare to hide in a forest and to wait for a chance to escape. In the forest the two lovers spend a few days together, though threatened by punishment, yet quite happy. There Tess is discovered and arrested, then tried and hanged. So "Justice" was done, and the President of the Immortals had ended his sport with Tess.

Some Comments on *Tess of the D'Urbervilles*

The novel has a cyclical pattern, which can be divided into three parts. But Hardy makes the novel into seven phases. The first part is a prelude, which contains two phrases, "The Maiden" and "Maiden No More". This part tells how Tess leaves home and encounters Alec. She was seduced by Alec and comes back home disgrace. This is the first cycle, beginning in May and ending in August. The second part includes three phases, "The Rally", "The Consequence" and "The Wman Pays", which represents the second cycle. In this part, Tess has a new life: she meets with Angel and they fall in love with each other. It begins in May, reaches its climax at the turning of the year and ends in the following winter. The last two phases, "The Convert" and "Fulfillment", belong to the third part which represents her decline. Forced by poverty, Tess returns to Alec until Angel comes to claim her. In shame and anger, Tess kills Alec, and is finally arrested and executed. This part starts in winter and ends in spring.

As for the theme, it is the bold exposure of the hypocritical morality of bourgeois society and the destruction of the English peasantry towards the end of the nineteenth century.

Tess, the heroine, is depicted as a victim of the society. Being beautiful, innocent, honest, and hard-working country girl, she is easily taken in and abused by the hypocritical bourgeoisie, constantly suppressed by the social conventions and moral values of the day, and eventually executed by the unfair legal system of the society. Her absolute obedience to Angel as her husband and her willing suffering and sacrifice to him are not only her weakness in character but also an evitability in a girl of her upbringing. And most important of all, it is the poverty of the family that forces her to improper relations once and again with Alec, and finally, to his murder and her execution.

On one hand, Tess's fate is personal, because she happens to be so beautiful, so pure, so innocent, so obedient, and so poor, and because she happens to get involved with the two men who, though apparent rivals, actually join their forces in bringing about her destruction. On the other hand, her fate is a social one. It can be the fate of any country girl like her. It can be the fate of all the peasants who are driven out of their land and home and forced to seek somewhere else for sustenance.

Major Characters

Tess Durbeyfield is the main character of the book. It is a book of hers. Through all the scenes and all the seasons of the year, our attention is focused on what happens to her. At the beginning, Tess, a sixteen-years-old girl is enjoying herself on holiday. Because of her physical attraction and innocence, she is seduced by Alec. Later she falls in love with Angel, but her confession of the past in the night of marriage brings the dreaded disaster. Angel's reappearance and his forgiveness set her in disgrace and shame. She kills Alec and she is executed.

Love and responsibility are Tess's leading characteristics. She will do in her power for those she loves, under all difficulties, and at the expense of her own wishes and comfort. Having got into difficulties, her pride and guilt prevent her from appealing for help, until it is too late. Yet she is not perfect. Still young and inexperienced, she idealizes Angel and accepts what he says and does without question. Nevertheless, Tess is indeed "a pure woman", loving and true, too young to be always wise, but ruined far more through the fault of Angel than through her own.

Angel is enraptured by Tess's beauty and being in the dairy-farm. He falls in love with her. In spring, when love naturally grows passionate, Angel embraces Tess uncontrollably. Once having done so, he decides, disregarding the wishes of his parents and brothers, to marry her. Fascinated as he is by her virginal beauty, he believes Tess to be absolutely chaste and pure like nature's very daughter.

The sleep-walking scene, symbolic of the working of the subconscious mind, reveals his intense love for Tess and the terrible disappointment caused by the discovery of her past. After his strange travel to Brazil, ashamed of his own weaknesses, he is struck with remorse for his past actions. He has now a clearer knowledge of his love for Tess, of her innocence, of his true self and that of Tess. The conflict thus resolved, he decides to return to Tess.

Angel is the main cause of Tess's tragedy. He has the inconsistencies, preconceptions, idealism, intellectualism, irrationality and impulsiveness of an ardent young man. Like Tess, though he goes astray, he has a general tendency to goodness, and chastened by experience he soberly accepts his new responsibility, the care of Liza-Lu.

Alec Stoke-D'Urberville is the villain of this novel, with his rolling and lascivious eye, diamond ring and black moustachios conventional of stage melodrama. He is thoroughly sensual, violent and headstrong, and determined on getting her own way at all costs. Tess's resistance to the fulfillment of his desires is puny when compared to his cunning maneuvers and ultimately fails. As Tess's first lover, he is frequently regarded as another of Hardy's Satan figures.

Alec never seeks Tess out as a loving, equal partener. Clearly he assumes a cultural right, by virtue of class and gender, to possess Tess's body. Later, after he has proposed to Tess, he reveals his motive tobe not love but a desire for power when he states: "I was your master once! I will be your master again."

Introduction to Chapter 58

Chapter 58 is approaching to the end of the story. After Tess murdered Alec, she and Angel Clare are busy in escape. They live in an estate and enjoy several happy days. Their peace is interrupted by the care-taker. Tess follows Angel's advice and goes on walking to the South. They arrive at the old Stonehenge and Tess is exhausted and unwilling to walk forward. Tess tells Angel to marry her younger sister after her death. While she is lying on the stone slate, the police arrest her and "the justice is done". This chapter shows two lovers powerlessness in face of destiny. Tess is determined to be a tragic character.

Chapter 58

The night was strangely solemn and still. In the *small hours*[1] she whispered to him the whole story of how he had walked in his sleep with her in his arms across *the Froom stream*[2], at the imminent risk of both their lives, and laid her down in the stone coffin at the ruined abbey. He had never known of that till now.

'Why didn't you tell me next day?' he said. 'It might have prevented much misunderstanding and *woe*[3].'

'Don't think of what's past!' said she. 'I am not going to think outside of now. Why should we! Who knows what to-morrow has in store?'

But it apparently had no sorrow. The morning was wet and foggy, and Clare, rightly informed that the *caretaker*[4] only opened the windows on fine days, ventured to creep out of their chamber, and explore the house, leaving Tess asleep. There was no food on the *premises*[5], but there was water, and he took advantage of the fog to emerge from the mansion, and fetch tea, bread, and butter from a shop in a little place two miles beyond, as also a small tin kettle and *spirit-lamp*[6], that they might get fire without smoke. His re-entry awoke her; and they breakfasted on what he had brought.

They were indisposed to stir abroad[7], and the day passed, and the night following, and the next, and next; till, almost without their being aware, five days had slipped by in absolute seclusion, not a sight or sound of a human being disturbing their peacefulness, such as it was. The changes of the weather were their only events, the birds of the New Forest their only company. By *tacit consent*[8] they hardly once spoke of any incident of the past subsequent to their wedding-day. The gloomy intervening time seemed to sink into chaos, over which the present and prior times closed as if it never had been. Whenever he suggested that they should leave their shelter, and go forwards towards Southampton or London, she showed a strange unwillingness to move.

'Why should we put an end to all that's sweet and lovely!' she *deprecated*[9]. 'What must come will come.' And, looking through the *shutter-chink*[10]: 'All is trouble outside there; inside here content.'

He peeped out also. It was quite true; within was affection, union, error forgiven: outside was the *inexorable*[11].

'And-and,' she said, pressing her cheek against his; 'I fear that what you think of me now may not last. I do not wish to outlive your present feeling for me. I would rather not. I would rather be dead and buried when the time comes for you to despise me, so that it may never be known to me that you despised me.'

'I cannot ever despise you.'

'I also hope that. But considering what my life has been I cannot see why any man should, sooner or later, be able to help despising me.... How wickedly mad I was! Yet formerly I never could bear to hurt a fly or a worm, and the sight of a bird in a cage used often to make me cry.'

They remained yet another day. In the night the dull sky cleared, and the result was that the old caretaker at the cottage awoke early. The brilliant sunrise made her unusually brisk, she decided to open the *contiguous*[12] mansion immediately, and to air it thoroughly on such a day. Thus it occurred that, having arrived and opened the lower rooms before six o'clock, she ascended to the bedchambers, and was about to turn the handle of the one wherein they lay. At that moment she fancied she could hear the breathing of persons within. Her slippers and her antiquity had rendered her progress a noiseless one so far, and she made for instant retreat; then, deeming that her hearing might have deceived her, she turned around, to the door and softly tried the handle. The lock was out of order, but a piece of furniture had been moved forward on the inside, which prevented her opening the door more than an inch or two. A stream of morning light through the shutter-chink fell upon the faces of the pair, wrapped in profound slumber, Tess's lips being parted like a half-opened flower near his cheek. The caretaker was so struck with their innocent appearance, and with the elegance of Tess's gown hanging across a chair, her silk stockings beside it, the pretty parasol, and the other *habits*[13] in which she bad arrived because she had none else, that her first indignation at the *effrontery*[14] of tramps and vagabonds gave way to a momentary sentimentality over this genteel elopement, as it seemed. She closed the door, and withdrew as softly as she had come, to go and consult with her neighbours on the odd discovery.

Not more than a minute had elapsed after her withdrawal when Tess woke, and then Clare. Both had a sense that something had disturbed them, though they could not say what; and the uneasy feeling which it engendered grew stronger. As soon as he was dressed he narrowly scanned the lawn through the two or three inches of shutter-chink.

'I think we will leave at once,' said he. 'It is a fine day. And I cannot help fancying somebody is about the house. At any rate, the woman will be sure to come to-day.'

She passively assented, and putting the room in order they took up the few articles that belong to them, and departed noiselessly. When they had got into the Forest she turned to take a last look at the house.

'Ah, happy house-good-bye!' she said. 'My life can only be a question of a few weeks. Why should we not have stayed there?'

'Don't say it, Tess! We shall soon get out of this district altogether. We'll continue our course as we've begun it, and keep straight north. Nobody will think of looking for us there. We shall be looked for at the Wessex ports if we are sought at all. When we are in the north we will get to a port and away.'

Having thus persuaded her the plan was pursued, and they kept *a bee line*[15] northward. Their long repose at the *manor-house*[16] lent them walking power now; and towards mid-day they found that they were approaching *the steepled city of Melchester*[17], which lay directly in their way. He decided to rest her in a clump of trees during the afternoon, and push onward under cover of darkness. At dusk Clare purchased food as usual, and their night march began, the boundary between Upper and Mid-Wessex being crossed about eight o'clock.

To walk across country without much regard to roads was not new to Tess, and she showed her old agility in the performance. The intercepting city, ancient Melchester, they were obliged to pass through in order to take advantage of the town bridge for crossing a large river that obstructed them. It was about midnight when they went along the deserted streets, lighted fitfully by the few lamps, keeping off the pavement that it might not echo their footsteps. The graceful pile of cathedral architecture rose dimly on their left hand, but it was lost upon them now. Once out of the town they followed the *turnpike-road*[18], which after a few miles plunged across an open plain.

Though the sky was dense with cloud a diffused light from some fragment of a moon had hitherto helped them a little. But the moon had now sunk, the clouds seemed to settle almost on their heads, and the night grew as dark as a cave. However, they found their way along, keeping as much on the turf as possible that their tread might not resound, which it was easy to do, there being no hedge or fence of any kind. All around was open loneliness and black solitude, over which a stiff breeze blew.

They had proceeded thus gropingly two or three miles further when on a sudden Clare became conscious of some vast erection close in his front, rising sheer from the grass. They had almost struck themselves against it.

'What monstrous place is this?' said Angel.

'It hums,' said she.'*Hearken*[19]！'

He listened. The wind, playing upon the edifice, produced a booming tune, like the note of some gigantic one-stringed harp. No other sound came from it, and lifting his hand and advancing a step or two, Clare felt the vertical surface of the structure. It seemed to be of solid stone, without joint or *moulding*[20]. Carrying his fingers onward he found that what he had come in contact with was a colossal rectangular pillar; by stretching out his left hand he could feel a similar one adjoining. At an indefinite height overhead something made the black sky blacker, which had the semblance of a vast architrave uniting the pillars horizontally. They carefully entered beneath and between; the surfaces echoed their soft rustle; but they seemed to be still out of doors. The place was roofless. Tess drew her breath fearfully, and Angel, perplexed, said—

'What can it be?'

Feeling sideways they encountered another tower-like pillar, square and uncompromising as the first; beyond it another and another. The place was all doors and pillars, some connected above by continuous *architraves*[21].

'A very *Temple of the Winds*[22],' he said.

The next pillar was isolated; others composed a *trilithon*[23]; others were prostrate, their flanks forming a causeway wide enough for a carriage; and it was soon obvious that they made up a forest of *monoliths*[24] grouped upon the grassy expanse of the plain. The couple advanced further into this pavilion of the night till they stood in its midst.

'It is *Stonehenge*[25]!' said Clare.

'The *heathen*[26] temple, you mean?'

'Yes. Older than the centuries; older than the d'Urbervilles! Well, what shall we do, darling? We may find shelter further on.' But Tess, really tired by this time, flung herself upon an oblong slab that lay close at hand, and was sheltered from the wind by a pillar. Owing to the action of the sun during the preceding day the stone was warm and dry, in comforting contrast to the rough and chill grass around, which had damped her skirts and shoes.

'I don't want to go any further, Angel,' she said stretching out her hand for his. 'Can't we *bide*[27] here?'

'I fear not. This spot is visible for miles by day, although it does not seem so now.'

'One of my mother's people was a shepherd hereabouts, now I think of it. And you used to say at Talbothays that I was a heathen. So now I am at home.'

He knelt down beside her outstretched form, and put his lips upon hers.

'Sleepy are you, dear? I think you are lying on an altar.'

'I like very much to be here,' she murmured. 'It is so solemn and lonely-after my great happiness-with nothing but the sky above my face. It seems as if there were no folk in the world but we two; and I wish there were not-except 'Liza-Lu.'

Clare thought she might as well rest here till it should get a little lighter, and he flung his overcoat upon her, and sat down by her side.

'Angel, if anything happens to me, will you watch over 'Liza-Lu for my sake?' she asked, when they had listened a long time to the wind among the pillars.

'I will.'

'She is so good and simple and pure. O, Angel-I wish you would marry her if you lose me, as you will do shortly. O, if you would!'

'If I lose you I lose all! And *she is my sister-in-law*[28].'

'That's nothing, dearest. People marry sister-laws continually about Marlott; and Liza-Lu is so gentle and sweet, and she is growing so beautiful. O I could share you with her willingly when we are spirits! If you would train her and teach her, Angel, and bring her up for your own self!... She has all the best of me without the bad of me; and if she were to become yours it would almost seem as if death had not divided us....Well, I have said it. I won't mention it again.'

She ceased, and he fell into thought. In the far north-east sky he could see between the pillars a level streak of light. The uniform *concavity*[29] of black cloud was lifting bodily like the lid of a pot, letting in at the earth's edge the coming day, against which the towering monoliths and trilithons began to be blackly defined.

'Did they sacrifice to God here?' asked she.

'No,' said he.

'Who to?'

'I believe to the sun. That lofty stone set away by itself is in the direction of the sun, which will presently rise behind it.'

'This reminds me, dear,' she said. 'You remember you never would interfere with any belief of mine before we were married? But I knew your mind all the same, and I thought as you thought-not from any reasons of my own, but because you thought so. Tell me now, Angel, do you think we shall meet again after we are dead? I want to know.'

He kissed her to avoid a reply at such a time.

'O, Angel-I fear that means no!' said she, with a suppressed sob. 'And I wanted so to see you again-so much, so much! What not even you and I, Angel, who love each other so well?' *Like a greater than himself, to the critical question at the critical time he did not answer*[30]; and they were again silent. In a minute or two her breathing became more regular, her clasp of his hand relaxed, and she fell asleep. The band of silver paleness along the east horizon made even the distant parts of the

Great Plain appear dark and near; and the whole enormous landscape bore that impress of reserve, *taciturnity*[31], and hesitation which is usual just before day. The eastward pillars and their architraves stood up blackly against the light, and the great flame-shaped Sun-stone beyond them; and the Stone of Sacrifice midway. Presently the night wind died out, and the quivering little pools in the cup-like hollows of the stones lay still. At the same time something seemed to move on the verge of the dip eastward-a mere dot. It was the head of a man approaching them from the hollow beyond the Sun-stone. Clare wished they had gone onward, but in the circumstances decided to remain quiet. The figure came straight towards the circle of pillars in which they were.

He heard something behind him, the brush of feet. Turning, he saw over the prostrate columns another figure; then before he was aware, another was at hand on the right, under a trilithon, and another on the left. The dawn shone full on the front of the man westward, and Clare could discern from this that he was tall, and walked as if trained. They all closed in with evident purpose. Her story then was true! Springing to his feet, he looked around for a weapon, loose stone, means of escape, anything. By this time the nearest man was upon him.

'It is no use, sir,' he said. 'There are sixteen of us on the Plain, and the whole country is reared.'

'Let her finish her sleep!' he implored in a whisper of the men as they gathered round.

When they saw where she lay, which they had not done till then, they showed no objection, and stood watching her, as still as the pillars around. He went to the stone and bent over her, holding one poor little hand; her breathing now was quick and small, like that of *a lesser creature than a woman*[32]. All waited in the growing light, their faces and hands as if they were silvered, the remainder of their figures dark, the stones glistening green-gray, the Plain still a mass of shade. Soon the light was strong, and a ray shone upon her unconscious form, peering under her eyelids and waking her.

'What is it, Angel?' she said, starting up. 'Have they come for me?'

'Yes, dearest,' he said. 'They have come.'

'It is as it should be,' she murmured. 'Angel, I am almost glad-yes, glad! This happiness could not have lasted. It was too much. I have had enough; and now I shall not live for you to despise me!' She stood up, shook herself, and went forward, neither of the men having moved.

'I am ready,' she said quietly.

Notes

[1] early in the moring, one or two o'clock.

[2] 佛鲁姆河。新婚之夜,Angel 梦游时抱着 Tess 走过佛鲁姆河,将她放在石棺上,后来又将她抱回。当时 Tess 醒着,但 Angel 却对此并不知晓。

[3] misfortune/pain

[4] 看门人

[5] 房屋,指 Angel 和 Tess 在逃亡途中暂时栖身的一座空房子。

[6] 酒精灯

[7] 他们都不想外出。

[8] 默准

[9] 反对

[10] 百叶窗窗缝

[11] 冷酷无情

[12] neighbouring

[13] clothes

[14] 放肆

[15] straight line

[16] 庄园,即他们暂时栖身的空屋。

[17] 尖塔之城梅尔切斯特

[18] 收税的道路

[19] hear

[20] 浇铸

[21] 柱顶过梁

[22] 风神庙

[23] 三根相连的巨石柱

[24] 独块巨石

[25] 巨石阵。英国南部索尔兹伯里附近一处史前巨石建筑遗址。

[26] 异教徒

[27] 停留

[28] 英国国会及法律禁止与已故妻子的妹妹结婚。该法律于 1906 年废止。

[29] 凹陷处

[30] 据《新约·约翰福音》记载,当耶稣被带到控告他的祭司长和长老们面前时,他拒绝回答他们的任何问题。

[31] 沉默寡言

[32] 不是妇女,而是小姑娘

Questions

1 Why do Tess and Angel escape?

2 Why is Tess unwilling to escape?

3 Why does Tess ask Angel to marry her sister, Liza-Lu after her death?

4 How is Tess arrested by the police?

5 What do you think the end of the story?

Analysis of Chapter 58

Tess of the D'Urbervilles is Hardy's masterpiece. In Chapter 58, Tess tells Angel about how he carried her while sleepwalking, and he regrets that he did not tell him about this earlier, for it might have prevented much misunderstanding and woe. Tess is unwilling to leave their shelter and go forward, for she wonders why they must put an end to all that sweet and lovely. She says that what must come will come. Angel decides that they must finally leave the mansion, but Tess wishes to stay, for she believes she will not last more than several weeks. Angel plans to take Tess north, where they sail from Wessex. They travel northward and reach Stonehenge. Tess wishes to remain there, for Angel used to say that she was a heathen and thus Stonehenge is appropriate for her. Tess asks Angel to look after Liza-Lu if he loses her and to marry her. Tess falls asleep there, as she sleeps a party come for her. Tess admits that she is almost glad, for her happiness could not have lasted. She tells them that she is ready.

The story of Tess herself ends with her capture. Her sentence of death is an inevitable consequence. Chapter 59 is but the end of the novel, placing Angel and Lisa-Lu together and thus adding a bright color to the whole account.

Unit 7
James Joyce (1882~1904)

Life

James Joyce, an Irish novelist and poet. He is considered to be one of the most influential writers in the modernist avant-garde of the early 20th century. Joyce is best known for *Ulysses* (1922), a landmark work in which the episodes of Homer's *Odyssey* are paralleled in an array of contrasting literary styles, perhaps most prominently the stream of consciousness technique he perfected. Other major works are the short-story collection *Dubliners* (1914), and the novels *A Portrait of the Artist as a Young Man* (1916) and *Finnegans Wake* (1939).

Joyce was born to a middle class family in Dublin, where he excelled as a student at the Jesuit schools Clongowes and Belvedere, then at University College Dublin. In his early twenties he emigrated permanently to continental Europe, living in Trieste, Paris and Zurich. Though most of his adult life was spent abroad, Joyce's fictional universe does not extend beyond Dublin, and is populated largely by characters who closely resemble family members, enemies and friends from his time there. Joyce is noted for his frank representation of reality. In addition, Joyce's language has always been a topic of immense interest to people. It is poetic, accurate, forceful, rhythmic, musical, picturesque and humorous beyond description.

Plot of *Eveline*

A nineteen-year-old girl, Eveline struggles with poverty and the difficulties of supporting her family. She works very hard, at a store and also at home. She is planning to leave Ireland forever; her means of escape is a sailor named Frank, who promises her a new life. Frank treats her with tenderness, and he entertains her with stories about his travels around the world. Still, she loves her father and regrets the idea of leaving him in his old age. She remembers her mother's death, when she promised her mother to keep the home together as long as she could. In the end, however, she is too paralyzed and too frightened to leave Dublin.

Major Character

It is a short story about a girl called Eveline. She works hard all day at the shop bullied by her supervisor, at home doing all the housework and looking after two brothers; Being the breadwinner and the woman of the house, she has so many responsibilities. She is passive. She seems to see Frank only as harsh "protector" for a kind one. Eveline is incapable of becoming wiser. We know her future will be one of those some "commonplace sacrifices" like her mother.

Eveline

She sat at the window watching the evening invade the avenue. Her head was leaned against the window curtains and in her nostrils was the odour of dusty cretonne. She was tired.

Few people passed. The man out of the last house passed on his way home; she heard his footsteps clacking along the concrete pavement and afterwards crunching on the cinder path before the new red houses. One time there used to be a field there in which they used to play every evening with other people's children. Then a man from Belfast bought the field and built houses in it—not like their little brown houses but bright brick houses with shining roofs. The children of the avenue used to play together in that field—the Devines, the Waters, the Dunns, little Keogh the cripple, she and her brothers and sisters. Ernest, however, never played: he was too grown up. Her father used often to hunt them in out of the field with his *blackthorn stick*[1]; but usually little Keogh used to keep nix and call out when he saw her father coming. Still they seemed to have been rather happy then. Her father was not so bad then; and besides, her mother was alive. That was a long time ago; she and her brothers and sisters were all grown up her mother was dead. Tizzie Dunn was dead, too, and the Waters had gone back to England. Everything changes. Now she was going to go away like the others, to leave her home.

Home! She looked round the room, reviewing all its familiar objects which she had dusted once a week for so many years, wondering where on earth all the dust came from. Perhaps she would never see again those familiar objects from which she had never dreamed of being divided. And yet during all those years she had never found out the name of the priest whose yellowing photograph hung on the wall above the broken harmonium beside the coloured print of the promises made to Blessed Margaret Mary Alacoque. He had been a school friend of her father. Whenever he showed the photograph to a visitor her father used to pass it with a casual word:

"He is in Melbourne now."

She had consented to go away, to leave her home. Was that wise? She tried to weigh each side of the question. In her home anyway she had shelter and food; she had those whom she had known all her life about her. O course she had to work hard, both in the house and at business. What would they say of her in the Stores when they found out that she had run away with a fellow? Say she was a fool, perhaps; and her place would be filled up by advertisement. Miss Gavan would be glad. She had always had an edge on her, especially whenever there were people listening.

"Miss Hill, don't you see these ladies are waiting?"

"Look lively, Miss Hill, please."

She would not cry many tears at leaving the Stores.

But in her new home, in a distant unknown country, it would not be like that. Then she would be married—she, Eveline. People would treat her with respect then. She would not be treated as her mother had been. Even now, though she was over nineteen, she sometimes felt herself in danger of her father's violence. She knew it was that that had given her the palpitations. When they were growing up he had never gone for her like he used to go for Harry and Ernest, because she was a girl but latterly he had begun to threaten her and say what he would do to her only for her dead mother's sake. And no she had nobody to protect her. Ernest was dead and Harry, who was in the church decorating business, was nearly always down somewhere in the country. Besides, the invariable squabble for money on Saturday nights had begun to weary her unspeakably. She always gave her entire wages—seven shillings—and Harry always sent up what he could but the trouble was to get any money from her father. He said she used to squander the money, that she had no head, that he wasn't going to give her his hard-earned money to throw about the streets, and much more, for he was usually fairly bad on Saturday night. In the end he would give her the money and ask her had she any intention of buying Sunday's dinner. Then she had to rush out as quickly as she could and do her marketing, holding her black leather purse tightly in her hand as she elbowed her way through the crowds and returning home late under her load of provisions. She had hard work to keep the house together and to see that the two young children who had been left to hr charge went to school regularly and got their meals regularly. It was hard work—a hard life—but now that she was about to leave it she did not find it a wholly undesirable life.

She was about to explore another life with Frank. Frank was very kind, manly, open-hearted. She was to go away with him by the night-boat to be his wife and to live with him in *Buenos Ayres*[2] where he had a home waiting for her. How well she remembered the first time she had seen him; he was lodging in a house on the main road where she used to visit. It seemed a few weeks ago. He was standing at the gate, his peaked cap pushed back on his head and his hair tumbled forward over a face of bronze. Then they had come to know each other. He used to meet her outside the Stores every evening and see her home. He took her to see *The Bohemian Girl*[3] and she felt elated as she sat in an unaccustomed part of the theatre with him. He was awfully fond of music and sang a little. People knew that they were courting and, when he sang about the lass that loves a sailor, she always felt pleasantly confused. He used to call her Poppens out of fun. First of all it had been an excitement for her to have a fellow and then she had begun to like him. He had tales of distant countries. He had started as a deck boy at a pound a month on a ship of the Allan Line going out to Canada. He told her the names of the ships he had been on and the names of the different services. He had sailed through *the Straits of Magellan*[4] and he told her stories of the terrible *Patagonians*[5]. He had fallen on his feet in Buenos Ayres, he said, and had come over to the old country just for a holiday. Of course, her father had found out the affair and had forbidden her to have anything to say to him.

"I know these sailor chaps," he said.

One day he had quarreled with Frank and after that she had to meet her lover secretly.

The evening deepened in the avenue. The white of two letters in her lap grew indistinct. One was to Harry; the other was to her father. Ernest had been her favourite but she liked Harry too. Her father was becoming old lately, she noticed; he would miss her. Sometimes he could be very nice. Not long before, when she had been laid up for a day, he had read her out a ghost story and made toast for her at the fire. Another day, when their mother was alive, they had all gone for a picnic to the Hill of Howth. She remembered her father putting on her mother's bonnet to make the children laugh.

Her time was running out but she continued to sit by the window, leaning her head against the window curtain, inhaling the odour of dusty cretonne. Down far in the avenue she could hear a street organ playing. She knew the air Strange that it should come that very night to remind her of the promise to her mother, her promise to keep the home together as long as she could. She remembered the last night of her mother's illness; she was again in the close dark room at the other side of the hall and outside she heard a melancholy air of Italy. The organ-player had been ordered to go away and given sixpence. She remembered her father strutting back into the sickroom saying:

"Damned Italians! Coming over here!"

As she mused the pitiful vision of her mother's life laid its spell on the very quick of her being—that life of commonplace sacrifices closing in final craziness. She trembled as she heard again her mother's voice saying constantly with foolish insistence:

"Derevaun Seraun! Derevaun Seraun!"

She stood up in a sudden impulse of terror. Escape! She must escape! Frank would save her. He would give her life, perhaps love, too. But she wanted to live. Why should she be unhappy? She had a right to happiness. Frank would take her in his arms, fold her in his arms. He would save her.

She stood among the swaying crowd in the station at the North Wall. He held her hand and she knew that he was speaking to her, saying something about the passage over and over again. The station was full of soldiers with brown baggages. Through the wide doors of the sheds she caught a glimpse of the black mass of the boat, lying in beside the quay wall, with illumined portholes. She answered nothing. She felt her cheek pale and cold and, out of a maze of distress, she prayed to God to direct her, to show her what was her duty. The boat blew a long mournful whistle into the mist. If she went, tomorrow she would be on the sea with Frank, steaming towards Buenos Ayres. Their passage had been booked. Could she still draw back after all he had done for her? Her distress awoke a nausea in her body and she kept moving her lips in silent fervent prayer.

A bell clanged upon her heart. She felt him seize her hand:

"Come!"

All the seas of the world tumbled about her heart. He was drawing her into them: he would drown her. She gripped with both hands at the iron railing.

"Come!"

No! No! No! It was impossible. Her hands clutched the iron in frenzy. Amid the seas she sent a cry of anguish.

"Eveline! Evvy!"

He rushed beyond the barrier and called to her to follow. He was shouted at to go on but he still called to her. She set her white face to him, passive, like a helpless animal. Her eyes gave him no sign of love or farewell or recognition.

Notes

[1] 李木手杖

[2] 布宜诺斯艾利斯,城市名,阿根廷的首都

[3] 波西米亚女孩

[4] 麦哲伦海峡,南美智利以南的一个海峡

[5] 南美洲南端的巴塔哥尼亚印第安人

Questions

1　Why did she want to escape?

2　Why didn't she escape?

3　If you were Eveline, what would you choose, to leave or not to leave home?

Analysis of *Eveline*

Eveline focuses on the theme of escape. She has been given a chance, yet in the end, the girl finds herself incapable of escape. Eveline has a complex psychological world. She lingers on the question whether to run away from home or not. On one hand, she wants to leave home, because she feels lonely and unhappy. Her father was not kind any longer, and mother was not alive. She had to work hard, both in the house and at business. She was in danger of her father's violence and threats and she always spent her entire wages (7shillings) on the whole family. The most important reason is that she wants to marry Frank and that means a new life, where she will be treated with respect. Eveline has learnt from her mother's experience—she sacrifices and ends life in craziness, so Eveline does not want to repeat her mother's life—she wants to escape.

However she can't make a decision to leave home. Home, for her means shelter and food. She had those whom she had known all her life about her and she has fear of being said as a fool to run away with a fellow. She was tortured by her promise to her mother—keep the home together as long as she could. The last reason is that she has a fear of being drowned in the seas. Maybe Frank is also a symbol of danger in her world. What kind of life Frank provides her is Sticl unknown. It is possible that she will be cheated by him and sold to whorehouse.

Powerlessness, Imprisonment and paralysis are themes of the story. Eveline, a young woman, is in some way imprisoned. The imprisonment is often caused by a combination of circumstances: poverty, social pressure and family situation.

In this story, the 19 year old girl, Eveline's mental world symbolizes the dream's disillusionment and Frank is a symbol of new life and new experience or maybe a potential danger in the life of Eveline.

Unit 8
Virginia Woolf (1882~1941)

Life

    Virginia Woolf was born in London, the daughter of Julia Jackson Duckworth, a member of the Duckworth publishing family, and Sir Leslie Stephen, a literary critic, and the founder of the *Dictionary of National Biography*. Leslie Stephen's first wife had been the daughter of the novelist William Makepeace Thackeray.

    Woolf, who was educated at home, grew up at the family home at Hyde Park Gate. From her early age, she was extremely attached to her father. Woolf's youth was shadowed by series of emotional shocks. Woolf's mother died from influenza, when Virginia was in her early teens. Stella Duckworth, her half sister, took her mother's place, but died two years later. Woolf's father suffered a slow death from stomach cancer, he died in 1904. When Virginia's brother Thoby died in 1906, she had a prolonged mental breakdown.

    Following the death of her father, Woolf moved with her sister and two brothers to the house in Bloomsbury.

The Voyage Out (1915) was Virginia Woolf's first novel. Set in South America, it tells of the emotions of tourists somewhere near the Amazon River. The whole scene is imaginary; Woolf had never been there, but the story can be read as an allegory of artistic creation. This work, which received mixed reviews, was followed by *Night and Day* (1919), a realistic novel about the lives of two friends, Katherine and Mary. *Jacob's Room* (1922) was based upon the life and death of her brother Thoby.

With *To the Lighthouse* (1927) and *The Waves* (1931) Woolf established herself as one of the leading writers of modernism. *The Waves* is perhaps Woolf's most difficult novel. It follows in soliloquies the lives of six persons from childhood to old age.

Much of her writing reflected her inner conflicts. Woolf developed innovative literary techniques in order to reveal women's experience and find an alternative to the dominating views of reality.

Mrs. Dalloway (1925) formed a web of boring and depressing thoughts of several groups of people. Like Joyce's *Ulysses*, the action takes place in a single day, in this case in June in 1923. There is little action, but much movement in time from present to past and back again. The central figure, Clarissa Dalloway, married to Richard Dalloway, is a wealthy London hostess, who spends her day in London preparing for her evening party. Clarissa recalls her life before World War I, her friendship with the unconventional Sally Seton, and her relationship with Peter Walsh. At her party she never meets the shell-shocked veteran Septimus Smith, one of the first Englishmen to enlist in the war. Sally returns as Lady Rossetter, Peter Walsh is still enamored with Mrs. Dalloway, the prime minister arrives, and Smith commits suicide.

After the final attack of mental illness, Woolf loaded her pockets full of stones and drowned herself in the river, near her Sussex home, on March 28, 1941. On her note to her husband she wrote: "I have a feeling I shall go mad. I cannot go on longer in these terrible times. I hear voices and cannot concentrate on my work. I have fought against it but cannot fight any longer. I owe all my happiness to you but cannot go on and spoil your life."

Virginia Woolf's concern with feminist themes is dominant in *A Room of One's Own* (1929). In it she made her famous statement: "A woman must have money and a room of her own if she is to write fiction."

As an essayist Woolf was prolific. She published some 500 essays in periodicals and collections, Since 1905. To find her own voice, she read and wrote voraciously, but it was not until Woolf was middle-aged she felt confident in her craft. Characteristic for Woolf's essays are dialogic nature of style. A number of her writings are autobiographical. In the essay on the art of Walter Sickert, which was inspired by her visit in his retrospective show, Woolf asked how words can express colour, and answered that all great writers are great colorists: "Each of Shakespeare's plays has its dominant colour. And each writer differs of course as a colourist..." (*Walter Sickert: A Conversation*, 1934). Woolf's rejection of an authoritative voice links her essays to the tradition of Montaigne.

Plot of *Mrs. Dalloway*

Mrs. Dalloway (published on 14 May 1925) is a novel by Virginia Woolf that details a day in the life of Clarissa Dalloway in post-World War I England. It is one of Woolf's best-known novels.

Clarissa Dalloway goes around London in the morning, getting ready to host a party that evening. The nice day reminds her of her youth at Bourton and makes her wonder about her choice of husband; she married the reliable Richard Dalloway instead of the enigmatic and demanding Peter Walsh and she "had not the option" to be with Sally Seton. Peter reintroduces these conflicts by paying a visit that morning.

Septimus Warren Smith, a veteran of World War I suffering from deferred traumatic stress, spends his day in the park with his Italian-born wife Lucrezia, where they are observed by Peter Walsh. Septimus is visited by frequent and indecipherable hallucinations, mostly concerning his dear friend Evans who died in the war. Later that day, after he is prescribed involuntary commitment to a psychiatric hospital, he commits suicide by jumping out of a window.

Clarissa's party in the evening is a slow success. It is attended by most of the characters she has met in the book, including people from her past. She hears about Septimus' suicide at the party and gradually comes to admire the act of this stranger, which she considers an effort to preserve the purity of his happiness.

Some Comments on *Mrs. Dalloway*

In *Mrs Dalloway*, all of the action, except flashbacks, takes place on a day in June. It is an example of free indirect discourse storytelling (not stream of consciousness because this story moves between the consciousnesses of every character in a form of discourse): every scene closely tracks the momentary thoughts of a particular character.

Because of structural and stylistic similarities, *Mrs Dalloway* is commonly thought to be a response to James Joyce's *Ulysses*, a text that is often considered one of the greatest novels of the twentieth century.

The novel has two main narrative lines involving two separate characters; within each narrative there is a particular time and place in the past that the main characters keep returning to in their minds. For Clarissa, it is her charmed youth at Bourton keeps intruding into her thoughts on this day in London. For Septimus, it is his time as a soldier during the Great War keeps intruding, especially in the form of Evans, his comrade.

The novel follows the themes as Mental illness and feminism. Septimus, as the shell-shocked war hero, operates as a pointed criticism of the treatment of mental illness and depression.

Woolf goes beyond criticizing the treatment of mental illness. Using the characters of Clarissa and Rezia, she makes the argument that people can only interpret Septimus' shell-shock according to their cultural norms. Throughout the course of the novel Clarissa does not meet Septimus. Clarissa's reality is vastly different from that of Septimus; his presence in London is unknown to Clarissa until his death becomes idle chat at her party. Her use of Septimus as the stereotypically traumatized man from the war is her way of showing that there were still reminders of the First World War in 1923 London.

As a commentary on inter-war society, Clarissa's character highlights the role of women as the proverbial "Angel in the House" and embodies sexual and economic repression and the narcissism of bourgeois women who have never known the hunger and insecurity of working women.

Her old friend Sally Seton, whom Clarissa admires dearly, is remembered as a great independent woman. She smoked cigars, once ran down a corridor naked to fetch her sponge-bag and made bold, unladylike statements to get a reaction from people. When Clarissa meets her in the present day, she turns out to be a perfect housewife, having married a self-made rich man and given birth to five sons.

Major Characters

Clarissa Dalloway is a fifty-one-year-old protagonist of the novel. She is the wife of Richard and mother of Elizabeth. She spends the day organizing a party that will be held that night while also reminiscing about the past. She is self-conscious about her role in London high society.

Richard Dalloway is the haughty husband of Clarissa. He is immersed in his work in government.

Elizabeth Dalloway is a seventeen-year-old daughter of Clarissa and Richard. She is said to look "oriental" and has great composure. Compared to her mother, she takes great pleasure in politics and modern history, hoping to be either a doctor or farmer in the future.

Septimus Warren Smith is a World War I veteran who suffers from "shell shock" and hallucinations of his deceased friend, Evans. Educated and decorated in the war, he is detached from society. He is married to Lucrezia from whom he has grown distant.

Lucrezia Smith is the Italian wife of Septimus. She is burdened by his mental illness and believes that she is judged because of it. During most of the novel she is homesick for family and country, which she left to marry Septimus after the Armistice.

Sally Seton had a strained relationship with her family and spent much time with Clarissa's family in her youth. Sally is married to Lord Rosseter and has five boys. She can be described as feisty as well as a youthful raga muffin.

Peter Walsh is an old friend of Clarissa. In the past, she rejected his marriage proposal. Now he has returned to England from India and is one of the guests at Clarissa's party. He is planning to marry Daisy.

Introduction to Chapter I (*An Excerpt*)

Clarissa Dalloway, an upper-class, fifty-two-year-old woman married to a politician, decides to buy flowers herself for the party she is hosting that evening instead of sending a servant to buy them. London is full of noise this Wednesday. Big Ben strikes. The king and queen are at the palace. It is a fresh mid-June morning, and Clarissa recalls one girlhood summer on her father's estate, Bourton. She sees herself at eighteen, standing at the window, feeling as if something awful might happen. Despite the dangers, Clarissa loves life. Her one gift, she feels, is an ability to know people by instinct.

She thinks affectionately of Peter, who once asked her to marry him. She refused. He made her cry when he said she would marry a prime minister and throw parties. Clarissa continues to feel the sting of his criticisms but now also feels anger that Peter did not accomplish any of his dreams.

Chapter I
(*An Excerpt*)

Mrs. Dalloway said she would buy the flowers herself.

For *Lucy*[1] had her work cut out for her. The doors would be taken off their hinges; *Rumpelmayer's men*[2] were coming. And then, thought Clarissa Dalloway, what a morning—fresh as if issued to children on a beach.

What a lark! What a plunge! For so it had always seemed to her, when, with a little *squeak*[3] of the hinges, which she could hear now, she had burst open *the French windows*[4] and plunged at *Bourton*[5] into the open air. How fresh, how calm, stiller than this of course, the air was in the early morning; like the flap of a wave; the kiss of a wave; chill and sharp and yet (for a girl of eighteen as she then was) solemn, feeling as she did, standing there at the open window, that something awful was about to happen; looking at the flowers, at the trees with the smoke winding off them and the rooks rising, falling; standing and looking until Peter Walsh said, "Musing among the vegetables?"—was that it? —"I prefer men to cauliflowers"— was that it? He must have said it at breakfast one morning when she had gone out on to the terrace—Peter Walsh. He would be back from India one of these days, June or July, she forgot which, for his letters were awfully dull; it was his sayings one remembered; his eyes, his pocket-knife, his smile, his *grumpiness*[6] and, when millions of things had utterly vanished—how strange it was! —a few sayings like this about cabbages.

She stiffened a little on the *kerb*[7], waiting for *Durtnall's van*[8] to pass. A charming woman, *Scrope Purvis*[9] thought her (knowing her as one does know people who live next door to one in *Westminster*[10]); a touch of the bird about her, of the *jay*[11], blue-green, light, *vivacious*[12], though she was over fifty, and grown very white since her illness. There she perched, never seeing him, waiting to cross, very upright.

For having lived in Westminster—how many years now? over twenty—one feels even in the midst of the traffic, or waking at night, Clarissa was positive, a particular hush, or solemnity; an indescribable pause; a suspense (but that might be her heart, affected, they said, by influenza) before *Big Ben*[13] strikes. There! Out it boomed. First a warning, musical; then the hour, *irrevocable*[14]. The leaden circles dissolved in the air. Such fools we are, she thought, crossing *Victoria Street*[15].

Notes

[1] 露西,达洛维夫人家里的女佣。

[2] "Rumpelmayer"是店名。Rumpelmayer's men 是指前来卸门的工人。

[3] 嘎吱嘎吱的响声

[4] 落地窗

[5] 英格兰度假胜地,这里指达洛维夫人少女时代其父母的居住地。

[6] bad temper

[7] 人行道

[8] 某商号的运货车

[9] 大概是运货车的驾驶员或其他雇员

[10] 威斯敏斯特,英国伦敦西部的贵族居住区,在泰晤士河北岸,区内有白金汉宫、议会大厦、首相府邸、政府各部门和威斯敏斯特大教堂。

[11] 松鸦,一种漂亮鸣鸟

[12] 活泼的

[13] 大本钟,伦敦英国议会大厦钟楼上的大钟

[14] 不可挽回的

[15] 维多利亚大街,在伦敦市中心

Questions

1 How does Woolf present Mrs. Dalloway to the reader?

2 What do you know about the personality of Peter Walsh?

3 What is the function of Big Ben?

Analysis of Chapter I (*An Excerpt*)

Woolf wrote much of *Mrs. Dalloway* in free indirect discourse. We are generally immersed in the subjective mental world of various characters, although the book is written in the third person, referring to characters by proper names, as well as the pronouns *he*, *she*, and *they*. Woolf allows us to evaluate characters from both external and internal perspectives: We follow them as they move physically through the world, all the while listening to their most private thoughts. The subjective nature of the narrative demonstrates the unreliability of memory.

In this excerpt, Clarissa is full of happy thoughts as she sets off to buy flowers that beautiful June morning, but her rapture reminds her of a similar June morning thirty years earlier, when she stood at the window at Bourton and felt something awful might happen. Tragedy is never far from her thoughts, and from the first page of the book Clarissa has a sense of impending tragedy. Indeed, one of the central dilemmas Clarissa will face is her own mortality. Even as Clarissa rejoices in life, she struggles to deal with aging and death. Then, by accident, she reads two lines about death from an open book in a shop window: "Fear no more the heat o' the sun / Nor the furious winter's rages." The words are from one of Shakespeare's later plays, *Cymbeline*, which is experimental since it has comic, romantic, and tragic elements, much like *Mrs. Dalloway*. The lines are from a funeral song that suggests death is a comfort after life's hard struggles.

Woolf reveals mood and character through unusual and complex syntax. The rush and movement of London are reflected in galloping sentences that go on for line after line in a kind of ecstasy. These sentences also reflect Clarissa's character, particularly her ability to enjoy life, since they forge ahead quickly and bravely, much as Clarissa does. As Clarissa sees the summer air moving the leaves like waves, sentences become rhythmic, full of dashes and semicolons that imitate the choppy movement of water. Parentheses abound, indicating thoughts within thoughts, sometimes related to the topic at hand and sometimes not.

Unit 9
Nathaniel Hawthorne (1804~1864)

Life

Nathaniel Hawthorne was an American novelist and short story writer. He was born in 1804 in the city of Salem, Massachusetts to Nathaniel Hathorne and the former Elizabeth Clarke Manning. His ancestors include John Hathorne, the only judge involved in the Salem witch trials who never repented of his actions. Nathaniel later added a ".w" to make his name "Hawthorne" in order to hide this relation. He entered Bowdoin College in 1821, where he met his two important friends, one is 13th American president Franklin Pierce and another is American poet Henry Longfellow. He graduated in 1825. Hawthorne anonymously published his first work, a novel titled *Fanshawe*, in 1828. He published several short stories in various periodicals which he collected in 1837 as *Twice-Told Tales*. The next year, he became engaged to Sophia Peabody. He worked at a Custom Housebefore marrying Peabody in 1842. The couple moved to The Old Manse in Concord, Massachusetts, later moving to Salem, the Berkshires, then to The Wayside in Concord. *The Scarlet Letter* was published in

1850, followed by a succession of other novels. A political appointment took Hawthorne and family to Europe before their return to The Wayside in 1860. Hawthorne died on May 19, 1864, and was survived by his wife and their three children.

Much of Hawthorne's writing centers on New England, many works featuring moral allegories with a Puritan inspiration. His fiction works are considered part of the Romantic movement and, more specifically, dark romanticism. His themes often center on the inherent evil and sin of humanity, and his works often have moral messages and deep psychological complexity. His published works include novels, short stories, and a biography of his friend Franklin Pierce.

Plot of *The Scarlet Letter*

The story starts during the summer of 1642, near Boston, in a Puritan village. A young woman, named Hester Prynne, has been led from the town prison with her infant daughter in her arms, and on the breast of her gown "a rag of scarlet cloth", a letter "A" The Scarlet Letter "A" represents adultery that she has committed and it is to be a symbol of her sin—a badge of shame—for all to see. A man, who is elderly and a stranger to the town, enters the crowd and asks another onlooker what's happening. The second man responds by explaining that Hester is being punished for adultery. Hester's husband, who is much older than she, and whose real name is unknown, has sent her ahead to America whilst settling affairs in Europe. However, her husband does not arrive in Boston. It is apparent that, while waiting for her husband, Hester has had an affair, leading to the birth of her daughter. She will not reveal her lover's identity, however, and the scarlet letter, along with her subsequent public shaming, is the punishment for her sin. On this day, Hester is led to the town scaffold, but she again refuses to identify her child's father.

The elderly onlooker is Hester's missing husband, who is now practicing medicine and calling himself Roger Chillingworth. He reveals his true identity to Hester and medicates her daughter. They have a frank discussion where Chillingworth states that it was foolish and wrong for a cold, old intellectual like him to marry a young lively woman like Hester. He expressly states that he thinks that they have wronged each other and that he is even with her—her lover is a completely different matter. Hester refuses to tell the name of her lover and Chillingworth does not press her stating that he will find out anyway. He settles in Boston to practice medicine there. Several years pass. Hester supports herself by working as a seamstress, and her daughter, Pearl, grows into a willful, naughty child, and is said to be the scarlet letter come to life as both Hester's love and her punishment. Shunned by the community, they live in a small cottage on the outskirts of Boston. Community officials attempt to take Pearl away from Hester, but with the help of Arthur Dimmesdale, an eloquent minister, the mother and daughter manage to stay together. Dimmesdale, however, appears to be wasting away and suffers from mysterious heart trouble, seemingly caused by psychological distress. Chillingworth attaches himself to the ailing minister and eventually moves in with him so that he can provide his patient with round-the-clock care. Chillingworth also suspects that there may be a connection between the minister's torments and Hester's secret, and he begins to test Dimmesdale to see what he can learn. One afternoon, while the minister sleeps, Chillingworth discovers something undescribed to the reader, supposedly an "A" burned into Dimmesdale's chest, which convinces him that his suspicions are correct.

Dimmesdale's psychological anguish deepens, and he invents new tortures for himself. In the meantime, Hester's charitable deeds and quiet humility have earned her a reprieve from the scorn of the community. One night, when Pearl is about seven years old, she and her mother are returning home from a visit to the deathbed of John Winthrop when they encounter Dimmesdale atop the town scaffold, trying to punish himself for his sins. Hester and Pearl join him, and the three link hands. Dimmesdale refuses Pearl's request that he acknowledge her publicly the next day, and a meteor marks a dull red "A" in the night sky as Dimmesdale sees Chillingworth in the distance. It is interpreted by the townsfolk to mean *Angel*, as a prominent figure in the community had died that night, but Dimmesdale sees it as meaning *adultery*. Hester can see that the minister's condition is worsening, and she resolves to intervene. She goes to Chillingworth and asks him to stop adding to Dimmesdale's self-torment. Chillingworth refuses. She suggests that she may reveal his true identity to Dimmesdale.

The former lovers decide to flee to Europe, where they can live with Pearl as a family. They will take a ship sailing from Boston in four days. Dimmesdale gives Pearl a kiss on the forehead, which Pearl immediately tries to wash off in the brook, because he again refuses to make known publicly their relationship. However, he clearly feels a release from the pretense of his former life, and the laws and sins he has lived with.

The day before the ship is to sail, the townspeople gather for a holiday in honor of an election and Dimmesdale preaches his most eloquent sermon ever. Meanwhile, Hester has learned that Chillingworth knows of their plan and has booked passage on the same ship. Dimmesdale, leaving the church after his sermon, sees Hester and Pearl standing before the town scaffold. He looks ill. Knowing his life is about to end, he mounts the scaffold with his lover and his daughter, and confesses publicly, exposing the mark supposedly seared into the flesh of his chest. He dies in Hester's arms after Pearl kisses him.

Frustrated in his revenge, Chillingworth dies within the year. Hester and Pearl leave Boston, and no one knows what has happened to them. Many years later, Hester returns alone, still wearing the scarlet letter, to live in her old cottage and resumes her charitable work. She receives occasional letters from Pearl, who was rumored to have married a European aristocrat and established a family of her own. Pearl also inherits all of Chillingworth's money even though he knows she is not his daughter. There is a sense of liberation in her and the townspeople, especially the women, who had finally begun to forgive Hester of her tragic indiscretion. When Hester dies, she is buried with a tombstone decorated with a letter "A", for Hester and Dimmesdale.

Some Comments on *The Scarlet Letter*

The experience of Hester and Dimmesdale recalls the story of Adam and Eve because, in both cases, sin results in suffering. But it also results in knowledge—specifically, in knowledge of what it means to be immortal. For Hester, the scarlet letter functions as "her passport into regions where other women dared not tread". It leads her to "speculate" about her society and herself more "boldly" than anyone else in New England.

As for Dimmesdale, the "cheating minister", his sin gives him "sympathies so intimate with the sinful brotherhood of mankind, so that his chest vibrates in unison with theirs." His eloquent and powerful sermons derive from this sense of empathy. The narrative of the Reverend Arthur Dimmesdale is quite in keeping with the oldest and most fully authorized principles in Christian thought.

The rosebush, its beauty a striking contrast to all that surrounds it—as later the beautifully embroidered scarlet A will be-is held out in part as an invitation to find "some sweet moral blossom" in the ensuing, tragic tale and in part as an image that "the deep heart of nature" (perhaps God) may look more kind on the errant Hester and her child than her Puritan neighbors do. Throughout the work, the nature images contrast with the darkness of the Puritans and their systems.

Chillingworth's misshapen body reflects the anger in his soul, which builds as the novel progresses, similar to the way Dimmesdale's illness reveals his inner turmoil. The outward man reflects the condition of the heart; an observation thought to be inspired by the deterioration of Edgar Allan Poe, whom Hawthorne "much admired".

Although Pearl is a complex character, her primary function within the novel is as a symbol. Pearl herself is the embodiment of the scarlet letter, and Hester rightly clothes her in a beautiful dress of scarlet, embroidered with gold thread, just like the scarlet letter upon Hester's bosom.

Major Characters

Hester Prynne is a women with complex characters. We know very little about Hester prior to her affair with Dimmesdale and her public shaming. We read that she married Chillingworth although she did not love him, but we never fully understand why. The early chapters of the book suggest that, prior to her marriage, Hester was a strong-willed and impetuous young woman—she remembers her parents as loving guides who frequently had to restrain her incautious behavior. The fact that she has an affair also suggests that she once had a passionate nature.

But it is what happens after Hester's affair that makes her into the woman with whom the reader is familiar. Shamed and alienated from the rest of the community, Hester becomes contemplative. She speculates on human nature, social organization, and larger moral questions.

Hester also becomes a kind of compassionate maternal figure as a result of her experiences. Hester is also maternal with respect to society: she cares for the poor and brings them food and clothing. By the novel's end, Hester has become a feminist mother figure to the women of the community. The shame attached to her scarlet letter is long gone. Women recognize that her punishment stemmed in part from the town fathers' sexism, and they come to Hester seeking shelter from the sexist forces under which they themselves suffer. Throughout *The Scarlet Letter* Hester is portrayed as an intelligent, capable, but not necessarily extraordinary woman. It is the extraordinary circumstances shaping her that make her such an important figure.

Roger Chillingworth is a man deficient in human warmth. His twisted and deformed shoulders mirror his distorted soul. From what the reader is told of his early years with Hester, he was a difficult husband. He ignored his wife for much of the time, yet expected her to nourish his soul with affection when he did condescend to spend time with her. Chillingworth's decision to assume the identity of a "leech," or doctor, is fitting. Chillingworth's death is a result of the nature of his character. After Dimmesdale dies, Chillingworth no longer has a victim.

Similarly, Dimmesdale's revelation that he is Pearl's father removes Hester from the old man's clutches. Having lost the objects of his revenge, the leech has no choice but to die.

Ultimately, Chillingworth represents true evil. He is interested in revenge, not justice, and he seeks the deliberate destruction of others rather than a redress of wrongs. His desire to hurt others stands in contrast to Hester and Dimmesdale's sin, which had love, not hate, as its intent. Any harm that may have come from the young lovers' deed was unanticipated, whereas Chillingworth reaps deliberate harm.

Arthur Dimmesdale, like Hester Prynne, is an individual whose identity owes more to external circumstances than to his innate nature. The reader is told that Dimmesdale was a scholar of some renown at Oxford University. His past suggests that he is probably somewhat aloof, the kind of man who would not have much natural sympathy for ordinary men and women. However, Dimmesdale has an unusually active conscience. The fact that Hester takes all of the blame for their shared sin goads his conscience, and mental anguish and physical weakness open up his mind and allow him to empathize with others. Consequently, he becomes an eloquent and emotionally powerful speaker and a compassionate leader.

Ironically, the townspeople do not believe Dimmesdale's protestations of sinfulness. This drives Dimmesdale to further internalize his guilt and self-punishment and leads to still more deterioration in his physical and spiritual condition. In his death, Dimmesdale becomes even more of an icon than he was in life. Many believe his confession was a symbolic act, while others believe Dimmesdale's fate was an example of divine judgment.

Pearl functions primarily as a symbol of living scarlet letter. She is quite young during most of the events of this novel—when Dimmesdale dies she is only seven years old—and her real importance lies in her ability to provoke the adult characters in the book. She asks them pointed questions and draws their attention, and the reader's, to the denied or overlooked truths of the adult world. In general, children in *The Scarlet Letter* are portrayed as more perceptive and more honest than adults, and Pearl is the most perceptive of them all.

Introduction to Chapter II

This first chapter contains little in the way of action, instead setting the scene. A crowd of somber, dreary-looking people has gathered outside the door of a prison in seventeenth-century Boston. As the crowd watches, Hester Prynne, a young woman holding an infant, emerges from the prison door and makes her way to a scaffold (a raised platform), where she is to be publicly condemned. The women in the crowd make disparaging comments about Hester; they particularly criticize her for the embroidered badge on her chest—a letter "A" stitched in gold and scarlet. From the women's conversation and Hester's reminiscences as she walks through the crowd, we can deduce that she has committed adultery and has borne an illegitimate child, and that the "A" on her dress stands for "Adulterer."

The beadle calls Hester forth. Children tease her and adults stare at her. Scenes from Hester's earlier life flash through her mind: she sees her parents standing before their home in rural England. Then she sees a "misshapen" scholar, much older than herself, whom she married and followed to continental Europe. But now the present floods in upon her, and she inadvertently squeezes the infant in her arms, causing it to cry out. She regards her current fate with disbelief.

Chapter II   The Market-Place

The grassplot before the jail, in Prison Lane, on a certain summer morning, not less than two centuries ago, was occupied by a pretty large number of the inhabitants of Boston; all with their eyes intently fastened on the iron-clamped oaken door. Amongst any other population, or at a later period in the history of New England, the grim rigidity that petrified the bearded *physiognomies*[1] of these good people would have augured some awful business in hand. It could have betokened nothing short of the anticipated execution of some noted culprit, on whom the sentence of a legal tribunal had but confirmed the verdict of public sentiment. But, in that early severity of the Puritan character, *an inference of this kind could not so indubitably be* drawn[2]. It might be that a sluggish bond-servant, or an undutiful child, whom his parents had given over to the civil authority, was to be corrected at the whipping-post. It might be, that an *Antinomian*[3], a Quaker, or other heterodox religionist, was to be scourged out of the town, or an idle and vagrant Indian, whom the white man's *fire-water*[4] had made riotous about the streets, was to be driven with stripes into the shadow of the forest. It might be, too, that a witch, like *old Mistress Hibbins*[5], the bitter-tempered widow of the magistrate, was to die upon the gallows. In either case, there was very much the same solemnity of demeanour on the part of the spectators; as befitted a people amongst whom *religion and law were almost identical*[6], and in whose character both were so thoroughly interfused, that the mildest and the severest acts of public discipline were alike made venerable and awful. Meagre, indeed, and cold, was the sympathy that a transgressor might look for, from such bystanders at the scaffold. On the other hand, a penalty which, in our days, would infer a degree of mocking infamy and ridicule, might then be invested with almost as stern a dignity as the punishment of death itself.

It was a circumstance to be noted, on the summer morning when our story begins its course, that the women, of whom there were several in the crowd, appeared to take a peculiar interest in whatever penal infliction might be expected to ensue. The age had not so much refinement, that any sense of impropriety restrained the wearers of petticoat and farthingale from stepping forth into the public ways, and wedging their not unsubstantial persons, if occasion were, into the throng nearest to the scaffold at an execution. Morally, as well as materially, there was a coarser fibre in those wives and maidens of old English birth and breeding, than in their fair descendants, separated from them by a series of six or seven generations; for, throughout that chain of ancestry, every successive mother had transmitted to her child a fainter bloom, a more delicate and briefer beauty, and a slighter physical frame, if not a character of less force and solidity, than her own. The women, who were now standing about the prison-door, stood within less than half a century of the period when the *man-like Elizabeth*[7] had been the not altogether unsuitable representative of the sex. They were her countrywomen; and the beef and ale of their native land, with a moral diet not a whit more refined, entered largely into their composition. The bright morning sun, therefore, shone on broad shoulders and well-developed busts, and on round and ruddy cheeks, that had ripened in the far-off island, and had hardly yet grown paler or thinner in the atmosphere of New England. There was, moreover, a boldness and rotundity of speech among these matrons, as most of them seemed to be, that would startle us at the present day, whether in respect to its purport or its volume of tone.

"Goodwives," said a hard-featured dame of fifty, "I'll tell ye a piece of my mind. It would be greatly for the public *behoof*[8], if we women, being of mature age and church-members in good repute, should have the handling of such *malefactresses*[9] as this Hester Prynne. What think ye, *gossips*[10]? If the hussy stood up for judgment before us five, that are now here in a knot together, would she come off with such a sentence as the worshipful magistrates have awarded? *Marry, I trow not*[11]!"

"People say," said another, "that the Reverend Master Dimmesdale, her godly pastor, takes it very grievously to heart that such a scandal should have come upon his congregation."

"The magistrates are God-fearing gentlemen, but merciful overmuch,—that is a truth," added a third autumnal matron. "At the very least, they should have put the brand of a hot iron on Hester Prynne's forehead. Madame Hester would have winced at that, I warrant me. But she,—the naughty baggage,—little will she care what they put upon the bodice of her gown! Why, look you, she may cover it with a brooch, or such like, heathenish adornment, and so walk the streets as brave as ever!"

"Ah, but," interposed, more softly, a young wife, holding a child by the hand, "let her cover the mark as she will, the pang of it will be always in her heart."

"What do we talk of marks and brands, whether on the bodice of her gown, or the flesh of her forehead?" cried another female, the ugliest as well as the most pitiless of these self-constituted judges. "This woman has brought shame upon us all, and ought to die. Is there not law for it? Truly there is, both in the Scripture and the statute-book. Then let the magistrates, who have made it of no effect, thank themselves if their own wives and daughters go astray!"

"Mercy on us, goodwife," exclaimed a man in the crowd, "is there no virtue in woman, save what springs from a wholesome fear of the gallows? That is the hardest word yet! Hush, now, gossips; for the lock is turning in the prison-door, and here comes Mistress Prynne herself."

The door of the jail being flung open from within, there appeared, in the first place, like a black shadow emerging into sunshine, the grim and grisly presence of the town-beadle, with a sword by his side and his staff of office in his hand. *This personage prefigured and represented in his aspect the whole dismal severity of the Puritanic code of law*[12] , which it was his business to administer in its final and closest application to the offender. Stretching forth the official staff in his left hand, he laid his right upon the shoulder of a young woman, whom he thus drew forward until, on the threshold of the prison-door, she repelled him, by an action marked with natural dignity and force of character, and stepped into the open air, as if by her own free-will. She bore in her arms a child, a baby of some three months old, who winked and turned aside its little face from the too vivid light of day; because its existence, heretofore, had brought it acquainted only with the gray twilight of a dungeon, or other darksome apartment of the prison.

When the young woman—the mother of this child—stood fully revealed before the crowd, it seemed to be her first impulse to clasp the infant closely to her bosom; not so much by an impulse of motherly affection, as that she might thereby conceal a certain token, which was wrought or fastened into her dress. In a moment, however, wisely judging that one token of her shame would but poorly serve to hide another, she took the baby on her arm, and, with a burning blush, and yet a haughty smile, and a glance that would not be abashed, looked around at her townspeople and neighbours. On the breast of her gown, in fine red cloth, surrounded with an elaborate embroidery and fantastic flourishes of gold thread, appeared the letter A. It was so artistically done, and with so much fertility and gorgeous luxuriance of fancy, that it had all the effect of a last and fitting decoration to the apparel which she wore; and which was of a splendor in accordance with the taste of the age, but greatly beyond what was allowed by the sumptuary regulations of the colony.

The young woman was tall, with a figure of perfect elegance, on a large scale. She had dark and abundant hair, so glossy that it threw off the sunshine with a gleam, and a face which, besides being beautiful from regularity of feature and richness of complexion, had the impressiveness belonging to a marked brow and deep black eyes. She was lady-like, too, after the manner of the feminine gentility of those days; characterized by a certain state and dignity, rather than by the delicate, evanescent, and indescribable grace, which is now recognized as its indication. And never had Hester Prynne appeared more lady-like, in the antique interpretation of the term, than as she issued from the prison. Those who had before known her, and had expected to behold her dimmed and obscured by a disastrous cloud, were astonished, and even startled, to perceive how her beauty shone out, and made a halo of the misfortune and ignominy in which she was enveloped. It may be true, that, to a sensitive observer, there was something exquisitely painful in it. Her attire, which, indeed, she had wrought for the occasion, in prison, and had modelled much after her own fancy, seemed to express the attitude of her spirit, the desperate recklessness of her mood, by its wild and picturesque peculiarity. But the point which drew all eyes, and, as it were, transfigured the wearer,—so that both men and women, who had been familiarly acquainted with Hester Prynne, were now impressed as if they beheld her for the first time,—was that SCARLET LETTER, so fantastically embroidered and illuminated upon her bosom. It had the effect of a spell, taking her out of the ordinary relations with humanity, and inclosing her in a sphere by herself.

"She hath good skill at her needle, that's certain," remarked one of the female spectators; "but did ever a woman, before this brazen hussy, contrive such a way of showing it! Why, gossips, what is it but to laugh in the faces of our godly magistrates, and make a pride out of what they, worthy gentlemen, meant for a punishment?"

"It were well," muttered the most *iron-visaged*[13] of the old dames, "if we stripped Madam Hester's rich gown off her dainty shoulders; and as for the red letter, which she hath stitched so curiously, *I'll bestow a rag of mine own rheumatic flannel*[14], to make a fitter one!"

"O, peace, neighbours, peace!" whispered their youngest companion. "Do not let her hear you! Not a stitch in that embroidered letter, but she has felt it in her heart."

The grim beadle now made a gesture with his staff.

"Make way, good people, make way, in the King's name," cried he. "Open a passage; and, I promise ye, Mistress Prynne shall be set where man, woman, and child may have a fair sight of her brave apparel, from this time till an hour past meridian. A blessing on the righteous Colony of the Massachusetts, where iniquity is dragged out into the sunshine! Come along, Madam Hester, and show your scarlet letter in the market-place!"

A lane was forthwith opened through the crowd of spectators. Preceded by the beadle, and attended by an irregular procession of stern-browed men and unkindly-visaged women, Hester Prynne set forth towards the place appointed for her punishment. A crowd of eager and curious schoolboys, understanding little of the matter in hand, except that it gave them a half-holiday, ran before her progress, turning their heads continually to stare into her face, and at the winking baby in her arms, and at the ignominious letter on her breast. It was no great distance, in those days, from the prison-door to the market-place. Measured by the prisoner's experience, however, it might be reckoned a journey of some length; for, haughty as her demeanour was, she perchance underwent an agony from every footstep of those that thronged to see her, as if her heart had been flung into the street for them all to spurn and trample upon. In our nature, however, there is a provision, alike marvellous and merciful, that the sufferer should never know the intensity of what he endures by its present torture, but chiefly by the pang that rankles after it. With almost a serene deportment, therefore, Hester Prynne passed through this portion of her ordeal, and came to a sort of scaffold, at the western extremity of the market-place. It stood nearly beneath the eaves of Boston's earliest church, and appeared to be a fixture there.

In fact, this scaffold constituted a portion of a penal machine, which now, for two or three generations past, has been merely historical and traditionary among us, but was held, in the old time, to be as effectual an agent in the promotion of good citizenship, as ever was the guillotine among *the terrorists of France*[15]. It was, in short, the platform of the pillory; and above it rose the framework of that instrument of discipline, so fashioned as to confine the human head in its tight grasp, and thus hold it up to the public gaze. The very ideal of ignominy was embodied and made manifest in this contrivance of wood and iron. There can be no outrage, methinks, against our common nature,—whatever be the delinquencies of the individual,—no outrage more flagrant than to forbid the culprit to hide his face for shame; as it was the essence of this punishment to do. In Hester Prynne's instance, however, as not unfrequently in other cases, her sentence bore, that she should stand a certain time upon the platform, but without undergoing that gripe about the neck and confinement of the head, the proneness to which was the most devilish characteristic of this ugly engine. Knowing well her part, she ascended a flight of wooden steps, and was thus displayed to the surrounding multitude, at about the height of a man's shoulders above the street.

Had there been a *Papist*[16] among the crowd of Puritans, he might have seen in this beautiful woman, so picturesque in her attire and mien, and with the infant at her bosom, an object to remind him of the image of *Divine Maternity*[17], which so many illustrious painters have vied with one another to represent; something which should remind him, indeed, but only by contrast, of that *sacred image of sinless motherhood, whose infant was to redeem the world*[18]. Here, there was the taint of deepest sin in the most sacred quality of human life, working such effect, that the world was only the darker for this woman's beauty, and the more lost for the infant that she had borne.

The scene was not without a mixture of awe, such as must always invest the spectacle of guilt and shame in a fellow-creature, before society shall have grown corrupt enough to smile, instead of shuddering, at it. The witnesses of Hester Prynne's disgrace had not yet passed beyond their simplicity. They were stern enough to look upon her death, had that been the sentence, without a murmur at its severity, but had none of the heartlessness of another social state, which would find only a theme for jest in an exhibition like the present. Even had there been a disposition to turn the matter into ridicule, it must have been repressed and overpowered by the solemn presence of men no less dignified than the Governor, and several of his counsellors, a judge, a general, and the ministers of the town; all of whom sat or stood in a balcony of the meeting-house, looking down upon the platform. When such personages could constitute a part of the spectacle, without risking the majesty or reverence of rank and office, it was safely to be inferred that the infliction of a legal sentence would have an earnest and effectual meaning. Accordingly, the crowd was sombre and grave. The unhappy culprit sustained herself as best a woman might, under the heavy weight of a thousand unrelenting eyes, all fastened upon her, and concentrated at her bosom. It was almost intolerable to be borne. Of an impulsive and passionate nature, she had fortified herself to encounter the stings and venomous stabs of public contumely, wreaking itself in every variety of insult; but there was a quality so much more terrible in the solemn mood of the popular mind, that she longed rather to behold all those rigid countenances contorted with scornful merriment, and herself the object. Had a roar of laughter burst from the multitude,—each man, each woman, each little shrill-voiced child, contributing their individual parts,—Hester Prynne might have repaid them all with a bitter and disdainful smile. But, under the leaden infliction which it was her doom to endure, she felt, at moments, as if she must needs shriek out with the full power of her lungs, and cast herself from the scaffold down upon the ground, or else go mad at once.

Yet there were intervals when the whole scene, in which she was the most conspicuous object, seemed to vanish from her eyes, or, at least, glimmered indistinctly before them, like a mass of imperfectly shaped and spectral images. Her mind, and especially her memory, was preternaturally active, and kept bringing up other scenes than this roughly hewn street of a little town, on the edge of *the Western wilderness*[19]; other faces than were lowering upon her from beneath the brims of those steeple-crowned hats. Reminiscences, the most trifling and immaterial, passages of infancy and school-days, sports, childish quarrels, and the little domestic traits of her maiden years, came swarming back upon her, intermingled with recollections of whatever was gravest in her subsequent life; one picture precisely as vivid as another; as if all were of similar importance, or all alike a play. Possibly, it was an instinctive device of her spirit to relieve itself, by the exhibition of these phantasmagoric forms, from the cruel weight and hardness of the reality.

Be that as it might, the scaffold of the pillory was a point of view that revealed to Hester Prynne the entire track along which she had been treading, since her happy infancy. Standing on that miserable eminence, she saw again her native village, in *Old England*[20], and her paternal home; a decayed house of gray stone, with a poverty-stricken aspect, but retaining a half-obliterated *shield of arms*[21] over the portal, in token of antique gentility. She saw her father's face, with its bold brow, and reverend white beard, that flowed over the old-fashioned *Elizabethan ruff*[22]; her mother's, too, with the look of heedful and anxious love which it always wore in her remembrance, and which, even since her death, had so often laid the impediment of a gentle remonstrance in her daughter's pathway. She saw her own face, glowing with girlish beauty, and illuminating all the interior of the dusky mirror in which she had been wont to gaze at it. There she beheld another countenance, of a man well stricken in years, a pale, thin, scholar-like visage, with eyes dim and bleared by the lamp-light that had served them to pore over many ponderous books. Yet those same bleared optics had a strange, penetrating power, when it was their owner's purpose to read the human soul. This figure of the study and the cloister, as Hester Prynne's womanly fancy failed not to recall, was slightly deformed, with the left shoulder a trifle higher than the right. *Next rose before her, in memory's picture-gallery, the intricate and narrow thoroughfares, the tall, gray houses, the huge cathedrals, and the public edifices, ancient in date and quaint in architecture, of a Continental city*[23]; where a new life had awaited her, still in connection with *the misshapen scholar*[24]; a new life, but feeding itself on time-worn materials, *like a tuft of green moss on a crumbling wall*[25]. Lastly, *in lieu of*[26] these shifting scenes, came back the rude market-place of the Puritan settlement, with all the townspeople assembled and levelling their stern regards at Hester Prynne,—yes, at herself,—who stood on the scaffold of the pillory, an infant on her arm, and the letter A, in scarlet, fantastically embroidered with gold thread, upon her bosom!

Could it be true? She clutched the child so fiercely to her breast, that it sent forth a cry; she turned her eyes downward at the scarlet letter, and even touched it with her finger, to assure herself that the infant and the shame were real. Yes! —these were her realities,—all else had vanished!

Notes

[1] 面孔

[2] such conclusion should not be drawn quickly.

[3] 唯信仰论者;道德律废弃者。其主要信条是,基督徒只是恪守《圣经》中的道德法律,无济于事,只有坚信上帝无所不知,无所不能,才能使自己的灵魂得到拯救。

[4] 烈酒

[5] 指真是的历史人物 Ann Hibbins。1655 年,她因被指控使用巫术而受审,1656 年被处以绞刑。

[6] 宗教和法律几乎完全相同,指 17 世纪北美殖民时期清教占统治地位时政教合一的神权政治。

[7] 英国女王伊丽莎白一世(Queen Elizabeth I 1558~1603),在位期间治国安邦,建树非凡,其管理社稷的才能不亚于男性君主,所以小说的叙述者称赞她具有男子气概。

[8] benefit

[9] bad woman;同下文的 hussy 和 naughty baggage 意思相近,指破靶、破烂货、坏女人、荡妇,咒骂有性违规行为的女人的词语,这里指 Hester。

[10] women friends

[11] Virgin Mary, I thought not.

[12] 这个角色的尊荣便是清教徒法典全部冷酷无情的象征和代表……

[13] 面孔板得紧

[14] 我患风湿病时用过的一块法兰绒;在古英语中,mine 意思是 my。

[15] 法国的恐怖分子,指法国资产阶级革命过程中雅各宾派曾于 1793 年至 1794 年采取恐怖政策。

[16] 罗马天主教徒(贬义)

[17] 圣母玛利亚

[18] 接受圣灵而孕的圣母玛利亚;whose infant 指耶稣;redeem the world,献给世界来赎罪的

[19] 指美国西部,欧洲移民初到北美时,是在东海岸建立殖民地,然后才逐步向西部开发。

[20] 指英国。英国移民初到北美时,常以本国的某些地名命名北美的殖民地,但在原有的地名前加 New,以示区别,例如:New England, New York, New Hampshire。

[21] 家族的识别物,由色彩、盾牌和图样组成,显示持有者的身份和生活环境,这段描写说明 Hester 出身没落贵族。

[22] 做工精美且坚硬的衣领,流行于 16、17 世纪的英国上流社会。

[23] a continental city 指阿姆斯特丹。英国的许多清教徒在移民北美之前需要在阿姆斯特丹逗留,等待许可证。这句意思是:在她回忆的画廊中接下来升到眼前的是欧洲大陆一座城市里的纵横交错又显得狭窄的街道,以及年深日久,古色古香的公共建筑物,宏伟的天主教堂和高大的灰色住宅。

[24] 指 Hester 的丈夫 Chillingworth。

[25] 像附在残垣上的一簇青苔,象征 Hester 嫁给 Chillingworth。

[26] instead of

Questions

1 What are the comments of the crowd on Hester?

2 Find out the description of Hester's Scarlet Letter on her bosom.

3 How does Hester release the pain of being ridiculed and teased?

4 What do appear in the memories Hester?

Analysis of Chapter II

This chapter introduces the reader to Hester Prynne and begins to explore the theme of sin. The chapters' use of symbols, as well as their depiction of the political reality of Hester Prynne's world, testifies to the contradictions inherent in Puritan society. This is a world that has already "fallen," that already knows sin: the colonists are quick to establish a prison and a cemetery in their "Utopia," for they know that misbehavior, evil, and death are unavoidable.

But the images of the chapters—the public gatherings at the prison and at the scaffold, both of which are located in central common spaces—also speak to another.

Yet, unlike her fellow townspeople, Hester accepts her humanity rather than struggles against it; in many ways, her "sin" originated in her acknowledgment of her human need for love, following her husband's unexplained failure to arrive in Boston and his probable death. The women of the town criticize her for embroidering the scarlet letter, the symbol of her shame, with such care and in such a flashy manner. It seems to declare that she is proud, rather than ashamed, of her sin. In reality, however, Hester simply accepts the "sin" and its symbol as part of herself, just as she accepts her child. And although she can hardly believe her present "realities," she takes them as they are rather than resisting them or trying to atone for them.

Pearl is a sign of a larger, more powerful order than that which the community is attempting to assert—be it nature, biology, or a God untainted by the corruptions of human religious practices. The fact that the townspeople focus on the scarlet letter rather than on the human child underlines their pettiness, and their failure to see the more "real" consequences of Hester's action.

From this point forward, Hester will be formally, officially set apart from the rest of society; yet these opening chapters imply that, even before her acquisition of the scarlet letter, she had always been unique. The text describes her appearance as more distinctive than conventionally beautiful: she is tall with a natural nobility that sets her apart from the women of the town.

This is the first of three important scenes involving the scaffold. Each of these scenes will show a character taking the first step toward a sort of Emersonian self-reliance, the kind of self-reliance that would come to replace Puritan ideology as the American ideal. In this scene, Hester confronts her "realities" and discovers a new self that does not fit with her old conceptions of herself. From now on, Hester will stand outside, if still surrounded by, the Puritan order.

Unit 10
Edgar Ellan Poe (1809 ~ 1849)

Life

    Edgar Ellan Poe is a prominent poet, fiction-writer and literary critic. But he led a poor life all through his life. Literary career did not make him wealthy. His works were not welcome in America when he was alive, but well received in Europe. His genius in literature didn't win recognition in his native country until early 20th century. As a poet, he wrote some very fine short lyrics, some acknowledged masterpieces in American literature; Poe was a master of the suspenseful short story and he introduced the detective story to American readers. Poe was the first great critic of America. His literary principles on poems and fiction writing are highly valued by contemporary writers.

    But he never seems able to find success or happiness. He led a life which was almost as usual as his writing. Poe was born in Boston, Massachusetts, 1809. He was two years old when his actor parents died. Poe became an orphan. John Allan, a wealthy tobacco merchant took him in, although he never really adopted the boy. Poe took his name as his middle name.

In 1820, he studied at a local academy and then attended the University of Virginia. However, because of gambling debts, he was forced to leave after only one-year study in University.

After a bitter quarrel between Poe and the Allan family over money matters, (sth. else or unwilling to pay gambling debts for him), he ran away in 1827 to Boston.

From 1827 to 1830 Poe enlisted in the Army for two years, served at West Point for about eight months. From 1830, Poe determined, without any other choice, to be dependent on his pen for his living. He worked as an editor for a number of popular magazines and won recognition for his magazines, stories and articles, yet his personal life continued to be a struggle with poverty.

In 1836 he married his thirteen-year-old cousin, Virginia Clemm, but she died prematurely from tuberculosis at the age of 25, in 1847. During her life time, Poe did his most inspired writing. Virginia's death left the poet in a state of despair. As his life became increasingly difficult, Poe sought to escape from it, often through alcohol. Two years after the death of his wife, in 1849 he was found dead in Baltimore in an alley near a tavern.

Poe's works which include fiction, legend, tales, poetry and critical articles, are prolific and versatile. Poe's poetry is a very small portion in his total work. In his opinion, the function of poetry is not to summarize and interpret the earthly experience but to create a mood in which the soul rises toward supernal beauty. Some of his poems have a narrative basis, but it is often difficult for the reader to find in it a complete plot. For Poe believes poetry must concern itself only with "supernatural beauty", not with the narration of story, not even with the beauty of particular things.

Best-known poems:

The Raven: This poem has long been considered to be one of Poe's best poetic works, and it is his most developed and clearest verse narrative. First published in the *New York Evening Mirror*, January 29, 1845. It soon became one of the most popular of Poe's poems. Its tone is sad and mournful and it is also highly symbolic. So it is difficult for readers to understand.

Annabel Lee on (1850)

To Helen: it was inspired by Mrs. Jane Stanard, one of his young neighbors. She died in 1824 at the age of 31. In order to commemorate her, Poe wrote this poem.

Poe and the Short Story:

Poe was also well-known for his short stories. He wrote about seventy stories: Poe bears two relations to the short stories; He gave the first definition of short story and in the second place he wrote memorable examples of this type of literature.

In his definition, he emphasized brevity and unity of impression. The latter is the more important element, and by unity, Poe means totality or oneness of impression. E.g. If an author wishes to give an impression of dreariness and melancholy, that impression must be stressed to the exclusion of all others. If the author wishes to leave a feeling of horror, every element must be kept out of the story that does not contribute to the dominant impression.

Poe stresses brevity because he thought quite rightly that unity of impression would be blurred and lost in the mass of details, which are certainly inevitable in a long story or novel. (It will be noted that Poe did not stress the plot or action in this definition of story)

He insisted that the writer must first determine the effect that he wished to produce and then deliberately choose incidents to assist in the creation of such an effect. e. g. *The Fall of the House of Usher*, one of Poe's most widely read and successful stories, is consisted with its author's definition in every respect.

As for the style of Poe's stories, it falls into two categories: those of mystery and horror; and those of ratiocination, which have set the standard for the modern detective story such as *The Cask of Amontillado* and *The Purloined Letter*.

Plot of *The Cask of Amontillado*

Montresor tells the story of the day that he took his revenge on Fortunato, a fellow nobleman. Angry over some unspecified insult, he plots to murder his friend during Carnival when the man is drunk, dizzy, and wearing a jester's motley.

He baits Fortunato by telling him he has obtained what he believes to be a pipe of rare Amontillado. He claims he wants his friend's expert opinion on the subject.

Fortunato goes with Montresor to the wine cellars of the latter's palazzo, where they wander in the catacombs. Montresor offers wine to Fortunato. At one point, Fortunato makes an elaborate, grotesque gesture with an upraised wine bottle. When Montresor appears not to recognize the gesture, Fortunato asks, "You are not of the masons?" Montresor says he is, and when Fortunato, disbelieving, requests a sign, Montresor displays a trowel he had been hiding.

Montresor warns Fortunato, who has a bad cough, of the damp, and suggests they go back; Fortunato insists on continuing, claiming that "[he] shall not die of a cough." During their walk, Montresor mentions his family arms: a foot in a blue background crushing a snake whose fangs are embedded in the foot's heel, with the motto *Nemo me impune lacessit* ("No one insults me with impunity"). When they come to a niche, Montresor tells his victim that the Amontillado is within. Fortunato enters and, drunk and unsuspecting, does not resist as Montresor quickly chains him to the wall. Montresor then declares that, since Fortunato won't go back, he must "positively leave him".

Montresor walls up the niche, entombing his friend alive. At first, Fortunato, who sobers up faster than Montresor anticipated he would, shakes the chains, trying to escape. Fortunato then screams for help, but Montresor mocks his cries, knowing nobody can hear them. Fortunato laughs weakly and tries to pretend that he is the subject of a joke and that people will be waiting for him. As the murderer finishes the topmost row of stones, Fortunato wails, "For the love of God, Montresor!" Montresor replies, "Yes, for the love of God!" He listens for a reply but hears only the jester's bells ringing. Before placing the last stone, he drops a burning torch through the gap. He claims that he feels sick at heart, but dismisses this reaction as an effect of the dampness of the catacombs.

In the last few sentences, Montresor reveals that it has been 50 years since that night, he has never been caught, and Fortunato's body still hangs from its chains in the niche where he left it.

Major Characters

Fortunato is the victim of the revenge. He seems a person with some deficiency of character. According to Montresor he insults Montresor. From his way of speaking, Fortunato is an arrogant person and he lacks respect for others. He has rich family background and he is crazy about wine. He is a very foolish and innocent person. So he is so easy to fall the trap of Montresor.

Montresor is the person to revenge. He is a cruel and cold-blooded murderer. In the beginning he told the audience he had received thousand of injuries from Fortunato. However, he refuses to describe the detail. So his so called "injuries" are not reliable. May what he called injuries can not be considered as injuries. The same with Fortunato, he is also a person with character deficiency. He knows nothing about communication and buries everything in his mind and does not speak out. His inner mind is dark and deep. He is a horrible narrow-mined person. His evil is secretly concealed, while Fortunato's is superficial. He is so horrible a person also because his way of carrying out revenge. He is the murderer and he is able to be free from the punishment of law.

The Cask of Amontillado

The thousand injuries of *Fortunato*[1] I had borne as I best could, but when he ventured upon insult, I vowed revenge. You, who so well know the nature of my soul, will not suppose, however, that I gave utterance to a threat. At length I would be avenged; this was a point definitively settled—but the very definitiveness with which it was resolved precluded the idea of risk. *I must not only punish, but punish with impunity*[2]. A wrong is unredressed when retribution overtakes its redresser. It is equally unredressed when the avenger fails to make himself felt as such to him who has done the wrong. It must be understood that neither by word nor deed had I given Fortunato cause to doubt my good will. I continued, as was my wont, to smile in his face and he did not perceive that *my smile now was at the thought of his immolation*[3].

He had a weak point—this Fortunato—although in other regards he was a man to be respected and even feared. He prided himself on his connoisseurship in wine. Few Italians have the true *virtuoso*[4] spirit. For the most part their enthusiasm is adopted to suit the time and opportunity to practice imposture upon the British and Austrian millionaires. In painting and gemmary, Fortunato, like his countrymen, was a quack, but in the matter of old wines he was sincere. In this respect I did not differ from him materially; I was skilful in the Italian vintages myself, and bought largely whenever I could.

It was about dusk, one evening during the supreme madness of the carnival season, that I encountered my friend. He accosted me with excessive warmth, for he had been drinking much. The man wore *motley*[5]. He had on a tight-fitting parti-striped dress, and his head was surmounted by the conical cap and bells. I was so pleased to see him that I thought I should never have done wringing his hand.

I said to him—"My dear Fortunato, you are luckily met. How remarkably well you are looking to-day! But I have received a pipe of what passes for Amontillado, and I have my doubts."

"How?" said he, "Amontillado? A pipe? Impossible! And in the middle of the carnival!"

"I have my doubts," I replied, "and I was silly enough to pay the full Amontillado price without consulting you in the matter. You were not to be found, and I was fearful of losing a bargain."

"Amontillado!"

"I have my doubts."

"Amontillado!"

"And I must satisfy them."

"Amontillado!"

"As you are engaged, I am on my way to Luchesi. If any one has a critical turn, it is he. He will tell me—"

"Luchesi cannot tell Amontillado from Sherry."

"And yet some fools will have it that his taste is a match for your own."

"Come let us go."

"Whither?"

"To your vaults."

"My friend, no; I will not impose upon your good nature. I perceive you have an engagement Luchesi—"

"I have no engagement; come."

"My friend, no. It is not the engagement, but the severe cold with which I perceive you are afflicted. The vaults are insufferably damp. They are encrusted with nitre."

"Let us go, nevertheless. The cold is merely nothing. Amontillado! You have been imposed upon; and as for Luchesi, he cannot distinguish Sherry from Amontillado."

Thus speaking, Fortunato possessed himself of my arm. Putting on a mask of black silk and drawing a *roquelaire*[6] closely about my person, I suffered him to hurry me to my *palazzo*[7]. There were no attendants at home; they had *absconded to make merry in honour of the time*[8]. I had told them that I should not return until the morning and had given them explicit orders not to stir from the house. These orders were sufficient, I well knew, to insure their immediate disappearance, one and all, as soon as my back was turned.

I took from their sconces two flambeaux, and giving one to Fortunato bowed him through several suites of rooms to the archway that led into the vaults. I passed down a long and winding staircase, requesting him to be cautious as he followed. We came at length to the foot of the descent, and stood together on the damp ground of the catacombs of the Montresors. The gait of my friend was unsteady, and the bells upon his cap jingled as he strode.

"The pipe," said he.

"It is farther on," said I; "but observe the white web work which gleams from these cavern walls."

He turned towards me and *looked into my eyes with two filmy orbs that distilled the rheum of intoxication*[9].

"Nitre?" he asked, at length

"Nitre," I replied. "How long have you had that cough!"

"Ugh! ugh! ugh! —ugh! ugh! ugh! —ugh! ugh! ugh! —ugh! ugh! ugh! —ugh! ugh! ugh!"

My poor friend found it impossible to reply for many minutes.

"It is nothing," he said, at last.

"Come," I said, with decision, "we will go back; your health is precious. You are rich, respected, admired, beloved; You are happy, as once I was. You are a man to be missed. For me it is no matter, we will go back; you will be ill, and I cannot be responsible. Besides, there is Luchesi—"

"Enough," he said; "the cough is a mere nothing; it will not kill me. I shall not die of a cough."

"True—true," I replied, "and, indeed, I had no intention of alarming you unnecessarily—but you should use all proper caution. A draught of this *Medoc*[10] will defend us from the damps."

Here I knocked off the neck of a bottle which I drew from a long row of its fellows that lay upon the mould.

"Drink," I said, presenting him the wine.

He raised it to his lips with a leer. He paused and nodded to me familiarly, while his bells jingled.

"I drink," he said, "to the buried that repose around us."

"And I to your long life."

He again took my arm and we proceeded.

"These vaults," he said, "are extensive."

"The Montresors," I replied, "were a great numerous family."

"I forget your arms."

"*A huge human foot d'or, in a field azure; the foot crushes a serpent rampant whose fangs are imbedded in the heel*[11] ."

"And the motto?"

"Nemo me impune lacessit."

"Good!" he said.

The wine sparkled in his eyes and the bells jingled. My own fancy grew warm with the Medoc. We had passed through walls of piled bones, with casks and puncheons intermingling, into the inmost recesses of the catacombs. I paused again, and this time I made bold to seize Fortunato by an arm above the elbow.

"The nitre!" I said: "See it increases. It hangs like moss upon the vaults. We are below the river's bed. The drops of moisture trickle among the bones. Come, we will go back ere it is too late. Your cough—"

"It is nothing." he said; "let us go on. But first, another draught of the Medoc."

I broke and reached him *a flagon of De Grave*[12] . He emptied it at a breath. His eyes flashed with a fierce light. He laughed and threw the bottle upwards with a gesticulation I did not understand. I looked at him in surprise. He repeated the movement—a grotesque one.

"You do not comprehend?" he said.

"Not I," I replied.

"Then you are not of the brotherhood."

"How?"

"You are not of the masons."

"Yes, yes," I said "yes! yes."

"You? Impossible! A mason?"

"A mason," I replied.

"A sign," he said.

"It is this," I answered, producing a trowel from beneath the folds of my roquelaire.

"You jest," he exclaimed, recoiling a few paces. "But let us proceed to the Amontillado."

"Be it so," I said, replacing the tool beneath the cloak, and again offering him my arm. He leaned upon it heavily. We continued our route in search of the Amontillado. We passed through a range of low arches, descended, passed on, and descending again, arrived at a deep crypt, in which the foulness of the air caused our flambeaux rather to glow than flame.

At the most remote end of the crypt there appeared another less spacious. Its walls had been lined with human remains piled to the vault overhead, in the fashion of the great catacombs of Paris. Three sides of this interior crypt were still ornamented in this manner. From the fourth the bones had been thrown down, and lay promiscuously upon the earth, forming at one point a mound of some size. Within the wall thus exposed by the displacing of the bones, we perceived a still interior recess, in depth about four feet, in width three, in height six or seven. It seemed to have been constructed for no especial use in itself, but formed merely the interval between two of the colossal supports of the roof of the catacombs, and was backed by one of their circumscribing walls of solid granite.

It was in vain that Fortunato, uplifting his dull torch, endeavored to pry into the depths of the recess. Its termination the feeble light did not enable us to see.

"Prooood," I said, "herein is the Amontillado. As for Luchesi—"

"He is an *ignoramus*[13]," interrupted my friend, as he stepped unsteadily forward, while I followed immediately at his heels. In an instant he had reached the extremity of the niche, and finding his progress arrested by the rock, stood stupidly bewildered. A moment more and I had fettered him to the granite. In its surface were two iron staples, distant from each other about two feet, horizontally. From one of these depended a short chain, from the other a padlock. Throwing the links about his waist, it was but the work of a few seconds to secure it. He was too much astounded to resist. Withdrawing the key I stepped back from the recess. "Pass your hand," I said, "over the wall; you cannot help feeling the nitre. Indeed it is very damp. Once more let me implore you to return. No? Then I must positively leave you. But I must first render you all the little attentions in my power."

"The Amontillado!" ejaculated my friend, not yet recovered from his astonishment.

"True," I replied; "the Amontillado."

As I said these words I busied myself among the pile of bones of which I have before spoken. Throwing them aside, I soon uncovered a quantity of building stone and mortar. With these materials and with the aid of my trowel, I began vigorously to wall up the entrance of the niche.

I had scarcely laid the first tier of my masonry when I discovered that the intoxication of Fortunato had in a great measure worn off. The earliest indication I had of this was a low moaning cry from the depth of the recess. It was NOT the cry of a drunken man. There was then a long and obstinate silence. I laid the second tier, and the third, and the fourth; and then I heard the furious vibrations of the chain. The noise lasted for several minutes, during which, that I might hearken to it with the more satisfaction, I ceased my labors and sat down upon the bones. When at last the clanking subsided, I resumed the trowel, and finished without interruption the fifth, the sixth, and the seventh tier. The wall was now nearly upon a level with my breast. I again paused, and holding the flambeaux over the mason-work, threw a few feeble rays upon the figure within.

A succession of loud and shrill screams, bursting suddenly from the throat of the chained form, seemed to thrust me violently back. For a brief moment I hesitated—I trembled. Unsheathing my rapier, I began to grope with it about the recess; but the thought of an instant reassured me. I placed my hand upon the solid fabric of the catacombs, and felt satisfied. I reapproached the wall. I replied to the yells of him who clamored. I reechoed—I aided—I surpassed them in volume and in strength. I did this, and the clamorer grew still.

It was now midnight, and my task was drawing to a close. I had completed the eighth, the ninth, and the tenth tier. I had finished a portion of the last and the eleventh; there remained but a single stone to be fitted and plastered in. I struggled with its weight; I placed it partially in its destined position. But now there came from out the niche a low laugh that erected the hairs upon my head. It was succeeded by a sad voice, which I had difficulty in recognizing as that of the noble Fortunato. The voice said—

"Ha! ha! ha! —he! he! —a very good joke indeed—an excellent jest. We will have many a rich laugh about it at the palazzo—he! he! he! —over our wine—he! he! he!"

"The Amontillado!" I said.

"He! he! he! —he! he! he! —yes, the Amontillado . But is it not getting late? Will not they be awaiting us at the palazzo, the Lady Fortunato and the rest? Let us be gone."

"Yes," I said "let us be gone."

"FOR THE LOVE OF GOD, MONTRESOR!"

"Yes," I said, "for the love of God!"

But to these words I hearkened in vain for a reply. I grew impatient. I called aloud—

"Fortunato!"

No answer. I called again—

"Fortunato!"

No answer still. I thrust a torch through the remaining aperture and let it fall within. There came forth in return only a jingling of the bells. My heart grew sick—on account of the dampness of the catacombs. I hastened to make an end of my labor. I forced the last stone into its position; I plastered it up. Against the new masonry I re-erected the old rampart of bones. For the half of a century no mortal has disturbed them. *In pace requiescat*[14] !

Notes

[1] 弗图纳多,有"幸运"之意。

[2] 我不仅必须要惩罚,而且要使自己不受伤害地实施惩罚。Montresor 一方面 发誓要报复 Fortunato,另一方面还想方设法使报复行为神不知鬼不觉,自己 不会因此而受到牵连。

[3] 笑里藏刀

[4] 鉴赏家

[5] 小丑五彩斑斓的衣服

[6] 披风;斗篷

[7] 豪华的宫殿或府邸

[8] escaped from here to enjoy themselves; "the time" refers to "carnival."

[9] 用他那双因醉酒而渗出黏液的朦胧的醉眼看着我。

[10] 产于法国波尔多的一种葡萄酒

[11] "or", 法语, 意为"金色"; 此句意思是: 蓝底儿金色大脚正把一条毒牙咬进
脚跟的巨蛇踩得粉身碎骨。

[12] 产于法国波尔多的一种白葡萄酒

[13] ignorant person, 笨蛋

[14] 拉丁语, 意思是"愿他安息"。

Questions

1　Why did Montresor vow to revenge?

2　What are Fortunato's weak points?

3　Under what conditions, "I" tempted Fortunato to follow me to go to my vaults?

4　What words do show my humble attitude toward Fortunato?

Analysis of *The Cask of Amontillado*

　　The narrator, Montresor, "I" opens the story by saying that he has been insulted by his acquaintance, Fortunato and he seeks revenge. He decided to use Fortunato's fondness for wine against him. During the carnival season, Montresor, wearing a mask of Black silk, approaches Fortunato. He said he acquired a cask of Amontillado, a light Spanish sherry.

　　Fortunate wears the multicolored costume of jester, a cone cap with bells. Montresor told him if he is too busy, he will ask a man named Luchesi to taste it. Fortunate claims that Luchesi could not tell Amotillado from other types of sherry. Fortunato is anxious to taste the wine and determines to go Montresor's vaults.

　　Montresor has planned this meeting by sending his servants away to the carnival. The two men descend into the damp vaults, which are covered with nitre. Fortunato began to cough. The narrator keeps asking Fortunato to be back home, but he refuses. The two men continue to walk into the deep of vaults which are full of dead bodies of Montresor family. Montresor shows the arm and motto of his family, implying his real intention.

Later in their journey, they see human bones decorate three of the four walls. The bones of the fourth wall have been thrown down on the ground. On the wall, there's a small recess, Montresor told Fortunato that the Amontillado is being stored. Fortunate, drunken, goes to the back of the recess and is suddenly chained by Montresor to the stone.

Cursing and walling up the entrance, therefore he trapped Fortunato inside. Fortunato awakens, moans, terrified and helpless. As the layers continue to rise, Fortunato falls silent. Just as Montresor is about to finish, Fortunato laughs just as if Montresor is playing joke on him, but Montresor is not joking. After his final plea, "For the love of God, Montresor", he has no response to Montresor by sound of bells.

It is a story full of horror. The enduring horror of the story is the fact of punishment without proof. Law is nowhere on Montresor's life. The results mentioned at the beginning have no evidence, so the narrator's account is not so reliable. That is a person's distorted psychological world; bones, dark vaults nitre create gothic atmosphere, peculiarly one is murdered by walling up another.

The story has several symbols. Montresor's face is covered with a black silk mask, which symbolizes Montresor's evil motivo of king Fortunato. The two men's underground travels are a metaphor for their trip to hell.

To build suspense in the story, Poe often employs foreshadowing. E.g. When Fortunato says: "I shall not die of cough", Montresor replies: "True," because he knows Fortunato will die from lacking Oxygen and starvation; the description of family arm: the family's coat of arms also foreshadows the future events: the shield features a human foot crushing a poisonous serpent. In this image, the foot represents Montresor and the serpent represents Fortunato. Fortunate has hurt Montresor with biting results; Montresor will ultimately crush him. By walling Fortunato up, Montresor becomes Fortunato's grave builder.

Unit 11
Mark Twain（1835~1910）

Life

Earnest Hemingway comments that all modern American literature comes from one book by Mark Twain called *Huckleberry Finn*. Mark Twain is an American writer, journalist and humorist, "Mark Twain" the pen name of Samuel Langhorne Clemens. He wrote about his own experiences and things he knew about from firsthand experience. Mark Twain won the worldwide audience for his stories of the youthful adventures of Tom Sawyer and Huckleberry Finn.

Twain was sensitive to the sound of language and introduced colloquial speech into American fiction.

Twain, the third of five children, was born on Nov. 30, 1835, in the village of Florida, Missouri. He grew up in the larger river town of Hannibal, on the bank of Mississippi. Hannibal was dusty and quiet with large forest nearby. He uses this place as the background of *The Adventures of Huckleberry Finn*. In it, "Pap", father of

Huck kidnaps Huck and hides him out in the great forest. The steamboats, which passed daily were the fascination of the town and became the subject matter of Twain's *Life on the Mississippi* (1883). His experience as a steamboat pilot on... the town of Hannibal is immortalized as St. Petersburg in Twain's *The Adventures of Tom Sawyer* (1876) (illustration: Mississippi River and forest; Twain's hometown and the background of his many novels)

Twain's father was an ambitious and respected but only mildly successful country lawyer and storekeeper. He was, however, a highly intelligent man. Twain's mother, a southern beauty in her youth, she has sense of humor, she was emotional and known to be particularly fond of animals and unfortunate human beings. Although the family was not wealthy, Mark Twain apparently had a happy childhood. Twain's father died when he was 12 years old and for the next 10 years, he was an apprentice printer and then a printer both in Hannibal and in New York City.

Hoping to find his fortune he conceived a wild scheme of making a fortune in South America. On his way, he met a famous riverboat pilot, who promised to teach him the trade for 500 dollars. After two-year-training, Mark Twain was a riverboat pilot for four years on the Mississippi river and during this time, he became familiar with all of the towns along the Mississippi River. It plays an important part in "Huck Finn" and he also became acquainted with every type of character which inhabits his various novels especially "Huck Finn".

But the civil war put an end to the riverboat business. He went to west with his brother. In California, he tried mining briefly. Eventually he became a reporter under the pen name of Mark Twain. And then writing and lecturing became his career.

The publication of the short story *The Celebrated Jumping Frog of Calaveras County* in *New York Magazine* in 1865, attracted favorable attention in the East, and soon Mark Twain became known as a writer of humorous western tales and newspaper sketches. After a trip to Europe as a correspondent, he published his famous travel book *The Innocents Abroad* (1869), and he was quickly becoming both renowned and rich.

In 1870, at 35, Mark Twain married Olivia Langdon, a daughter of a wealthy merchant. They settled down and in the following 17 years he produced his greatest works, *The Adventures of Tom Sawyer* (1876), *The Adventures of Huckleberry Finn* (1884) and *Life on the Mississippi* (1883), *The Prince and the Pauper* (1881).

Among them, "Huck Finn", rich and deep in its view of life and beautiful in its use of vernacular English, so it is considered by some critics to be the greatest American novel, a work that reaches out beyond the limitations of time and place and touches the readers of any age or country.

Twain's personal life in later years was tortured by trouble. He went bankrupt through bad investments, largely in publishing, so he had to set out an around-the-world lecture tour to pay off his debts. The death of his wife and two daughters left him lonely and weary of the world. So his later works are becoming increasingly critical and satirical, culmination in the bitterness, disillusionment and pessimism of his last works. *The Man that Corrupted Hadleyburg* (1900) and *The Mysterious Stranger* (published posthumously in 1916) (see illustrations of Mark Twain and his daughters and the estate where Twain lives and works out his great novels)

During the final years of his life, Mark Twain—the first literary giant born west of the Mississippi—was without doubt the most celebrated personality in America. His birthdays became national events; Yale University and Oxford University awarded him a Doctor of Letters degree. The self-educated son of poor parents was immensely proud of the honor he obtained.

That is life of Mark Twain, a printer, pilot, soldier, silver-miner, reporter, lecturer, traveler, businessman, novelist and autobiographer. Mark Twain had led an active life, in the very center of the American experience. He died of heart attack on April 21 1910. 1835 Nov. 30–1910 April 21, Haley comet was seen in the sky. In the interval years, Mark Twain had become one of the greatest and most famous American authors.

Plot of *The Adventures of Huckleberry Finn*

Through a novel called *The Adventures of Tom Sawyer*, readers must have heard about Huck Finn. Now he decides to tell his own story in "Huckleberry Finn", so he is the protagonist and narrator of the book.

The novel centers two escapes. One is Huck's escape from "civilization" and his father's ill-treatment; another is black Jim's escape from "being sold as a slave". Both share the same pursuit—pursuit for freedom.

Huck is the son of the town drunkard of Hannibal, Missouri. On the east boundary of Hannibal is the Mississippi River. He lives with the widow Douglas and her sister Miss Watson. They both want to civilize him—dress cleanly, to eat on time, and go to school; but he prefers the easy and free manner of living wild.

When his father discovers that Huck has some money, Huck is kidnapped and held as prisoner in a small house across river. His father beats him so brutally that Huck decides he must escape, otherwise his father will kill him someday. He thinks of a plan. When he left the house, he left it as if he were murdered by robbers. Then he goes to hide on the Jackson's island.

On the island, he discovers Jim, Miss Watson's runaway slave. Jim wants to go to free states and dreams to get a job there to earn money to buy his wife and children out of slavery. Huck promises to keep Jim's secrets. They became good friends. On the river, they feel free and easy as they travel during the night and hide during the day. They have funs and adventures. Our selection given here writes that feeling dull and boring on the river, Huck ventures to go to the town to get some news. Dressed as a girl, Huck knocks on the door of the house. The woman lets him in, believing him to be a young girl. Huck learns there's someone after them. He returns to Jim and both run away. After that they have experienced many adventures with so called "King" and "Duke". Finally, Huck acquires freedom according to Ms. Watson's will.

Some Comments on *The Adventures of Huckleberry Finn*

When the book was published, it is attacked by critics because it was not morally uplifting; because it showed low life; because it had no larger-than-life hero. However, these are just the points that the greatness of this novel lies in.

Twain portrays the ordinary Americans, the actual, the average. He expresses them, accepts their values and describes their hopes, fears, decencies and indecencies.

He deals with low life, with criminals, with all the mentions of common men. He depicts man as he is in everyday life, man as you and I.

He is different from writers before him. Before Mark Twain, serious literature was not expected to do this. There was an implicit understanding that it should devote itself to the high class of people, depicting larger-than-life heroic protagonists. And the worth of art should be to show man as he is expected to be and no as he is.

Huckleberry Finn was severely criticized by the critics for not moral uplifting and for Mark Twain depicted too many murders and Huck was not sufficiently a heroic protagonist. But Mark Twain, as a realist writer, believes that plots, events, actions, characters of the novel must be believable, not miraculous on strange. What he is trying to do is to bring the novel closer to life, to have the novel truly represent life. He enormously widens the area, the subject matter of serious literature.

This is one reason why he is called the first truly modern American writer. That is for the democracy of his work.

Twain writes in one of the great styles of American literature. He helps to develop the modern American style. He is the first writer who used the American vernacular at the level of art.

Romantic writers such as Hawthorne, Melville writes in the classical tradition, and uses very formal dialogue. As a realist, Mark Twain handles the dialogue in a different way. *Huckleberry Finn* probably is the supreme example of successful dialogue. Twain used 65 dialects in that book very accurately because he tried to recreate the reality as he saw it: the society, the common people, and the way they spoke.

Huck's narrating in this book in his own language with its poor idioms and bad grammar, with his strong expressions is Twain's genius. The language of Huck is effective and refreshingly alive. If Mark Twain had written his book in his own voice, that is, using his own point of view rather than that of Huck's point of view it would not today enjoy the status like that. It is the language of Huck that is the book's supreme achievement.

Major Characters

Huck Finn is a "bad" boy who comes from the lowest levels of white society. Huck himself is dirty and frequently homeless, for his father is a drunkard and cruel to him. Widow Douglas attempts to adopt him and "civilize" him—schooling and religious training; Huck resists her attempts and maintains his independent ways, because he can not accustom himself to the social values. Huck's distance from the mainstream society makes him skeptical of the world around him. E.g. According to the law, Jim is Miss Watson's property, but according to Huck's sense of fairness, it seems "right" to help him, even helping him will go to hell, Huck follows his principle not the principle of the society.

He is imperfect, smoking, fighting, cheating, being mischievous and making fun of others, however, such bad habits are formed by the corrupted and dirty environment. Though from the appearance, Huck is more mature and adult-like, deep in his heart, he has the child-like innocence. His so-called "evil-doings", such as telling lies to others without thinking, are not for the purpose of hurting others but purely for protecting himself in the sophisticated society.

Jim is a run-away slave and Huck's companion as he travels down the river, is a man of remarkable intelligence and compassion. He has a family, although he has been separated from his wife and children, he misses them terribly, and it is only the thought of a permanent separation from them that motivates his criminal act of running away from Miss Watson.

On the river, Jim becomes a considerate father and friend to Huck, taking care of him. He cooks for the boy and shelters him from some of the worst horrors they encounter. Jim consistently acts as a noble human being and a loyal friend. In fact, Jim could be described as the only real adult in the novel and the only one who provides a positive, respectable example for Huck to follow.

Mrs. Judith Loftus is a minor character in the book and a major in Chapter 11. She is a common talkative housewife in the town, but she receives Huck with kindness, consideration and hospitality. She is an adult with keen observation, by which, she found Huck is in the disguise of a girl. Due to Huck's witty remarks, she believes his last lie and Huck. Through her mouth, learns what happens in the town. So he makes a haste returning journey and tells Jim some one is after him and they must escape.

Introduction to Chapter 11

Chapter 11 is a humorous episode of the book. Having been on the Jackson's Island for long time, Huck feels boring and he tells Jim he would inquire about some information in the village. He disguises himself as a girl and knocks at a door. A middle-aged woman opens the door and tells him some information about the murder of Huck. What Huck concerns is that someone found there's smoke on the Jackson's Island and the villagers' doubt that must be the run-away slave. That makes Huck nervous and he has to reveal to the woman that he is not the girl but a boy. Then he hurries back to find Jim and they start their way to escape again.

Chapter 11

"COME in," says the woman, and I did. She says:
"*Take a cheer.*"[1]
I done it. She looked me all over with her little shiny eyes, and says:
"What might your name be?"
"Sarah Williams."

"*Where' bouts*[2] do you live? In this neighborhood?"

"*No'm*[3]. In Hookerville, seven mile below. I've walked all the way and I'm all tired out."

"Hungry, too, I reckon. I'll find you something."

"No'm, I ain't hungry. I was so hungry I had to stop two miles below here at a farm; so I ain't hungry no more. It's what makes me so late. My mother's down sick, and out of money and everything, and I come to tell my uncle Abner Moore. He lives at the upper end of the town, she says. I hain't ever been here before. Do you know him?"

"No; but I don't know everybody yet. I haven't lived here quite two weeks. It's a considerable ways to the upper end of the town. You better stay here all night. Take off your bonnet."

"No," I says; "I'll rest a while, I reckon, and go on. I ain't afeared of the dark."

She said she wouldn't let me go by myself, but her husband would be in by and by, maybe in a hour and a half, and she'd send him along with me. Then she got to talking about her husband, and about her relations up the river, and her relations down the river, and about how much better off they used to was, and how *they didn't know but*[4] they'd made a mistake coming to our town, instead of *letting well alone*[5]—and so on and so on, till I was afeard I had made a mistake coming to her to find out what was going on in the town; but by and by she dropped on to pap and the murder, and then I was pretty willing to let her clatter right along. She told about me and Tom Sawyer finding the six thousand dollars (only she got it ten) and all about pap and what *a hard lot*[6] he was, and what a hard lot I was, and at last she got down to where I was murdered. I says:

"Who done it? We've heard *considerable*[7] about these goings on down in Hookerville, but we don't know who't was that killed Huck Finn."

"Well, I reckon *there's a right smart chance of people*[8] HERE that'd like to know who killed him. Some think old Finn done it himself."

"No—is that so?"

"*Most*[9] everybody thought it at first. He'l never know how nigh he come to getting lynched. But before night they changed around and judged it was done by a runaway nigger named Jim."

"Why HE—"

I stopped. I reckoned I better keep still. She run on, and never noticed I had put in at all:

"The nigger run off the very night Huck Finn was killed. So there's a reward out for him—three hundred dollars. And there's a reward out for old Finn, too—two hundred dollars. You see, he come to town the morning after the murder, and told about it, and was out with 'em on the ferryboat hunt, *and right away after he up and left*[10]. Before night they wanted to lynch him, but he was gone, you see. Well, next day they found out the nigger was gone; they found out *he hadn't ben seen sence ten o'clock*[11] the night the murder was done. So then they put it on him, you see; and while they was full of it, next day, back comes old Finn, and went boo-hooing to Judge Thatcher to get money to hunt for the nigger all over Illinois with. The judge gave him some, and that evening he got drunk, and was around till after midnight with a couple of mighty hard-looking strangers, and then went off with them. Well, he hain't come back sence, and they ain't looking for him back till this thing blows over a little, for people thinks now that he killed his boy and fixed things so folks would think robbers done it, and then he'd get Huck's money without having to bother a long time with a lawsuit. People do say he *warn't*[12] any too good to do it. Oh, he's sly, I reckon. If he don't come back for a year he'll be all right. You can't prove anything on him, you know; everything will be quieted down then, and he'll walk in Huck's money as easy as nothing."

"Yes, I reckon so, 'm. I don't see nothing in the way of it. Has everybody guit thinking the nigger done it?"

"Oh, no, not everybody. A good many thinks he done it. But they'll get the nigger pretty soon now, and maybe they can scare it out of him."

"Why, are they after him yet?"

"Well, you're innocent, ain't you! Does three hundred dollars lay around every day for people to pick up? Some folks think the nigger ain't far from here. I'm one of them—but I *hain't*[13] talked it around. A few days ago I was talking with an old couple that lives next door in the log shanty, and they happened to say hardly anybody ever goes to that island over yonder that they call Jackson's Island. Don't anybody live there? says I. No, nobody, says they. I didn't say any more, but I done some thinking. I was pretty near certain I'd seen smoke over there, about the head of the island, a day or two before that, so I says to myself, like as not that nigger's hiding over there; anyway, says I, it's worth the trouble to give the place a hunt. I hain't seen any smoke sence, so I reckon maybe he's gone, if it was him; but husband's going over to see—him and another man. He was gone up the river; but he got back to-day, and I told him as soon as he got here two hours ago."

I had got so uneasy I couldn't *set*[14] still. I had to do something with my hands; so I took up a needle off of the table and went to threading it. My hands shook, and I was making a bad job of it. When the woman stopped talking I looked up, and she was looking at me pretty curious and smiling a little. I put down the needle and thread, and *let on*[15] to be interested—and I was, too—and says:

"Three hundred dollars is a power of money. I wish my mother could get it. Is your husband going over there to-night?"

"Oh, yes. He went up-town with the man I was telling you of, to get a boat and see if they could borrow another gun. They'll go over after midnight."

"Couldn't they see better if they was to wait till daytime?"

"Yes. And couldn't the nigger see better, too? After midnight he'll likely be asleep, and they can slip around through the woods and hunt up his camp fire all the better for the dark, if he's got one."

"I didn't think of that."

The woman kept looking at me pretty curious, and I didn't feel a bit comfortable. Pretty soon she says"

"What did you say your name was, honey?"

"M—Mary Williams."

Somehow it didn't seem to me that I said it was Mary before, so I didn't look up—seemed to me I said it was Sarah; so I felt sort of cornered, and was afeared maybe I was looking it, too. I wished the woman would say something more; the longer she *set*[16] still the uneasier I was. But now she says:

"Honey, I thought you said it was Sarah when you first come in?"

"Oh, yes'm, I did. Sarah Mary Williams. Sarah's my first name. Some calls me Sarah, some calls me Mary."

"Oh, that's the way of it?"

"Yes'm."

I was feeling better then, but I wished I was out of there, anyway. I couldn't look up yet.

Well, the woman fell to talking about how hard times was, and how poor they had to live, and how the rats was as free as if they owned the place, and so forth and so on, and then I got easy again. She was right about the rats. You'd see one stick his nose out of a hole in the corner every little while. She said she had to have things handy to throw at them when she was alone, or they wouldn't give her no peace. She showed me a bar of lead twisted up into a knot, and said she was a good shot with it *generly*[17], but she'd wrenched her arm a day or two ago, and didn't know whether she could throw true now. But she watched for a chance, and directly banged away at a rat; but she missed him wide, and said "Ouch!" it hurt her arm so. Then she told me to try for the next one. I wanted to be getting away before the old man got back, but of course I didn't *let on*[18]. I got the thing, and the first rat that showed his nose I let drive, and *if he'd a stayed where he was he'd a been a tolerable sick rat*[19]. She said that was first-rate, and she reckoned I would *hive*[20] the next one. She went and got the lump of lead and fetched it back, and brought along a hank of yarn which she wanted me to help her with. I held up my two hands and she put the hank over them, and went on talking about her and her husband's matters. But she broke off to say:

"Keep your eye on the rats. You better have the lead in your lap, handy."

So she dropped the lump into my lap just at that moment, and I clapped my legs together on it and she went on talking. But only about a minute. Then she took off the hank and looked me straight in the face, and very pleasant, and says:

"Come, now, what's your real name?"

"Wh—what, mum?"

"What's your real name? Is it Bill, or Tom, or Bob? —or what is it?"

I reckon I shook like a leaf, and I didn't know hardly what to do. But I says:

"Please to don't poke fun at a poor girl like me, mum. If I'm in the way here, I'll—"

"No, you won't. Set down and stay where you are. I ain't going to hurt you, and I ain't going to tell on you, *nuther*[21]. You just tell me your secret, and trust me. I'll keep it; and, what's more, I'll help you. So'll my old man if you want him to. You see, you're a runaway' *prentice*[22], that's all. It ain't anything. There ain't no harm in it. You've been treated bad, and you made up your mind to *cut*[23]. Bless you, child, I wouldn't tell on you. Tell me all about it now, that's a good boy."

So I said it wouldn't be no use to try to play it any longer, and I would just make a clean breast and tell her everything, but she mustn't go back on her promise. Then I told her my father and mother was dead, and the law had bound me out to a mean old farmer in the country thirty mile back from the river, and he treated me so bad I couldn't stand it no longer; he went away to be gone a couple of days, and so I took my chance and stole some of his daughter's old clothes and cleared out, and I had been three nights coming the thirty miles. I traveled nights, and hid daytimes and slept, and the bag of bread and meat I carried from home lasted me all the way, and I had a-plenty. I said I believed my uncle Abner Moore would take care of me, and so that was why I struck out for this town of Goshen.

"Goshen, child? This ain't Goshen. This is *St. Petersburg*[24]. Goshen's ten mile further up the river. Who told you this was Goshen?"

"Why, a man I met at daybreak this morning, just as I was going to turn into the woods for my regular sleep. He told me when the roads forked I must take the right hand, and five mile would fetch me to Goshen."

"He was drunk, I reckon. He told you just exactly wrong."

"Well, he did act like he was drunk, but it ain't no matter now. I got to be moving along. I'll fetch Goshen before daylight."

"Hold on a minute. I'll put you up a snack to eat. You might want it."

So she put me up a snack, and says:

"Say, when a cow's laying down, which end of her gets up first? Answer up prompt now—don't stop to study over it. Which end gets up first?"

"The hind end, mum."

"Well, then, a horse?"

"The *for'ard*[25] end, mum."

"Which side of a tree does the moss grow on?"

"North side."

"If fifteen cows is browsing on a hillside, how many of them eats with their heads pointed the same direction?"

"The whole fifteen, mum."

"Well, I reckon you HAVE lived in the country. I thought maybe you was trying to hocus me again. What's your real name, now?"

"George Peters, mum."

"Well, try to remember it, George. Don't forget and tell me it's Elexander before you go, and then get out by saying it's George Elexander when I catch you. And don't go about women in that old calico. You do a girl tolerable poor, but you might fool men, maybe. Bless you, child, when you set out to thread a needle don't hold the thread still and fetch the needle up to it; hold the needle still and poke the thread at it; that's the way a woman most always does, but a man always *does t'other way*[26]. And when you throw at a rat or anything, hitch yourself up *a tiptoe*[27] and fetch your hand up over your head as awkward as you can, and miss your rat about six or seven foot. Throw stiff-armed from the shoulder, like there was a pivot there for it to turn on, like a girl; not from the wrist and elbow, with your arm out to one side, like a boy. And, mind you, when a girl tries to catch anything in her lap she throws her knees apart; she don't clap them together, the way you did when you catched the lump of lead. Why, I spotted you for a boy when you was threading the needle; and I contrived the other things just to make certain. Now trot along to your uncle, Sarah Mary Williams George Elexander Peters, and if you get into trouble you send word to Mrs. Judith Loftus, which is me, and I'll do what I can to get you out of it. Keep the river road all the way, and next time you tramp take shoes and socks with you. The river road's a rocky one, and your feet'll be *in a condition*[28] when you get to Goshen, I reckon."

I went up the bank about fifty yards, and then *I doubled on my tracks*[29] and slipped back to where my canoe was, a good piece below the house. I jumped in, and was off in a hurry. I went up-stream far enough to make the head of the island, and then started across. I took off the sun-bonnet, for I didn't want no blinders on then. When I was about the middle I heard the clock begin to strike, so I stops and listens; the sound come faint over the water but clear—eleven. When I struck the head of the island I never waited *to blow*[30], though *I was most winded*[31], but I shoved right into the timber where my old camp used to be, and started a good fire there on a high and dry spot.

Then I jumped in the canoe and *dug out*[32] for our place, a mile and a half below, as hard as I could go. I landed, and *slopped through the timber*[33] and up the ridge and into the cavern. There Jim laid, sound asleep on the ground. I roused him out and says:

"*Git up and hump yourself, Jim*![34] There ain't a minute to lose. They're after us!"

Jim never asked no questions, he never said a word; but the way he worked for the next half an hour showed about how he was scared. By that time everything we had in the world was on our raft, and she was ready to be shoved out from the willow cove where she was hid. We put out the camp fire at the cavern the first thing, and didn't show a candle outside after that.

I took the canoe out from the shore a little piece, and took a look; but if there was a boat around I couldn't see it, for stars and shadows ain't good to see by. Then we got out the raft and slipped along down in the shade, past the foot of the island dead still—never saying a word.

Notes

[1] Take a chair

[2] whereabouts

[3] No, mum. (here, "mum" means "ma'am").

[4] they didn't know that.

[5] staying in their old place and not moving to our own

[6] a difficult person; a person who is difficult to get along with.

[7] considerably

[8] There are a lot of people.

[9] Almost

[10] and soon afterward he suddenly left ("up" is used as a verb to express suddenness and surprise)

[11] he hadn't been seen since then o'clock.

[12] wasn't

[13] haven't

[14] sit

[15] pretended

[16] sat

[17] generally

[18] let out the secret

[19] if he should have stayed where he was he would have been a rather sick rat.

[20] hit

[21] neither

[22] apprentice

[23] run away

[24] Huck's hometown. This is a fictitious name, and is based on the small riverside township of Hannibal, Missouri, where Twain lived from the age of four to eighteen.

[25] forward

[26] does it the other way

[27] on tip-toe

[28] in a poor conditon

[29] I returned along the same path

[30] to pant; to take breath

[31] I was almost breathless.

[32] rowed out

[33] went awkwardly through the wood (because it was dark).

[34] get up and brace yourself, Jim!

Questions

1   Who are supposed to be the murderer of Huckleberry Finn?

2   How much reward will be given, if one catches Jim? And how much if Huck's father is caught?

3   After learning there are persons in the town after Jim, how nervous Huck is? Point out the related details from the textbook.

4   What's the name of the 40-year-old woman whom Huck talks to in town?

5   How does the woman know that Huck is not a girl?

6   How does the woman know Huck is a country boy?

Analysis of Chapter 11

Chapter11 displays another aspect of Huck's humor; that is the ability of Huck to disguise himself and convince adult to believe his stories. Huck is, indeed an imaginative liar who lies his way along the Mississippi River, so some authors and critics condemned his character as being unsuitable for young readers, however, Huck is also prone to forget his early stories, and therefore he is forced to invent new tales in order to continue his deception. The constantly changing fabrication is certainly comical and displays the creative ability of Huck and also reveals the ignorance of people he meets.

The narration that the woman fools Huck into revealing his identity as a boy also provides much of the humor in the chapter. Huck is a product of the environment. The tricks (the inability to thread a needle; improper action of throwing things) that the woman uses force Huck to reveal his male nature, his "boy" characteristics. Even though the woman discovers Huck is not a girl, Huck is still able to save his story by making another disguise as an orphaned and mistreated apprentice. The added story is another example of Huck's ability to succeed and adapt in a world of scams.

You should note that chapter 11 ends with Huck and Jim functioning as a team. When Huck discovers that Jim is in danger, he does not think about society's judgment and simply reacts. In Huck's view, the pursuing men are after both of them, even though the consequences for Huck would be minimal. In other words, Huck unconsciously places Jim's safety above his own, and their separate struggles for freedom become one. As Huck and Jim slip *past the foot of the island dead still*, *never saying a word*, Twain takes another step away form the childish *Adventures of Tom Sawyer* and strengthens the relationship between the two outcasts.

This novel has an anti-slavery theme. It is the most well-known aspect of this novel. Since its first publication, Twain's perspective on slavery and ideas on racism have been hotly debated. In his personal and public life, Mark Twain was anti-slavery. Considering this, it is easy to see that "Huck Finn" provides an allegory to explain how and why slavery is wrong. Twain uses Jim, a main character and a slave, to demonstrate the humanity of slaves. Jim expresses the complicated emotion and struggles with the path of his life. To prevent being sold and forced to separate from his family, Jim runs away form Miss Watson, and works towards obtaining freedom, so he can buy his family's freedom. All along their journey down river, Jim cares for and protects Huck, not as a servant, but as a friend. Thus, Mark Twain encourages the reader to feel sympathy for Jim and outrage at the society that has enslaved him and threatened his life. However, although Mark Twain attacks slavery his portrayal of Jim, he never directly addresses the issue. Huck and Jim never debate slavery, and all the other slaves in the novel are very minor characters. Only in the final section of the novel does Mark Twain develop the central conflict concerning slavery: Should Huck free Jim and then be condemned to go to hell? This decision is life-altering for Huck, as it forces him to reject everything "civilization" has taught him. Huck chooses to free Jim, based on his personal experiences rather than the social norms.

This novel belongs to local Color literature. From 1860 to early 20th century, it is a blend of Romanticism, realism and humor and a nostalgic feeling for past traditions. It explores the tensions between rural and urban values with an emphasis on the characters, dialect, customs, and other features particular to a specific area. E.g. Hardy "Wessex" novels, Faulkner "Yoknapatawpha town" and Mark Twain's "The Mississippi River" novels.

The Mississippi River has a symbolic Meaning. The majority of the plot takes place on the river or its banks. For Huck and Jim, the river represents freedom. On the raft, they are completely independent and determine their own courses of action.

Jim looks forward to reaching the free states, and Huck is eager to escape his abusive drunkard father and the "civilization" of Miss Watson. But the towns along the river bank influence them much. Eventually, Huck and Jim meet criminals, shipwreck, dishonesty and great danger. Originally, the river is a safe place for the two travelers, but it becomes increasingly dangerous, so the river soon becomes only a short-term escape, and the novel concludes on the safety of dry land, where ironically, Huck and Jim find their true freedom.

Unit 12
F. Scott Fitzgerald (1896~1940)

Life

Francis Scott Fitzgerald was born in St. Paul, Minnesota, on September 24, 1896. During 1911~1913 he attended the Newman School, a Catholic prep school in New Jersey. As a member of the Princeton Class of 1917, Fitzgerald neglected his studies for his literary apprenticeship. He wrote the scripts and lyrics for the Princeton Triangle Club musicals and was a contributor to the *Princeton Tiger* humor magazine and the *Nassau Literary Magazine*. Fitzgerald joined the army in 1917. Convinced that he would die in the war, he rapidly wrote a novel, *The Romantic Egotist*.

In June 1918 Fitzgerald was assigned to Camp Sheridan. There he fell in love with a celebrated belle, eighteen-year-old Zelda, the youngest daughter of a judge. The war ended just before he was to be sent overseas; after his discharge in 1919 he went to New York City to seek his fortune in order to marry. Unwilling to wait while Fitzgerald succeeded in the advertisement business and unwilling to live on his small salary, Zelda Sayre broke their engagement.

Fitzgerald quit his job in July 1919 and returned to St. Paul to rewrite his novel as *This Side of Paradise*. It was accepted by editor in September. The publication of *This Side of Paradise* on March 26, 1920, made the twenty-four-year-old Fitzgerald famous almost overnight, and a week later he married Zelda Sayre in New York. They embarked on an extravagant life as young celebrities.

After a riotous summer in Westport, Connecticut, the Fitzgeralds took an apartment in New York City; there he wrote his second novel, *The Beautiful and Damned*. When Zelda Fitzgerald became pregnant they took their first trip to Europe in 1921 and then settled in St. Paul for the birth of their only child, Frances Scott (Scottie) Fitzgerald, who was born in October 1921.

The chief theme of Fitzgerald's work is aspiration of the idealism he regarded as defining American character. Another major theme was mutability or loss. As a social historian Fitzgerald became identified with the Jazz Age: "It was an age of miracles, it was an age of art, it was an age of excess, and it was an age of satire," he wrote in "*Echoes of the Jazz Age.*"

Seeking tranquility for his work the Fitzgeralds went to France in the spring of 1924. He wrote *The Great Gatsby* during the summer. The Fitzgeralds spent the winter of 1924 1925 in Rome, where he revised *The Great Gatsby*; *The Great Gatsby* marked a striking advance in Fitzgerald's technique, utilizing a complex structure and a controlled narrative point of view. Fitzgerald's achievement received critical praise, but sales of *Gatsby* were disappointing, though the stage and movie rights brought additional income.

In Paris Fitzgerald met Ernest Hemingway with whom he formed a friendship based largely on his admiration for Hemingway's personality and genius. The Fitzgeralds remained in France until the end of 1926, alternating between Paris and the Riviera. Since 1926 Fitzgerald can not make significant progress on his novel. In 1930 his wife Zelda suffered mental breakdown. When F. Scott Fitzgerald died he believed himself a failure. By 1960 he had achieved a secure place among America's enduring writers. *The Great Gatsby*, a work that seriously examines the theme of aspiration in an American setting, defines the classic American novel.

Plot of *The Great Gatsby*

The story is told in the first person by Nick Carraway, a quiet young Midwesterner who comes east to work on the New York exchange and rents a house in 1922 at West Egg, Lang Island. His house is next to an extravagant mansion owned by the mysterious but wealthy Jay Gatsby. Gatsby's real name is James Gats and he was a poor boy from the west. When he was an army officer, he had fallen in love with Daisy, who was charming and polished, but whose "voice is full of money". Daisy later married Tom Buchanan, a wealthy and cold arrogant young Midwesterner who has recently come east. And Gatsby became rich through bootlegging and other criminal activities. However he has never stopped loving Daisy and has taken a house to be near her to attract her attention. Through Dick, Daisy's cousin, he finds a way to meet her again her favor. When he is overjoyed, he feels that he has Daisy back again. Her husband Tome has an affair with Mrs. Wilson, wife of a garage man. When Wilson has finally become suspicious of her fidelity and began to bully her, in panic she runs out into the highway and under the wheels of the car in which Daisy is driving. Gatsby manages to protect Daisy and Tom. But Tom revenged upon her lover by telling Wilson that it was Gatsby who killed his wife and also tells him where to find Gatsby, Wilson kills off Gatsby and then kills himself by shooting. The only person to go to the funeral besides Nick is Gatsby's father, Henry Gats, for all of Gatsby's acquaintances desert him and the party guests vanish.

Some Comments on *The Great Gatsby*

The Great Gatsby is the best novel of F.S. Fitzgerald. As a novel with strong tragic flavor, it keeps in step with the time and its criticism of America society is really penetrating.

The importance of the setting in *The Great Gatsby* lays in the fact that Fitzgerald's world setting revealed characters. The story took place during the Roaring Age, and there were four major settings in this novel: (1) West Egg including Gatsby's mansion and Nick's House that decide character's personality and status. They are new rich and not fashionable. Gatsby and Nick are not rich enough to buy house in the East Egg. (2) East Egg (3) The Valley of Ashes (4) New York City: The offices, Tom and Myrtle's apartment. Within each of these major settings were two or more sub-settings. West Egg included both Gatsby's mansion and Nick's House; while East Egg was limited to Daisy's house; The Valley of Ashes incorporated the Wilson's garage, Michaels' restaurant, and the advertising billboard with the eyes of Dr. T.J. Ecklebury; New York included the offices, the apartment Tom keeps for Myrtle and the Plaza Hotel.

Each setting reflected and also determined the values of the people who lived or worked there. West Egg, where Gatsby and Nick lived, was the "less fashionable" side of Lang Island. Gatsby lives there because he belonged to the "New Rich" and was temporarily unable to be accepted in East Egg; Nick lived there because he was too poor to afford a house in East Egg. Their houses are vulgar and would be totally out of place in the more refined world of East Egg. This explained the reason why in the end Gatsby was ruined by the East Egg and Nick decided to go back home.

East Egg was the "fashionable" side of Long Island.

The Valley of Ashes in contrast to both East Egg and West Egg was the desolate wasteland where the poor people like the Wilsons lived. In fact, those poor people were the victims of the rich. For instance, the Wilsons were the very victims of the Buchanans. The valley, with the eyes of Dr. T. J Eckleburg, also represented the spiritual emptiness and dryness of the world.

New York city stood as a symbol of what America had become in the roaring twenties: a place where money was made and bootleggers flourished, where parties and affairs came after another, and where bizarre and colorful character who appeared from time to time at Gatsby's parties. *The Great Gatsby* is considered by many critics to be one of the most well-written and tightly structured novels in American literature.

Fitzgerald begins the novel in the presents, offering the reader in the first three chapters, a glimpse of the four main settings of the novel, that is, the East Egg, the Valley of Ashes, the West Egg and the New York City. He uses flashback to narrate the main events of the story in chapter 4, 6 and 7 to gradually exhibit the past of Gatsby. In Chapter 9, the past and present combine to end the novel.

The combination of the first person narrative and the gradual revelation of the past as the narrator gets more and more, constitutes the key to the structure of the novel. The two devices work effectively together, and neither would work well separately.

The novel shows the disillusion of "American Dream" in the 1920s. At that age, it was impossible for Gatsby to succeed. The novel also shows that in the American society of 1920s, the commons were in total depravity. It tells us that there is no way to go from money to love, from material to spirit. In a split world, love could neither make up the split nor replace the value. It is full of realistic meanings.

The clues of the novel are very clear, while the specific events are mysterious. In addition, the novel is intensely lyrical. With colorful musical elements, the author composed a tragic song, leaving a lot of questions for us to think about.

Major Characters

Nick Carraway (narrator) is a man from the Midwest, a Yale graduate, a World War I veteran, and a resident of West Egg. He is Gatsby's next-door neighbor and a bonds salesman.

Jay Gatsby (originally James Gatz) is a young, mysterious millionaire with shady business connections later revealed to be a bootlegger, originally from North Dakota. He is obsessed with Daisy Buchanan, whom he had met when he was a stationed as a young officer in World War I.

Daisy Buchanan is an attractive and shallow young woman; Nick's second cousin, once removed; and the wife of Tom Buchanan. Daisy once had a romantic relationship with Gatsby, before she married Tom. Therefore, her choice between Gatsby and Tom is one of the central conflicts in the novel.

Tom Buchanan is a millionaire who lives on East Egg, and Daisy's husband. He is also an arrogant and irresponsible man.

Jordan Baker is Daisy Buchanan's long-time friend, a professional golfer with a slightly shady reputation.

George B. Wilson is a mechanic and owner of a garage. When he learns of the death of his wife, he shoots and kills Gatsby, wrongly believing he had been driving the car that killed Myrtle, and then kills himself.

Myrtle Wilson is George's wife, and Tom Buchanan's mistress. She is accidentally killed after being hit by a car, driven by Daisy, though Gatsby takes the blame for it.

Introduction to Chapter 9

Chapter 9 is the last chapter of *The Great Gatsby*. Gatsby's death has attracted many people's attention. These people include photographers, police, newspapermen, detective, and boy from his neighbourhood; however, these people come to visit Gatsby not out of their care for Gatsby but out of curiosity for murder. As a friend and neighbour of Gatsby, Nick hopes Gatsby to have others' respect like the days when he is alive. The result disappoints Nick so much that all suddenly desert Gatsby and none is willing to attend his funeral. Daisy and Tom took baggage away and left no address.

Gatsby's friend, Wolfsheim pretends not to be at office; Nick keeps looking for him, finally Nick succeeds in seeing him, but Wolfsheim is determined not to attend Gatsby's funeral. Slagle (Gatsby's business partner), hearing the death of Gatsby hang the phone. Nick and the man with owl-eyed glassed are only guests to attend Gatsby's funeral. After that Nick decides to go back his hometown, the west.

Chapter 9

After two years $I^{[1]}$ remember the rest of that day, and that night and the next day, only as an endless drill of police and photographers and newspaper men in and out of Gatsby's front door. A rope stretched across the main gate and a policeman by it kept out the curious, but little boys soon discovered that they could enter through my yard, and there were always a few of them clustered open-mouthed about the pool. Someone with a positive manner, perhaps a detective, used the expression "madman." as he bent over $Wilson^{[2]}$'s body that afternoon, and the adventitious authority of his voice set the key for the newspaper reports next morning.

Most of those reports were a nightmare—grotesque, circumstantial, eager, and untrue. When $Michaelis^{[3]}$'s testimony at the inquest brought to light Wilson's suspicions of his wife I thought the whole tale would shortly be served up in racy pasquinade—but $Catherine^{[4]}$, who might have said anything, didn't say a word. She showed a surprising amount of character about it too—looked at the coroner with determined eyes under that corrected brow of hers, and swore that her sister had never seen Gatsby, that her sister was completely happy with her husband, that her sister had been into no mischief whatever. She convinced herself of it, and cried into her handkerchief, as if the very suggestion was more than she could endure. S. Wilson was reduced to a man "deranged by grief." in order that the case might remain in its simplist form. And it rested there.

But all this part of it seemed remote and unessential. I found myself on Gatsby's side, and alone. From the moment I telephoned news of the catastrophe to $West\ Egg$ $village^{[5]}$, every surmise about him, and every practical question, was referred to me. At first I was surprised and confused; then, as he lay in his house and didn't move or breathe or speak, hour upon hour, it grew upon me that I was responsible, because no one else was interested—interested, I mean, with that intense personal interest to which every one has some vague right at the end.

I called up $Daisy^{[6]}$ half an hour after we found him, called her instinctively and without hesitation. But she and $Tom^{[7]}$ had gone away early that afternoon, and taken baggage with them.

"Left no address?"

"No."

"Say when they'd be back?"

"No."

"Any idea where they are? How I could reach them?"

"I don't know. Can't say."

I wanted to get somebody for him. I wanted to go into the room where he lay and reassure him: "I'll get somebody for you, Gatsby. Don't worry. Just trust me and I'll get somebody for you—"

Meyer Wolfsheim[8]'s name wasn't in the phone book. The butler gave me his office address on Broadway, and I called Information, but by the time I had the number it was long after five, and no one answered the phone.

"Will you ring again?"

"I've rung them three times."

"It's very important."

"Sorry. I'm afraid no one's there."

I went back to the drawing-room and thought for an instant that they were chance visitors, all these official people who suddenly filled it. But, as they drew back the sheet and looked at Gatsby with unmoved eyes, his protest continued in my brain:

"Look here, old sport, you've got to get somebody for me. You've got to try hard. I can't go through this alone."

Some one started to ask me questions, but I broke away and going up-stairs looked hastily through the unlocked parts of his desk—he'd never told me definitely that his parents were dead. But there was nothing—only the picture of *Dan Cody*[9], a token of forgotten violence, staring down from the wall.

Next morning I sent the butler to New York with a letter to Wolfsheim, which asked for information and urged him to come out on the next train. That request seemed superfluous when I wrote it. I was sure he'd start when he saw the newspapers, just as I was sure there'd be a wire from Daisy before noon—but neither a wire nor Mr. Wolfsheim arrived; no one arrived except more police and photographers and newspaper men. When the butler brought back Wolfsheim's answer I began to have a feeling of defiance, of scornful solidarity between Gatsby and me against them all.

Dear Mr. Carraway. This has been one of the most terrible shocks of my life to me I hardly can believe it that it is true at all. Such a mad act as that man did should make us all think. I cannot come down now as I am tied up in some very important business and cannot get mixed up in this thing now. If there is anything I can do a little later let me know in a letter by Edgar. I hardly know where I am when I hear about a thing like this and am completely knocked down and out.

Yours truly

Meyer Wolfshiem

and then hasty addenda beneath:

Let me know about the funeral etc. do not know his family at all.

When the phone rang that afternoon and Long Distance said Chicago was calling I thought this would be Daisy at last. But the connection came through as a man's voice, very thin and far away.

"This is *Slagle*[10] speaking…"

"Yes?" The name was unfamiliar.

"Hell of a note, isn't it? Get my wire?"

"There haven't been any wires."

"Young *Parke*[11]'s in trouble," he said rapidly. "They *picked him up*[12] when he handed the bonds over the counter. They got a circular from New York giving 'em the numbers just five minutes before. What d'you know about that, hey? You never can tell in these hick towns—"

"Hello!" I interrupted breathlessly. "Look here—this isn't Mr. Gatsby. Mr. Gatsby's dead."

There was a long silence on the other end of the wire, followed by an exclamation… then a quick squawk as the connection was broken.

I think it was on the third day that a telegram signed Henry C. Gatz arrived from a town in Minnesota. It said only that the sender was leaving immediately and to postpone the funeral until he came.

It was Gatsby's father, a solemn old man, very helpless and dismayed, bundled up in a long cheap ulster against the warm September day. His eyes leaked continuously with excitement, and when I took the bag and umbrella from his hands he began to pull so incessantly at his sparse gray beard that I had difficulty in getting off his coat. He was on the point of collapse, so I took him into the music room and made him sit down while I sent for something to eat. But he wouldn't eat, and the glass of milk spilled from his trembling hand.

"I saw it in the Chicago newspaper," he said. "It was all in the Chicago newspaper. I started right away."

"I didn't know how to reach you." His eyes, seeing nothing, moved ceaselessly about the room.

"It was a madman," he said. "He must have been mad."

"Wouldn't you like some coffee?" I urged him.

"I don't want anything. I'm all right now, Mr.—"

"Carraway."

"Well, I'm all right now. Where have they got Jimmy?" I took him into the drawing-room, where his son lay, and left him there. Some little boys had come up on the steps and were looking into the hall; when I told them who had arrived, they went reluctantly away.

After a little while Mr. Gatz opened the door and came out, his mouth ajar, his face flushed slightly, his eyes leaking isolated and unpunctual tears. He had reached an age where death no longer has the quality of ghastly surprise, and when he looked around him now for the first time and saw the height and splendor of the hall and the great rooms opening out from it into other rooms, his grief began to be mixed with an awed pride. I helped him to a bedroom up-stairs; while he took off his coat and vest I told him that all arrangements had been deferred until he came.

"I didn't know what you'd want, Mr. Gatsby—"

"Gatz is my name."

"—Mr. Gatz. I thought you might want to take the body West."

He shook his head.

"Jimmy always liked it better down East. He rose up to his position in the East.

Were you a friend of my boy's, Mr.—?"

"We were close friends."

"He had a big future before him, you know. He was only a young man, but he had a lot of brain power here."

He touched his head impressively, and I nodded.

"*If he'd of lived, he'd of been a great man*[13]. A man like *James J. Hill*[14]. He'd of helped build up the country."

"That's true," I said, uncomfortably.

He fumbled at the embroidered coverlet, trying to take it from the bed, and lay down stiffly—was instantly asleep.

That night an obviously frightened person called up, and demanded to know who I was before he would give his name.

"This is Mr. Carraway," I said.

"Oh!" He sounded relieved. "This is *Klipspringer*[15]." I was relieved too, for that seemed to promise another friend at Gatsby's grave. I didn't want it to be in the papers and draw a sightseeing crowd, so I'd been calling up a few people myself. They were hard to find.

"The funeral's to-morrow," I said. "Three o'clock, here at the house. I wish you'd tell anybody who'd be interested."

"Oh, I will," he broke out hastily. "Of course I'm not likely to see anybody, but if I do."

His tone made me suspicious.

"Of course you'll be there yourself."

"Well, I'll certainly try. What I called up about is—"

"Wait a minute," I interrupted. "How about saying you'll come?"

"Well, the fact is—the truth of the matter is that I'm staying with some people up here in *Greenwich*[16], and they rather expect me to be with them to-morrow. In fact, there's a sort of picnic or something. Of course I'll do my very best to get away."

I ejaculated an unrestrained "Huh!" and he must have heard me, for he went on nervously:

"What I called up about was a pair of shoes I left there. I wonder if it'd be too much trouble to have the butler send them on. You see, they're tennis shoes, and I'm sort of helpless without them. My address is care of B. F.—"

I didn't hear the rest of the name, because I hung up the receiver.

After that I felt a certain shame for Gatsby—one gentleman to whom I telephoned implied that he had got what he deserved. However, that was my fault, for he was one of those who used to sneer most bitterly at Gatsby on the courage of Gatsby's liquor, and I should have known better than to call him.

The morning of the funeral I went up to New York to see Meyer Wolfsheim; I couldn't seem to reach him any other way. The door that I pushed open, on the advice of an elevator boy, was marked "The Swastika Holding Company," and at first there didn't seem to be any one inside. But when I'd shouted "hello." several times in vain, an argument broke out behind a partition, and presently a lovely Jewess appeared at an interior door and scrutinized me with black hostile eyes.

"Nobody's in," she said. "Mr. Wolfsheim's gone to Chicago."

The first part of this was obviously untrue, for someone had begun to whistle "The Rosary," tunelessly, inside.

"Please say that Mr. Carraway wants to see him."

"I can't get him back from Chicago, can I?"

At this moment a voice, unmistakably Wolfsheim's, called "Stella!" from the other side of the door.

"Leave your name on the desk," she said quickly. "I'll give it to him when he gets back."

"But I know he's there."

She took a step toward me and began to slide her hands indignantly up and down her hips.

"You young men think you can force your way in here any time," she scolded. "We're getting *sickantired*[17] of it. When I say he's in Chicago, he's in Chicago."

I mentioned Gatsby.

"Oh—h!" She looked at me over again. "Will you just—What was your name?"

She vanished. In a moment Meyer Wolfsheim stood solemnly in the doorway, holding out both hands. He drew me into his office, remarking in a reverent voice that it was a sad time for all of us, and offered me a cigar.

"My memory goes back to when I first met him," he said. "A young major just out of the army and covered over with medals he got in the war. He was so hard up he had to keep on wearing his uniform because he couldn't buy some regular clothes. First time I saw him was when he come into Winebrenner's poolroom at Forty-third Street and asked for a job. He hadn't eat anything for a couple of days. 'come on have some lunch with me,' *I sid*[18]. He ate more than four dollars' worth of food in half an hour."

"Did you start him in business?" I inquired.

"Start him! I made him."

"Oh."

"I raised him up out of nothing, right out of the gutter. I saw right away he was a fine-appearing, gentlemanly young man, and when he told me he was at *Oggsford*[19] I knew I could use him good. I got him to join up in the *American Legion*[20] and he used to stand high there. Right off he did some work for a client of mine up to Albany. We were so thick like that in everything."—he held up two bulbous fingers—" always together."

I wondered if this partnership had included *the World's Series transaction*[21] in 1919.

"Now he's dead," I said after a moment. "You were his closest friend, so I know you'll want to come to his funeral this afternoon."

"I'd like to come."

"Well, come then."

The hair in his nostrils quivered slightly, and as he shook his head his eyes filled with tears.

"I can't do it—I can't get mixed up in it," he said.

"There's nothing to get mixed up in. It's all over now."

"When a man gets killed I never like to get mixed up in it in any way. I keep out. When I was a young man it was different—if a friend of mine died, no matter how, I stuck with them to the end. You may think that's sentimental, but I mean it—

to the bitter end."

I saw that for some reason of his own he was determined not to come, so I stood up.

"Are you a college man?" he inquired suddenly.

For a moment I thought he was going to suggest a "*gonnegtion*[22]," but he only nodded and shook my hand.

"Let us learn to show our friendship for a man when he is alive and not after he is dead," he suggested. "After that my own rule is to let everything alone."

When I left his office the sky had turned dark and I got back to West Egg in a drizzle. After changing my clothes I went next door and found Mr. Gatz walking up and down excitedly in the hall. His pride in his son and in his son's possessions was continually increasing and now he had something to show me.

"Jimmy sent me this picture." He took out his wallet with trembling fingers. "Look there."

It was a photograph of the house, cracked in the corners and dirty with many hands. He pointed out every detail to me eagerly. "Look there!" and then sought admiration from my eyes. He had shown it so often that I think it was more real to him now than the house itself.

"Jimmy sent it to me. I think it's a very pretty picture. It shows up well."

"Very well. Had you seen him lately?"

"He come out to see me two years ago and bought me the house I live in now. Of course we was broke up when he run off from home, but I see now there was a reason for it. He knew he had a big future in front of him. And ever since he made a success he was very generous with me." He seemed reluctant to put away the picture, held it for another minute, lingeringly, before my eyes. Then he returned the wallet and pulled from his pocket a ragged old copy of a book called *Hopalong Cassidy*.

"Look here, this is a book he had when he was a boy. It just shows you."

He opened it at the back cover and turned it around for me to see. On the last fly-leaf was printed the word *Schedule*, and the date September 12, 1906. and underneath:

   Rise from bed...............   6.00 *a.m.*

Dumbbell exercise and wall-scaling......	6.15–6.30
Study electricity, etc............	7.15–8.15
Work.....................	8.30–4.30 *p.m.*
Baseball and sports.............	4.30–5.00
Practice elocution, poise and how to attain it	5.00–6.00
Study needed inventions..........	7.00–9.00

General Resolves

No wasting time at Shafters or [a name, indecipherable]

No more smoking or chewing

Bath every other day

Read one improving book or magazine per week

Save $5.00 [crossed out] $3.00 per week

Be better to parents

"I come across this book by accident," said the old man. "It just shows you, don't it?"

"It just shows you."

"Jimmy was bound to get ahead. He always had some resolves like this or something. Do you notice what he's got about improving his mind? He was always great for that. He told me *I et like a hog*[23] once, and I beat him for it."

He was reluctant to close the book, reading each item aloud and then looking eagerly at me. I think he rather expected me to copy down the list for my own use.

A little before three the Lutheran minister arrived from Flushing, and I began to look involuntarily out the windows for other cars. So did Gatsby's father. And as the time passed and the servants came in and stood waiting in the hall, his eyes began to blink anxiously, and he spoke of the rain in a worried, uncertain way. The minister glanced several times at his watch, so I took him aside and asked him to wait for half an hour. But it wasn't any use. Nobody came.

About five o'clock our procession of three cars reached the cemetery and stopped in a thick drizzle beside the gate—first a motor hearse, horribly black and wet, then Mr. Gatz and the minister and I in the limousine, and a little later four or five servants and the postman from West Egg in Gatsby's station wagon, all wet to the skin. As we started through the gate into the cemetery I heard a car stop and then the sound of someone splashing after us over the soggy ground. I looked around. It was *the man with owl-eyed glasses*[24] whom I had found marvelling over Gatsby's books in the library one night three months before.

I'd never seen him since then. I don't know how he knew about the funeral, or even his name. The rain poured down his thick glasses, and he took them off and wiped them to see the protecting canvas unrolled from Gatsby's grave.

I tried to think about Gatsby then for a moment, but he was already too far away, and I could only remember, without resentment, that Daisy hadn't sent a message or a flower. Dimly I heard someone murmur, "Blessed are the dead that the rain falls on," and then the owl-eyed man said "Amen to that," in a brave voice.

We straggled down quickly through the rain to the cars. Owl-eyes spoke to me by the gate.

"I couldn't get to the house," he remarked.

"Neither could anybody else."

"Go on!" He started. "Why, my God! they used to go there by the hundreds." He took off his glasses and wiped them again, outside and in.

"The poor son-of a bitch," he said.

One of my most vivid memories is of coming back West from prep school and later from college at Christmas time. Those who went farther than Chicago would gather in the old dim Union Station at six o'clock of a December evening, with a few Chicago friends, already caught up into their own holiday gayeties, to bid them a hasty good-by. I remember the fur coats of the girls returning from Miss This-or-that's and the chatter of frozen breath and the hands waving overhead as we caught sight of old acquaintances, and the matchings of invitations: "Are you going to the Ordways'? the Herseys'? the Schultzes'?" and the long green tickets clasped tight in our gloved hands. And last the murky yellow cars of the Chicago, Milwaukee and St. Paul railroad looking cheerful as Christmas itself on the tracks beside the gate.

When we pulled out into the winter night and the real snow, our snow, began to stretch out beside us and twinkle against the windows, and the dim lights of small Wisconsin stations moved by, a sharp wild brace came suddenly into the air. We drew in deep breaths of it as we walked back from dinner through the cold vestibules, unutterably aware of our identity with this country for one strange hour, before we melted indistinguishably into it again.

That's my Middle West—not the wheat or the prairies or the lost Swede towns, but the thrilling returning trains of my youth, and the street lamps and sleigh bells in the frosty dark and the shadows of holly wreaths thrown by lighted windows on the snow. I am part of that, a little solemn with the feel of those long winters, a little complacent from growing up in the Carraway house in a city where dwellings are still called through decades by a family's name. I see now that this has been a story of the West, after all—Tom and Gatsby, Daisy and *Jordan*[25] and I, were all Westerners, and perhaps we possessed some deficiency in common which made us subtly unadaptable to Eastern life.

Even when the East excited me most, even when I was most keenly aware of its superiority to the bored, sprawling, swollen towns beyond the Ohio, with their interminable inquisitions which spared only the children and the very old—even then it had always for me a quality of distortion. West Egg, especially, still figures in my more fantastic dreams. I see it as a night scene by *El Greco*[26]: a hundred houses, at once conventional and grotesque, crouching under a sullen, overhanging sky and a lustreless moon. In the foreground four solemn men in dress suits are walking along the sidewalk with a stretcher on which lies a drunken woman in a white evening dress. Her hand, which dangles over the side, sparkles cold with jewels. Gravely the men turn in at a house—the wrong house. But no one knows the woman's name, and no one cares.

After Gatsby's death the East was haunted for me like that, distorted beyond my eyes' power of correction. So when the blue smoke of brittle leaves was in the air and the wind blew the wet laundry stiff on the line I decided to come back home.

There was one thing to be done before I left, an awkward, unpleasant thing that perhaps had better have been let alone. But I wanted to leave things in order and not just trust that obliging and indifferent sea to sweep my refuse away. I saw Jordan Baker and talked over and around what had happened to us together, and what had happened afterward to me, and she lay perfectly still, listening, in a big chair.

She was dressed to play golf, and I remember thinking she looked like a good illustration, her chin raised a little jauntily, her hair the color of an autumn leaf, her face the same brown tint as the fingerless glove on her knee. When I had finished she told me without comment that she was engaged to another man. I doubted that, though there were several she could have married at a nod of her head, but I pretended to be surprised. For just a minute I wondered if I wasn't making a mistake, then I thought it all over again quickly and got up to say good-bye.

"Nevertheless you did throw me over," said Jordan suddenly. "You threw me over on the telephone. I don't give a damn about you now, but it was a new experience for me, and I felt a little dizzy for a while."

We shook hands.

"Oh, and do you remember."—she added—"a conversation we had once about driving a car?"

"Why—not exactly."

"You said a bad driver was only safe until she met another bad driver? Well, I met another bad driver, didn't I? I mean it was careless of me to make such a wrong guess. I thought you were rather an honest, straightforward person. I thought it was your secret pride."

"I'm thirty," I said. "I'm five years too old to lie to myself and call it honor."

She didn't answer. Angry, and half in love with her, and tremendously sorry, I turned away.

One afternoon late in October I saw Tom Buchanan. He was walking ahead of me along Fifth Avenue in his alert, aggressive way, his hands out a little from his body as if to fight off interference, his head moving sharply here and there, adapting itself to his restless eyes. Just as I slowed up to avoid overtaking him he stopped and began frowning into the windows of a jewelry store. Suddenly he saw me and walked back, holding out his hand.

"What's the matter, Nick? Do you object to shaking hands with me?"

"Yes. You know what I think of you."

"You're crazy, Nick," he said quickly. "Crazy as hell. I don't know what's the matter with you."

"Tom," I inquired, "what did you say to Wilson that afternoon?" He stared at me without a word, and I knew I had guessed right about those missing hours. I started to turn away, but he took a step after me and grabbed my arm.

"I told him the truth," he said. "He came to the door while we were getting ready to leave, and when I sent down word that we weren't in he tried to force his way up-stairs. He was crazy enough to kill me if I hadn't told him who owned the car. His hand was on a revolver in his pocket every minute he was in the house—" He broke off defiantly. "What if I did tell him? That fellow had it coming to him. He threw dust into your eyes just like he did in Daisy's, but he was a tough one. He ran over Myrtle like you'd run over a dog and never even stopped his car."

There was nothing I could say, except the one unutterable fact that it wasn't true.

"And if you think I didn't have my share of suffering—look here, when I went to give up that flat and saw that damn box of dog biscuits sitting there on the sideboard, I sat down and cried like a baby. By God it was awful—"

I couldn't forgive him or like him, but I saw that what he had done was, to him, entirely justified. It was all very careless and confused. They were careless people, Tom and Daisy—they smashed up things and creatures and then retreated back into their money or their vast carelessness, or whatever it was that kept them together, and let other people clean up the mess they had made....

I shook hands with him; it seemed silly not to, for I felt suddenly as though I were talking to a child. Then he went into the jewelry store to buy a pearl necklace— or perhaps only a pair of cuff buttons—rid of my provincial squeamishness forever.

Gatsby's house was still empty when I left—the grass on his lawn had grown as long as mine. One of the taxi drivers in the village never took a fare past the entrance gate without stopping for a minute and pointing inside; perhaps it was he who drove Daisy and Gatsby over to *East Egg*[27] the night of the accident, and perhaps he had made a story about it all his own. I didn't want to hear it and I avoided him when I got off the train.

I spent my Saturday nights in New York because those gleaming, dazzling parties of his were with me so vividly that I could still hear the music and the laughter, faint and incessant, from his garden, and the cars going up and down his drive. One night

I did hear *a material car*[28] there, and saw its lights stop at his front steps. But I didn't investigate. Probably it was some final guest who had been away at the ends of the earth and didn't know that the party was over.

On the last night, with my trunk packed and my car sold to the grocer, I went over and looked at that huge incoherent failure of a house once more. On the white steps an obscene word, scrawled by some boy with a piece of brick, stood out clearly in the moonlight, and I erased it, drawing my shoe raspingly along the stone. Then I wandered down to the beach and sprawled out on the sand.

Most of the big shore places were closed now and there were hardly any lights except the shadowy, moving glow of a ferryboat across *the Sound*[29]. And as the moon rose higher the inessential houses began to melt away until gradually I became aware of *the old island*[30] here that flowered once for Dutch sailors' eyes—a fresh, green breast of the new world. Its vanished trees, the trees that had made way for Gatsby's house, had once pandered in whispers to the last and greatest of all human dreams; for a transitory enchanted moment man must have held his breath in the presence of this continent, compelled into an aesthetic contemplation he neither understood nor desired, face to face for the last time in history with something commensurate to his capacity for wonder.

And as I sat there brooding on the old, unknown world, I thought of Gatsby's wonder when he first picked out *the green light*[31] at the end of *Daisy's dock*[32]. He had come a long way to this blue lawn, and his dream must have seemed so close that he could hardly fail to grasp it. He did not know that it was already behind him, somewhere back in that vast obscurity beyond the city, where the dark fields of the republic rolled on under the night.

Gatsby believed in the green light, the orgastic future that year by year recedes before us. It eluded us then, but that's no matter—to-morrow we will run faster, stretch out our arms farther.... And one fine morning—

So we beat on, boats against the current, borne back ceaselessly into the past.

Notes

[1] I 是故事的叙述者 Nick Carraway。

[2] Wilson 是汤姆情妇的丈夫。黛西驾车时将他妻子撞死。他误认为是盖茨比

将他妻子撞死,在枪杀盖茨比之后自杀(见第二章、第七章和第八章)。

[3] 咖啡店店主,汽车肇事时他在现场,但连汽车的颜色都没看清(第七章)。

[4] 车祸受害者 Myrtle 的妹妹

[5] 西卵镇,小说主人公盖茨比和叙述者尼克居住的地方。

[6] 曾是盖茨比的情人后来嫁给了汤姆。

[7] 汤姆

[8] 非法操纵比赛的赌徒,盖茨比做非法生意的合作伙伴。

[9] 曾在内华达州开银矿发财,盖茨比年轻时遇到他并为他工作。

[10] 盖茨比非法生意伙伴

[11] 盖茨比非法生意伙伴

[12] 他们逮捕了他,这证实了盖茨比参加了非法生意。

[13] If he'd lived, he'd have been a great man.

[14] 詹姆斯·J·希尔(1838~1916) 美国金融家和铁路建筑家。

[15] 一个经常寄住在盖茨比家的人(第四章)。

[16] 格林尼治,美国康涅狄格州西南部城镇。

[17] sick and tired

[18] I said

[19] Oxford

[20] 美国军团(美国退伍军人组织)

[21] World Series:世界系列赛(美国棒球系列比赛);transaction:这里指操纵比赛的非法交易。

[22] connection

[23] I ate like a hog.

[24] 盖茨比宴会上的客人(第三章)

[25] 乔丹,高尔夫球运动员,曾与尼克有恋爱关系(第一章)

[26] El Greco(1541~1614):西班牙画家,这里是尼克以画中变形了的景物暗喻东部地区的扭曲的生活方式。

[27] 东卵镇,黛西夫妇居住的富人区。

[28] 真实而不是幻觉中的汽车

[29] Long Island Sound 长岛海峡

[30] Long Island

[31] 绿色在英语里象征青春和生命。书中多次提到盖茨比对绿色光明的向往
（第一章），他以为黛西就是他向往的光明。

[32] 这里既指黛西住所外码头上的指示灯（其实应该是红色的）又指盖茨比心
中理想的停泊港湾。

Questions

1　What's people's attitude toward the death of Gatsby?

2　What do you think the personality of Daisy and Tom?

3　How does Gatsby's schedule relate with the American Dream?

4　Why does the author call Gatsby "the great Gatsby"?

Analysis of Chapter 9

As this chapter opens, Nick reminds us that this is a memoir of events that took place two years previously. He remembers the rest of the day of Gatsby's murder as "an endless drill of police and photographers and newspapermen."

At the coroner's inquest the connection between Myrtle Wilson and Tom Buchanan is never discovered.

Nick is left to make Gatsby's funeral arrangements. Tom and Daisy have left town. Meyer Wolfsheim, Gatsby's gangster mentor, lets Nick know via letter that he does not care to be involved any further in Gatsby's affairs.

Gatsby's father, "a solemn old man very helpless and dismayed," arrives on Long Island.

Nick goes to New York to see Mr. Wolfsheim. Wolfsheim refuses to even attend the funeral.

He gives Nick one of the last pieces of information about Gatsby. He and Gatsby met after the war in a pool hall. Gatsby was penniless and looking for work. Wolfsheim realized right away that someone with Gatsby's appearance, Oxford manner, and good war record would be useful to him.

The last information about Gatsby comes from his father, who shows Nick an old copy of a boy's book—the young Gatsby's schedule for the day and resolutions for improving himself are written on the fly leaf in back.

Nick, Gatsby's father, a minister, servants from Gatsby's big house, and the local postman attend the funeral ceremony. One stray party-goer makes it to the actual burial.

Nick sums up Gatsby's story in terms of how it has affected him, he speaks of prep school and college days, and of returning home to the Midwest in winter on the train, of balancing between the exciting glamorous East and the reassuring solid Midwest.

He speaks of the pull of the Midwest and his decision to go home after Gatsby's death. Perhaps, he tells us, his personality is "subtly unadaptable to Eastern life." He sees Jordan Baker one more time and tells her goodbye.

And before he leaves he runs into Tom Buchanan on the sidewalk in New York. He comes to some final understanding or comprehension of Tom and Daisy: "careless people... they smashed up things and creatures and then retreated back into their money or their vast carelessness or whatever it was that kept them together..."

On Nick's last night in the East, he walks over to Gatsby's place and looks over the grounds one last time. He walks down to the shore of the bay and sits in the sand. In a single terrific compressed moment of personal empathy and historical sensibility and insight, he merges Gatsby's story with the American dream of hopefulness and striving.

Unit 13
Earnest Hemingway (1899~1961)

Life

Hemingway was born on 21st July 1899 in Oak Park, Chicago. At the age of 17, he started his career as a writer in *The Kansas City Star* newspaper office. He entered the First World War in 1918 as a volunteer ambulance driver in the Italian army. He was wounded near the Italian-Austrian front and as a result, awarded the Italian Silver Medal for Valor. He spent considerable time in hospitals and fell in love with a nurse who was seven years older than him.

These dramatic personal events against the backdrop of a brutal war became the basis of Hemingway's first widely successful novel *A Farewell to Arms*, published in 1929. After his return to the United States, he became a reporter for Canadian and American newspapers and was soon sent back to Europe to cover such events as the Greek Revolution.

From 1925 to 1926 Hemingway produced some of the most important works of

20th century fiction, including the landmark short story collection *In Our Time*, published in 1925. In 1926 he came out his first novel—*The Sun Also Rises*. He followed that book with *Men Without Women* in 1927. *A Farewell to Arms*, known as the finest novel to emerge from WWI, came out in 1929. In four short years he went from being an unknown writer to being the most important writer of his generation, and perhaps of the 20th century.

After growing success with his great style, Hemingway wrote out of his own direct experience on three continents about bull-fighting, big game hunting and deep-sea fishing in the 1930s. his works in this period include *The Fifth Column*, *The First Forty-Nine Stories* (1930), *Death in the Afternoon* (1932), *Winner Takes Nothing* (1933), *Green Hills of Africa* (big game hunting 1935) and *To Have and Have Not* (1937).

In the 1940s, he wrote about war again and a representative work is *For Whom the Bell Tolls* (1940《战地钟声》) inspired by his experience in the Spanish Civil War. After World War II, many critics said Hemingway's best writing period was past. But in September 1952, his Pulitzer winning novella—*The Old Man and the Sea*, surprised the critics. It first appeared in "life" magazine, later printed out by his exclusive publisher the Scribners. The book was a huge success both critically and commercially.

On October 28, 1954, he received the Nobel Prize "for his mastery of the art of narrative most recently demonstrated in *The Old Man and Sea*, and for the influence, that he has exerted on contemporary style" (由于他现代叙述艺术的高超技艺和他在当代风格中所发挥的影响). But due to his injuries in a plane crash, he was unable to attend the ceremonies in Sweden and asked the US Ambassador John Cabot to read for him acceptance speech instead.

Hemingway died in Ketchum, Idaho, in July 1961, by shooting himself. It is a mystery that Hemingway's father, grandfather and he himself all ended their life by committing suicide. However his works live on. They have been translated into many languages, read by numerous people and studied by students of literature all around the world.

Hemingway's first major novel, written when he was in Paris is *The Sun Also*

Rises. The title is from "Bible", means "No matter what sufferings human people meet, the sun also rises, we are unable to change the reality of disillusionment, disorder and despair." It is a typically representative work of the Lost Generation writers.

However, novels of Hemingway seem less important than his influence as a craftsman, for his style of writing is striking, characterized by short and terse sentences, simple diction with emotion and vivid colloquialism, like Mark Twain in his "Huckleberry Finn".

His style, to large extent is based on his experience as a journalist and his belief that "The dignity of movement of an iceberg is due to only one eighth of it being above water". 1/8 refers little labor of writing and minimal use of words; 7/8 refers to the feeling or implication—foundation of the novel. Hemingway describes his writing style as "Iceberg on the sea". What readers reading are precise and terse expressions in literary works. It is their implied meanings and reader's profound understanding that can give dignity and magnificence to the literary work. So in style, Hemingway refuses abundant adjective and prepositional phrases and he advocates the telegram-like expressions.

His subjects and themes spoke for the Lost Generation. Due to the profound impact of world war I, Hemingway's works are cynical and disillusioned. His characters become involved in war and in the competitive games such as hunting or bull-fighting. His characters are all "tough", courageous, and honest, but broken physically by the brutality of war and disillusioned by the hollowness of civilized society.

Plot of *A Clean, Well-lighted Place*

The story happens in a clean well-lighted cafe. It makes a contrast between the inner world of the old man and the outside world.. Hemingway contrasts light and dark to show the difference between this man and the young people around him. The main focus of *A Clean, Well-Lighted Place* is on the pain of old age suffered by a man that we meet in a cafe late one night. The old man is afraid of the darkness and loneliness.

He need cafe's whiskey to encourage himself to live. Two waiters are disscussing the old man while he is drinking in the cafe..the younger waiter and the older one are different. the older one has more experience in the world, so he can understand the old man better. While the young waiter is impolite, unsympathetic and naïve, he knows nothing about the pain of the old man. The young looks down upon the old and intends to go back home as early as possible. What he concerns is his own happiness and he does not care about the feelings of the old man.

Major Characters

The old man is a poor deaf man who suffers loneliness and darkness from the rest of the world. He is unwilling to sleep. Maybe he is afraid of something so he chooses to use whiskey to keep alive. He is afraid of death so he committed suicide to end the dread of death.However,he failed. He can't choose anything even his death. He can't do anything but wait. He uses his deafness as an image if his separation from the rest of the world. This old man is a typical Hemingway's tough guy. He keeps graceful manners even under the pressure of old age and death. What he wants is nothing but a clean and well-lighted place to enjoy calmness.

The old waiter has more experience in the world so he could understand the old man. He is more understanding and sympathetic than the young waiter.

The younger waiter can't understand the old man. His attitude toward the old man is impatient and cold. He disgusted him, treated the old man badly and even thought he should have already died.

A Clean, Well-lighted Place

It was late and everyone had left the cafe except an old man who sat in the shadow the leaves of the tree made against the electric light. In the daytime the street was dusty, but at night the dew settled the dust and the old man liked to sit late because he was deaf and now at night it was quiet and he felt the difference. The two waiters inside the cafe knew that the old man was a little drunk, and while he was a good client they knew that if he became too drunk he would leave without paying, so they kept watch on him.

"Last week he tried to commit suicide," one waiter said.

"Why?"

"He was in despair."

"What about?"

"Nothing."

"How do you know it was nothing?"

"He has plenty of money."

They sat together at a table that was close against the wall near the door of the cafe and looked at the terrace where the tables were all empty except where the old man sat in the shadow of the leaves of the tree that moved slightly in the wind. A girl and a soldier in the street. The street light shone on the brass number on his collar. The girl wore no head covering and hurried beside him.

"The guard will *pick him up*[1]," one waiter said.

"*What does it matter if he gets what he's after?*"[2]

"He had better get off the street now. the guard will get him. They went by finve minutes ago."

The old man sitting in the shadow rapped on his saucer with his glass. The younger waiter went over to him.

"What do you want?"

The old man looked at him. "Another brandy," he said.

"You'll be drunk," the waiter said. The old man looked at him. The waiter went away.

"He'll stay all night," he said to his colleague. "I'm sleepy now. I never get into bed before three o'clock. He should have killed himself last week."

The waiter took the brandy bottle and another saucer from the counter inside the cafe and marched out to the old man's table. He put down the saucer and poured the glass full of brandy.

"You should have killed yourself last week," he said to the deaf man. The old man motioned with his finger, "A little mare," he said. *The waiter poured on into the glass so that the brandy slopped over and ran down the stem into the top saucer of the pile.*[3] "Thank you," the old man said. The waiter took the bottle back inside the café. He sat down at the table with his colleague again.

"He's drunk now," he said.

"He's drunk every night."

"What did he want to kill himself for?"

"How should I know."

"How did he do it?"

"He jimg himself with a rope."

"Who cut him down?"

"His niece."

"Why did they do it?"

"*Fear for his soul*[4]."

"How much money hes he got?"

"He's got plenty."

"He must be eighty years old."

"Anyway I should say he was eighty."

"I wish he would go home. I never get to bed before three o'clock. What kind of hour is that to go to bed?"

"He stays up because he likes it."

"He's lonely. I'm not lonely. I have a wife waiting in bed for me."

"He had a wife once too."

"*A wife would be no good to him now*[5]."

"You can't tell. He might be better with a wife."

"I wouldn't want to be that old. An old man is a nasty thing."

"Not always. This old man is clean. He drinks without spilling. Even now, drunk. Look at him."

"I don't want to look at him. I wish he would go home. He has no regard for those who must work."

The old man looked from his glass across the square, then over at the waiters.

"Another brandy," he said, pointing to his glass. The waiter who was in a hurry came over.

"Finished," he said, speaking with that omission of syntax stupid people employ when talking to drunken people or foreigners. "No more tonight. Close now."

"Another," said the old man.

"No. Finished." The waiter wiped the edge of the table with a towel and shook his head.

The old man stood up, slowly counted the saucers, took a leather coin purse from his pocket and paid for the drinks, leaving half a *peseta*[6] tip.

The waiter watched him go down the street, a very old man walking unsteadily but with dignity.

"Why didn't you let him stay and drink?" the unhurried waiter asked. They were putting up the shutter. "It is not half past two."

"I want to go home to bed."

"*What is an hour?*[7]"

"*More to me than to him*[8]."

"An hour is the same."

"You talk like an old man yourself. He can buy a bottle and drink at home."

"It's not the same."

"No, it is not," agreed the waiter with a wife. He did not wish to be unjust. He was only ina hurry.

"And you? *You have no fear of going home before your usual hour?*[9]"

"Are you trying to insult me?"

"No, *hombre*[10], only to make a joke."

"No," the waiter who was in a hurry said, rising from pulling down the metal shutters. "I have confidence. I am all confidence."

"You have youth, confidence, and a job," the older waiter said. "You have everything."

"And what do you lack?"

"Everything but work."

"You have everything I have."

"No. I have never had confidence and I am not young."

"Come on. Stop talking nonsense and lock up."

"I am of those who like to stay late at the café," the older waiter said. "With all those who do not want to go to bed, with all those who need a light for the night."

"I want to go home and into bed."

"We are of two different kinds," the old waiter said. He was now dressed to go home. "It is not only a question of youth and confidence although those things are very beautiful. Each night I am reluctant to close up because there may be someone who needs the cafe."

"Hombre, there are bodegas open all night long."

"You do not understand. This is a clean and pleasant cafe. It is well lighted. The light is very good and also, now, there are shadows of the leaves."

"Good night," said the younger waiter.

"Good night," the other said. Turning off the electric light he continued the conversation with himself. It is the light of course, but it is necessary that the place be clean and pleasant. Certainly you do not want music. Nor can you stand before a bar with dignity although that is all that is provided for these hours. What did he fear? It was not fear or dread. It was a nothing that he knew too well. It was all a nothing and a man was nothing too. It was only that the light was all it needed and a certain cleanness and order. Some lived in it and never felt it but he knew it all was nada[11] y[12] pues[13] nada y nada y pues nada. *Our nada who art in nada, nada be thy name thy kingdom nada thy will be nada in nada as it is in nada. Give us this nada our daily nada and nada us our data as we nada our nadas and nada us not into nada but deliver us from nada; pues nada. Hail nothing full of nothing, nothing is with thee.*[14]

He smiled and stood before a bar with a shining steam pressure coffee machine.

He smiled and stood before a bar with a shining steam pressure coffee machine.

"What yours?" asked the barman.

"Nada."

"*Otro loco mas*[15]," said the barman and turned away.

"A little cup," said the waiter.

The barman poured it for him.

"The light is very bright and pleasant but the bar is unpolished," the waiter said.

The barman looked at him but did not answer. It was too late at night for conversation.

"You want another *copita*[16]?" the barman asked.

"No, thank you," said the waiter and went out. He disliked bars and bodegas. A clean, well-lighted cafe was a very different thing. Now, without thinking further, he would go home to his room. He would lie in the bed and finally, with daylight, he would go to sleep. After all, he said to himself, it was probably only insomnia. Many must have it.

Notes:

[1] (宵禁)卫兵会逮捕他的

[2] 如果他能得到他想要的东西,这又有什么关系呢? 这句暗示那个士兵想满足自己的欲望。

[3] 此句表现年轻侍者很不耐烦,有意将酒倒出杯子外。这一邋遢行为与后面年长侍者谈到老者的整洁、从不将酒洒出成对比。

[4] 为他的灵魂不能得救而担心。基督教认为自杀是一种犯罪,是对上帝行为的干涉。

[5] 年轻侍者认为这样一把年纪就是有妻子也没用。

[6] 比塞塔(西班牙货币单位)

[7] 晚一个小时又有什么关系呢?

[8] 对我比对他重要得多。

[9] 这是年长侍者开了个玩笑,暗示如果回家比平时早可能会撞见妻子偷情。

[10]（西班牙文）男人，老兄

[11]（西班牙文）nothing or nothingness

[12]（西班牙文）和，所以，那么

[13]（西班牙文）既然，那么。

[14]这一段模仿祷告词，表明一切事物和行为都是虚无。

[15]（西班牙文）又一个疯子。这句话表明以世人的标准来看，年长侍者的行为是"不正常"的。

[16]西班牙等地所产浅黄或深褐色葡萄酒。

Questions

1　Why did the old commit suicide?

2　What is the attitude of the young waiter toward the old man?

3　How did the attitude of the young waiter and the attitude of the middle-aged waiter form a sharp contrast?

4　Why did the old man choose a clean and well-lighted place to drink?

Analysis of *A Clean, Well-lighted Place*

We sympathize with the content. The plot of this novel is concise and legible. The story takes place in a cafe: "it was very late. Everyone had left the cafe except an old man who sat in the shadow, the leaves of the tree made against the electric light." These descriptions establish a kind of lonely tone which was unfolded by means of the dialogue between two waiters (one, young and full of energy, the other, old and feeble) revolve around the old man.

Some critics perceived that the theme accused the war: "the war not only destroyed a whole generation's dreams, but also aroused them to pursue the failure and death." Undoubtedly, these opinions, in various degrees, shed light on the understanding of the tale.

"He was desperate," "what about," "nothing," "how do you know it was nothing" and "he was plenty of money". The young waiter consider that "the more money you have, the more happiness you get". However, in fact, the rich old man has no happiness, even wants to kill himself. In society, many people always regard the money as the spring of happiness. Undeniably, we can't do many things without money. There are two things can satisfy us: substance and spirit. Money can only content our need for substance but not the spiritual need. The rich always lack of the satisfaction of spirit.

The poor old man maybe has a great family, enjoying family relationships and associating with many friends. At present, as the growing of age, love, friendly feeling and affection of family members dump him. While, the young waiter said, "I'm not lonely, I have a wife waiting in bed for me." Time takes away all the things the old man had before, and gives him an unique thing: friendless and wretched life. Human, as a member of the society, never like to be lonely. During several years, we often heard that many old men kill themselves because they can't suffer loneliness. The phenomenon becomes ordinary. In modern society, the children leave their hometown and go to strive for a bright future when they grow up and seldom go back home. On the other hand, the old people feel rather lonely because they are too old to strive. So, the old parents need more care from their children.

For us, to be young is greatest wealth, we can make many attempts. Even if we fail, we can say that we are young and we still have a lot of time. So, we are always full of confidence. While, as a result of age, the aged man has no energy to try new things, no time to do something they want have no qualifications to be confident. Others think so, and they think so, too.

A clean, well-lighted place seems like happy and serene. However, if we connect it with the blue tone, we are grieved. The old man escaped away from the ice-clod reality, self-satisfying in the imagined scene like the match girl absorbed in the hope of the firelight, but be continually cut in by the waiter. What the old man is suffering can not be understood by the youth.

The word "nothing" is repeated in this article. Some people think it expresses the world-weariness and nihility which lick up everything. Nihility which exists everywhere represents darkness, loneliness, hopeless, meaningless and rootless maze.

中文参考译文

第一单元　鲁宾逊漂流记　第四章

我的思想这时完全集中在怎样安全防御野人或者野兽。假如岛上有野人出现，或者有野兽出没的话。我想了许多方法，考虑造什么样的住所，还是在土里掘一个洞呢，还是在地上支一个帐篷呢？总之，我决定两个都做。至于什么样子，怎么作法，不妨在这里谈谈。

首先，我感到目前居住的地方不太合适。一则因离海太近，地势低湿，不大卫生；二则附近没有淡水。我得找一个比较卫生，比较方便的地方建造自己的住所。

我根据自己的情况，拟定了选择住所的几个条件：第一，必须如我上面所说的，要卫生，要有淡水；第二，要能遮阴；第三，要能避免猛兽或人类的突然袭击；第四，要能看到大海，万一上帝让什么船只经过，我就不至于失去脱险的机会，因为我始终存有一线希望，迟早能摆脱目前的困境。

我按上述条件去寻找一个合适的地点，发现在一个小山坡旁，有一片平地。小山靠平地的一边又陡又直，像一堵墙，不论人或野兽都无法从上面下来袭击我。在山岩上，有一块凹进去的地方，看上去好像是一个山洞的进口，但实际上里面并没有山洞。

在这山岩凹进去的地方，前面是一片平坦的草地，我决定就在此搭个帐篷。这块平地宽不过一百码，长不到二百码。

若把住所搭好，这块平坦的草地犹如一块草皮，从门前起伏连绵向外伸展形成一个缓坡，直至海边的那块低地。这儿正处小山西北偏北处，日间小山正好挡住阳光，当太阳转向西南方向照到这儿时，也就快要落下去了。

搭帐篷前，我先在石壁前面划了一个半圆形，半径约十码，直径有二十码。

沿这个半圆形，我插了两排结实的木桩；木桩打入泥土，仿佛像木橛子，大头朝下，高约五尺半，顶上都削得尖尖的。两排木桩之间的距离不到六英寸。然后，我用从船上截下来的那些缆索，沿着半圆形，一层一层地堆放在两排木桩之间，一直堆到顶上，再用一些两英尺半高的木桩插进去支撑住缆索，仿佛柱子上的横茬。这个篱笆十分结实牢固，不管是人还是野兽，都无法冲进来或攀越篱笆爬进来。这项工程，花了我不少时间和劳力，尤其是我得从树林里砍下粗枝做木桩，再运到草地上，又一一把它们打入泥土，这工作尤其费力费时。

至于住所的进出口，我没有在篱笆上做门，而是用一个短梯从篱笆顶上翻进来，进入里面后再收好梯子。这样，我四面都受保护，完全与外界隔绝，夜里就可高枕无忧了。不过，我后来发现，对我所担心的敌人，根本不必如此戒备森严。

我又花了极大的力气，把前面讲到的我的全部财产，全部粮食、弹药武器和补给品，一一搬到篱笆里面，或者可以说搬到这个堡垒里来。我又给自己搭了一个大帐篷用来防雨，因为这儿一年中有一个时期常下倾盆大雨。我把帐篷做成双层的；也就是说，里面一个小的，外面再罩一个大的，大帐篷上面又盖上一大块油布。那油布当然也是我在船上搜集帆布时一起拿下来的。

现在我不再睡在搬上岸的那张床上了，而是睡在一张吊床上，这吊床原是船上大副所有，质地很好。

我把粮食和一切可能受潮损坏的东西都搬进了帐篷。完成这工作后，就把篱笆的出入口堵起来。此后，我就像上面所说，用一个短梯翻越篱笆进出。

做完这些工作后，我又开始在岩壁上打洞，把挖出来的土石方从帐篷里运到外面，沿篱笆堆成一个平台，约一英尺高。这样，帐篷算是我的住房，房后的山洞就成了我的地窖。

这些工作既费时又费力，但总算一一完成了。现在，我再回头追述一下其他几件使我煞费苦心的事情。在我计划搭帐篷打岩洞的同时，突然乌云密布，暴雨如注，雷电交加。在电光一闪，霹雳突至时，一个思想也像闪电一样掠过我的头脑，使我比对闪电本身更吃惊："哎哟，我的火药啊！"想到一个霹雳就会把我的火药全部炸毁时，我几乎完全绝望了。因为我不仅要靠火药自卫，还得靠其猎取食物为生。当时，我只想到火药，而没有想到火药一旦爆炸自己也就完了。假如真的火药爆炸，我自己都不知道死在谁的手里呢。

这场暴风雨使我心有余悸。因此，我把所有其他工作，包括搭帐篷、筑篱笆等都先丢在一边。等雨一停，我立刻着手做一些小袋子和匣子，把火药分成许许多多小包。这样，万一发生什么情况，也不致全部炸毁。我把一包包的火药分开贮藏起来，免得一包着火危及另一包。这件工作我足足费了两个星期的时间。火药大约有二百四十磅，我把它们分成一百多包。至于那桶受潮的火药，我倒并不担心会发生什么危险，所以我就把它放到新开的山洞里；我把这山洞戏称为我的厨房，其余的火药我都藏在石头缝里，以免受潮，并在储藏的地方小心地做上记号。

在包装和储藏火药的两星期中，我至少每天带枪出门一次。这样做可以达到三个目的：一来可以散散心；二来可以猎获点什么东西吃；三来也可以了解一下岛上的物产。第一次外出，我便发现岛上有不少山羊，使我十分满意。可我也发现这于我来说并非是件大好事。因为这些山羊胆小而又狡猾，而且跑得飞快，实在很难靠近它们。但我并不灰心，我相信总有办法打到一只的。不久我真的打死了一只。我首先发现了山羊经常出没之地，就采用打埋伏的办法来获取我的猎物。我注意到，如果我在山谷里，哪怕它们在山岩上，它们也准会惊恐地逃窜；但若它们在山谷里吃草，而我站在山岩上，它们就不会注意到我。我想，这是由于小羊眼睛生的部位，使它们只能向下看，而不容易看到上面的东西吧。因此，我就先爬到山上，从上面打下去，往往很容易打中。我第一次开枪，打死了一只正在哺小羊的母羊，使我心里非常难过。母羊倒下后，小羊呆呆地站在它身旁；当我背起母羊往回走时，那小羊也跟着我一直走到围墙外面。于是我放下母羊，抱起小羊，进入木栅，一心想把它驯养大。可是小山羊就是不肯吃东西，没有办法，我只好把它也杀了吃了。这两只一大一小的山羊肉，供我吃了好长一段时间，因为我吃得很省，我要尽量节省粮食，尤其是面包。

住所建造好了，我就想到必须要有一个生火的地方，还得准备些柴来烧。至于我怎样做这件事，怎样扩大石洞，又怎样创造其他一些生活条件，我想以后在适当的时候再详谈。

现在想先略微谈谈自己，谈谈自己对生活的看法。在这些方面，你们可以想象，确实有不少感触可以谈的。

我感到自己前景暗淡。因为，我被凶猛的风暴刮到这荒岛上，远离原定的航线，远离人类正常的贸易航线有数百海里之遥。我想，这完全是出于天意，让我孤苦伶仃，在凄凉中了却余生了。想到这些，我眼泪不禁夺眶而出。有时我不禁犯疑，苍天为什么要这样作践自己所创造的生灵，害得他如此不幸，如此孤立无援，又如此沮丧寂寞呢！在这样的环境中，有什么理由要我们认为生活于我们是一种恩赐呢？

可是，每当我这样想的时候，立刻又有另一种思想出现在我的脑海里，并责怪我不应有上述这些念头。特别有一天，当我正带枪在海边漫步时，我思考着自己目前的处境。这时，理智从另一方面劝慰我："的确，你目前形单影只，孑然一身，这是事实。可是，你不想想，你的那些同伴呢？他们到哪儿去了？你们一同上船时，不是有十一个人吗？那么，其他十个人到哪儿去了呢？为什么他们死了，唯独留下你一个人还活着呢？是在这孤岛上强呢，还是到他们那儿去好呢？"说到去他们那儿时，我用手指了指大海——"他们都已葬身大海了！真是，我怎么不想想祸福相倚和祸不单行的道理呢？"这时，我又想到，我目前所拥有的一切，殷实充裕，足以维持温饱。要是那只大船不从触礁的地方浮起来漂近海岸，并让我有时间从船上把一切有用的东西取下来，那我现在的处境又会怎样呢？要知道，像我现在的这种机遇，真是千载难逢的。假如我现在仍像我初上岸时那样一无所有；既没有任何生活必需品，也没有任何可以制造生活必需品的工具，那我现在的情况又会怎么样呢？"尤其是，"我大声对自己说，"如果我没有枪，没有弹药，没有制造东西的工具，没有衣服穿，没有床睡觉，没有帐篷住，甚至没有任何东西可以遮身，我又该怎么办呢？"可是现在，这些东西我都有，而且相当充足，即使以后弹药用尽了，不用枪我也能活下去。我相信，我这一生决不会受冻挨饿，因为我早就考虑到各种意外，考虑到将来的日子；不但考虑到弹药用尽之后的情况，甚至想到我将来体衰力竭之后的日子。

我得承认，在考虑这些问题时，并未想到火药会被雷电一下子炸毁的危险；因此雷电交加之际，忽然想到这个危险，着实使我惊恐万状。这件事我前面已叙述过了。

现在，我要开始过一种寂寞而又忧郁的生活了；这种生活也许在这世界上是前所未闻的。因此，我决定把我生活的情况从头至尾，按时间顺序一一记录下来。我估计，我是九月三十日踏上这可怕的海岛的；当时刚入秋分，太阳差不多正在我头顶上。所以，据我观察，我在北纬九度二十二分的地方。

上岛后约十一二天，我忽然想到，我没有书、笔和墨水，一定会忘记计算日期，甚至连安息日和工作日都会忘记。为了防止发生这种情况，我便用刀子在一根大柱子上用大写字母刻上以下这句话："我于一六五九年九月三十日在此上岸。"我把柱子做成一个大十字架，立在我第一次上岸的地方。

（郭建中　译）

第二单元　格列佛游记　第四部分　第六章

[再谈女王统治下的英国——欧洲宫廷中一位首相大臣的性格。]

　　我的主人还是完全不能明白这一帮律师为什么仅仅为了迫害自己的同类而不厌其烦地组织这么一个不义的组织？他们究竟有什么目的呢？它也搞不明白我说他们干这事是受人之雇究竟又是怎么回事。于是我又只好不厌其烦向它说明钱的作用。解释钱是由哪些材料制成的，各种不同金属的价值如何。我对它说，当一只"野胡"储有大量这样的贵重物质时，它想买什么就都能买到，比如最好的衣服、最华丽的房屋以及大片的土地，最昂贵的肉食和酒类，还可以挑选到最漂亮的女人。所以，既然金钱一项就能建立这种种功劳，我们的"野胡"就认为，不论是用钱还是储蓄，钱总是越多越好，永远也不会有满足的时候，因为他们发现自己天性就是这样，不是挥霍浪费就是贪得无厌。富人享受着穷人的劳动成果，而穷人和富人在数量上的比例是一千比一。我们的大多数人民被迫过悲惨的日子，为了一点点报酬每天都得辛苦劳作，为的是能让少数人过富裕的生活。我在这些问题以及许多别的类似的细节上谈了很多，可土人阁下还要往下问，因为它是这样推想的：地球上出产的东西，所有动物都有权享受一份，尤其是主宰其他动物的统治者更有享受的权利。因此它要我告诉它，那些昂贵的肉食到底是些什么肉？我们怎么偏偏就吃不到？我于是就把能想得到的各种肉类一一列举出来，同时还列举了各种不同的烹调的方法；如果不是派船只航海到世界各地去采办酒类、调料以及数不清的其他食品，这一切是办不到的。我对他讲，给我们的一只境况较好的雌"野胡"做一顿早餐或者弄一只盛早餐的杯子，至少得绕地球转三圈才能办到。它说，一个国家连自己居民的饭都供不起，肯定是个悲惨的国家。但更使它感到奇怪的是，在像我描述的这么大片的土地上怎么竟然完全没有淡水，人们必须到海外去弄饮料？我回答说，英国（那是我亲爱的出生地）生产的粮食据估算是那里居民消费需求的三倍；从谷物和某种树木的果实中提取或榨取的液体可制成极好的饮料，它们和每一样别的日常用品一样，也都是居民消费需求的三倍。但是，为了满足男人的奢侈无度和女人的虚荣，我们都把绝大部分的必需品送到国外去，而由此换回疾病、愚蠢、罪恶的材料供自己消费。于是我们大多数人民就没有生存的依靠，只好靠讨饭、抢劫、偷窃、欺骗、拉皮条、作伪证、谄媚、教唆、伪造、赌博、说谎、奉承、威吓、搞选举、胡写文章、星象占卜、放毒、卖淫、侈谈、诽谤、想入非非以及各种相似的事来糊口过日子。这其中的每一个名词我都费了不少劲来解释，最后它终于明白了。

我又说，我们从国外进口酒类倒并不是因为我们缺少淡水或其他饮料，而是因为酒是一种喝了可以使人麻木而让人高兴的液体；它可以消遣我们所有的忧愁，在脑海中唤起狂野奔放的想象，增加希望，驱除恐惧，使每一点理智暂时都失去效用，四肢不能运动，直到我们昏睡过去。可是我们必须承认，一觉醒来总是精神萎靡，而总喝这种流体只会给我们带来种种疾病，使我们的生命痛苦而短暂。

然而除了所有这一切之外，我们的大多数人民还得靠向富人提供日常必需品或者互相之间提供这些东西来维持自己的生活。比如我在家的时候，身上穿得像模像样，那一身衣服就是一百名工匠的手艺；我的房子和房子里的家具也同样需要这么多人来制造，而把我的妻子打扮一下，则需要五百名工匠付出劳动。

接下来我又跟他谈到另一类人，他们是靠侍候病人来维持生活的，我在前面也曾有几次跟主人说过，我船上有许多水手就是因生病才死的。可是我真是费了九牛二虎之力才使它明白了我的意思。一个"慧骃"在临死前几天会慢慢变得衰弱无力、行动迟缓，或者遇上什么意外会弄伤一条腿，这它都是很容易就能理解的。可是，为什么大自然将万事万物都创造得非常完美，竟会让我们的身体遭受痛苦？它不相信这些，所以它就想知道如此不可解释的灾难，究竟是什么原因呢？我就对它说，我们吃的东西不下千种，吃下去却互不相容；还有，我们肚子不饿却还要吃，嘴巴不渴却只管喝；通宵达旦坐在那儿喝烈性酒，东西却不吃一点儿，喝得人慵懒松散，身体发烧，不是消化太快就是无法消化。卖淫的女"野胡"身上有一种病，谁要是投进她们的怀抱就得烂骨头，而这种病和许多别的病一样，都是遗传的，所以许多人生到这个世上来，身上就已经带有种种复杂的疾病了。要是把人身上的所有疾病全都讲给它听，一时真还说不完，因为这些病不下五六百种，人的四肢和每一个关节——总之，身体的每一部分都各有毛病。为了治疗这些疾病，我们中间就培养了一类专以治病为业的人，不过也有冒充的。因为我在这一行上有点本事，为了感谢主人对我的恩德，我愿意把那些人行医的秘密和方法全都说给它听。

　　但是，除了这些真正的疾病之外我们还会生许多仅仅是空想的病，对此医生们则发明了空想的治疗的方法；这些病各有其不同的名称，并且也有对症的药品。我们的女"野胡"们就老是会染上这样的空想病。

　　这帮人有超人的本事，他们能预测病症的后果，这方面难得会弄错。真正的疾病症状恶化，通常死亡就在眼前了，没有办法治好，那他们的预言就总是有把握的。所以，要是他们已经宣判了病的死刑，而病人却出乎意料地渐有好转的迹象，他们也不会就这样任人去骂他们是骗子；他们知道如何及时地给病人用上一剂药就可以向世人证明，他们还是有先见之明的。

　　对自己的配偶已感到厌倦的丈夫或妻子，对长子。大臣，而尤其是对君王，他们也都有特别的用处。我前面已经跟我的主人谈过政府的一般性质，特别是我们那优越的宪法，那真是值得全世界赞叹和羡慕的。这里我又偶然提到了大臣这个词，它就要我下面跟它说说，我所称的"大臣"到底是一种什么样的"野胡"。

　　我说，我要描述的这位首相大臣是这样一个人：他整个儿是哀乐无动于衷、爱恨不明、不同情不动怒；至少你可以说，他除了对财富、权力和爵位有强烈的欲望外，别的一概不动感情。他说的话当什么用都可以，就是不表明他的心。他每说一句实话，却总要想你会把它当成谎言，而每次说谎又都以为你会信以为真。那些被他在背后说得一塌糊涂的人，实际上是他最喜欢的人，而每当他向别人或当你的面夸奖你时，从那天起你就要倒霉。最糟糕的标志是你得到了他的一个许诺，如果他在向你许诺时还发了誓，那就更为糟糕；他这么做，每一个聪明人都会自行引退，一切希望全都放弃。

　　一个人可以通过三种办法爬上首相大臣的位置。第一，要知道怎样以比较慎重的方式出卖自己的妻女和姐妹；第二，背叛或者暗杀前任首相大臣；第三，在公开集会上慷慨激昂地抨击朝廷的各种腐败。但是英明的君王一定愿意挑选惯于采用第三种办法的人，因为事实证明，那些慷慨激昂的人总是最能顺从其主子的旨意和爱好。这些大臣一旦控制了所有的要职，就会贿赂元老院或者大枢密院中的大多数人，以此来保全自己的势力。最后，他们还借一种"免罚法"（我向它说明了这条法令的性质）以保证自己事后免遭不测，满载着从国民身上贪污来的赃物从公职上悄然引退下来。

　　首相官邸是他培养同伙的学校。他的随从、仆人和看门人通过效仿其主子，也都在各自的区域内作起大官来。他们向主人学习蛮横、说谎和贿赂这三种主要本领而能更胜一筹，于是他们也就有了自己的小朝廷，受到贵族的奉承。有时他们还靠机巧和无耻，一步步往上爬，终于做上了他们老爷的继承人。

首相大臣往往受制于色衰的荡妇或者自己的亲信仆人，趋炎附势、企求恩宠的人都得通过这个渠道，所以说到底，讲他们是王国的统治者，倒是很恰当的。

有一天，我的主人听我谈到我国的贵族，它倒是说了我一句好话，不过我是不敢当。它说，它敢肯定我是出身于贵族家庭，因为我模样好，肤色白，身上干净，这几方面都远远超过它们国内所有的"野胡"；虽然我似乎不及它们那样身强力壮、动作敏捷，可那是因为我的生活方式与那些通讯畜生完全不一样。除此之外，我不但具有说话的能力，而且还有几分理性，以致它所有的相识都认为我是一个难得的人才。

它叫我注意，"慧骃"中的白马、栗色马和铁青马样子长得跟火红马、深灰色斑纹马和黑马并不完全一样，这是天生的，也没有变好的可能，所以它们永远处在仆人的地位。它们如果妄想出人头地，那样的话，在这个国家中就要被认为是一件可怕而反常的事。

我的主人十分看重我，对此我向它表示万分的感激；不过我同时又告诉它，我其实出身低微，父母都是普普通通的老百姓，只能供我接受一些还说得过去的教育。我说我们那里的贵族可跟它想象的完全不一样；我们的年轻贵族从孩子时代起就过着游手好闲、奢侈豪华的生活；一到成年，他们就在淫荡的女人中鬼混，消耗精力，并染上一身恶病；等到自己的财产所剩无几时，就娶一个出身卑贱、脾气乖戾而身体还不好的女人做妻子，那只是因为她有几个钱，其实他对这女人是既恨又瞧不起。这种婚姻的产物，生下来的孩子通常不是患瘰疬病、佝偻病、就是残废。做妻子的如果不注意在邻居或佣人中给她的孩子找一个身体强健的父亲以改良品种传宗接代的话，那这家人一般是传不到三代就要断子绝孙。身体虚弱多病，面貌瘦削苍白，是一个常见贵族的标志。健康强壮的外表在一位贵族看来反倒是一种极大的耻辱，因为世人会认为他真正的父亲一定是个马夫或者车夫。他的头脑也和他的身体一样大有缺陷，那是古怪、迟钝、无知、任性、荒淫和傲慢的合成品。

不得到这一帮贵族的同意，任何法令都不能颁布，既不能废除，也不能修改。这些贵族还对我们所有的财产拥有决定权，而不用征求我们的意见。

（林纾　译）

第三单元　傲慢与偏见　第一章

凡是有钱的单身汉，总想娶位太太，这已经成了一条举世公认的真理。这样的单身汉，每逢新搬到一个地方，四邻八舍虽然完全不了解他的性情如何，见解如何，可是，既然这样的一条真理早已在人们心目中根深蒂固，因此人们总是把他看作自己某一个女儿理所应得的一笔财产。

有一天班纳特太太对她的丈夫说："我的好老爷，尼日斐花园终于租出去了，你听说过没有？"

班纳特先生回答道，他没有听说过。

"的确租出去了，"她说，"朗格太太刚刚上这儿来过，她把这件事的底细一五一十地告诉了我。"

班纳特先生没有理睬她。

"你难道不想知道是谁租去的吗？"太太不耐烦地嚷起来了。

"既是你要说给我听，我听听也无妨。"

这句话足够鼓励她讲下去了。

"哦！亲爱的，你得知道，郎格太太说，租尼日斐花园的是个阔少爷，他是英格兰北部的人；听说他星期一那天，乘着一辆驷马大轿车来看房子，看得非常中意，当场就和莫理斯先生谈妥了；他要在'米迦勒节'以前搬进来，打算下个周末先叫几个佣人来住。"

"这个人叫什么名字？"

"彬格莱。"

"有太太的呢，还是单身汉？"

"噢！是个单身汉，亲爱的，确确实实是个单身汉！一个有钱的单身汉；每年有四五千磅的收入。真是女儿们的福气！"

"这怎么说？关女儿们什么事？"

"我的好老爷，"太太回答道，"你怎么这样叫人讨厌！告诉你吧，我正在盘算，他要是挑中我们一个女儿做老婆，可多好！"

"他住到这儿来，就是为了这个打算吗？"

"打算！胡扯，这是哪儿的话！不过，他倒作兴看中我们的某一个女儿呢。他一搬来，你就得去拜访拜访他。"

"我不用去。你带着女儿们去就得啦，要不你干脆打发她们自己去，那或许倒更好些，因为你跟女儿们比起来，她们哪一个都不能胜过你的美貌，你去了，彬格莱先生倒可能挑中你呢？"

"我的好老爷，你太捧我啦。从前也的确有人赞赏过我的美貌，现在我可有敢说有什么出众的地方了。一个女人家有了五个成年的女儿，就不该对自己的美貌再转什么念头。"

"这样看来，一个女人家对自己的美貌也转不了多少念头喽。"

"不过，我的好老爷，彬格莱一搬到我们的邻近来，你的确应该去看看他。"

"老实跟你说吧，这不是我分内的事。"

"看女儿的份上吧。只请你想一想，她们不论哪一个，要是攀上了这样一个人家，够多么好。威廉爵士夫妇已经决定去拜望他，他们也无非是这个用意。你知道，他们通常是不会拜望新搬来的邻居的。你的确应该去一次，要是你不去，叫我们怎么去。"

"你实在过分心思啦。彬格莱先生一定高兴看到你的；我可以写封信给你带去，就说随便他挑中我哪一个女儿，我都心甘情愿地答应他把她娶过去；不过，我在信上得特别替小丽莎吹嘘几句。"

"我希望你别这么做。丽莎没有一点儿地方胜过别的几个女儿；我敢说，论漂亮，她抵不上吉英一半；论性子，她抵不上丽迪雅一半。你可老是偏爱她。""她们没有哪一个值得夸奖的，"他回答道；"他们跟人家的姑娘一样，又傻，又无知；倒是丽莎要比她的几个姐妹伶俐些。"

"我的好老爷，你怎么舍得这样糟蹋自己的亲生女儿？你是在故意叫我气恼，好让你自己得意吧。你半点儿也不体谅我的神经衰弱。"

"你真错怪了我，我的好太太。我非常尊重你的神经。它们是我的老朋友。至少在最近二十年以来，我一直听到你郑重其事地提到它们。"

"啊！你不知道我怎样受苦呢！"

"不过我希望你这毛病会好起来，那么，像这种每年有四千镑收入的阔少爷，你就可以眼看着他们一个个搬来做你的邻居了。"

"你既然不愿意去拜访他们，即使有二十个搬了来，对我们又有什么好处！"

"放心吧，我的好太太，等到有了二十个，我一定去一个个拜望到。"

班纳特先生真是个古怪人，他一方面喜欢插科打诨，爱挖苦人，同时又不苟言笑，变幻莫测，真使他那位太太积二十三年之经验，还摸不透他的性格。太太的脑子是很容易加以分析的。她是个智力贫乏、不学无术、喜怒无常的女人，只要碰到不称心的事，她就以为神经衰弱。她生平的大事就是嫁女儿；她生平的安慰就是访友拜客和打听新闻。

（张玲　张扬　译）

第四单元 简·爱 第三十七章（节选）

第二天一早，我听见他起来走动了，从一个房间摸到另一个房间。玛丽一下楼，我就听见他问："爱小姐在这儿吗？"接着又问："你把她安排在哪一间？里面干燥吗？她起来了吗？去问问是不是需要什么，什么时候下来？"

我一想到还有一顿早餐，便下楼去了。我轻手轻脚进了房间，他还没有发现我，我就已瞧见他了。说实在目睹那么生龙活虎的人沦为一个恹恹的弱者，真让人心酸。他坐在椅子上——虽然一动不动，却并不安分，显然在企盼着。如今，习惯性的愁容，已镌刻在他富有特色的脸庞上。他的面容令人想起一盏熄灭了的灯，等待着再度点亮——唉！现在他自己已无力恢复生气勃勃、光彩照人的表情了，不得不依赖他人来完成。我本想显得高高兴兴、无忧无虑，但是这个强者那么无能为力的样子，使我心碎了。不过我还是尽可能轻松愉快地跟他打了招呼：

"是个明亮晴朗的早晨呢，先生，"我说。"雨过天晴，你很快可以去走走了。"

我已唤醒了那道亮光，他顿时容光焕发了。

"呵，你真的还在，我的云雀！上我这儿来。你没有走，没有飞得无影无踪呀？一小时之前，我听见你的一个同类在高高的树林里歌唱，可是对我来说，它的歌声没有音乐，就像初升的太阳没有光芒。凡我能听到的世间美妙的音乐，都集中在简的舌头上，凡我能感受到的阳光，都全聚在她身上。"

听完他表示对别人的依赖，我不禁热泪盈眶。他仿佛是被链条锁在栖木上的一头巨鹰，竟不得不企求一只麻雀为它觅食。不过，我不喜欢哭哭啼啼，抹掉带咸味的眼泪，便忙着去准备早餐了。

大半个早上是在户外度过的。我领着他走出潮湿荒凉的林子，到了令人心旷怡艳的田野。我向他描绘田野多么苍翠耀眼，花朵和树篱多么生机盎然，天空又多么湛蓝闪亮。我在一个隐蔽可爱的地方，替他找了个座位，那是一个干枯的树桩。坐定以后，我没有拒绝他把我放到他膝头上。既然他和我都觉得紧挨着比分开更愉快，那我又何必要拒绝呢？派洛特躺在我们旁边，四周一片寂静。他正把我紧紧地搂在怀里时突然嚷道：

"狠心呀，狠心的逃跑者！呵，简，我发现你出走桑菲尔德，而又到处找不着你，细看了你的房间，断定你没有带钱，或者能换钱的东西，我心里是多么难受呀！我送你的一根珍珠项链，原封不动地留在小盒子里。你的箱子捆好了上了锁，像原先准备结婚旅行时一样。我自问，我的宝贝成了穷光蛋，身上一个子儿也没有，她该怎么办呢？她干了些什么呀？现在讲给我听听吧。"

于是在他的敦促之下，我开始叙述去年的经历了。我大大淡化了三天的流浪和挨饿的情景，因为把什么都告诉他，只会增加他不必要的痛苦。但是我确实告诉他的一丁点儿，也撕碎了他那颗忠实的心，其严重程度超出了我的预料。

他说，我不应该两手空空地离开他，我应该把我的想法跟他说说。我应当同他推心置腹，他决不会强迫我做他的情妇。尽管他绝望时性情暴烈，但事实上，他爱我至深至亲，绝不会变成我的暴君。与其让我把自己举目无亲地抛向茫茫人世，他宁愿送我一半财产，而连吻一下作为回报的要求都不提。他确信，我所忍受的比我说给他听的要严重得多。

"嗯，我受的苦不多，时间都不长。"我回答。随后我告诉他如何被接纳进沼泽居；如何得到教师的职位，以及获得财产，发现亲戚等，按时间顺序，——叙述。当然随着故事的进展，圣·约翰·里弗斯的名字频频出现。我一讲完自己的经历，这个名字便立即被提出来了。

"那么，这位圣·约翰是你的表兄了？"

"是的，"

"你常常提到他，你喜欢他吗？"

"他是个大好人，先生，我不能不喜欢他。"

"一个好人？那意思是不是一个体面而品行好的五十岁男人？不然那是什么意思？"

"圣·约翰只有二十九岁，先生。"

"Jeune encore，"就像法国人说的。"他是个矮小、冷淡、平庸的人吗？是不是那种长处在于没有过错，而不是德行出众的人？"

"他十分活跃，不知疲倦，他活着就是要成就伟大崇高的事业。"

"但他的头脑呢？大概比较软弱吧？他本意很好，但听他谈话你会耸肩。"

"他说话不多，先生。但一开口总是一语中的。我想他的头脑是一流的，不易打动，却十分活跃。"

"那么他很能干了?"

"确实很能干。"

"一个受过良好教育的人?"

"圣·约翰是一个造诣很深、学识渊博的学者。"

"他的风度,我想你说过,不合你的口味?" "——一本正经,一副牧师腔调。"

"我从来没有提起过他的风度。但除非我的口味很差,不然是很合意的。他的风度优雅、沉着,一副绅士派头,"

"他的外表——我忘了你是怎么样描述他的外表的了——那种没有经验的副牧师,扎着白领巾,弄得气都透不过来;穿着厚底高帮靴,顶得像踩高跷似的,是吧?"

"圣·约翰衣冠楚楚,是个漂亮的男子,高个子,白皮肤,蓝眼睛,鼻梁笔挺。"

(旁白)"见他的鬼!——"(转向我)"你喜欢他吗,简?"

"是的,罗切斯特先生,我喜欢他。不过你以前问过我了。"

当然,我觉察出了说话人的用意。妒忌已经攫住了他,刺痛着他。这是有益于身心的,让他暂时免受忧郁的咬啮。因此我不想立刻降服嫉妒这条毒蛇。

"也许你不愿意在我膝头上坐下去了,爱小姐?"接着便是这有些出乎意料的话。

"为什么不愿意呢,罗切斯特先生?"

"你刚才所描绘的图画,暗示了一种过分强烈的对比。你的话已经巧妙地勾勒出了一个漂亮的阿波罗。他出现在你的想象之中,——'高个子,白皮肤,蓝眼睛,笔挺的鼻梁。'而你眼下看到的是一个火神——一个道地的铁匠,褐色的皮肤,宽阔的肩膀,瞎了眼睛,又瘸了腿。"

"我以前可从来没有想到过这点,不过你确实像个火神,先生?"

"好吧——你可以离开我了,小姐。但你走之前(他把我搂得更紧了),请你回答我一两个问题。"他顿了一下。

"什么问题,罗切斯特先生?"

接踵而来的便是这番盘问:

"圣·约翰还不知道你是他表妹,就让你做莫尔顿学校的教师?"

"是的。"

"你常常见到他吗？他有时候来学校看看吗？"

"每天如此。"

"他赞同你的计划吗，简？——我知道这些计划很巧妙，因为你是一个有才干的家伙。"

"是的，——他赞同了。"

"他会在你身上发现很多预料不到的东西，是吗？你身上的某些才艺不同寻常。"

"这我不知道。"

"你说你的小屋靠近学校，他来看你过吗？"

"不时来。"

"晚上来吗？"

"来过一两次。"

他停顿了一下。

"你们彼此的表兄妹关系发现后，你同他和他妹妹们又住了多久？"

"五个月。"

"里弗斯同家里的女士们在一起的时候很多吗？"

"是的，后客厅既是他的书房，也是我们的书房。他坐在窗边，我们坐在桌旁。"

"他书读得很多吗？"

"很多。"

"读什么？"

"印度斯坦语。"

"那时候你干什么呢？"

"起初学德语。"

"他教你吗？"

"他不懂德语。"

"他什么也没有教你吗？"

"教了一点儿印度斯坦语。"

"里弗斯教你印度斯坦语？"

"是的，先生。"

"也教他的妹妹们吗？"

"没有。"

"光教你？"

"光教我。"

"是你要求他教的吗？"

"没有。"

"他希望教你？"

"是的。"

他又停顿了一下。

"他为什么希望教你？印度斯坦语对你会有什么用处？"

"他要我同他一起去印度。"

"呵！这下我触到要害了。他要你嫁给他吗？"

"他求我嫁给他。"

"那是虚构的——胡编乱造来气气我。"

"请你原谅，这是千真万确的事实。他不止一次地向我求婚，而且在这点上像你一样寸步不让。"

"爱小姐，我再说一遍，你可以离开我了。这句话我说过多少次了？我已经通知你可以走了，为什么硬赖在我膝头上？"

"因为在这儿很舒服。"

"不，简，你在这儿不舒服，因为你的心不在我这里，而在你的这位表兄，圣·约翰那里了，呵，在这之前，我以为我的小简全属于我的，相信她就是离开我了也还是爱我的，这成了无尽的苦涩中的一丝甜味，尽管我们别了很久，尽管我因为别离而热泪涟涟，我从来没有料到，我为她悲悲泣泣的时候，她却爱着另外一个人！不过，心里难过也毫无用处，简，走吧，去嫁给里弗斯吧！"

"那么，甩掉我吧，先生，一把推开我，因为我可不愿意自己离开你。"

"简，我一直喜欢你说话的声调，它仍然唤起新的希望，它听起来又那么真诚。我一听到它，便又回到了一年之前。我忘了你结识了新的关系。不过我不是傻瓜——走吧——。"

"我得上哪儿去呢，先生？"

"随你自己便吧——上你看中的丈夫那儿去。"

"谁呀？"

"你知道——这个圣·约翰·里弗斯。"

"他不是我丈夫，也永远不会是，他不爱我，我也不爱他。他爱（他可以爱，跟你的爱不同）一个名叫罗莎蒙德的年轻漂亮小姐。他要娶我只是由于以为我配当一个传教士的妻子，其实我是不行的。他不错，也很了不起，但十分冷峻，对我来说冷同冰山一般冷。他跟你不一样，先生。在他身边，接近他，或者同他在一起，我都不会愉快。他没有迷恋我——没有溺爱我。在我身上，他看不到吸引人的地方，连青春都看不到——他所看到的只不过心理上的几个有用之处罢了。那么，先生，我得离开你上他那儿去了？"

我不由自主地哆嗦了一下，本能地把我亲爱的瞎眼主人搂得更紧了。他微微一笑。

"什么，简！这是真的吗？这真是你与里弗斯之间的情况吗？"

"绝对如此，先生。呵，你不必嫉妒！我想逗你一下让你少伤心些。我认为愤怒比忧伤要好。不过要是你希望我爱你，你就只要瞧一瞧我确实多么爱你，你就会自豪和满足了。我的整个心儿是你的，先生，它属于你，即使命运让我身体的其余部分永远同你分离，我的心也会依然跟你在一起。"

他吻我的时候，痛苦的想法使他的脸又变得阴沉了。

"我烧毁了的视力！我伤残了的体力！"他遗憾地咕哝着。

我抚摸着他给他以安慰。我知道他心里想些什么，并想替他说出来，但我又不敢。他的脸转开的一刹那，我看到一滴眼泪从封闭着的眼睑滑下来，流到了富有男子气的脸颊上。我的心膨胀起来了。

"我并不比桑菲尔德果园那棵遭雷击的老栗子树好多少，"没有过多久他说。"那些残枝，有什么权利吩咐一棵爆出新芽的忍冬花以自己的鲜艳来掩盖它的腐朽呢？"

"你不是残枝，先生——不是遭雷击的树。你碧绿而苗壮。不管你求不求，花草会在你根子周围长出来，因为它们乐于躲在你慷慨的树荫下。长大了它们会偎依着你，缠绕着你，因为你的力量给了它们可靠的支撑。"

他再次笑了起来，我又给了他安慰。

"你说的是朋友吗，简？"他问。

"是的，是朋友，"我迟迟疑疑地回答。我知道我的意思超出了朋友，但无法判断要用什么字。他帮了我忙。

"呵？简。可是我需要一个妻子。"

"是吗，先生？"

"是的，对你来说是桩新闻吗？"

"当然，先前你对此什么也没说。"

"是一桩不受欢迎的新闻？"

"那就要看情况了，先生——要看你的选择。"

"你替我选择吧，简。我会遵从你的决定。"

"先生，那就挑选最爱你的人。"

"我至少会选择我最爱的人，简。你肯嫁给我吗？"

"肯的，先生。"

"一个可怜的瞎子，你得牵着手领他走的人。"

"是的，先生。"

"一个比你大二十岁的瘸子，你得侍候他的人。"

"是的，先生。"

"当真，简？"

"完全当真，先生。"

"呵，我的宝贝？愿上帝祝福你，报答你！"

"罗切斯特先生，如果我平生做过一件好事——如果我有过一个好的想法——如果我做过一个真诚而没有过错的祷告——如果我曾有过一个正当的心愿——那么现在我得到了酬报。对我来说，做你的妻子是世上最愉快的事了。"

"因为你乐意做出牺牲。"

"牺牲！我牺牲了什么啦？牺牲饥饿而得到食品，牺牲期待而得到满足。享受特权搂抱我珍重的人——亲吻我热爱的人——寄希望于我信赖的人。那能叫牺牲吗？如果说这是牺牲，那当然乐于做出牺牲了。"

"还要忍受我的体弱，简，无视我的缺陷。"

"我毫不在乎，先生。现在我确实对你有所帮助了，所以比起当初你能自豪地独立自主，除了施主与保护人，把什么都不放在眼里时，要更爱你了。"

"我向来讨厌要人帮助——要人领着，但从今起我觉得我不再讨厌了。我不喜欢把手放在雇工的手里，但让简的小小的指头挽着，却很愉快。我不喜欢佣人不停地服侍我，而喜欢绝对孤独。但是简温柔体贴的照应却永远是一种享受。简适合我，而我适合她吗？"

"你与我的天性丝丝入扣。"

"既然如此，就根本没有什么好等的了，我们得马上结婚。"

他的神态和说话都很急切，他焦躁的老脾气又发作了。

"我们必须毫不迟疑地化为一体了，简。只剩下把证书拿到手——随后我们就结婚——"

"罗切斯特先生，我刚发现，日色西斜，太阳早过了子午线。派洛特实际上已经回家去吃饭了，让我看看你的手表。"

"把它别在你腰带上吧，珍妮特，今后你就留着，反正我用不上。"

"差不多下午四点了，先生。你不感到饿吗？"

"从今天算起第三天，该是我们举行婚礼的日子了，简。现在，别去管豪华衣装和金银首饰了，这些东西都一钱不值。"

"太阳已经晒干了雨露，先生。微风止了，气候很热。"

"你知道吗，简，此刻在领带下面青铜色的脖子上，我戴着你小小的珍珠项链。自从失去仅有的宝贝那天起，我就戴上它了，作为对她的怀念。"

"我们穿过林子回家吧，这条路最荫凉。"

他顺着自己的思路去想，没有理会我。

"简！我想，你以为我是一条不敬神的狗吧，可是这会儿我对世间仁慈的上帝满怀感激之情。他看事物跟人不一样，要清楚得多；他判断事物跟人不一样，而要明智得多。我做错了，我会玷污清白的花朵——把罪孽带给无辜，要不是上帝把它从我这儿抢走的话。我倔强地对抗，险些儿咒骂这种处置方式，我不是俯首听命，而是全不放在眼里。神的审判照旧进行，大祸频频临头。我被迫走过死阴的幽谷，"他的惩罚十分严厉，其中一次惩罚是使我永远甘于谦卑。你知道我曾对自己的力量非常自傲，但如今它算得了什么呢？我不得不依靠他人的指引，就像孩子的孱弱一样。最近，简——只不过是最近——我在厄运中开始看到并承认上帝之手。我开始自责和忏悔，情愿听从造物主。有时我开始祈祷了，祷告很短，但很诚恳。

"已经有几天了，不，我能说出数字来——四天。那是上星期一晚上——我产生了一种奇怪的心情：忧伤，也就是悲哀和阴沉代替了狂乱。我早就想，既然到处找不着你，那你一定已经死了。那天深夜——也许在十一二点之间——我闷闷不乐地去就寝之前，祈求上帝，要是他觉得这么做妥当的话，可以立刻把我从现世收去，准许我踏进未来的世界，那儿仍有希望与简相聚。"

"我在自己的房间，坐在敞开着的窗边，清香的夜风沁人心脾。尽管我看不见星星，只是凭着一团模糊发亮的雾气，才知道有月亮。我盼着你，珍妮特！呵，无论是肉体还是灵魂，我都盼着你。我既痛苦而又谦卑地问上帝，我那么凄凉、痛苦、备受折磨，是不是已经够久了，会不会很快就再能尝到幸福与平静。我承认我所忍受的一切是应该的——我恳求，我实在不堪忍受了。我内心的全部愿望不由自主地崩出了我的嘴巴，化作这样几个字——'简！简！简！'"

"你大声说了这几个字吗？"

"我说了，简。谁要是听见了，一定会以为我在发疯，我疯也似的使劲叫着那几个字。"

"而那是星期一晚上，半夜时分！"

"不错，时间倒并不重要，随后发生的事儿才怪呢。你会认为我相信迷信吧——从气质来看，我是有些迷信，而且一直如此。不过，这回倒是真的——我现在说的都是我听到的，至少这一点是真的。"

"我大叫着'简！简！简！'的时候，不知道哪儿传来了一个声音，但听得出是谁的，这个声音回答道，'我来了，请等一等我！'过了一会儿，清风送来了悄声细语——'你在哪儿呀？'"

"要是我能够，我会告诉你这些话在我的心灵中所展示的思想和画面，不过要表达自己的想法并不容易。你知道，芬丁庄园深藏在密林里，这儿的声音很沉闷，没有回荡便会消失。'你在哪儿呀？'这声音似乎来自于大山中间，因为我听到了山林的回声重复着这几个字。这时空气凉爽清新，风似乎也朝我额头吹来。我会认为我与简在荒僻的野景中相会。我相信，在精神上我们一定已经相会了。毫无疑问，当时你睡得很熟，说不定你的灵魂脱离了它的躯壳来抚慰我的灵魂。因为那正是你的口音——千真万确——是你的！"

读者呀，正是星期一晚上——将近午夜——我也接到了神秘的召唤，而那些也正是我回答的话。我倾听着罗切斯特先生的叙述，却并没有向他吐露什么，我觉得这种巧合太令人畏惧，令人费解了，因而既难以言传，也无法议论。要是我说出什么来，我的经历也必定会在聆听者的心灵中留下深刻的印象，而这饱受痛苦的心灵上容易忧伤了，不需要再笼罩更深沉的超自然阴影了。于是我把这些纵情留在心里，反复思量。

"这会儿你不会奇怪了吧，"我主人继续说，"那天晚上你出乎意外地在我面前冒出来时。我难以相信你不只是一个声音和幻象，不只是某种会销声匿迹的东西，就像以前已经消失的夜半耳语和山间回声那样。现在我感谢上帝，我知道这回可不同了。是的，我感谢上帝！"

他把我从膝头上放下来。虔敬地从额头摘下帽子，向大地低下了没有视力的眼睛，虔诚地默默站立着，只有最后几句表示崇拜的话隐约可闻。

"我感谢造物主，在审判时还记着慈悲。我谦恭地恳求我的救世主赐予我力量，让我从今以后过一种比以往更纯洁的生活！"随后他伸出手让我领着，我握住了那只亲爱的手，在我的嘴唇上放了一会儿，随后让它挽住我肩膀，我个子比他矮得多，所以既做立支撑，又当了向导。我们进了树林，朝家里走去。

第五单元　呼啸山庄　第十五章

又过了一个星期——我更接近了健康和春天！我现在已经听完了我的邻人的全部历史，因为这位管家可以从比较重要的工作中腾出空闲常来坐坐。我要用她自己的话继续讲下去，只是压缩一点。总的说，她是一个讲故事的能手，我可不认为我能把她的风格改得更好。

晚上，（她说）：就是我去山庄的那天晚上，我知道希刺克厉夫先生又在附近，就像是我看到了他；我不出去，因为我还把他的信搁在口袋里，而且不愿再被吓唬或被揶揄了。我决定现在不交这信，一直等到我主人到什么地方去后再说，因为我拿不准凯瑟琳收到这信后会怎么样。结果是，这信过了三天才到她的手里。第四天是星期日，等到全家都去教堂后，我就把信带到她屋里。还有一个男仆留下来同我看家。我们经常在做礼拜时把门锁住，可是那天天气是这么温暖宜人，我就把门都大开，而且，我既然知道谁会来，为了履行我的诺言，我就告诉我的同伴的说女主人非常想吃橘子，他得跑到村里去买几个，明天再付钱。他走了，我就上了楼。

林惇夫人穿着一件宽大的白衣服，和往常一样，坐在一个敞开着窗子的凹处，肩上披着一条薄薄的肩巾。她那厚厚的长发在她初病时曾剪去一点，现在她简单地梳梳，听其自然地披在她的鬓角和颈子上。正如我告诉过希刺克厉夫的一样，她的外表是改变了；但当她是宁静的时候，在这种变化中仿佛具有非凡的美。她眼里的亮光已经变成一种梦幻的、忧郁的温柔；她的眼睛不再给人这种印象：她是在望着她四周的东西；而是显现出总是在凝视着远方，遥远的地方——你可以说是望着世外。还有她脸上的苍白——她恢复之后，那种憔悴的面貌是消失了——还有从她心境中所产生的特别表情，虽然很凄惨地暗示了原因，却使她格外令人爱怜；这些现象——对于我，我知道，对于别的看见她的人都必然认为——足以反驳那些说是正在康复的明证，却标明她是注定要凋谢了。

一本书摆在她面前的窗台上，打开着，简直令人感觉不到的风间或掀动着书页。我相信是林惇放在那儿的：因为她从来不想读书，或干任何事，他得花上许多钟头来引她注意那些以前曾使她愉快的事物。她明白他的目的，在她心情较好时，就温和地听他摆布；只是时不时地压下一声疲倦的叹息，表示这些是没有用的，到最后就用最悲惨的微笑和亲吻来制止他。在其他时候，她就突然转身，用手掩着脸，或者甚至愤怒地把他推开；然后他就小心翼翼地让她自己待着，因为他确信自己是无能为力的了。

吉默吞的钟还在响着；山谷里那涨满了的水溪传来的潺潺流水声非常悦耳。这美妙的声音代替了现在还没有到来的夏日树叶飒飒声，等到树上生了果子，这声音就湮没了田庄附近的那种音乐。在呼啸山庄附近，在风雪或雨季之后的平静日子里，这小溪总是这样响着的。在凯瑟琳倾听时，那就是，如果她是在想着或倾听着的话；她所想的就是呼啸山庄！可是她有着我以前提到过的那种茫然的、捉摸不到的神气，这表明她的耳朵或眼睛简直不能辨识任何外界的东西。

"有你一封信，林惇夫人，"我说，轻轻把信塞进她摆在膝上的一只手里。"你得马上看它，因为等着回信呢。我把封漆打开好吗？""好吧，"她回答，没改变她的目光的方向。我打开它——信很短。"现在，"我接着说，"看吧。"她缩回她的手，任这信掉到地上。我又把它放在她的怀里，站着等她乐意朝下面看看的时候；可是她总是不动，终于我说——

"要我念吗，太太？是从希刺克厉夫先生哪儿来的。"

她一惊，露出一种因回忆而苦恼的神色，竭力使自己镇定卜来。她拿起信，仿佛是在阅读；当她看到签名的地方，她叹息着；但我还是发现她并没有领会到里面的意思，因为我急着要听她的回信，她却只指着署名，带着悲哀的、疑问的热切神情盯着我。

"唉，他想见见你，"我说，心想她需要一个人给她解释，"这时候他在花园里，急想知道我将给他带去什么样的回信呢？"

在我说话的时候，我看见躺在下面向阳的草地上的一只大狗竖起了耳朵，仿佛正要吠叫，然后耳朵又向后平下去。它摇摇尾巴算是宣布有人来了，而且它不把这个人当作陌生人看待。林惇夫人向前探身，上气不接下气地倾听着。过了一分钟，有脚步声穿过大厅；这开着门的房子对于希刺克厉夫是太诱惑了，他不能不走进来；大概他以为我有意不履行诺言，就决定随心所欲地大胆行事了。凯瑟琳带着紧张的热切神情，盯着她卧房的门口。他并没有马上发现应该走进哪间屋子；她示意要我接他进来，可是我还没走到门口，他已经找到了，而且大步走到她身边，把她搂在自己怀里了。

有五分钟左右，他没说话，也没放松他的拥抱，在这段时间我敢说他给予的吻比他有生以来所给的还多：但是先吻他的是我的女主人，我看得清清楚楚，他由于真正的悲痛，简直不能直瞅她的脸！他一看见她，就跟我同样地确信，她是没有最后复原的希望了——她命中注定，一定要死了。

"啊，凯蒂！啊，我的命！我怎么受得了啊？"这是他说出的第一句话，那声调并不想掩饰他的绝望。现在他这么热切地盯着她，他的凝视是这么热烈，我想他会流泪的。但是那对眼睛却燃烧着极度的痛苦：并没化作泪水。

"现在还要怎么样呢？"凯瑟琳说，向后仰着，以突然阴沉下来的脸色回答他的凝视：她的性子不过是她那时常变动的精神状态的风信标而已。"你和埃德加把我的心都弄碎了，希刺克厉夫！你们都为那件事来向我哀告，好像你们才是该被怜悯的人！我不会怜悯你的，我才不。你已经害了我——而且，我想，还因此心满意足吧。你多强壮啊！我死后你还打算活多少年啊？"

希刺克厉夫本来是用一条腿跪下来搂着她的。他想站起来，可是她抓着他的头发，又把他按下去。

"但愿我能抓住你不放，"她辛酸地接着说，"一直到我们两个都死掉！我不应该管你受什么苦。我才不管你的痛苦哩。你为什么不该受苦呢？我可在受呀！你会忘掉我吗？等我埋在地里的时候，你会快乐吗？二十年后你会不会说，'那是凯瑟琳·恩萧的坟。很久以前我爱过她，而且为了失去她而难过；可是这都过去了。那以后我又爱过好多人：我的孩子对于我可比她要亲多了；而且，到了死的时候，我不会因为我要去她那儿就高兴：我会很难过，因为我得离开他们了！'你会不会这么说呢，希刺克厉夫？"

"不要把我折磨得跟你自己一样地发疯吧，"他叫，扭开他的头，咬着牙。

在一个冷静的旁观者看来，这两个人形成了一幅奇异而可怕的图画。凯瑟琳很有理由认为天堂对于她就是流放之地，除非她的精神也随同她的肉体一起抛开。在她现在的面容上，那白白的双颊，没有血色的唇，以及闪烁的眼睛都显出一种狂野的要复仇的心情；在她的握紧的手指中间还留有她刚才抓住的一把头发。至于她的同伴，他一只手撑住自己，一只手握着她的胳膊；他对她那种温存，对于她当时的健康状况是很不适合的。在他松手时，我看见在那没有血色的皮肤上留下了四条清清楚楚的紫痕。

"你是不是被鬼缠住了，"他凶暴地追问着，"在你要死的时候还这样跟我说话？你想没想到所有这些话都要烙在我的记忆里，而且在你丢下我之后，将要永远更深地啮食着我？你明知道你说的我害死你的话是说谎；而且，凯瑟琳，你知道我只要活着就不会忘掉你！当你得到安息的时候，我却要在地狱的折磨里受煎熬，这还不够使你那狠毒的自私心得到满足吗？"

"我不会得到安息的，"凯瑟琳哀哭着，感到她身体的衰弱，因为在这场过度的激动下，她的心猛烈地、不规则地跳动着，甚至跳得能觉察出来。她说不出话来，直到这阵激动过去，才又接着说，稍微温和一些了。

"我并不愿意你受的苦比我受的还大，希刺克厉夫。我只愿我们永远不分离：如果我有一句话使你今后难过，想想我在地下也感到一样的难过，看在我自己的份上，饶恕我吧！过来，再跪下去！你一生从来没有伤害过我。是啊，如果你生了气，那今后你想起你的气愤就要比想起我那些粗暴的话更难受！你不肯再过来吗？来呀！"

希刺克厉夫走到她椅子背后，向前探身，却让她看不见他那因激动而变得发青的脸。她回过头望他；他不许她看；他突然转身，走到炉边，站在那儿，沉默着，背对着我们。林惇夫人的目光疑惑不解地跟着他：每一个动作在她心里都唤起一种新的感情。在一阵沉默和长久的凝视之后，她又讲话了；带着愤慨的失望声调对我说——

"啊，你瞧，耐莉，他都不肯暂时发发慈悲好让我躲开坟墓。我就是这样被人爱啊！好吧，没关系。那不是我的希刺克厉夫。我还是要爱我那个，我带着他：他是在我灵魂里。而且，"她沉思地又说，"使我最厌烦的到底还是这个破碎的牢狱，我不愿意被关在这儿了。我多想躲避到那个愉快的世界里，永远在那儿：不是泪眼模糊地看到它，不是在痛楚的心境中渴望着它；可是真的跟它在一起，在它里面。耐莉，你以为你比我好些，幸运些；完全健康有力：你为我难过——不久这就要改变了。我要为你们难过。我将要无可比拟地超越你们，在你们所有的人之上。我奇怪他不肯挨近我？"她自言自语地往下说，"我以为他是愿意的。希刺克厉夫，亲爱的！现在你不该沉着脸。到我这儿来呀，希刺克厉夫。"

她异常激动地站起身来，身子靠着椅子的扶手。听了那真挚的乞求，他转身向她，神色是完全不顾一切了。他睁大着双眼，含着泪水，终于猛地向她一闪，胸口激动地起伏着。他们各自站住一刹那，然后我简直没看清他们是怎么合在一起的，只见凯瑟琳向前一跃，他就把她擒住了，他们拥抱得紧紧的，我想我的女主人绝不会被活着放开了：事实上，据我看，她仿佛立刻就不省人事了。他投身到最近处的椅子上，我赶忙走上前看看她是不是昏迷了，他就对我咬牙切齿，像个疯狗似的吐着白沫，带着贪婪的嫉妒神色把她抱紧。我简直不觉得我是在陪着一个跟我同类的动物：看来即使我跟他说话，他也不会懂；因此我只好非常惶惑地站开，也不吭声。

凯瑟琳动弹了一下，这才使我立刻放了心：她伸出手搂住他的脖子，他抱住她，她把脸紧贴着他的脸；他回报给她无数疯狂的爱抚，又狂乱地说——

"你现在才使我明白你曾经多么残酷——残酷又虚伪。你过去为什么瞧不起我呢？你为什么欺骗你自己的心呢，凯蒂？我没有一句安慰的话。这是你应得的。你害死了你自己。是的，你可以亲吻我，哭，又逼出我的吻和眼泪：我的吻和眼泪要摧残你——要诅咒你。你爱过我——那么你有什么权力离开我呢？有什么权利——回答我——对林惇存那种可怜的幻想？因为悲惨、耻辱和死亡，以及上帝或撒旦所能给的一切打击和痛苦都不能把我们分开，而你，却出于你自己的心意，这样做了。我没有弄碎你的心——是你弄碎了的；而在弄碎它的时候，你把我的心也弄碎了。因为我是强壮的，对于我就格外苦。我还要活吗？那将是什么样的生活，当你——

啊，上帝！你愿意带着你的灵魂留在坟墓里吗？"

"别管我吧，别管我吧，"凯瑟琳抽泣着。"如果我曾经做错了，我就要为此而死去的。够啦！你也丢弃过我的，可我并不要责备你！我饶恕你。饶恕我吧！"

"看看这对眼睛，摸摸这双消瘦的手，要饶恕是很难的，"他回答。"再亲亲我吧；别让我看见你的眼睛！我饶恕你对我做过的事。我爱害了我的人——可是害了你的人呢？我又怎么能够饶恕他？"

他们沉默着——脸紧贴着，用彼此的眼泪在冲洗着。至少，我猜是双方都在哭泣；在这样一个不同寻常的场合中，就连希刺克厉夫仿佛也能哭泣了。

同时我越来越心焦；因为下午过得很快，我支使出去的人已经完成使命回来了，而且我从照在山谷的夕阳也能分辨出吉默吞教堂门外已有一大堆人涌出了。

"做完礼拜了，"我宣布。"我的主人要在半个钟头内到家啦。"

希刺克厉夫哼出一声咒骂，把凯瑟琳抱得更紧，她一动也不动。

不久我看见一群仆人走过大路，向厨房那边走去。林惇先生在后面不远；他自己开了大门，慢慢溜达过来，大概是要享受这风和日丽、宛如夏日的下午。

"现在他到这儿来了，"我大叫。"看在老天爷的份上，快下去吧！你在前面楼梯上不会遇到什么人的。快点吧，在树林里待着，等他进来你再走。"

"我一定得走了，凯蒂，"希刺克厉夫说，想从他的伴侣的胳臂中挣脱出来。"可是如果我还活着，在你睡觉以前，我还要来看你的。我不会离开你的窗户五码之外的。"

"你决不能走！"她回答，尽她的全力紧紧地抓住他。"我告诉你，你不要走。"

"只走开一个钟头，"他热诚地恳求着。

"一分钟也不行，"她回答。

"我非走不可——林惇马上就要来了，"这受惊的闯入者坚持着。

他想站起来，要松开她的手指——但她紧紧搂住，喘着气：在她脸上现出疯狂的决心。

"不！"她尖叫。"啊，别，别走。这是最后一次了！埃德加不会伤害我们的。希刺克厉夫，我要死啦！我要死啦！"

"该死的混蛋！他来了，"希刺克厉夫喊着，倒在他的椅子上。"别吵，我亲爱的！别吵，别吵，凯瑟琳！我不走了。如果他就这么拿枪崩了我，我也会在嘴唇上带着祝福咽气的。"

他们又紧紧地搂在一起。我听见我主人上楼了——我的脑门上直冒冷汗；我吓坏了。

"你就听她的胡话吗？"我激动地说。"她不知道她说什么。就因为她神志丧失，不能自主，你要毁了她吗？起来！你马上就可以挣脱的。这是你所做过的最恶毒的事。我们——主人、女主人、仆人——可都给毁啦！"

我绞着手，大叫；林惇先生一听声音，加快了脚步，在我的震动之中，我衷心欢喜地看见凯瑟琳的胳臂松落下来，她的头也垂下来"她是昏迷了，或是死了，"我想，"这样还好些。与其活着成为周围人的负担，成为不幸的制造者，那还不如让她死了的好。"

埃德加冲向这位不速之客，脸色因惊愕与愤怒而发白。他打算怎么样，我也不知道；可是，另一个人把那看来已没有生命的东西往他怀里一放，立刻停止了所有的示威行动。

"瞧吧！"他说。"除非你是一个恶魔，不然就去救救她吧——然后你再跟我说话!"

他走到客厅里坐下来。林惇先生召唤我去,费了好大劲,用了好多方法,我们才使她醒过来;可是她完全精神错乱了;她叹息,呻吟,谁也不认识。埃德加一心为她焦急,也忘了她那可恨的朋友。我可没有忘。我找了个最早的机会劝他离开:肯定说凯瑟琳已经好些了,他明天早晨可以听我告诉他她这一夜过得怎么样。

"我不会拒绝出这个门,"他回答,"可是我要待在花园里:耐莉,记着明天你要遵守诺言。我将在那些落叶松下面,记住!不然我还要来,不管林惇在不在家。"

他急急地向卧房的半开的门里投去一瞥,证实了我所说的是真实的,这不吉利的人才离开了这所房子。

第六单元　德伯家的苔丝　第五十八章

那天的夜晚尤其阴沉，尤其宁静。半夜过后，苔丝悄悄地向他讲述了他梦游的故事，说他怎样在睡梦里抱着她，冒着两个人随时都会掉进河里淹死的危险，从佛卢姆河的桥上走过，把她放在寺庙废墟中的一个石头棺材里。直到现在苔丝告诉了他，他才知道了这件事。

"第二天你为什么不告诉我呢？"他说。"如果你告诉了我，许多误会和痛苦也许就避免了。"

"过去了的事就不要再想了吧！"她说。"除了我们的此时此刻而外，我什么都不去想。我们不要去想！又有谁知道明天会发生什么事呢？"

不过第二天显然没有悲伤痛苦。早上潮湿多雾，克莱尔昨天已经听人说过，看管房子的人只是在天晴的时候才来开窗户，所以他就把苔丝留在房间里继续睡觉，自己大胆地走出房间，把整座房子查看了一遍，屋内虽然没有食物，但是有水。于是他就利用有雾的天气，走出屋外，到两三英里以外的一个小地方的店铺里，买了茶点、面包和黄油，还买了一个铁皮水壶和一个酒精灯，这样他们就有了不冒烟的火了。他回来时把苔丝惊醒了；于是他们就一起吃他买回来的东西，当了一顿早饭。

他们都不想到外面去，只是待在屋里；白天过去了，夜晚来临了，接着是另一天，然后又是另一天；在不知不觉中，他们差不多就这样在绝对隐蔽的地方度过了五天，看不见一个人影，也听不到一点人声，没有谁来打扰他们的平静。天气变化是他们唯一的大事，陪伴他们的也只有森林的鸟儿。他们都心照不宣，几乎一次也没有提起过婚后的任何一件事情。他们中间那段悲伤的日子似乎在天地开辟之前的混沌中消失了，现在的和过去的欢乐时光又重新连接起来，仿佛从来就没有中断似的。每当他提出离开他们躲藏的屋子到南桑普顿或者伦敦去，她总是令人奇怪地表示不愿意离开。

"一切都是这样恩爱甜蜜，我们为什么要结束它呢！"她恳求说。"要来的总是躲不掉的。"她从百叶窗的缝隙中看着外面说："你看，屋外都是痛苦，屋内才是美满啊。"

他也向外面看去。她说得完全对：屋内是爱情、和谐、宽恕，屋外却是冷酷、无情。

"而且——而且,"她把自己的脸贴在他的脸上说;"你现在这样对待我,我担心也许不会长久。我希望永远拥有你现在这份情意。我不愿意失去它。我情愿在你瞧不起我的那一天到来的时候,我已经死了,埋掉了,那样我就永远不会知道你瞧不起我了。"

"我永远也不会瞧不起你的。"

"我也希望如此,可是一想到我这一生的遭遇,我总以为别人早晚都要瞧不起我的。……我真是一个可恶的疯子呀!可是从前,我连一只苍蝇、一条小虫都不敢伤害,看见关在笼子里的小鸟,也常常要悲伤流泪。"

他们在那座屋子里又待了一天。晚上,阴沉的天气晴朗了,因此照看房子的老太太很早就在她的茅屋里醒了。灿烂的朝阳使她精神异常爽快,于是决定立即就去把那座屋子的窗户打开,在这样好的天气里让空气流通。因此在六点钟以前,她就来到那座屋子,把楼下房间的窗户打开了,接着又上楼去开卧室的窗户;她来到克莱尔和苔丝躲藏的那个房间,就用手去转动门上的把手。就在这个时候,她认为自己听见房间里有人呼吸的声音。她脚上穿着便鞋,年纪又大,所以走到房间门口也没有弄出一点儿声音。她听见声音,就急忙退了回去。后来,她想也许是自己听错了,就又转身走到门口,轻轻地转动门上的把手。门锁已经坏了,但是有一件家具被搬过来,从里面把门挡住。老太太无法完全把门打开,只打开了一两英寸。早上太阳的光线穿过百叶窗的缝隙,照射在一对正在酣睡着的人的脸上,苔丝的嘴半张着,就像是在克莱尔的脸旁半开的一朵鲜花。照看房子的老太太看见他们睡在那儿,样子是那样纯真;她看见苔丝挂在椅子上的长袍,看见长袍旁边的丝织长袜和漂亮的小阳伞,还有苔丝没有别的可穿而穿来的其他几件衣服,被它们的华美高雅深深打动了;她最初以为他们是妓女和流氓,心里十分生气,现在看来他们好像是上流社会一对私奔的情侣,于是心中的愤怒便化作了一阵怜爱。她把门关上,像来的时候那样轻轻地离开,找她的邻居商量她的奇怪发现去了。

老太太走后不到一分钟,苔丝就醒了,接着克莱尔也醒了。他们两个人都觉得出现过打扰他们的事,但是他们又说不清楚是什么事;因此他们心中产生的不安情绪也就越来越强烈了。克莱尔穿好衣服,立即从百叶窗上两三寸宽的窄缝中向外仔细观察。

"我想我们要立即离开了,"他说。"今天是一个晴天。我总觉得房子里有什么人来过。无论如何，那个老太太今天肯定是要来的。"

苔丝只好同意，于是他们收拾好房间，带上属于他们的几件物品，不声不响地离开了那座屋子。在他们走进新林的时候，苔丝回过头去，向那座屋子望了最后一眼。

"啊，幸福的屋子啊——再见吧！"她说。"我只能活上几个礼拜了。我们为什么不待在那儿呢？"

"不要说这种话，苔丝！不久我们就要完全离开这个地方了。我们要按照我们当初的路线走，一直朝北走。谁也不会想到上那儿去缉拿我们的。他们要是缉拿我们，一定是在威塞克斯各个港口寻找。等我们到了北边，我们就可以从一个港口离开。"

苔丝被说服以后，他们就按计划行事，径直朝北走。他们在那座屋子里休息了这样长的时间，现在走路也有了力气；到了中午，他们走到了恰好挡住他们去路的尖塔城梅尔彻斯特的附近。克莱尔决定下午让苔丝在一个树丛里休息，到了晚上在黑夜的掩护下赶路。克莱尔在黄昏时又像往常一样去买了食物，开始在夜晚中往前走。到了八点左右，他们就走过了上威塞克斯和中威塞克斯之间的边界。

苔丝早就习惯在乡野里走路而不管道路如何，因此她走起路来就显得轻松自如。他们必须从阻挡着他们的那座古老城市梅尔彻斯特穿过去，这样他们就可以从城里那座桥上通过挡住他们去路的大河。到了午夜时候，街道上空无一人，他们借着几盏闪烁不定的街灯走着，避开人行道，免得走路的脚步声引起回响。朦胧中出现在他们左边的那座堂皇雄伟的大教堂，现在已经从他们的眼前消失了。他们出了城，沿着收税栅路走，往前走了几英里，就进了他们要穿过的广阔平原。

先前虽然天上乌云密布，但是月亮仍然洒下散光，对他们走路多少有一些帮助。现在月亮已经落下去了，乌云似乎就笼罩在他们的头上，天黑得伸手不见五指。但是他们摸索着往前走，尽量走在草地上，免得脚步发出响声。这是容易做到的，因为在她们周围，既没有树篱，也没有任何形式的围墙。他们四周的一切都是空旷的寂静和黑夜的孤独，还有猛烈的风不停吹着。

他们就这样摸索着又往前走了两三英里，克莱尔突然感觉到，他的面前有一座巨大的建筑物，在草地上顶天而立。他们几乎撞到了它的上面。

"这是一个什么古怪地方呢？"安琪尔说。

"还在嗡嗡响呢,"她说。"你听!"

他听了听。风在那座座巨大的建筑物中间吹着,发出一种嗡嗡的音调,就像是一张巨大的单弦竖琴发出的声音。除了风声,他们听出还有其他的声音。克莱尔把一双手伸着,向前走了一两步,摸到了那座建筑物垂直的表面。它似乎是整块的石头,没有接缝,也没有花边。他继续用手摸去,发现摸到的是一根巨大的方形石柱;他又伸出左手摸去,摸到附近还有一根同样的石柱。在他的头顶上,高高的空中还有一件物体,使黑暗的天空变得更加黑暗了,它好像是把两根石柱按水平方向连接起来的横梁。他们小心翼翼地从两根柱子中间和横梁底下走了进去;他们走路的沙沙声从石头的表面发出回声,但他们似乎仍然还在门外。这座建筑是没有屋顶的。苔丝感到害怕,呼吸急促起来,而安琪尔也感到莫名其妙,就说——

"这里是什么地方呢?"

他们向旁边摸去,又摸到一根和第一根石柱同样高大坚硬的方形石柱,然后又摸到一根,再摸到一根。这儿全是门框和石柱,有的石柱上面还架着石梁。

"这是一座风神庙!"克莱尔说。

下面一根石柱孤零零地矗立着;另外有些石柱都是两根竖着的石柱上面横着一根石柱;还有一些石柱躺在地上,它们的两边形成了一条通道,宽度足可以通过马车;不久他们就弄明白了,原来在这块平原的草地上竖立的石柱,一起形成了一片石林。他们两个人继续往前走,一直走进黑夜中这个由石柱组成的亭台中间。

"原来是史前神庙。"克莱尔说。

"你是说这是一座异教徒的神庙?"

"是的。比纪元前还要古老;也比德贝维尔家族还要古老!啊,我们怎么办哪,亲爱的?再往前走我们也许就可以找到一个栖身的地方了。"

但是苔丝这一次倒是真正累了,看见附近有一块长方形石板,石板的一头有石柱把风挡住,于是她就在石板上躺下来。由于白天太阳的照射,这块石板既干燥又暖和,和周围粗糙冰冷的野草相比舒服多了,那时候她的裙子和鞋子已经被野草上的露水弄湿了。

"我再也不想往前走了,安琪尔,"她把手伸给克莱尔说。"我们不能在这儿过一夜吗?"

"恐怕不行。这个地点现在虽然觉得别人看不见，但是在白天，好几英里以外都能够看见的。"

"现在我想起来了，我母亲娘家有一个人是这儿附近的一个牧羊人。在泰波塞斯你曾经说我是一个异教徒，所以我现在算是回了老家啦。"

克莱尔跪在苔丝躺着的身旁，用自己的嘴唇吻着她的嘴唇。

"亲爱的，想睡了吧？我想你正躺在一个祭坛上。"

"我非常喜欢躺在这儿，"她嘟哝着说。"这儿是这样庄严，这样僻静，头上只有一片苍天——我已经享受过巨大的幸福了。我觉得，世界上除了我们两个而外，仿佛没有其他的人了；我希望没有其他的人，不过丽莎·露除外。"

克莱尔心想，她不妨就躺在这儿休息，等到天快亮的时候再走；于是他把自己的外套脱下来盖在她的身上，在她的身旁坐下。

"安琪尔，要是我出了什么事，你能不能看在我的分儿上照看丽莎·露？"风声在石柱中间响着，他们听了好久，苔丝开口说。

"我会照顾她的。"

"她是那样善良，那样天真，那样纯洁。啊，安琪尔——要是你失去了我，我希望你会娶了她。啊，要是你能够娶她的话！"

"要是我失去了你，我就失去了一切！她是我的姨妹啊。"

"那是没有关系的，亲爱的。在马洛特村一带时常有跟小姨子结婚的；丽莎·露是那样温柔、甜美，而且还越长越漂亮了。啊，当我们大家都变成了鬼魂，我也乐意和她一起拥有你啊！安琪尔，你只要训练她，教导她，你就可以把她也培养得和你自己一样了！……我的优点她都有，我的坏处她一点儿也没有；如果她将来做了你的妻子，我就是死了，我们也是无法分开的了。……唉，我已经说过了。我不想再提了。"

她住了口，克莱尔听了也陷入了深思。从远处东北方向的天上，他看见石柱中间出现了一道水平的亮光。满天的乌云像一个大锅盖，正在整个地向上揭起，把姗姗来迟的黎明从大地的边上放进来，因此矗立在那儿的孤独石柱和两根石柱加一根横梁的牌坊，也露出了黑色的轮廓。

"他们就是在这儿向天神献祭吗？"她问。

"不！"他说。

"那么向谁呢？"

"我认为是向太阳献祭的。那根高高的石头柱子不就是朝着太阳的方向安放的吗，一会儿太阳就从它的后面升起来了。"

"亲爱的，这让我想起一件事来，"她说。"在我们结婚以前，你说你永远不会干涉我的信仰，你还记不记得？其实我一直明白你的思想，像你一样去思考——而不是从我自己的判断去思考，因为你怎样想。我就怎样想。现在告诉我吧，安琪尔，你认为我们死后还能见面吗？我想知道这件事。"

他吻她，免得在这种时候去回答这个问题。

"啊，安琪尔——恐怕你的意思是不能见面了！"她尽力忍着哽咽说。"我多想再和你见面啊——我想得多厉害啊，多厉害啊！怎么，安琪尔，即使像你和我这样相爱，都还不能再见面吗？"

安琪尔也像一个比他自己更伟大的人物一样，在这样一个关键时候对于这样一个关键问题，不作回答，于是他们两个人又都沉默起来。过了一两分钟，苔丝的呼吸变得更加均匀了，她握着安琪尔的那只手放松了，因为她睡着了。东方的地平线上出现了一道银灰色的光带，大平原上远处的部分在那道光带的映衬下，变得更加黑暗了，也变得离他更近了。那一片苍茫的整个景色，露出了黎明到来之前的常有的特征，冷漠、含蓄、犹豫。东边的石柱和石柱上方的横梁，迎着太阳矗立着，显得黑沉沉的。在石柱的外面可以看见火焰形状的太阳石，也可以看见在石柱和太阳石之间的牺牲石。晚风很快就停止了，石头上由杯形的石窝形成的小水潭也不再颤抖了。就在这个时候，东边低地的边缘上似乎有什么东西在移动——是一个黑色的小点。那是一个人的头，正在从太阳石后面的洼地向他们走来。克莱尔后悔没有继续往前走，但是现在只好决定坐着不动。那个人影径直向他们待的那一圈石柱走来。

他听见他的后面传来声音，那是有人走路的脚步声。他转过身去，看见躺在地上的柱子后面出现了一个人影；他还看见在他附近的右边有一个，在他左边的横梁下也有一个。曙光完全照在从西边走来的那个人的脸上，克莱尔在曙光里看见他个子高大，走路像军人的步伐。他们所有的人显然是有意包围过来的。苔丝说的话应验了！克莱尔跳起来，往四周看去，想寻找一件武器，寻找一件松动的石头，或者寻找一种逃跑的方法什么的，就在这个时候，那个离他最近的人来到了他的身边。

"这是没有用的，先生，"他说，"在这个平原上我们有十六个人，这儿整个地区都已经行动起来了。"

"让她把觉睡完吧！"在他们围拢来的时候，他小声地向他们恳求说。

　　直到这个时候，他们才看见她睡觉的地方，因此就没有表示反对，而是站在一旁守着，一动也不动，像周围的柱子一样。他走到她睡觉的那块石头跟前，握住她那只可怜的小手；那时候她的呼吸快速而又细弱，和一个比女人还要弱小的动物的呼吸一样。天越来越亮了，所有的人都在那儿等着，他们的脸和手都仿佛镀上了一层银灰色，而他们身体的其他部分则是黑色的，石头柱子闪耀着灰绿色的光，平原仍然是一片昏暗。不久天大亮了，太阳的光线照射在苔丝没有知觉的身上，透过她的眼睑射进她的眼里，把苔丝唤醒了。

　　"怎么啦，安琪尔？"她醒过来说。"他们已经来抓我了吧？"

　　"是的，最亲爱的，"他说。"他们已经来啦。"

　　"他们是该来啦，"她嘟哝着说。"安琪尔，我一直感到高兴——是的，一直感到高兴！这种幸福是不能长久的，因为它太过分了。我已经享够了这种幸福；现在我不会活着等你来轻视我了！"

　　她站起来，抖了抖身子，就往前走，而其他的人一个也没有动。

　　"现在可以走了。"她从容地说。

第七单元　伊 芙 琳

　　她临窗而坐，看着夜色慢慢降临在林荫道上。她脑袋靠在窗帘上，嗅得出它肮脏的霉味。她累了。

　　有几个人走过，最后一个下班的人走在回家的路上，听得见水泥板人行道上响着他啪啪的脚步声，然后是踏在那幢新的红砖房子前面小径的沙沙声。

　　那儿曾经是一块空旷地，每天傍晚他们常和别家的孩子在那儿玩耍。后来从贝尔法斯特来了一个人，买了这块地，建了一幢房——不像他们这样的小灰色房子，而是明亮的砖房，有光闪闪的屋顶。

　　街上的孩子们以前总在那空地上做游戏，有狄怀恩家的、瓦特家的、但恩家的，还有瘸子小吉奥，以及她的兄弟姐妹们。然而，恩尼斯从来不玩——他太大了。她父亲总是用藤条才能把他们赶回家去。尽管如此，那时大家似乎都很快活，父亲也不见得脾气那么坏。

　　现在，她和兄弟姐妹们早已长大成人，母亲去世了，但恩也不在人间，瓦特一家搬回了英格兰——一切都变了样。如今，她也要像其他人一样走了，要离开她的家。

　　啊，家！她的目光扫视屋里四围，仔细观察这些多年来她每礼拜掸扫一遍灰尘的每一件熟悉的家具和陈设。她老是觉得奇怪——这些灰尘是从什么鬼地方来的？也许她再也见不到这些东西了，她从未想过有跟它们分手的一天。

　　她已经答应离家出走。这明智吗？她努力衡量利弊。在家里，她好歹头上有片瓦顶着，有顿饭充饥肠，还有这些与她生活密切相关的熟悉东西。当然啰，她得卖力做工，不管在家里还是外头，都得拼命干。一旦店里人发现她与人私奔了，会说些什么闲话呢？也许会议论她傻，而报纸会登个广告，雇人来顶她的空位。嘉雯小姐会幸灾乐祸，她对她说话总那么刻薄苛求，特别是有人在旁听的时候更如此。

　　"希尔小姐，你没看见这些女顾客在等买东西吗？"

　　"手脚放麻利点，希尔小姐！"

　　她对离开店铺一点也不觉得不安和留恋。

　　可是，在那个新的家，在遥远异国的家，情况就迥然不同了。

她——伊夫琳，将要结婚，人们会敬重她，她不用忍受和母亲同样的遭遇。她已经十九岁了，可是还时常处于父亲粗暴举止的威胁下，她常常为之心惊肉跳。长大后，父亲不会像殴打哈里和恩尼斯那样揍她了，因为她毕竟是个大姑娘。但近来父亲也开始恐吓她说，为了对得起死去的妈妈，要教训教训她一顿。

现在没有人保护她了：恩尼斯死了，哈里是教堂的装修工，总是在乡下的什么地方干活。而且，那固定不变的每礼拜六晚上为了钱引起的争吵。也使她不厌其烦。她把干活挣来的钱（每周七先令）全部交给父亲，哈里也尽量往家里多寄点钱。但是从父亲手里拿一个毫子也不容易，他说她花钱大手大脚，一点头脑也没有，说他不想把自己辛辛苦苦挣来的钱让女儿扔到大街上，等等，等等。

所以一到礼拜六晚上，父亲的脾气总是特别不好。一场争吵之后，他掏出钱来，问女儿到底还想不想去买礼拜天的面包。她只好尽快跑步去做她的买办。她手里紧捏着黑皮钱袋子，一边用胳膊肘在人群里挤开一条路，很迟很迟，她才挎着沉甸甸的粮食口袋回到家里。

维持这个家，还照顾下面两个小弟妹，让他们能继续上学，不让他们有一天饿肚皮，对她的确不是件简单的事。真艰难啊——艰难的生活！可是，如今她当即将告别这种生活，反而觉得生活并不那么令人不快了。

她就要和弗朗科一起开拓另一种新的生活。弗朗科既善良又有男子气概，还慷慨大方，她要和他乘夜班船走，去当他的妻子，一道在布宜诺斯艾利斯生活。在那儿，他早已为她准备了一个新的家。

初次见他的情景她记得多清楚啊；那时他在大路上，一所她常去拜访的房子暂住。想起来就跟几个礼拜前的事儿一样。他站在大门边，尖顶帽子向脑后推着，头发翻在前面，盖住古铜色的脸庞。接着他们认识了对方。每天傍晚他都在仓库外面等她，送她回家。他带着她去看波希米亚姑娘，当她跟他坐在剧院里那个陌生的座位区，她是那么开心。他对音乐极其痴迷，自己还唱一点儿。别人都知道他俩是在谈恋爱，而且，当他唱到那个爱上水手的少女，她总是感觉又快活又迷糊。他过去老是开玩笑叫她的绰号。刚一开始，身边有个小伙子让她兴奋，后来她就开始喜欢他了。他有来自遥远国度的故事。他是在爱轮轮船公司的一艘跑加拿大线的船上，从一个月领一英镑的甲板手开始做起的。他跟她列数他上过的船和干过的活儿。他跟她讲他穿越麦哲伦海峡和遇到可怕的巴塔哥尼亚人的故事。他曾在布宜诺斯艾利斯安然脱险，他说，然后就来到了这个古老的国度，只待一个假期。自然，她父亲发现了这一切，接着便严禁她再跟他说一句话。

"我清楚这些海上的小子们是怎么一回事儿。"他说。

有一天他跟弗兰克吵了一架，那之后，她就只能跟她的恋人悄悄地相会了。

街上的夜色更深了。她腿上那两封原本是呈白色的信慢慢地看不清了。一封是给哈里的，另一封给她的父亲。尔尼斯特一直是她最爱的哥哥，但是她也喜欢哈里。她父亲最近老了许多，她注意到了；他会想念她的。有时候他也可以很好。不是太久以前，她因病躺倒了一整天，他给她读了一个鬼故事，还在火边给她烤了土司。还有一天，那是他们的母亲还在世的时候，一家人跑到豪特山野餐。她记得她父亲戴上了她母亲的软帽来逗孩子们笑。

她没剩什么时间了，但她还是坐在窗边，把头抵着窗帘，吸着棉布灰尘的气味。从大街的远处她可以听到有人拉着街头风琴。她识得那旋律。出奇的是那一个晚上响起的也是这个旋律，让她想起了对母亲的承诺，她许诺会尽力让这个家尽可能长的不散掉。她想起母亲病重的最后一夜；她又是在厅的那一边的那个封闭，幽暗的房间里，而外面传来了一支意大利的悲哀旋律。他们勒令那风琴手走得远远的，塞给了他六便士。她记得父亲撑回病房，嘴里说着："意大利人都该死！跑到这儿来了！"

当她眼前浮现着她母亲下世的那最后一小会儿——就是她平凡的生命终于在最后的疯狂闭幕中牺牲掉的那一刻，她颤抖着，好像耳畔又响起母亲愚顽的坚持重复着的声音：

"德日王色朗！德日王色朗！"

她在惊怖的推动中一下子站起来。逃！她一定得逃！弗兰克会拯救她的。他会给她生命，或许，还有爱。可她想要活着。为什么她就该不快活？她有权幸福。弗兰克会拥她入怀，紧紧包住她。他会拯救她。

她站在北墙区码头摇晃攒动的人群里。他拉着她的手，她知道他在跟她说着些关于船票的什么话，翻来覆去的。码头上满是背着棕色行囊的士兵。穿过候船室的道道阔门，她瞥到轮船的巨大黑影，停靠在码头垣边，上面是一个个亮堂堂的舷窗。她没有答他的话。她感觉到自己的脸颊苍白寒冷，而且，出于让她困惑的苦恼，她祈祷神指引她，指示她什么才是她的职责。船上一声悲怆的汽笛透入雾层。如果走，明天她就跟弗兰克在海上，在船冒出的蒸气中驶向布宜诺斯艾利斯。他们已经订好了船票。在他为她做了这一切以后她还可以反悔么？她的苦恼在她身体里唤起一阵反胃，而她在无声又炙热的祷告中不停地动着嘴唇。

铃声叮咚打在她的心上。她感觉到他一把抓住她的手：

"来！"

全世界全部的海都在她的心头翻滚。他正拉着她往那里面去。他会淹死她的。她用两手抓住铁栏杆。

"来呀！"

不！不！不！不可能的。她狂暴地死死抠住那铁条。向着海中间发出一声痛苦的大喊。

"伊芙琳！伊芙！"

他冲过大堤，喊着叫她跟上来。他被人吼着催着往前走，可他还是在叫她。她把白白的脸庞转向他，被动的，像只无助的动物。她的眼睛没有给他或是爱或是告别或是认识他的任何讯号。

第八单元　达洛维夫人　第一章（选段）

达洛维夫人说他要自己去买花。

因为露西有很多事情要做。几扇屋门将从合页上卸下；朗波尔迈耶店里的工人要来。再说，克拉丽莎·达洛维想，今天早晨多么清新啊，好像是专为海滩上的孩子们准备的。

多有意思！多么痛快！因为她过去总有这样的感觉，每当合页吱扭一声——她现在还能听见那合页的轻微声响——她猛地推开伯尔顿村住宅的落地窗置身于户外的时候。早晨的空气多么清新，多么宁静，当然比现在要沉寂些；像微浪拍岸，像浮波轻吻，清凉刺肤然而（对于当时的她，一个十八岁的姑娘来说）又有几分庄严肃穆；当时她站在敞开的落地窗前，预感到有某种可怕的事就要发生；她观赏着鲜花，观赏着烟雾缭绕的树丛和上下翻飞的乌鸦；他站着，看着，直到彼得·沃尔什说："对着蔬菜想什么心事呢？"——是那么说的吧？——"我感兴趣的是人，不是花椰菜。"——是那么说的吧？这一定是他在那天吃早餐的时候说的，在她走到屋外的台地之后——彼得·沃尔什。他过些天就要从印度回来了，是六月还是七月，她记不清了，因为他的来信总是那么枯燥无味；倒是他常说的几句话让人忘不掉；她记得他的眼睛、他的折叠小刀、他的微笑、他的坏脾气，还有，在忘掉了成千上万件事情之后，还记得他说过的关于卷心菜的诸如此类的话——多奇怪呀！

她站在人行道的石沿上挺了挺身子，等着达特诺尔公司的小货车开过去。一个有魅力的女人，斯科洛普·派维斯这样评价她（他了解她的程度就跟威斯敏斯特市的居民了解自己紧邻的程度差不多）；她有几分像小鸟，像只樫鸟，蓝绿色，体态轻盈，充满活力，尽管她已经年过五十，而且自患病以来面色苍白。她站在人行道边上，从未看见过他，她在等着过马路，腰背直挺。

由于在威斯敏斯特住了——有多少年呢？二十多年了——克拉丽莎相信，你即使在车流之中，或在夜半醒来，总能感觉到一种特殊的寂静，或者说是肃穆；总能感觉到一种不可名状的停顿、一种牵挂（但有可能是因为她的心脏，据说是流行性感冒所致），等待着国会大厦上的大本钟敲响。听！那深沉洪亮的钟声响了。先是前奏，旋律优美；然后报时，铿锵有力。那深沉的音波逐渐消逝在空中。我们是如此愚蠢，穿过维多利亚街时她这样想。

（谷启楠 译）

第九单元　红字　第二章

　　二百多年前一个夏日的上午，狱前街上牢房门前的草地上，满满地站着好大一群波士顿的居民，他们一个个都紧盯着布满铁钉的橡木牢门。如若换成其他百姓，或是推迟到新英格兰后来的历史阶段，这些蓄着胡须的好心肠的居民们板着的冷冰冰的面孔，可能是面临凶险的征兆，至少也预示着某个臭名昭著的罪犯即将受到人们期待已久的制裁，因为在那时，法庭的判决无非是认可公众舆论的裁处。但是，由于早年清教徒性格严峻，这种推测未免过于武断。也许，是一个奴隶或是被家长送交给当局的一名逆子要在这笞刑柱上受到管教。也许，是一位唯信仰论者、一位教友派的教友或信仰其他异端的教徒被鞭挞出城，或是一个闲散的印第安游民，因为喝了白人的烈酒满街胡闹，要挨着鞭子给赶进树林。也许，那是地方官的遗孀西宾斯老夫人那样生性恶毒的巫婆，将要给吊死在绞架上。无论属于哪种情况，围观者总是摆出分毫不爽的庄严姿态；这倒十分符合早期移民的身份，因为他们将宗教和法律视同一体，二者在他们的品性中融溶为一，凡涉及公共纪律的条款，不管是最轻微的还是最严重的都同样令他们肃然起敬和望而生畏，确实，一个站在刑台上的罪人能够从这样一些旁观看身上谋得的同情是少而又少、冷而又冷的。另外，如今只意味着某种令人冷嘲热讽的惩罚，在当时却可能被赋予同死刑一样严厉的色彩。

　　就在我们的故事发生的那个夏天的早晨，有一情况颇值一书：挤在人群中的好几位妇女，看来对可能出现的任何刑罚抱有特殊的兴趣。那年月没有那么多文明讲究，身着衬裙和撑裙的女人们公然出入于大庭广众之中，只要有可能，便要撅动娘们那并不娇弱的躯体，挤进最靠近刑台的人群中去，也不会锻入什么不成体统的感觉。那些在英伦故土上出生和成长的媳妇和姑娘们，比起她们六七代之后的漂亮的后裔来，身体要粗壮些，精神也要粗犷些；因为通过家系承袭的链条，每代母亲遗传给她女儿的，即使不是较她为少的坚实有力的性格，总会是比较柔弱的体质、更加娇小和短暂的美貌和更加纤细的身材。当时在牢门附近站着的妇女们，和那位堪称代表女性的男子气概的伊丽莎白相距不足半个世纪。她们是那位女王的乡亲：她们家乡的牛肉和麦酒，佐以未经提炼的精神食粮，大量充实进她们的躯体。因此，明亮的晨光所照射着的，是宽阔的肩膀、发育丰满的胸脯和又圆又红的双颊——她们都是在遥远的祖国本岛上长大成人的，远还没有在新英格兰的气氛中变得白皙与瘦削些。尤其令人瞩目的是，这些主妇们多数人一开口便是粗喉咙、大嗓门，要是在今天，她们的言谈无论是含义还是音量，都足以使我们瞠目结舌。

"婆娘们，"一个满脸横肉的五十岁的老婆子说，"我跟你们说说我的想法。要是我们这些上了一把年纪、名声又好的教会会友，能够处置海丝特·白兰那种坏女人，倒是给大伙办了件好事。你们觉得怎么样，婆娘们？要是那个破靶站在眼下咱们这五个姐们儿跟前听候判决，她能够带着那些可敬的官老爷们赏给她的判决溜过去吗？老天爷，我才不信呢！"

"听人说，"另一个女人说，"尊敬的丁梅斯代尔教长，就是她的牧师，为了在他的教众中出了这桩丑事，简直伤心透顶啦。"

"那帮官老爷都是敬神的先生，可惜慈悲心太重——这可是真事，"第三个人老珠黄的婆娘补充说。"最起码，他们应该在海丝特·白兰的脑门上烙个记号。那总能让海丝特太太有点怕，我敢这么说。可她——那个破烂货——她才不在乎他们在她前襟上贴个什么呢！哼，你们等着瞧吧，她准会别上个胸针，或者是异教徒的什么首饰，挡住胸口，照样招摇过市！"

"啊，不过，"一个手里领着孩子的年轻媳妇轻声插嘴说，"她要是想挡着那记号就随她去吧，反正她心里总会受折磨的。"

"我们扯什么记号不记号的，管它是在她前襟上还是脑门上呢？"另一个女人叫嚷着，她在这几个自命的法官中长相最丑，也最不留情。"这女人给我们大伙都丢了脸，她就该死。难道说没有管这种事的法律吗？明明有嘛，圣经里和法典上全都写着呢。那就请这些不照章办事的官老爷们的太太小姐们去走邪路吧，那才叫自作自受呢！"

"天哪，婆娘们，"人群中一个男人惊呼道，"女人看到绞刑架就害怕，除去这种廉耻之心，她们身上难道就没有德行了吗？别把话说得太重了！轻点，喂，婆娘们！牢门的锁在转呢，海丝特太太本人就要出来了。"

牢门从里面给一下子打开了，最先露面的是狱吏，他腰侧挎着剑，手中握着权杖，那副阴森可怖的模样像个暗影似的出现在日光之中。这个角色的尊容便是清教徒法典全部冷酷无情的象征和代表，对触犯法律的人最终和最直接执法则是他的差事。此时他伸出左手举着权杖，右手抓着一个年轻妇女的肩头，挽着她向前走；到了牢门口，她用了一个颇能说明她个性的力量和天生的尊严的动作，推开狱吏，像是出于她自主的意志一般走进露天地。她怀里抱着一个三个月左右的婴儿，那孩子眨着眼睛，转动她的小脸躲避着过分耀眼的阳光——自从她降生以来，还只习惯于监狱中的土牢或其他暗室那种昏晦的光线呢。

当那年轻的妇女——就是婴儿的母亲——全身伫立在人群面前时，她的第一个冲动似乎就是把孩子抱在胸前；她这么做与其说是出于母爱的激情，不如说可以借此掩盖钉在她衣裙上的标记。然而，她很快就醒悟过来了，用她的耻辱的一个标记来掩盖另一个标记是无济于事的，于是，索性用一条胳膊架着孩子，她虽然面孔红得发烧，却露出高傲的微笑，用毫无愧色的目光环视着她的同镇居民和街坊邻里。她的裙袍的前胸上露出了一个用红色细布做就、周围用金丝线精心绣成奇巧花边的一个字母 A。这个字母制作别致，体现了丰富的想象力和华美的匠心，佩在衣服上构成尽美尽善的装饰，而她的衣服把她那年月的情趣衬托得恰到好处，只是其艳丽程度大大超出了殖民地俭补标准的规定。

那年轻妇女身材颀长，体态优美之极。她头上乌黑的浓发光彩夺目，在阳光下说说熠熠生辉。她的面孔不仅皮肤滋润、五官端正、容貌秀丽，而且还有一对鲜明的眉毛和一双漆黑的深目，十分楚楚动人。就那个时代女性举止优雅的风范而论，她也属贵妇之列；她自有一种端庄的风韵，并不同子如今人们心目中的那种纤巧、轻盈和不可言喻的优雅。即使以当年的概念而吉，海丝特·白兰也从来没有像步出监狱的此时此刻这样更像贵妇。那些本来就认识她的人，原先满以为她经历过这一磨难，会黯然失色，结果却惊得都发呆了，因为他们所看到的，是她焕发的美丽，竟把笼罩着她的不幸和耻辱凝成一轮光环。不过，目光敏锐的旁观者无疑能从中觉察出一种微妙的痛楚。她在狱中按照自己的想象，专门为这场合制作的服饰，以其特有的任性和别致，似乎表达了她的精神境界和由绝望而无所顾忌的心情。但是，吸引了所有的人的目光而且事实上使海丝特·白兰焕然一新的，则是在她胸前额频闪光的绣得妙不可言的那个红字，以致那些与她熟识的男男女女简直感到是第一次与她谋面。这个红字具有一种震慑的力量，竟然让她从普通人中超脱出来，紧裹在自身的氛围里。

"她倒做得一手好针线，这是不用说的，"一个旁观的女人说，"这个厚脸皮的淫妇居然想到用这一手来显示自己，可真是从来没见过我说，婆娘们，这纯粹是当面笑话我们那些规规矩矩的官老爷，这不是借火入先生们判的刑罚来大出风头吗?"

"我看啊!"一个面孔板得最紧的老太婆咕哝着,"要是我们能把海丝特太太那件讲究的衣袍从她秀气的肩膀上扒下来,倒挺不值钱;至于她绣的稀奇古怪的那个红字嘛,我倒愿意借给她一块我害风湿病用过的法兰绒破布片,做出来才更合适呢!"

"噢,安静点,街坊们,安静点!"她们当中最年轻的同伴悄声说;"别让她听见咱们的话!她绣的那个字,针针线线全都扎到她心口上呢。"

狱吏此时用权杖做了个姿势。

"让开路,好心的人们,让开路,看在国王的份上!"他叫嚷着。"让开一条队,我向诸位保证,白兰太太要站的地方,无论男女老少都可以看清她的漂亮的衣服,从现在起直到午后一点,保你们看个够。祝福光明正大的马萨诸塞殖民地,一切罪恶都得拉出来见见太阳!过来,海丝特太太,在这市场上亮亮你那鲜红的字母吧!"

围观的人群中挤开了一条通路。海丝特·白兰跟着在前面开路的狱吏,身后跟随着拧眉攒目的男人和心狠面恶的女人的不成形的队伍,走向指定让她示众的地方。一大群怀着好奇心来凑热闹的小男孩,对眼前的事态不明,所以,只晓得学校放了他们半天假,他们一边在头前跑着,一边不时回过头来盯着她的脸、她怀中抱着的眨着眼的婴儿,还有她胸前那个丢人现眼的红字。当年,从牢门到市场没有几步路。然而,要是以囚犯的体验来测量,恐怕是一个路途迢迢的旅程;因为她虽说是高视阔步,但在人们逼视的目光下,每迈出一步都要经历一番痛苦,似乎她的心已经给抛到满心,任凭所有的人碾踩践踏。然而,在我们人类的本性中,原有一条既绝妙又慈悲的先天准备:遭受苦难的人在承受痛楚的当时并不能觉察到其剧烈的程度,反倒是过后延绵的折磨最能使其撕心裂肺。因此,海丝特·白兰简直是以一种安详的举止,度过了此时的磨难,来到市场西端的刑台跟前。这座刑台几乎就竖在波士顿最早的教堂的檐下,看上去像是教堂的附属建筑。

事实上,这座刑台是构成整个惩罚机器的一个组成部分,时隔二、三代人的今天,它在我们的心目中只不过是一个历史和传统的纪念,但在当年,却如同法国大革命时期恐怖党人的断头台一样,被视为教化劝善的有效动力。简言之,这座刑台是一座枷号示众的台子,上面竖着那个惩罚用的套枷,做得刚好把人头紧紧卡死,以便引颈翘首供人观瞻。设计这样一个用铁和木制成的家伙显然极尽羞辱之能事。依我看来，无论犯有何等过失，再没有比这种暴行更违背我们的人性的了，其不准罪人隐藏他那羞惭的面容的险恶用心实在无以复加；而这恰恰是这一刑罚的本意所在。不过，就海丝特·白兰的例子而论，和多数其他案子相仿，她所受到的惩处是要在刑台上罚站示众一段时间，而无须受扼颈囚首之苦，从而幸免于这一丑陋的机器最为凶残的手段。她深知自己此时的角色的意义，举步登上一段木梯，站到齐肩高的台上，展示在围观人群的众目睽睽之前。

设若在这一群清教徒之中有一个罗马天主教徒的话，他就会从这个服饰和神采如画、怀中紧抱婴儿的美妇身上，联想起众多杰出画家所竞相描绘的圣母的形象，诚然，他的这种联想只能在对比中才能产生，因为圣像中那圣洁清白的母性怀中的婴儿是献给世人来赎罪的。然而在她身上，世俗生活中最神圣的品德，却被最深重的罪孽所玷污了，其结果，只能使世界由于这妇人的美丽而更加晦默，由于她生下的婴儿而越发沉沦。

在人类社会尚未腐败到极点之前，目睹这种罪恶与羞辱的场面，人们还不致以淡然一笑代替不寒而栗，总会给留下一种敬畏心理。亲眼看到海丝特·白兰示众的人们尚未失去他们的纯真。如果她被判死刑，他们会冷冷地看着她死去，而不会咕哝一句什么过于严苛；但他们谁也不会像另一种社会形态中的人那样，把眼前的这种示众只当作笑柄。即使有人心里觉得这事有点可笑，也会因为几位至尊至贵的大人物的郑重出席，而吓得不敢放肆。总督、他的几位参议、一名法官、一名将军和镇上的牧师们就在议事厅的阳台上或坐或立，俯视着刑台。能有这样一些人物到场，而不失他们地位的显赫和职务的威严，我们可以有把握地推断，所做的法律判决肯定具有真挚而有效的含义。因之，人群也显出相应的阴郁和庄重。这个不幸的罪人，在数百双无情的目光紧盯着她、集中在她前胸的重压之下，尽一个妇人的最大可能支撑着自己。这实在是难以忍受的。她本是一个充满热情、容易冲动的人，此时她已使自己坚强起来，以面对用形形色色的侮辱来发泄的公愤的毒刺和利刃；但是，人们那种庄重的情绪反倒隐含着一种可做得多的气氛，使她宁可看到那一张张僵刻的面孔露出轻蔑的嬉笑来嘲弄她。如果从构成这一群人中的每一个男人、每一个女人和每一个尖嗓门的孩子的口中爆发出哄笑，海丝特·白兰或许可以对他们所有的人报以倨傲的冷笑。可是，在她注定要忍受的这种沉闷的打击之下，她时时感到要鼓起胸腔中的全部力量来尖声呼号，并从刑台上翻到地面，否则，她会立刻发疯的。

　　然而，在她充当众目所瞩的目标的全部期间，她不时感到眼前茫茫一片，至少，人群像一大堆支离破碎、光怪陆离的幻象般地朦胧模糊。她的思绪，尤其是她的记忆，却不可思议地活跃，越出这蛮荒的大洋西岸边缘上的小镇的祖创的街道，不断带回来别的景色与场面；她想到的，不是那些尖顶高帽下藐视她的面孔。她回忆起那些最琐碎零散、最无关紧要的事情；孩提时期和学校生活，儿时的游戏和争吵，以及婚前在娘家的种种琐事蜂拥回到她的脑海，其中还混杂着她后来生活中最重大的事件的种种片断，一切全都历历如在目前；似乎全都同等重要，或者全都像一出戏。可能，这是她心理上的一种本能反应：通过展现这些各色各样、变幻莫测的画面，把自己的精神从眼前这残酷现实的无情重压下解脱出来。

　　无论如何，这座示众刑台成了一个瞭望点，在海丝特·白兰面前展现出自从她幸福的童年以来的全都轨迹。她痛苦地高高站在那里，再次看见了她在老英格兰故乡的村落和她父母的家园：那是一座破败的灰色石屋，虽说外表是一派衰微的景象，但在门廊上方还残存着半明半暗的盾形家族纹章，标志着远祖的世系。她看到了她父亲的面容：光秃秃的额头和飘洒在伊丽莎白时代老式环状皱领上的威风凛凛的白须；她也看到了她母亲的面容，那种无微不至和牵肠挂肚的爱的表情，时时在她脑海中萦绕，即使在母亲丢世之后，仍在女儿的人生道路上经常留下温馨忆念的告诫。她看到了自己少女时代的光彩动人的美貌，把她惯于映照的那面昏暗的镜子的整个镜心都照亮了。她还看到了另一副面孔，那是一个年老力衰的男人的面孔，苍白而瘦削，看上去一副学者模样，由于在灯光下研读一册册长篇巨著而老眼昏花。然而正是这同一双昏花的烂眼，在窥测他人的灵魂时，又具有那么奇特的洞察力。尽管海丝特·白兰那女性的想象力竭力想摆脱他的形象，但那学者和隐士的身影还是出现了：他略带畸形，左肩比右肩稍高。在她回忆的画廊中接下来升到她眼前的，是欧洲大陆一座城市里的纵横交错又显得狭窄的街道，以及年深日久、古色古香的公共建筑物，宏伟的天主教堂和高大的灰色住宅；一种崭新的生活在那里等待着她，不过仍和那个畸形的学者密切相关；那种生活像是附在颓垣上的一簇青苔，只能靠腐败的营养滋补自己。最终，这些接踵而至的场景烟消云散，海丝特·白兰又回到这片清教徒殖民地的简陋的市场上，全镇的人都聚集在这里，一双双严厉的眼睛紧紧盯着她——是的，盯着她本人——她站在示众刑台上，怀中抱着婴儿，胸前钉着那个用金丝线绝妙地绣着花边的鲜红的字母 A！

这一切会是真的吗？她把孩子往胸前猛地用力一抱，孩子哇地一声哭了；她垂下眼睛注视着那鲜红的字母，甚至还用指头触摸了一下，以便使自己确信婴儿和耻辱都是实实在在的。是啊——这些便是她的现实，其余的一切全都消失了！

第十单元　阿蒙提拉多的酒桶

福吐纳托对我百般迫害，我都尽量忍在心头，可是一旦他胆敢侮辱我，我就发誓要报仇了，您早就摸熟我生性脾气，总不见得当我说说吓唬人。总有一天我要报仇雪恨；这个主意坚定不移，既然拿定主意不改，就没想到会出危险。我不仅要给他吃吃苦头，还要干得绝了后患。报仇的自己得到报应，这笔仇就没了清。复仇的不让冤家知道是谁害他，这笔仇也没了清。

不消说，我一言一语，一举一动都没引起福吐纳托怀疑是存心不良。还是照常对他笑脸相迎，可他没看出如今我是想到要送他命才笑呢。

福吐纳托这人在某些方面虽令人尊重，甚至令人敬畏，可就是有个弱点。他自夸是品酒老手。意大利人没几个具有真正行家的气质。他们的热诚，多半都用来随机应变，看风使舵，好让英国和奥地利的大财主上当。谈到古画和珠宝方面，福吐纳托跟他同胞一样，夸夸其谈，不过谈到陈酒方面，倒是真正识货。这点我跟他大致相同——对意大利葡萄酒，我也算内行，只要办得到的话，就大量买进。

在热闹的狂欢节里，有天傍晚，正当暮色苍茫，我碰到了这位朋友。他亲热地招呼我，因为他肚里灌饱了酒。这家伙扮成小丑，身穿杂色条纹紧身衣，头戴圆尖帽，上面系着铃铛。我看见他真是高兴极了，不由想握着他的手久久不放。

我对他说："老兄啊，幸会，幸会。你今天气色真是好到极点。我弄到一大桶所谓白葡萄酒（西班牙蒙蒂利亚生产的一种甜酒），可我不放心。"

"怎的？"他说，"白葡萄酒？一大桶？不见得吧！在狂欢节期间哪儿弄得到？"

"我不放心，"我答道，"我真笨透了，居然没跟你商量，就照白葡萄酒的价钱全付清了。找又找不到你，可又生怕错过这笔买卖。"

"白葡萄酒！"

"我不放心。"

"白葡萄酒！"

"我一定得放下这条心！"

"白葡萄酒!"

"瞧你有事,我正想去找卢克雷西呢。只有他才能品酒。他会告诉我——"

"可有些傻瓜硬说他眼力跟你不相上下呢。"

"快,咱们走吧。"

"上哪儿?"

"上你地窖去。"

"老兄,这不行;我不愿欺你心好就麻烦你啊。我看出你有事。卢克雷西——"

"我没事,来吧。"

"老兄,这不行。有事没事倒没什么,就是冷得够呛,我看你受不了。地窖里潮得不得了。四壁都是硝。"

"咱们还是走吧,冷算不了什么。白葡萄酒!你可上当啦。说到卢克雷西,他连雪梨酒跟白葡萄酒都分不清。"

说着福吐纳托就架住我胳膊;我戴上黑绸面具,把短披风紧紧裹住身子,就由他催着我上公馆去了。

家里听差一个也不见,都趁机溜出去过节了。我对他们说过我要到第二天早晨才回家,还跟他们讲明,不准出门。我心里有数,这么一吩咐,包管我刚转身,马上就一个个都跑光了。

我从烛台上拿了两个火把,一个给福吐纳托,领他穿过几套房间,走进拱廊,通往地窖,走下长长一座回旋楼梯,请他一路跟着,随加小心。我们终于到了楼梯脚下,一块站在蒙特里梭府墓窖的湿地上。

我朋友的脚步摇摇晃晃,跨一步,帽上铃铛就丁零当啷响。

"那桶酒呢?"他说。

"在前面,"我说,"可得留神墙上雪白的蛛网在发光。"

他朝我回过身来,两只醉意蒙眬的眼睛水汪汪地盯着我。

"硝?"他终于问道。

"硝,"我答道,"你害上那种咳嗽有多久了?"

"呃嘿!呃嘿!——呃嘿!呃嘿!呃嘿!——呃嘿!呃嘿!呃嘿!——呃嘿!呃嘿!呃嘿!——呃嘿!呃嘿!呃嘿!"

我那可怜的朋友老半天答不上口。

"没什么，"最后他说道。

"噗，"我依然答道，"咱们回去吧，你的身体要紧。你有钱有势，人人敬慕，又得人心；你像我从前一样幸福。要有个三长两短，那真是非同小可。我倒无所谓，咱们回去吧，你害病，我可担待不起。再说，还有卢克雷西——"

"别说了，"他说，"咳嗽可不算什么，咳不死的。我不会咳死。"

"对——对，"我答，"说真的，我可不是存心吓唬你——可总得好好预防才是。喝一口美道克酒去去潮气吧。"

说着我就从泥地上的一长溜酒瓶里，拿起一瓶酒，砸了瓶颈。

"喝吧，"我把酒递给他。

他瞟了我一眼，就将酒瓶举到唇边。他歇下手，亲热地向我点点头，帽上铃铛就丁零当啷响了。

"我为周围那些长眠地下的干杯。"他说。

"我为你万寿无疆干杯。"

他又挽着我胳膊，我们就继续往前走。

"这些地窖可真大。"他说。

"蒙特里梭家是大族，子子孙孙多。"我答。

"我忘了你们府上的家徽啦。"

"偌大一只人脚，金的，衬着一片天蓝色的背景，把一条腾起的蝰蛇踩烂了，蛇牙就咬着脚跟。"

"那么家训呢？"

"凡伤我者，必遭惩罚。"

"妙啊！"他说。

喝了酒，他眼睛亮闪闪的，帽上铃铛又丁零当啷响了。我喝了美道克酒，心里更加胡思乱想了。我们走过尸骨和大小酒桶堆成的一长条夹弄，进了墓窖的最深处，我又站住脚，这回竟放胆抓住福吐纳托的上臂。

"硝！"我说，"瞧，越来越多了。像青苔，挂在拱顶上。咱们在河床下面啦。水珠子滴在尸骨里呢。快走，咱们趁早回去吧。你咳嗽——"

"没什么，"他说，"咱们往下走吧。不过先让我再喝口美道克酒。"

我打开一壶葛拉维酒，递给他。他一口气喝光了，眼睛里顿时杀气腾腾，呵呵直笑，把酒瓶往上一扔，那个手势，我可不明白是什么意思。

我吃惊地看着他。他又做了那个手势——一个稀奇古怪的手势。

"你不懂？"他说。

"我不懂。"我答。

"那你就不是同道。"

"怎的？"

"你不是泥瓦工。"

"是的，是的，"我说，"是的，是的。"

"你？不见得吧！你是？"

"我是，"我答。

"暗号呢，"他说，"暗号呢？"

"就是这个，"我边说边从短披风的褶裥下拿出把泥刀。

"你开玩笑呐，"他倒退几步，喊着说。"咱们还是往前去看白葡萄酒吧。"

"好吧，"我说，一边把泥刀重新放在披风下面，一边伸过胳膊给他扶着。他沉沉地靠在我胳膊上。这就继续向前走，再往下走，到了一个幽深的墓穴里，这里空气浑浊，手里火把顿时不见火光，只剩火焰了。

在墓穴的尽头，又出现了更狭窄的墓穴。四壁成排堆着尸骨，一直高高堆到拱顶，就跟巴黎那些人墓窖一个样。里头这个墓穴有三面墙，仍然这样堆着。还有一面的尸骨都给推倒了，乱七八糟的堆在地上，积成相当大的一个尸骨墩。在搬开尸骨的那堵墙间，只见里头还有一个墓穴，或者壁龛，深约四英尺，宽达三英尺，高六七英尺。看上去当初造了并没打算派什么特别用处，不过是墓窖顶下两根大柱间的空隙罢了，后面却靠着一堵坚固的花岗石垣墙。

福吐纳托举起昏暗的火把，尽力朝壁龛深处仔细探看，可就是白费劲，火光微弱，看不见底。

"往前走，"我说，"白葡萄酒就在这里头。卢克雷西——"

"他是个充内行，"我朋友一面摇摇晃晃地往前走，一面插嘴道，我紧跟在他屁股后走进去。一眨眼工夫，他走到壁龛的尽头了，一见给岩石挡住了道，就一筹莫展地发着愣。隔了片刻，我已经把他锁在花岗石墙上了。墙上装着两个铁环，横里相距两英尺左右。一个环上挂着根短铁链，另一个挂着把大锁。不消一刹那工夫，就把他拦腰拴上链子了。他惊慌失措，根本忘了反抗，我拔掉钥匙，就退出壁龛。

"伸出手去摸摸墙，"我说，"保你摸到硝。真是湿得很。让我再一次求求你回去吧。不回去？那我得离开你啦。可我还先得尽份心，照顾你一下。"

"白葡萄酒！"我朋友惊魂未定，不由失声喊道。

"不错，"我答，"白葡萄酒。"

说着我就在前文提过的尸骨堆间忙着。我把尸骨扔开，不久就掏出好些砌墙用的石块和灰泥。我便用这些材料，再靠那把泥刀，一个劲地在壁龛入口处砌起一堵墙来。

我连头一层石块也没砌成，就知道福吐纳托的醉意八成醒了。最先听到壁龛深处传出幽幽一声哼叫。这不像醉鬼的叫声。随即一阵沉默，久久未了。我砌了第二层，再砌第三层，再砌第四层；接着就听到拼命摇晃铁链的声音。一直响了好几分钟，我索性歇下手中的活，在骨堆上坐下，为的是听得更加称心如意，待等当啷当啷的声音终于哑寂，才重新拿起泥刀，不停手的砌上第五层，第六层，第七层。这时砌得差不多齐胸了。我又歇下手来，将火把举到石墙上，一线微弱的火光就照在里头那个人影上。

猛然间，那个上了锁链的人影从嗓子眼里发出一连串尖利响亮的喊声，仿佛想拼命吓退我。刹那间，我拿不定主意，簌簌直抖，不久就拔出长剑，手执长剑在壁龛里摸索起来；转念一想，又放下了心。我的手搁在墓窖那坚固的建筑上，就安心了。再走到墙跟前，那人大声嚷嚷，我也对他哇哇乱叫。他叫一声，我应一声，叫得比他响，比他亮。这一叫，对方叫嚷的声音就哑了。

这时已经深更半夜了，我也快干完了。第八层，第九层，第十层早砌上了，最后一层，也就是第十一层，也快砌完了；只消嵌进最后一块石块，再抹上灰泥就行了。我拼了命托起这块沉甸甸的石块，把石块一角放在原定地位。谁知这时壁龛里传来一阵低沉的笑声，吓得我头发根根直立。接着传来凄厉的一声，好容易才认出那是福吐纳托老爷的声音。只听得说——

"哈！哈！哈！——嘻！嘻！嘻！——这倒真是个天大的笑话——绝妙的玩笑，回头到了公馆，就好笑个痛快啦——嘻！嘻！嘻！——边喝酒边笑——嘻！嘻！嘻！"

"白葡萄酒！"我说。

"嘻！嘻！嘻！——嘻！嘻！嘻！——对，白葡萄酒。可还来得及吗？福吐纳托夫人他们不是在公馆里等咱们吗？咱们走吧！"

"对，"我说，"咱们走吧！"

"看在老天爷分儿上走吧，蒙特里梭！"

"对，"我说，"看在老天爷分儿上。"

谁知我说了这句话，怎么听都听不到一声回答。心里渐渐沉不住气了，便出声喊道：

"福吐纳托！"

没搭腔。我再唤一遍。

"福吐纳托！"

还是没搭腔。我将火把塞进还没砌上的墙孔，扔了进去。谁知只传来丁零当啷的响声。我不由恶心起来，这是由于墓窖里那份湿气的缘故。我赶紧完工。把最后一块石头塞好，抹上灰泥。再紧靠着这堵新墙，重新堆好尸骨。五十年来一直没人动过。愿死者安息吧！

第十一单元　哈克贝利·费恩历险记　第十一章

"进来"，那个妇女说。我就走了进去。她说：

"请坐。"

我坐了下来。她那亮亮的小眼睛把我端详了个仔细，接着说："你叫什么名字啊？"

"莎拉·威廉斯。"

"你住哪里？是在这儿附近么？"

"不。是在霍克维尔，这儿下面七英里地。我一路走得来，实在累了。"

"我看也饿了吧。我给你找点东西吃。"

"不，我不饿。本来我倒是饿得很。我在离这儿两英里路的一家农庄不能不歇了一口气，所以不饿了。这样我才会弄得这么晚。我妈在家有病，又没有钱，我是来把情况告诉我叔叔阿勃纳·摩尔的。我妈对我说，他住在这个镇上的那一头。这儿我还没有来过呢。你认识他吧？"

"不，我还不认识什么人哩。我住在这里还不到两个星期。要到镇上那一头，还有不少路呢。你最好这晚上便歇在这里。把你的那顶帽子给取下来吧。"

"不"，我说，"我看我歇一会儿，便往前走。天黑我不怕。"

她说她可不能放我一个人走。不过，她丈夫一会儿便会回来，大概是一个半钟头左右吧。她会让她丈夫陪我一起走。接下来便讲她的丈夫，讲她沿河上游的亲戚，讲她下游的亲戚，讲她们过去的光景怎样比现在好得多，怎样自己对这一带并没有搞清楚，怎样打错了主意到了这个镇上来，放了好日子不知道过——如此等等，说得没有个完。这样，我就担起心来，生怕这回找到她打听镇上的情况，也许这个主意是错了。不过，不一会儿，她提到了我爸爸以及那件杀人案，我就很乐意听她唠叨下去。她说到我和汤姆·索亚怎样弄到六千块钱的事（只是她说成了一万块钱），讲到了有关爸爸的种种情况，以及他多么命苦，我又是多么命苦。到后来，她讲到了我怎样被杀害。我说："是谁干的？在霍克维尔，我们听到过很多有关这件事的说法，不过是谁杀了哈克·芬的，我们可不知道。"

"嗯，据我看，就在这儿，也有不少人想要知道是谁杀了他的。有些人认为，是老芬头儿自己干的。"

"不吧——真是这样么?"

"开头，几乎谁都是这么想的。他自己永远不会知道他怎样差一点儿就会落到个私刑处死。不过，到了天黑以前，那些人主意变了。据他们判断，认为是一个逃跑的黑奴名叫杰姆的干的。"

"怎么啦，他——"

我把话打住了。我看，最好我别作声。她滔滔不绝讲下去，根本没有注意到我的插话。

"那个黑奴逃跑的那一个晚上，正是哈克·芬被杀害的日子。因此，悬赏捉拿他——悬赏三百块钱。还为了捉拿老芬头儿——悬赏两百块钱。你知道吧，他在杀人后第二天早上来到了镇上，讲了这件事，然后和他们一起在渡轮上去寻找，可是一完事，人就走了，马上不见人了。在天黑以前，人家要给他处私刑，可是他跑掉了，你知道吧。嗯，到第二天，人家发现那个黑奴跑了。他们发现，杀人的那个晚上，十点钟以后，就不见这个黑奴的人影了。知道吧，人家就把罪名安在他头上。可是他们正嚷得起劲的时候，第二天，老芬头儿又回来了，又哭又喊地找到了撒切尔法官，索要那笔钱，为了走遍伊利诺伊州寻找那个黑奴。法官给了他几个钱，而当天晚上，他就喝得醉醺醺的，在半夜前一直在当地。半夜后，他和一些相貌凶恶的外地人在一起，接下来便和他们一起走掉了。啊，从此以后，再没见他回来过。人家说，在这件案子的风头过去以前，他未必会回来。因为人家如今认为，正是他杀了自己的孩子，把现场布置了一番，让人家以为是强盗干的，这样，他就能得到哈克的那笔钱，不用在诉讼案件上花费很长一段时间了。人家说，他是个窝囊废，干不了这个。哦，我看啊，这人可是够刁的了。他要是在一年之内不回来，他就不会有什么事了。你知道吧，你拿不出什么证据来定他的罪。一切便会烟消云散。他就会不费气力地把哈克的钱弄到手。"

"是的，我也这么看。我看不出他会有什么不好办的。是不是人家不再认为是黑奴干的呢?"

"哦，不。不是每个人都这么个看法。不少人认为是他干的。不过，人家很快便会逮到那个黑奴，说不定人家会逼着他招出来的。"

"怎么啦，人家还在搜捕他么?"

"啊，你可真是不懂事啊! 难道三百大洋是能天天摆在那里让人随手一拣就到手的么？有些人认为那个黑奴离这儿不远呢。我就是其中的一个——不过我没有到处说就是了。才几天前，我对隔壁木棚里的一对老年夫妇说过话，他们随口讲到，人们如今没有去附近那个叫作杰克逊岛的小岛。我问道，那里有人住么？他们说没有。我没有接下去说什么，不过我倒是想过一想的。我可以十分肯定，我曾望见过那儿冒烟，是在岛的尖端那边，时间是在这以前的一两天。我因此曾自个儿盘算过，那个黑奴多半就在那边啊。这样就值得花工夫到岛上去来个搜捕，在这以后，就没有再见到冒烟了。我寻思，说不定他溜走了，要是他就是那个黑奴的话。不过，我丈夫反正就要上那边去看一趟——他和另外一个人要去。他出门到上游去了，不过今天回来了，两个钟点以前，他一回到家，我就对他说过了。"

我搞得心神不安，坐也坐不住了。我这双手该干点什么才好啊。我就从桌子上拿起了一只针，想要穿通一根线头，我的手抖抖的，怎么也穿不好。那个妇女话头停了下来，我抬头一望，她正看着我，一脸好奇的神气，微微一笑。我把针和线往桌子上一放，装作听得出神的样子，——其实我也确实听得出神——接着说："三百块大洋可是一大笔钱啊。但愿我妈能得这笔钱。你丈夫今晚上去那么？"

"是啊。他和那个我跟你讲起的人到镇上去了，去搞一只小船，还要想想办法，看能不能弄到一支枪。他们半夜以后动身。"

"他们白天去不是能看得更清楚么？"

"是啊。可是那个黑奴不是也会看得更清楚么？半夜以后，他兴许会睡着了吧。他们就好穿过林子，轻手轻脚溜到那边，寻找到他的宿营地，乘着黑夜，找起来更方便些，如果他真有宿营之处的话。"

"这我倒没有想到。"

那个妇女还是带着好奇的神色看着我，这叫我很不舒服。

"亲爱的，你的名字叫什么来着？"

"玛——玛丽·威廉斯。"

我仿佛觉得，我最初说的时候并没有说是玛丽，所以我没有抬起头来。我觉得，我最初说的是莎拉。我因此觉得很窘，并且怕脸上露出了这样的神气。我但愿那个妇女能接着说点什么。她越是一声不响坐在那里，我越是局促不安。可是她这时说：

"亲爱的，你刚进门的时候，说的是莎拉吧？"

"啊，那是的，我是这么说了的。莎拉·玛丽·威廉斯。莎拉是我第一个名字。有人叫我莎拉，有人叫我玛丽。"

"哦，是这样啊。"

"是的。"

这样，我就觉得好过了一些。不过，我但愿能离开这里。

我还抬不起头来。

接下来，那个妇女就谈起了时势多么艰难，她们生活又多么穷困，老鼠又多么猖狂，仿佛这里就是它们的天下，如此等等。这样，我觉得又舒坦了起来。说到老鼠，她讲的可是实情。在角落头一个小洞里，每隔一会儿，就能见到一只老鼠，把脑袋伸出洞口探望一下。她说，她一个人在家时，手边必须准备好东西扔过去，不然得不到安生的时候。她给我看一根根铅丝拧成的一些团团，说扔起来很准。不过，一两天前，她把胳膊扭了，如今还不知道能不能扔呢。她看准了一个机会，朝一只老鼠猛然扔了过去，不过，她扔得离目标差一截子，一边叫了起来："噢！胳膊扭痛了。"她接着要我扔下一个试试看。我一心想的是在她家里的老头儿回来以前就溜之大吉，不过自然不便表露出来。我把铅团子拿到了手里，老鼠一探头，我就猛地扔过去，它要是迟一步，准会被砸成一只病歪歪的老鼠。她说我扔得挺准，还说她估摸，下一个我准能扔中。她把一些铅团子拿过来，又拿来一绞毛线，叫我帮她绕好。我伸出了双手，她把毛线套在我手上，一边讲起她自己和她丈夫的事。不过，她打听了话说："眼睛看准了老鼠。最好把铅团团放在大腿上，好随时扔过去。"

说着，她便把一些铅团子扔到我大腿上，我把双腿一并接住了。她接着说下去，不过才只说了一分钟。接下来她取下了毛线，眼睛直盯着我的脸，不过非常和颜悦色地问："说吧——你的真名字叫什么？"

"什——什么，大娘？"

"你真名是什么？是比尔还是汤姆？还是鲍勃？——还是什么？"

我看我准定是抖得像一片树叶子。我实在不知所措。可是我说：

"大娘，别作弄我这样一个穷苦的女孩吧，要是我在这里碍事，我可以——"

"哪有的事？你给我坐下，别动。我不会害你，也不会告发你。把你的秘密一五一十告诉我，相信我，我会保守秘密的。还不只这样，我会帮你忙的，我家老头儿也会的，只要你需要他的话。要知道，你是个逃出来的学徒——就是这么一回事。这有什么大不了的，这算得了什么啊。人家亏待了你，你就决心一跑了之。孩子，但愿你交好运，我不会告发的。原原本本告诉我——这才是一个好孩子。”

这样，我就说，事已如此，也不用再装了。还说，我会把一切的一切原原本本都倒给她听，只是她答应了的不许反悔。随后我告诉她，我父母双亡，按照法律，把我给栓住在乡下一个卑鄙的农民手里，离大河有三十英里。他虐待我，我再也不能忍受了。他出门几天，我便乘机偷了他女儿的几件旧衣服，溜出了家门。这三十英里，我走了三个晚上。我只在晚上走，白天躲起来，找地方睡，家里带出来的一袋面包和肉供我一路上食用。东西是足够的。我相信我的叔叔阿勃纳·摩尔会照看我的。这就是为什么我要上高申镇来。

“高申？孩子。这儿可不是高申啊！这是圣彼得堡啊。高申还在大河上边十英里地呢。谁跟你说这里是高申来着？”

“怎么啦？今天拂晓我遇到的一个男人这么说的。他对我说，那里是岔路口，需得走右手这一条路，走五英里便能到高申。”

“我看他准是喝醉了，他指给你的恰好是相反的路。”

“哦，他那样子真像是喝醉了的。不过，如今也无所谓了，我反正得往前走。天亮以前，我能赶到高申。”

“等一会儿，我给你准备点儿吃的带着，你也许用得着。”

她就给我弄了点儿吃的，还说：“听我说——一头奶牛趴在地上，要爬起来时，哪一头先离地？赶快答——不用停下来想。哪一头先起来？”

“牛屁股先离地，大娘。”

“好，那么一匹马呢？”

“前头的，大娘。”

“一棵树，哪一侧青苔长得最盛？”

“北边的一侧。”

“假如有十五头牛在一处小山坡上吃草，有几头是冲着同一个方向的？”

“十五头全冲着一个方向，大娘。”

“嗯，我看啊，你果真是住在乡下的。我还以为你又要哄我呢。现在你说，你的真姓名是什么？”

“乔治·彼得斯，大娘。”

　　"嗯，要把这名字记住了，乔治。别把这忘了，弄得在走以前对我说你的名字叫亚历山大，等出了门给我逮住了，便说是乔治·亚历山大。还有，别穿着这样旧的花布衣服装成女人啦。你装成一个姑娘家可装得蹩脚，不过你要是糊弄一个男人，也许还能对付。上天保佑，孩子，你穿起针线来，可别捏着线头不动，光是捏着针鼻往线头上凑，而是要捏着针头不动，把线头往针鼻上凑——妇女多半是这么穿针线的，男人多半倒过来。打老鼠或者别的什么，应当踮着脚尖，手伸到头顶上，越高越好。打过去之后，离老鼠最好有六七英尺远。胳膊挺直，靠肩膀的力扔出去。肩膀就好比一个轴，胳膊就在它上面转——这才像一个女孩扔东西的姿势，可不是用手腕子和胳膊后的力，把胳膊朝外伸，像一个男孩子扔东西的姿势。还要记住，一个女孩，人家朝她膝盖上扔东西，她接的时候，两腿总是张开的，不是像男孩那样把两腿并拢，不像你接铅团那样把两腿并拢。啊，你穿针线的时候，我就看出你是个男孩子了。我又想出了一些别的法子来试试你，就为的是弄得确实无误。现在你跑去找你的叔叔去吧，莎拉·玛丽·威廉斯·乔治·亚历山大·彼得斯。你要是遇到什么麻烦，不妨给裘第丝·洛芙特丝一个信，那就是我的名字。我会想方设法帮你解决的，顺着大河，一直往前走。下回出远门，要随身带好袜子、鞋子。沿河的路尽是石头路。我看啊，走到高申镇，你的脚可要遭殃了。"

　　我沿河岸往上游走了五十码，然后急步走回来，溜到了系独木舟的地方，就是离那家人家相当远的一个去处。我跳上船，急急忙忙开船。我朝上水划了相当一段路，为的是能划到岛的顶端，然后往对岸划去。我取下了遮阳帽，因为我这时候已经不需要这遮眼的东西了。我划到大河的水中央的时候，听到钟声响起来了。我便停了下来，仔细听着。声音从水上传来，很轻，可是很清楚——十一下子。我一到了岛尖，尽管累得喘不过气来，不敢停下来缓一口气，便直奔我早先宿营的林子那里，拣一个干燥的高处生起一堆大火。

　　随后便跳进独木舟，使出全身的劲儿，往下游一英里半我们藏身的地方划去。我跳上了岸，窜过树林，爬上山脊，冲进山洞。杰姆正躺着。在地上睡得正香，我把他叫了起来，对他说：

　　"杰姆，快起来，收拾好东西。一分钟也拖延不得，人家来搜捕我们啦！"

　　杰姆一个问题也没有问，一句话也没有说。不过，从接下来半小时中收拾东西的那个劲儿来看，他准是吓坏了。等到我们把所有的家当全都放到木排上的时候，我们准备从隐藏着的柳树弯子里撑出去，我们第一件事是把洞口的火堆灰烬熄灭。在这以后，在外边，连一点烛光也不敢点。

　　我把独木舟划到离岸不远的地方，然后往四下里张望了一下。不过嘛，当时即便附近有一只小船吧，我也不会看到，因为星光黯淡，浓影深深，看不清。随后我们就把木筏撑出去，溜进了阴影里，朝下游漂去，悄没声地漂过了岛尾，两人一句话也没有说。

第十二单元　了不起的盖茨比　第九章

事隔两年，我回想起那天其余的时间，那一晚以及第二天，只记得一批又一批的警察、摄影师和新闻记者在盖茨比家的前门口来来往往。外面的大门口有一根绳子拦住，旁边站着一名警察，不让看热闹的人进来，但是小男孩们不久就发现他们可以从我的院子里绕过来，因此总有几个孩子目瞪口呆地挤在游泳池旁边。那天下午，有一个神态自信的人，也许是一名侦探，低头检视威尔逊的尸体时用了"疯子"两个字，而他的语气偶然的权威就为第二天早上所有报纸的报道定了调子。

那些报道大多数都是一场噩梦——离奇古怪，捕风捉影，煞有介事，而且不真实。等到米切里斯在验尸时的证词透露了威尔逊对他妻子的猜疑以后，我以为整个故事不久就会被添油加醋在黄色小报上登出来了——不料凯瑟琳，她本可以信口开河的，却什么都不说，并且表现出惊人的魄力——她那描过的眉毛底下的两只坚定的眼睛笔直地看着验尸官，又发誓说她姐姐从来没见过盖茨比，说她姐姐和她丈夫生活在一起非常美满，说她姐姐从来没有什么不端的行为。她说得自己都信以为真了，又用手帕捂着脸痛哭了起来，仿佛连提出这样的疑问都是她受不了的，于是威尔逊就被归结为一个"悲伤过度精神失常"的人，以便这个案子可以保持最简单的情节。案子也就这样了结了。

但是事情的这个方面似乎整个都是不痛不痒、无关紧要的。我发现自己是站在盖茨比一边的，而且只有我一人。从我打电话到西卵镇报告惨案那一刻起，每一个关于他的揣测、每一个实际的问题，都提到我这里来。起初我感到又惊讶又迷惑，后来一小时又一小时过去，他还是躺在他的房子里，不动，不呼吸，也不说话，我才渐渐明白我在负责，因为除我以外没有任何人有兴趣——我的意思是说，那种每个人身后多少都有权利得到的强烈的个人兴趣。

在我们发现他的尸体半小时之后我就打了电话给黛西，本能地、毫不迟疑地给她打了电话。但是她和汤姆那天下午很早就出门了，还随身带了行李。

"没留地址吗?"

"没有。"

"说他们几时回来吗?"

"没有。"

"知道他们到哪儿去了吗？我怎样能和他们取得联系？"

"我不知道，说不上来。"

我真想给他找一个人来。我真想走到他躺着的那间屋子里去安慰他说："我一定给你找一个人来，盖茨比。别着急。相信我好了，我一定给你找一个人来……"

迈耶·沃尔夫山姆的名字不在电话簿里。男管家把他百老汇办公室的地址给我，我又打电话到电话局问讯处，但是等到我有了号码时已经早就过了五点，没有人接电话了。

"请你再摇一下好吗？"

"我已经摇过三次了。"

"有非常要紧的事。"

"对不起，那儿恐怕没有人。"

我回到客厅里去，屋子里突然挤满了官方的人员，起先我还以为是一些不速之客。虽然他们掀开被单，用惊恐的眼光看着盖茨比，可是他的抗议继续在我脑子里回响：

"我说，老兄，你一定得替我找个人来。你一定得想想办法。我一个人可受不了这个罪啊。"

有人来找我提问题，我却脱了身跑上楼去，匆匆忙忙翻了一下书桌上没锁的那些抽屉——他从没明确地告诉我他的父母已经死了，但是什么也找不到——只有丹·科迪的那张相片，那已经被人遗忘的粗野狂暴生活的象征，从墙上向下面凝视着。

第二天早晨我派男管家到纽约去给沃尔夫山姆送一封信，信中向他打听消息，并恳请他搭下一班火车就来。我这样写的时候觉得这个请求似乎是多此一举。我认为他一看见报纸肯定马上就会赶来的，正如我认为中午以前黛西肯定会有电报来的——可是电报也没来，沃尔夫山姆先生也没到。什么人都没来，只有更多的警察、摄影师和新闻记者。等到男管家带回来沃尔夫山姆的回信时，我开始感到傲视一切，感到盖茨比和我可以团结一致横眉冷对他们所有的人。

亲爱的卡罗威先生：这个消息使我感到万分震惊，我几乎不敢相信是真的。那个人干的这种疯狂行为应当使我们大家都好好想想。我现在不能前来，因为我正在办理一些非常重要的业务，目前不能跟这件事发生牵连。过一些时候如有我可以出力的事，请派埃德加送封信通知我。我听到这种事后简直不知道自己身在何处，感到天昏地暗了。

您的忠实的迈耶·沃尔夫山姆

下面又匆匆附了一笔：关于丧礼安排请告知。又及：根本不认识他家里人。

那天下午电话铃响，长途台说芝加哥有电话来，我以为这总该是黛西了，但等到接通了一听却是一个男人的声音，很轻很远。

"我是斯莱格……"

"是吗？"这名字很生疏。

"那封信真够呛，是不？收到我的电报了吗？"

"什么电报也没有。"

"小派克倒霉了，"他话说得很快，"他在柜台上递证券的时候给逮住了。刚刚五分钟之前他们收到纽约的通知，列上了号码。你想得到吗？在这种乡下地方你没法料到……"

"喂！喂！"我上气不接下气地打断了他的话，"你听我说——我不是盖茨比先生。盖茨比先生死了。"

电话线那头沉默了好久，接着是一声惊叫……然后咔嗒一声电话就挂断了。

我想大概是第三天，从明尼苏达州的一个小城镇来了一封署名亨利·C·盖兹的电报。上面只说发电人马上动身，要求等他到达后再举行葬礼。

来的是盖茨比的父亲，一个很庄重的老头子，非常可怜，非常沮丧，这样暖和的九月天就裹上了一件蹩脚的长外套。他激动得眼泪不住地往下流，我从他手里把旅行包和雨伞接过来时，他不停地伸手去拉他那撮稀稀的花白胡须。我好不容易才帮他脱下了大衣。他人快要垮了，不是我一面把他领到音乐厅里去，让他坐下，一面打发人去搞一点吃的来，但是他不肯吃东西，那杯牛奶也从他哆哆嗦嗦的手里泼了出来。

"我从芝加哥报纸上看到的，"他说，"芝加哥报纸上全都登了出来，我马上就动身了。"

"我没法子通知您。"

他的眼睛视而不见，可是不停地向屋子里四面看。

"是一个疯子干的，"他说，"他一定是疯了。"

"您喝杯咖啡不好吗？"我劝他。

"我什么都不要。我现在好了，您是……"

"卡罗威。"

"呃，我现在好了。他们把杰米放在哪儿？"

我把他领进客厅里他儿子停放的地方，把他留在那儿。有几个小男孩爬上了台阶，正在往门厅里张望。等到我告诉他们是谁来了，他们才勉勉强强地走开了。

过了一会儿盖兹先生打开门走了出来，他嘴巴张着，脸微微有点红，眼睛断断续续洒下几滴泪水。他已经到了并不把死亡看作一件骇人听闻的事情的年纪，于是此刻他第一次向四周一望，看见门厅如此富丽堂皇，一间间大屋子从这里又通向别的屋子，他的悲伤就开始和一股又惊讶又骄傲的感情交织在一起了。我把他搀到楼上的一间卧室里。他一面脱上衣和背心，我一面告诉他一切安排都推迟了，等他来决定。

"我当时不知道您要怎么办，盖茨比先生……"

"我姓盖兹。"

"盖兹先生，我以为您也许要把遗体运到西部去。"

他摇了摇头。

"杰米一向喜欢待在东部。他是在东部上升到他这个地位的。你是我孩子的朋友吗，先生？"

"我们是很知己的朋友。"

"他是大有前程的，你知道。他只是个年轻人，但是他在这个地方很有能耐。"

他郑重其事地用手碰碰脑袋，我也点了点头。

"假使他活下去的话，他会成为一个大人物的，像詹姆斯·J·希尔那样的人，他会帮助建设国家的。"

"确实是那样，"我局促不安地说。

他笨手笨脚地把绣花被单扯来扯去，想把它从床上拉下来，接着就硬邦邦地躺下去——立刻就睡着了。

那天晚上一个显然害怕的人打电话来，一定要先知道我是谁才肯报他自己的姓名。

"我是卡罗威"我说。

"哦!"他似乎感到宽慰,"我是克利普斯普林格。"

我也感到宽慰,因为这一来盖茨比的墓前可能会多一个朋友了。我不愿意登报,引来一大堆看热闹的人,所以我就自己打电话通知了几个人。他们可真难找到。

"明天出殡,"我说,"下午三点,就在此地家里。我希望你转告凡是有意参加的人。"

"哦,一定,"他忙说,"当然啦,我不大可能见到什么人,但是如果我碰到的话。"

他的语气使我起了疑心。

"你自己当然是要来的。"

"呃,找一定想法子来。我打电话来是要问……"

"等等,"我打断了他的话,"先说你一定来怎么样?"

"呃,事实是……实际情况是这样的,我目前待在格林尼治这里朋友家里,人家指望我明天和他们一起玩。事实上,明天要去野餐什么的。当然我走得开一定来。"

我忍不住叫了一声"嘿",他也一定听到了,因为他很紧张地往下说:

"我打电话来是为了我留在那里的一双鞋。不知道能不能麻烦你让男管家给我寄来,你知道,那是双网球鞋,我离了它简直没办法。我的地址是B·F……"

我没听他说完那个名字就把话筒挂上了。

在那以后我为盖茨比感到羞愧——还有一个我打电话去找的人竟然表示他是死有应得的。不过,这是我的过错,因为他是那些当初喝足了盖茨比的酒就大骂盖茨比的客人中的一个,我本来就不应该打电话给他的。

出殡那天的早晨,我到纽约去找迈耶·沃尔夫山姆。似乎用任何别的办法都找不到他。在开电梯的指点之下,我推开了一扇门,门上写着"控股公司",可是起先里面好像没有人,但是,我高声喊了几声"喂"也没人答应之后,一扇隔板后面突然传出争辩的声音,接着一个漂亮的犹太女人在里面的一个门口出现,用含有敌意的黑眼睛打量我。

"没人在家,"她说,"沃尔夫山姆先生到芝加哥去了。"

前一句话显然是撒谎,因为里面有人已经开始不成腔地用口哨吹奏《玫瑰经》。

"请告诉他卡罗威要见他。"

"我又不能把他从芝加哥叫回来，对不对？"

正在这时有一个声音，毫无疑问是沃尔夫山姆的声音，从门的那边喊了一声"斯特拉"。

"你把名字留在桌上，"她很快地说，"等他回来我告诉他。"

"可是我知道他就在里面。"

她向我面前跨了一步，开始把两只手气冲冲地沿着臀部一上一下地移动。

"你们这些年轻人自以为你们随时可以闯进这里来，"她骂道，"我们都烦死了。我说他在芝加哥，他就是在芝加哥。"

我提了一下盖茨比的名字。

"哦……啊！"她又打量了我一下，"请您稍……您姓什么来着？"

她不见了。过了一会，迈耶·沃尔夫山姆就庄重地站在门口，两只手都伸了出来。他把我拉进他的办公室，一面用虔诚的口吻说在这种时候我们大家都很难过，一面敬我一支雪茄烟。

"我还记得我第一次见到他的情景，"他说，"刚刚离开军队的一名年轻的少校，胸口挂满了在战场上赢得的勋章。他穷得只好继续穿军服，因为他买不起便服。我第一次见到他是那天他走进四十三号街怀恩勃兰纳开的弹子房找工作。他已经两天没吃饭了。'跟我一块吃午饭去吧。'我说。不到半个钟头他就吃了四块多美元的饭菜。"

"是你帮他做起生意来的吗？"我问。

"帮他！我一手造就了他。"

"哦"。

"是我把他从零开始培养起来，从阴沟里捡起来的。我一眼就看出他是个仪表堂堂、文质彬彬的年轻人，等他告诉我他上过牛劲，我就知道我可以派他大用场。我让他加入了美国退伍军火协会，后来他在那平面地位挺高的。他一出马就跑到奥尔巴尼去给我的一个主顾办了一件事。我们俩在一切方面都像这样亲密，"他举起了两个肥胖的指头，"永远在一起。"

我心里很纳罕，不知这种搭档是否也包括一九一九年世界棒球联赛那笔交易在内。

"现在他死了，"我隔了一会才说，"你是他最知己的朋友，因此我知道今天下午你一定会来参加他的葬礼的。"

"我很想来。"

"那么，来就是啦。"

他鼻孔里的毛微微颤动，他摇摇头，泪水盈眶。

"我不能来……我不能牵连进去。"他说。

"没有什么事可以牵连进去的。事情现在都过去了。"

"凡是有人被杀害，我总不愿意有任何牵连。我不介入。我年轻时就大不一样——如果一个朋友死了，不管怎么死的，我总是出力出到底。你也许会认为这是感情用事，可是我是说到做到的——一直拼到底。"

我看出了他决意不去，自有他的原因。于是我就站了起来。

"你是不是大学毕业的？"他突然问我。

有一会儿工夫我还以为他要提出搞点什么"关系"，可是他只点了点头，握了握我的手。

"咱们大家都应当学会在朋友活着的时候讲交情，而不要等到他死了之后，"他表示说，"在人死以后，我个人的原则是不管闲事。"

我离开他办公室的时候，天色已经变黑，我在蒙蒙细雨中回到了西卵。我换过衣服之后就到隔壁去，看到盖兹先生兴奋地在门厅里走来走去。他对他儿子和他儿子的财物所感到的自豪一直在不断地增长，现在他又有一样东西要给我看。

"杰米寄给我的这张照片。"他手指哆嗦着掏出了他的钱包，"你瞧吧。"

是这座房子的一张照片，四角破裂，也给许多手摸脏了。他热切地把每一个细节都指给我看。"你瞧！"随即又看我眼中有没有赞赏的神情。他把这张照片给人家看了那么多次数，我相信在地看来现在照片比真房子还要真。

"杰米把它寄给我的，我觉得这是一张很好看的照片，照得很好"。

"非常好。您近来见过他吗？"

"他两年前回过家来看我，给我买下了我现在住的房子。当然，他从家里跑走的时候我们很伤心，但是我现在明白他那样做是有道理的。他知道自己有远大的前程，他发迹之后一走对我很大方。"

他似乎不愿意把那张照片放回去，依依不舍地又在我眼前举了一会工夫。然后他把钱包放了回去，又从口袋小掏出一本破破烂烂的旧书，书名是《生仔卡西迪》。

"你瞧瞧，这本书是他小时候看的。真是从小见大。"

他把书的封底翻开，掉转过来让我看，在最后的空白页上端端正正地写着"时间表"几个字和一九零六年九月十二日的日期。下面是：

起床	上午6:00
哑铃体操及爬墙	6:15-6:30
学习电学等	7:15-8:15
工作	8:50-下午4:30
棒球及其他运动	下午4:30-5:00
练习演说、仪态	5:00-6:00
学习有用的新发明	7:00-9:00

个人决心

不要浪费时间去沙夫特家或（另一姓，字迹不清）

不再吸烟或嚼烟

每隔一天洗澡

每周读有益的书或杂志一份

每周储蓄五元（涂去）三元

对父母更加体贴

"我无意中发现这本书，"老头说，"真是从小见大，是不是？"

"真是从小见大。"

"杰米是注定了要出人头地的，他总是订出一些诸如此类的决心。你注意没有，他用什么办法提高自己的思想？他在这方面一向是了不起的。有一次他说我吃东西像猪一样，我把他揍了一顿。"

他舍不得把书合上，把每一条大声念了一遍，然后眼巴巴地看着我。我想他满以为我会把那张表抄下来给我自己用。

快到三点的时候，路德教会的那位牧师从弗勒兴来了，于是我开始不由自主地向窗户外面望，看看有没有别的车子来。盖茨比的父亲也和我一样。随着时间过去，佣人都走进来站在门厅等候，老人的眼睛顿时焦急地眨起来，同时他又忐忑不安地说到外面的雨。牧师看了好几次表，我只好把他拉到一旁，请他再等半个钟头，但是毫无用处。没有一个人来。

五点钟左右我们三辆车子的行列驶到基地，在密密的小雨中在大门旁边停了下来——第一辆是灵车，又黑又湿，怪难看的，后面是盖兹先生、牧师和我坐在大型轿车里，再后面一点的是四五个佣人和西卵镇的邮差坐在盖茨比的旅行车里，大家都淋得透湿。正当我们穿过大门走进墓地时，我听见一辆车停下来，接着是一个人踩着湿透的草地在我们后面追上来的声音。我回头一看，原来是那个戴猫头鹰眼镜的人，三个月以前的一个晚上我发现他一边看着盖茨比图书室里的书一边惊叹不已。

从那以后我没再见过他。我不知道他怎么会知道今天安葬的，我也不知道他的姓名。雨水顺着他的厚眼镜流下来，他只好把眼镜摘下探一擦，再看着那块挡雨的帆布从盖茨比的坟上卷起来。

这时我很想回忆一下盖茨比，但是他已经离得太远了，我只记得黛西既没来电报，也没送花，然而我并不感到气恼。我隐约听到有人喃喃念道："上帝保佑雨中的死者。"接着那个戴猫头鹰眼镜的人用洪亮的声音说了一声："阿门！"

我们零零落落地在雨中跑回到车子上。戴猫头鹰眼镜的人在大门口跟我说了一会话。

"我没能赶到别墅来。"他说。

"别人也都没能来。"

"真的！"他大吃一惊，"啊，我的上帝！他们过去一来就是好几百嘛。"

他把眼镜摘了下来，里里外外都擦了一遍。

"这家伙真他妈的可怜。"他说。

我记忆中最鲜明的景象之一就是每年圣诞节从预备学校，以及后来从大学回到西部的情景。到芝加哥以外的地方去的同学往往在一个十二月黄昏六点钟聚在那座古老、幽暗的联邦车站，和几个家在芝加哥的朋友匆匆话别，只见他们已经裹入了他们自己的节日欢娱气氛。我记得那些从东部某某私立女校回来的女学生的皮大衣以及她们在严寒的空气中喊喊喳喳的笑语，记得我们发现熟人时抢手呼唤，记得互相比较收到的邀请："你到奥德威家去吗？赫西家呢？舒尔茨家呢？"还记得紧紧抓在我们戴了手套的手里的长条绿色车票。最后还有停在月台门口轨道上的芝加哥—密尔沃基—圣保罗铁路的朦胧的黄色客车，看上去就像圣诞节一样地使人愉快。

火车在寒冬的黑夜里奔驰，真正的白雪、我们的雪，开始在两边向远方伸展，迎着车窗闪耀，威斯康星州的小车站暗灰的灯火从眼前掠过，这时空中突然出现一股使人神清气爽的寒气。我们吃过晚饭穿过寒冷的通廊往回走时，一路深深地呼吸着这寒气，在奇异的一个小时中难以言喻地意识到自己与这片乡土之间的血肉相连的关系，然后我们就要重新不留痕迹地融化在其中了。

这就是我的中西部——不是麦田，不是草原，也不是瑞典移民的荒凉村镇，而是我青年时代那些激动人心的还乡的火车，是严寒的黑夜里的街灯和雪橇的铃声，是圣诞冬青花环被窗内的灯火映在雪地的影子。我是其中的一部分，由于那些漫长的冬天我为人不免有点矜持，由于从小在卡罗威公馆长大，态度上也不免有点自满。在我们那个城市里，人家的住宅仍旧世世代代称为某姓的公馆。我现在才明白这个故事到头来是一个西部的故事——汤姆和盖茨比、黛西、乔丹和我，我们都是西部人，也许我们具有什么共同的缺陷使我们无形中不能适应东部的生活。

即使东部最令我兴奋的时候，即使我最敏锐地感觉到比之俄亥俄河那边的那些枯燥无味、乱七八糟的城镇，那些只有儿童和老人可幸免于无止无休的闲话的城镇，东部具有无比的优越性——即使在那种时候，我也总觉得东部有畸形的地方，尤其西卵仍然出现在我做的比较荒唐的梦里。在我的梦中，这个小镇就像埃尔·格列柯画的一幅夜景：上百所房屋，既平常又怪诞，蹲伏在阴沉沉的天空和黯淡无光的月亮之下。在前景里有四个板着面孔、身穿大礼服的男人沿人行道走着，抬着一副担架，上面躺着一个喝醉酒的女人，身上穿着一件白色的晚礼服。她一只手耷拉在一边，闪耀着珠宝的寒光。那几个人郑重其事地转身走进一所房子——走错了地方。但是没人知道这个女人的姓名，也没有人关心。

盖茨比死后，东部在我心目中就是这样鬼影憧憧，面目全非到超过了我眼睛矫正的能力，因此等到烧枯叶的蓝烟弥漫空中，寒风把晾在绳上的湿衣服吹得邦邦硬的时候，我就决定回家来了。

在我离开之前还有一件事要办，一件尴尬的、不愉快的事，本来也许应当不了了之的，但是我希望把事情收拾干净，而不指望那个乐于帮忙而又不动感情的大海来把我的垃圾冲掉。我去见了乔丹·贝克，从头到尾谈了围绕着我们两人之间发生的事情，然后谈到我后来的遭遇，而她躺在一张大椅子里听着，一动也不动。

她穿的是打高尔夫球的衣服，我还记得我当时想过她活像一幅很好的插图，她的下巴根神气地微微翘起，她头发像秋叶的颜色，她的脸和她放在膝盖上的浅棕色无指手套一个颜色。等我讲完之后，她告诉我她和另一个人订了婚，别的话一句没说。我怀疑她的话，虽然有好几个人是只要她一点头就可以与她结婚的，但是我故作惊讶。一刹那间我寻思自己是否正在犯错误，接着我很快地考虑了一番就站起来告辞了。

"不管怎样，还是你甩掉我的，"乔丹忽然说，"你那天打电话把我甩了。我现在拿你完全不当回事了，但是当时那倒是个新经验，我有好一阵子感到晕头转向的。"

我们俩握了握手。

"哦，你还记得吗，"她又加了一句，"我们有过一次关于开车的谈话？"

"啊……记不太清了。"

"你说过一个开车不小心的人只有在碰上另一个开车不小心的人之前才安全吧？瞧，我碰上了另一个开车不小心的人了，是不是？我是说我真不小心，竟然这样看错了人。我以为你是一个相当老实、正直的人。我以为那是你暗暗引以为荣的事。"

"我三十岁了，"我说，"要是我年轻五岁，也许我还可以欺骗自己，说这样做光明正大。"

她没有回答。我又气又恼，对她有几分依恋，同时心里又非常难过，只好转身走开了。

十月下旬的一个下午我碰到了汤姆·布坎农。他在五号路上走在我前面，还是那样机警和盛气凌人，两手微微离开他的身体，仿佛要打退对方的碰撞一样，同时把头忽左忽右地转动，配合他那双溜溜转的眼睛。我正要放慢脚步免得赶上他，他停了下来，皱着眉头向一家珠宝店的橱窗里看。忽然间他看见了我，就往回走，伸出手来。

"怎么啦，尼克？你不愿意跟我握手吗？"

"对啦。你知道我对你的看法。"

"你发疯了，尼克，"他急忙说，"疯得够呛。我不明白你是怎么回事。"

"汤姆，"我质问道，"那天下午你对威尔逊说了什么？"

他一言不发地瞪着我，于是我知道我当时对于不明底细的那几个小时的猜测果然是猜对了。我掉头就走，可是他紧跟上一步，抓住了我的胳臂。

"我对他说了实话，"他说，"他来到我家门口，这时我们正准备出去，后来我让人传话下来说我们不在家，他就想冲上楼来。他已经疯狂到可以杀死我的地步，要是我没告诉他那辆车子是谁的。到了我家里他的手每一分钟都放在他口袋里的一把手枪上……"他突然停住了，态度强硬起来，"就算我告诉他又该怎样？那家伙自己找死。他把你迷惑了，就像他迷惑了黛西一样，其实他是个心肠狠毒的家伙。他撞死了茉特尔就像撞死了一条狗一样，连车子都不停一下。"

我无话可说，除了这个说不出来的事实：事情并不是这样的。

"你不要以为我没有受痛苦——我告诉你，我去退掉那套公寓时，看见那盒倒霉的喂狗的饼干还搁在餐具柜上，我坐下来像小娃娃一样放声大哭。我的天，真难受……"

我不能宽恕他，也不能喜欢他，但是我看到，他所做的事情在他自己看来完全是有理的。一切都是粗心大意、混乱不堪的。汤姆和黛西，他们是粗心大意的人——他们砸碎了东西，毁灭了人，然后就退缩到自己的金钱或者麻木不仁或者不管什么使他们留在一起的东西之中，让别人去收拾他们的烂摊子……

我跟他握了握手。不肯握手未免太无聊了，因为我突然觉得仿佛我是在跟一个小孩子说话。随后他走进那家珠宝店去买一串珍珠项链——或者也许只是一副袖扣——永远摆脱了我这乡下佬吹毛求疵的责难。

我离开的时候，盖茨比的房子还是空着——他草坪上的草长得跟我的一样高了。镇上有一个出租汽车司机载了客人经过大门口没有一次不把车子停一下，用手向里面指指点点。也许出事的那天夜里开车送黛西和盖茨比到东卵的就是他，也许他已经编造了一个别出心裁的故事。我不要听他讲，因此我下火车时总躲开他。

每星期六晚上我都在纽约度过，因为盖茨比那些灯火辉煌、光彩炫目的宴会我记忆犹新，我仍然可以听到微弱的百乐和欢笑的声音不断地从他园子里飘过来，还有一辆辆汽车在地的车道上开来开去。有一晚我确实听见那儿真有一辆汽车，看见车灯照在门口台阶上，但是我并没去调查。大概是最后的一位客人，刚从天涯海角归来，还不知道宴会早已收场了。

在最后那个晚上，箱子已经装好，车子也卖给了杂货店老板，我走过去再看一眼那座庞大而杂乱的、意味着失败的房子。白色大理石台阶上有哪个男孩用砖头涂了一个脏字眼儿，映在月光里分外触目，于是我把它擦了，在石头上把鞋子刮得沙沙作响。后来我又溜达到海边，仰天躺在沙滩上。

那些海滨大别墅现在大多已经关闭了，四周几乎没有灯火，除了海湾上一只渡船的幽暗、移动的灯光。当明月上升的时候，那些微不足道的房屋慢慢消逝，直到我逐渐意识到当年为荷兰水手的眼睛放出异彩的这个古岛——新世界的一片清新碧绿的地方。它那些消失了的树木，那些为盖茨比的别墅让路而被砍伐的树木，曾经一度迎风飘拂，低声响应人类最后的也是最伟大的梦想，在那昙花一现的神妙的瞬间，人面对这个新大陆一定屏息惊异，不由自主地堕入他既不理解也不企求的一种美学的观赏中，在历史上最后一次面对着和他感到惊奇的能力相称的奇观。

当我坐在那里缅怀那个古老的、未知的世界时，我也想到了盖茨比第一次认出了黛西的码头尽头的那盏绿灯时所感到的惊奇。他经历了漫长的道路才来到这片蓝色的草坪上，他的梦一定就像是近在眼前，他几乎不可能抓不住的。他不知道那个梦已经丢在他背后了，丢在这个城市那边那一片无垠的混沌之中不知什么地方了，那里合众国的黑黝黝的田野在夜色中向前伸展。

盖茨比信奉这盏绿灯，这个一年年在我们眼前渐渐远去的极乐的未来。它从前逃脱了我们的追求，不过那没关系——明天我们跑得更快一点，把胳臂伸得更远一点……总有一天……

于是我们奋力向前划，逆流向上的小舟，不停地倒退，进入过去。

第十三单元　一个干净、明亮的地方

　　时间很晚了，大家都离开餐馆，只有一个老人还坐在树叶挡住灯光的阴影里。白天里，街上尽是尘埃，到得晚上，露水压住了尘埃。这个老人喜欢坐得很晚，因为他是个聋子，现在是夜里，十分寂静，他感觉得到跟白天的不同。餐馆里的两个侍者知道这老人有点儿醉了，他虽然是个好主顾，可是，他们知道，如果他喝得太醉了，他会不付账就走，所以他们一直在留神他。

　　"上个星期他想自杀，"一个侍者说。

　　"为什么？"

　　"他绝望啦。"

　　"干吗绝望？"

　　"没事儿。"

　　"你怎么知道是没事儿？"

　　"他有很多钱。"

　　他们一起坐在紧靠着餐馆大门墙边的桌旁，眼睛望着平台，那儿的桌子全都空无一人，只有那个老人坐在随风轻轻飘拂的树叶的阴影里。有个少女和一个大兵走过大街。街灯照在他那领章的铜号码上。那个少女没戴帽子，在他身旁匆匆走着。

　　"警卫队会把他带走，"一个侍者说。

　　"如果他到手了他要找的东西，那又有什么关系呢？"

　　"他这会儿还是从街上溜走为好。警卫队会找他麻烦，他们五分钟前才经过这里。"

　　那老人坐在阴影里，用杯子敲敲茶托。那个年纪比较轻的侍者上他那儿去。

　　"你要什么？"

　　老人朝他看了看。"再来杯白兰地，"他说。

　　"你会喝醉的，"侍者说。老人朝他看了一看。侍者走开了。

　　"他会通宵待在这里，"他对他的同事说。"我这会儿真想睡。我从来没有在三点钟以前睡觉过。他应该在上星期就自杀了。"

侍者从餐馆里的柜台上拿了一瓶白兰地和另一个茶托，大步走了出来，送到老人桌上。他放下茶托，把杯子倒满了白兰地。

"你应该在上星期就自杀了，"他对那个聋子说。老人把手指一晃。"再加一点，"他说。侍者又往杯子里倒酒，酒溢了出来，顺着高脚杯的脚流进了一叠茶托的第一只茶托。"谢谢你，"老人说。侍者把酒瓶拿回到餐馆去。他又同他的同事坐在桌旁。

"他这会儿喝醉了，"他说。

"他每天晚上都喝醉。"

"他干吗要自杀呀？"

"我怎么知道。"

"他上次是怎样自杀的？"

"他用绳子上吊。"

"谁把他放下来的？"

"他侄女。"

"干吗要把他放下来？"

"为他的灵魂担忧。"

"他有多少钱？"

"他有很多钱。"

"他准有八十岁喽。"

"不管怎样，我算准他有八十岁。"

"我真希望他回家去。我从来没有在三点钟以前睡觉过。那是个什么样的睡觉时间呀？"

"他因为不喜欢睡觉所以才不睡觉。"

"他孤孤单单。我可不孤单。我有个老婆在床上等着我呢。"

"他从前也有过老婆。"

"这会儿有老婆对他可没好处。"

"话可不能这么说。他有老婆也许会好些。"

"他侄女会照料他。"

"我知道。你刚才说是她把他放下来的。"

"我才不要活得那么老。老人邋里邋遢。"

"不一定都是这样。这个老人干干净净。他喝啤酒来并不滴滴答答往外漏。哪怕这会儿喝醉了。你瞧他。"

"我才不想瞧他。我希望他回家去。他并不关心那些非干活不可的人。"

那老人从酒杯上抬起头来望望广场，又望望那两个侍者。

"再来杯白兰地，"他指着杯子说。那个着急的侍者跑了过去。

"没啦，"他不顾什么句法地说，蠢汉在对醉汉或外国人说话时就这么说法。"今晚上没啦。打烊啦。"

"再来一杯，"那老人说。

"不，没啦，"侍者一边拿块毛巾揩揩桌沿，一边摇摇头。

老人站了起来，慢慢地数着茶托，打口袋里摸出一只装硬币的起夹子来，付了酒账，又放下半个比塞塔作小费。

那个侍者瞅着他顺着大街走去，这个年纪很大的人走起路来，虽然脚步不太稳，却很有神气。

"你干吗不让他待下来喝酒呢？"那个不着急的侍者问道。他们这会儿正在拉下百叶窗。"还不到二点半呢。"

"我要回家睡觉了。"

"一个钟头算啥？"

"他无所谓，我可很在乎。"

"反正是 个钟头。"

"你说得就像那个老人一模一样。他可以买啤酒回家去喝嘛。"

"这可不一样。"

"是呀，这是不一样的。"那个有老婆的侍者表示同意说。他不希望做得不公道，他只是有点儿着急。

"那么你呢？你不怕不到你通常的时间就回家吗？"

"你想侮辱我吗？"

"不，老兄，只是开开玩笑。"

"不，"那个着急的侍者一边说，一边拉下了铁百叶窗后站了起来。"我有信心。我完全有信心。"

"你有青春，信心，又有工作，"那个年纪大些的侍者说，

"你什么都有了。"

"那么，你缺少什么呢？"

"除了工作，什么都缺。"

"我有什么，你也都有了。"

"不，我从来就没有信心，我也不年轻了。"

"好啦，好啦，别乱弹琴了，把门锁上吧。"

"我是属于那种喜欢在餐馆呆得很晚的人，"那个年纪大些的侍者说。"我同情那种不想睡觉的人，同情那种夜里要有亮光的人。"

"我要回家睡觉去了。"

"我们是不一样的，"那个年纪大些的侍者说。这会儿，他穿好衣服要回家了。"这不光是个年轻和信心的问题，虽然青春和信心都是十分美妙的。我每天晚上都很不愿意打烊，因为可能有人要上餐馆。"

"老兄，开通宵的酒店有的是。"

"你不懂。这儿是个干净愉快的餐馆。十分明亮。而且这会儿，灯光很亮，还有缥缈的树影。"

"再见啦，"那个年轻的侍者说。

"再见，"年纪大些的侍者说。他关了电灯，继续在自说自话。亮固然要很亮，但也必须是个干净愉快的地方。你不要听音乐。你肯定不要听音乐。你也不会神气地站在酒吧前面，虽然这会儿那里应有尽有。他怕什么？他不是怕，也不是发慌。他心里很有数，这是虚无缥缈。全是虚无缥缈，人也是虚无缥缈的。人所需要的只是虚无缥缈和亮光以及干干净净和井井有条。有些人生活于其中却从来没有感觉到，可是，他知道一切都是虚无缥缈的，一切都是为了虚无缥缈，虚无缥缈，为了虚无缥缈。我们的虚无缥缈就在虚无缥缈中，虚无缥缈是你的名字，你的王国也叫虚无缥缈，你将是虚无缥缈中的虚无缥缈，因为原来就是虚无缥缈。给我们这个虚无缥缈吧，我们日常的虚无缥缈，虚无缥缈是我们的，我们的虚无缥缈，因为我们是虚无缥缈的，我们的虚无缥缈，我们无不在虚无缥缈中，可是，把我们打虚无缥缈中拯救出来吧；为了虚无缥缈。欢呼全是虚无缥缈的虚无缥缈，虚无缥缈与汝同在。他含笑站在一个酒吧前，那儿有台闪光的蒸气压咖啡机。

"你要什么？"酒吧招待问道。

"虚无缥缈。"

"又是个神经病，"酒吧招待说过后，转过头去。

"来一小杯，"那个侍者说。

酒吧招待倒了一杯给他。

"灯很亮，也很愉快，只是这个酒吧没有擦得很光洁，"侍者说。

酒吧招待看看他，但是，没有搭腔，夜深了，不便谈话。

"你要再来一小杯吗?"酒吧招待问道。

"不，谢谢你，"侍者说罢，走出去了。他不喜欢酒吧和酒店。一个干净明亮的餐馆又是另一回事。现在他不再想什么了，他要回家，到自己屋里去。他要去躺在床上，最后，天亮了，他就要睡觉了。到头来，他对自己说，大概又只是失眠。许多人一定都失眠。

Bibliography

Abrams, M.H.*A Glossary of Literary Terms* (7th ed) [C]. Beijing: Foreign Language Teaching and Research Press, 2004.

Bradbury, Malcolm. *The Modern British Novel* [C]. Beijing: Foreign Language Teaching and Research Press, 2005.

Brooks, Cleanth. *Understanding Fiction* [M]. Beijing: Foreign Language Teaching and Research Press, 2005.

D.Hart, James *The Oxford Companion to American Literature* [M]. Beijing: Foreign Language Teaching and Research Press, 2005.

Drabble, Margaret *The Oxford Companion to English Literature* [M] Beijing: Foreign Language Teaching and Research Press, 2005.

Rogers, Pat. *An Outline of English Literature* [M] Oxford University Press, 1998.

奥斯丁著: 傲慢与偏见 [M], 张玲、张扬译, 人民文学出版社, 1993 年.

常耀信: 漫话英美文学——英美文学史考研指南 [M], 南开大学出版社, 2005 年.

常耀信著: 英国文学简史 [C], 南开大学出版社, 2006 年.

弗吉尼亚. 伍尔夫著: 达洛维太太 [M], 谷启楠译, 人民文学出版社, 2005 年.

胡荫桐, 刘树森主编: 美国文学教程 [C], 南开大学出版社, 1995 年.

马克·吐温著: 哈克贝利·费恩历险记 [M], 成时译, 人民文学出版社, 1989 年.

斯威夫特著: 格列佛游记 [M], 林纾译, 上海译文出版社, 2006 年.

苏煜编: 英国诗歌赏析 [C], 新华出版社, 2006 年.

王守仁编: 英国文学选读 [C], 高等教育出版社, 2005 年.

王誉公主编: 美国经典短篇小说选 [C], 漓江出版社, 1997 年.

王佐良等编: 英国文学选注 [C], 商务印书馆, 1983 年.

吴翔林编: 英美文学选读 [C], 中国对外翻译公司, 2005 年.

徐晓东 主编: 英文观止 [C], 世界图书出版社, 2006 年.

张伯香，龙江编：英美经典小说赏析 ［C］，武汉大学出版社，2005 年.

Javascript：scrollingpopup　Http：//www. sparknotes. com/shakespeare/romeojuliet/
　　terms/chara_3.html/

http：//www.luminarium.org/sevenlit/donne/donnebib.htm#

http：//www.gradesaver.com/classicnates/titles/tess/essays/html

http：//ishare.iask.sina.com.cn/f/9896245.html

http：//www.baidu.com/s? tn＝06008006_2_pg&bs＝The＋Celebrated＋Jumping＋Frog
　　＋of＋Calaveras＋County&f＝8&rsv_bp＝1&wd

图片来源：

http：//image. baidu. com/i? tn＝baiduimage&ct＝201326592&lm＝-1&cl＝2&nc＝
　　1&word